Praise for the novels of Michelle Major

"Major's charming small town is packed with salt-of-the-earth people readers will embrace, and each sister's journey is beautifully imagined."
—*Publishers Weekly* on *The Wish List*

"A dynamic start to a series with a refreshingly original premise."
—*Kirkus Reviews* on *The Magnolia Sisters*

"A sweet start to a promising series, perfect for fans of Debbie Macomber."
—*Publishers Weekly* (starred review) on *The Magnolia Sisters*

"*The Magnolia Sisters* is sheer delight, filled with humor, warmth and heart.... I loved everything about it."
—RaeAnne Thayne, *New York Times* bestselling author

"This enjoyable romance is perfect for voracious readers who want to dive into a new small-town series."
—*Library Journal* on *The Magnolia Sisters*

Also by Michelle Major

The Carolina Girls

A Carolina Promise
Wildflower Season
A Carolina Christmas
Mistletoe Season
Wedding Season
A Lot Like Christmas

The Magnolia Sisters

A Magnolia Reunion
The Magnolia Sisters
The Road to Magnolia
The Merriest Magnolia
A Carolina Valentine
The Last Carolina Sister

Look for Michelle Major's next novel
The Christmas Cabin
available soon from Canary Street Press.

MICHELLE MAJOR

The Front Porch Club

CANARY STREET PRESS

PLEASE RECYCLE
THIS PRODUCT IS RECYCLABLE

Recycling programs for this product may not exist in your area.

ISBN-13: 978-1-335-43065-6

For questions and comments about the quality of this book, please contact us at CustomerService@Harlequin.com.

Canary Street Press
22 Adelaide St. West, 41st Floor
Toronto, Ontario M5H 4E3, Canada
CanaryStPress.com

Printed in Lithuania

CONTENTS

THE FRONT PORCH CLUB

To Lee and Jo. I'm grateful for both of you—
this author journey is better with the three of us!

CHAPTER ONE

"YOUR CARD HAS been declined."

"That's impossible. Run it again."

Annalise Haverford, of the Charlotte Haverfords, she used to proudly tell people, swallowed down the embarrassment that threatened to choke off her ability to breathe. She'd managed to hold her head high in the face of far worse trials than a defective credit card machine or a teenager who didn't know how to work it.

"Ma'am, I've tried it twice now." The girl handed the card back to Annalise. It was heavy—platinum because that was the most exclusive membership level available to her—but the weight and prestige were no comfort right now. Not when a crumpled ten-dollar bill would have done the job with far less struggle. "Do you have another card?"

"Mommy, I'm hungry."

Annalise automatically put a hand on her daughter's shoulder and gently squeezed. "Just a moment, sweetheart."

"I want a cookie *now*, Mommy."

Annalise glanced down at the eight-year-old girl's head. Margo's hair was starting to darken at the roots, just as Annalise's had when she was that age. She'd been in third grade, just like Margo, the first time her mother had taken her to the salon for highlights.

Carolann Fluk had insisted that her only daughter would succeed on the beauty pageant circuit and had been convinced Annalise would do better with sun-kissed highlights than as a dishwater blond.

Despite her mother's efforts, Annalise hadn't made it through more than a handful of competitions before even Carolann admitted that her daughter didn't have what it took to make it as a beauty queen.

Unlike her mother's, Annalise's smile wasn't perky enough, and she had no real talent despite endless piano and voice lessons. There were some things that couldn't be overcome with training, and Annalise's lack of coordination and tone deafness fell into that category.

She eventually found other ways to make her mother proud, habits she carried into adulthood and had passed on to her daughter. Until a few months ago, she hadn't cared that most people considered Margo a brat.

Annalise had encouraged her daughter's precociousness and sense of entitlement, falsely believing those personality traits went hand in hand with confidence.

She'd encouraged a lot of things that were coming back to bite her in the tush—the habit of not carrying cash was proving to be one of them. Cash was dirty, and the way regular people—those without platinum cards—paid for purchases. Too bad germ-laden dollar bills weren't the worst way money could be dirty.

Who would have thought that a skinny latte, strawberry lemonade and cookie order at the local bakery in Magnolia, North Carolina, would be what finally brought Annalise low? Moisture pooled under the arms of her silk blouse, but she smiled benignly at the barista.

"I don't have another card with me."

The young girl furrowed her brow as if the words didn't make sense. "We take cash," she said and pulled the two drinks that sat on the counter between them closer to her side.

"Mommy."

"Hush, Margo," Annalise whispered. "Well, this is a bit of a quandary." A sense of amusement she didn't feel colored her tone. If she didn't think she'd be overplaying it, she would have added a "fiddle-dee-dee" into the mix like she was channeling her inner Scarlett O'Hara.

What a shame she had no Tara to retreat to and the windows of the house she was due to move out of by the end of the week had plantation shutters for blinds. She could have used some curtains for repurposing.

"I just need to run over to the bank and straighten things out," she told the guardian of her order. "I'll return with the money in a jiffy."

The girl rolled her eyes with such precision, Annalise wondered if she'd been practicing the gesture in the mirror. Either way, the barista had definitely heard the promise before.

"I'll keep your drinks to the side."

"Or we could take them with us," Annalise suggested, giving the girl her own practiced stare, the one that had cowed dozens of volunteer committees into doing Annalise's bidding over the past decade. "I'm a longtime member of this community. You can trust me."

There was a cough that sounded more like a muffled swear word behind her, and she turned to see her former best friend, Everly Mae Tinsdale, standing a few feet away. Certainly close enough to have overheard the entire exchange with the girl behind the counter.

Unlike Annalise, who was by this time dripping with anxious, sticky sweat as she shoved her useless credit card into her designer purse, Everly Mae appeared to have stepped out of the salon minutes earlier. Maybe she had.

What day of the week was it anyway?

She and Everly Mae used to go for blowouts and manicures every Wednesday afternoon. She glanced at the other woman's shiny peach nails and resisted the urge to shove her ignored hands into the pockets of her slim jeans.

"You can trust her until she screws you over," Everly Mae said.

Margo gasped. "Mommy, Mrs. Tinsdale said a bad word."

As if Annalise hadn't heard. As if she had the power to stop the public comeuppance.

"Ignore it, darlin'. Sometimes adults forget that little pitchers have big ears." She inclined her head toward Everly Mae. "You know I was not involved." Annalise let the Southern belle lilt she'd worked so hard to cultivate seep into her tone. Like a few elongated vowels would soften this moment.

"Mm-hmm." Everly Mae's smile was lethal. "You chose to ignore the behavior. Does that make it any better?"

"I can't ignore something I have no knowledge of," Annalise insisted, then glanced at the barista, who was watching the exchange with wide eyes. "I'll run to the bank and be right back."

She saw the bakery's longtime owner, Mary Ellen Winkler, standing near the entrance to the back office. She had the power to override the teen and allow Annalise to take her coffee, or at least give Margo the damn cookie.

But, no. The woman just watched.

No one would come to Annalise's rescue. Not in this town. Not anywhere.

"Let's go, Margo."

"No, Mommy. You promised me a cookie." Her daughter's voice went up in volume a few notches.

"I'll get you a cookie. Just not here."

"But Sunnyside has the cookies I like best. You promised."

Annalise could write a book on broken promises, so why was a cookie pushing her over the edge of her self-control?

"You may put the child's cookie on my tab," Everly Mae said, her voice deceptively sweet.

Annalise shook her head and brushed a strand of limp blond hair behind her ear. Did she look as pathetic as she felt at the moment?

"You don't have to—"

"Thank you, Mrs. Tinsdale," Margo said. The girl looked to be blinking away delicate tears.

Good gravy. Annalise had taught her daughter the art of getting her way better than she'd even realized. Her heart sank. How was she going to undo the damage she'd done? Certainly not by allowing Everly Mae Tinsdale to exert any influence over Margo.

"I told you I would get you a cookie. Not now. Not here," she repeated.

"Can I have the lemonade, too?" Margo addressed Everly Mae, a tremble in her tone as she ignored Annalise. "I am parched."

How did an eight-year-old's vocabulary include the word *parched*?

"Of course, sweet girl." Everly Mae nodded to the barista. "But leave the coffee."

"Thank you, Mrs. Tinsdale," Margo repeated with a beaming smile as the shop girl handed her the wrapped cookie and cup of lemonade. "We will not forget your kindness in our moment of need."

Annalise felt a muscle cramp in her jaw. She knew Margo had watched *Gone with the Wind* the last time she spent the weekend at her Gigi's house in Charlotte, but she had no idea the child would take the mannerisms of Scarlett to heart so effortlessly. There were more profound lessons to be learned from both life and the silver screen, but this wasn't the time or place for them.

"Let's go," Annalise repeated, and this time her daughter followed her through the coffee shop. "I'll hold the rest of your order," the barista called.

"No need." Annalise held up a hand to wave and managed not to offer a rude gesture with her middle finger. She was not the type of woman to communicate her emotions with degrading actions, and the girl was only doing her job.

Mary Ellen also owed her nothing, but Everly Mae... Annalise could not deny that it burned to have a friend—one of the few women in Magnolia she considered a true friend—treat her so shabbily.

"Mommy, you should have been nicer to Mrs. Tinsdale," Margo told her, unwrapping the cookie and taking a big bite. "Gigi always says you catch more flies with honey than vinegar."

"Sweetie, there was nothing kind about Mrs. Tinsdale buying that cookie for you." Magnolia's picturesque main street seemed to taunt her with its cheery displays in the windows of local merchants. Planters already overflowed with spring flowers and there were colorful arrangements hanging from every light post. The town was warm and welcoming to everyone but her. "She wanted to rub it in my face that my credit card had been declined."

"We can go to the bank and get it worked out." Margo's rosebud mouth closed over the straw. "In a jiffy, just like you said."

After all they'd been through the past few months, could her daughter believe that? And was Annalise actually hurting or helping the girl if she told her the truth?

As they walked toward the car, she watched Margo lick a cookie crumb off her wrist. Her daughter and son were innocent of the mess their father had created, and Annalise had done her best to shield them from the fallout of his actions. Sometimes though, the things that were hardest to accept and understand were the most helpful in the long run.

She stopped in a small alcove between two businesses, a light breeze tickling her skin, and crouched down to look her daughter straight in the eye.

"I do not believe it was a mistake by the bank," she told Margo. "My credit card does not work because we haven't..." She rolled her lips together and forced herself to confront the entire truth. Yes, it hurt, but Margo deserved to know.

"I have not been able to make the payments necessary since your father's bad business dealings impacted our circumstances."

Margo looked confused, her feathery brows drawing together in a severe line. Carolann would have admonished the girl for scrunching up her face, but Annalise only reached out and squeezed her darling baby's shoulder. "I'll figure it out."

"You don't have to, Mommy. Daddy will fix everything when he comes back. I'm sure until then, the bank can give you a new card and maybe some extra money."

Wasn't that exactly what Carolann had taught Annalise? Money could fix anything and everything.

"The bank is not going to give me a loan. It's not their responsibility, Margo. It's my responsibility to figure out our circumstances—only me. We've discussed this. Your father is not coming back for several years. He and I are officially divorced. It's just you and Trey and me now. I should have realized the card would be denied."

"Denied," Margo repeated. "That doesn't sound nice."

Annalise swallowed back a laugh. "It's not, but it will get better." It couldn't get much worse.

"Is that why nobody wants to sit with me anymore at the lunch table, and why I didn't get invited to Becky Bush's slumber party last weekend?"

Annalise thought her heart had turned to stone the day federal agents had raided her house and hauled her husband away to prison. She went through her days showing very little emotion and feeling less, which seemed like a protective instinct she hadn't realized she possessed. But her daughter's sad words and trembling chin broke through all of the walls she'd erected so she could stay functional in the wake of her ex-husband's deceptions.

"I didn't realize Becky had a slumber party. I'm sorry, sweetheart."

Becky's father, Nathaniel, had been one of Jonathan's biggest clients, so she understood exactly why Margo had been excluded.

Annalise had managed to avoid many of her former friends and neighbors in the past several months while she sorted through the legal ramifications of her ex-husband's Ponzi scheme. As bad as the legal and financial implications of Jonathan's criminal activity were, it was quickly becoming clear that Annalise had bigger fish to fry. She thought that Trey, her ten-year-old son, was acting out because he missed his daddy. She'd believed Margo when the girl told her she was fine.

None of them were fine.

"When we move into our new place, you can host a sleepover, Margs. We'll invite all your friends for a spa night and an ice cream sundae bar. Things will get back to normal."

"I don't want to move," her daughter whined as she stared at the half-eaten cookie. "Our house is the biggest one on the street. Daddy always said size matters."

"Your father said a lot of things." Annalise smoothed back Margo's hair as she straightened. "I've explained this. We don't have a choice. Our lives have changed, which means we will all need to roll with it. We'll be okay because we have each other."

The girl didn't look convinced but nodded. "Will I still have my own bathroom?"

"No, I don't believe so. But we can ask the landlord for permission to paint your bedroom, and you can choose whatever color you want."

"Purple." Margo followed Annalise to the used Subaru hatchback she'd bought when the dealership had confiscated her Mercedes SUV.

The car, while not fancy, was reliable and had the cargo space Annalise hoped she'd need to haul merchandise for her interior design business.

Of course, in order to afford merchandise, she needed clients.

Given that she'd been deemed more of a social pariah than her daughter, paying clients seemed like a lofty goal.

But Annalise had always been ambitious. It wasn't a skill she could pull out for a beauty pageant talent show, but it would serve her well as she worked to reinvent her life.

To take care of her children.

To leave her past behind.

As God as her witness, she would figure out a way to give them all a bright future.

No matter what she had to do to ensure it.

CHAPTER TWO

SHAUNA MYER SURVEYED the damaged kitchen and tried not to burst into tears.

A single mother of nearly six-year-old twin boys did not have time for tears. Certainly not the kind brought on by something as inconsequential as a busted pipe and flooded kitchen.

Growing up first with an addict mother and then in a series of foster-care homes, Shauna had an expansive capacity to deal with trouble.

Did a situation even count as an emergency if there was no risk of bodily harm?

"Can we get a duck?" her son Timmy asked as he came to stand next to her in the doorway. "A duck would like to swim in the water."

"We saw a mama and her babies at the park yesterday," Zach, her other son, explained. "Some dummy-head kids kept trying to catch them when they came near shore. They'd be safe in our kitchen."

Safe.

A word that had a deeper meaning for Shauna than her boys would ever know.

It was the reminder she needed. She could deal with anything as long as her sons were safe. She was safe.

"As soon as the plumber comes, this water is going away for good." She placed a hand on each boy's head. "Your duck would be out of luck."

"It's a lot of water," Zach said slowly.

"Yep," Shauna agreed. And the plumbing company she'd called had said they wouldn't be able to send someone over until early this evening, which meant she'd be paying overtime for the work.

She loved her kitchen, its ancient six-burner stove and yellow laminate countertops with chrome trim along the edges. Like most of the house's interior, it was past due for a renovation, last updated in the era of *Father Knows Best* and Donna Reed. But she'd painted the old wood cabinets a bright robin's-egg blue and added colorful accessories she'd found at thrift stores and garage sales to make the space look happy.

Happy was more important than new, although not when it came to a nonworking dishwasher.

Things had been fine that morning, and Shauna hadn't given a second thought to starting the dishwasher when she'd stopped home for lunch. Who knew the main pipe would give up the ghost midcycle?

She should have expected something along those lines. Owning a historic house had its challenges, although she'd avoided needing significant repairs on the main home for the year she'd owned the property.

Challenges could be overcome with willpower and a little grit—a lot of grit in some cases.

She'd managed to get the water main turned off, so at least that was something, although having no water was less than ideal for the twins. She had not-so-fond memories of utilities being shut off various months when her mom had forgotten or neglected to pay the bills.

So much neglect, but not on Shauna's watch.

"I'm going to grab a mop and bucket," she told her sons. "You two grab towels from the linen closet. Let's see if we can get this mess cleaned up."

The hardwood throughout the first floor was also original to the house, nearly a hundred years old. A soft whimper escaped her mouth as she thought of the potential damage waiting under the pond of water pooling in front of her dishwasher and sink. She'd need fans to dry everything and prayed she wouldn't have to involve insurance or a restoration company. Dollar signs floated in her vision.

If someone looked up the term *money pit* in the dictionary, would a photo of her house accompany the definition?

"I'll get my swimmy suit on," Zach announced.

"Me, too," Timmy echoed.

"I don't think..." Shauna forced a smile. "That's a great idea. Swimsuits will make it an adventure."

The twins cheered and headed for their shared room at the top of the stairs.

Timmy paused a few steps up. "Mommy, you should put on your swimmy suit, too. Your overalls are already wet, and you need more 'ventures."

Like she needed a hole in the head.

"I'll leave the adventuring up to you and your brother, sweetie. Don't forget the towels."

With a nod, her younger-by-two-minutes son ran up the stairs.

Shauna had just pulled the mop out of the closet in the laundry room when the doorbell rang.

Could the plumber have arrived early?

She practically sprinted to the door, reminding herself not to throw her arms around the busted-pipe white knight.

Only it wasn't the plumber on the other side.

"Annalise?"

She felt a blush creep into her cheeks as Annalise Haverford, the Magnolia mom crowd's recently disgraced queen bee, gaped at Shauna for a brief moment, then snapped shut her mouth, which curved into a subtle, patronizing smile.

Did the woman do condescension on purpose, or was that just how her face was made?

Shauna didn't hang with the town's mom brigade, although she did her part by signing up to bring baked goods for the various fundraisers the school held throughout the year.

"I apologize for interrupting." Annalise tucked her phone into the expensive-looking purse hanging from her shoulder. "You have me at a bit of a loss." Another full-frontal appraisal. "I don't believe we've met."

A lock of Annalise's glossy blond hair rustled in the early-April breeze, then fell back into place as if realizing the head on which it was lucky enough to rest would disapprove.

"I'm Shauna Myer." Shauna automatically started to offer her hand then remembered she was already holding the mop handle. "My boys are in first grade at the school. I recognize you from PTO meetings."

"You're a part of PTO?"

Annalise Haverford needed to fix her bitch face, resting and otherwise.

"Aren't all parents a part of PTO by virtue of having students at the school?"

"Yes, of course." Annalise had that Southern lilt down to a science, the cadence that could agree with a person while clearly communicating they were out of their mind.

"You might also know me because I was commissioned last fall to create a nursery mural at the Littleton estate outside of town. You intervened and convinced Charmaine Littleton that she needed to hire a painter out of Raleigh."

Fine lines appeared at the edges of Annalise's mouth as

her lips pursed. "That wasn't personal," she said, her diction crisper than it had been moments earlier. "I simply recommended an experienced artist who I heard had an excellent reputation."

"As I understand it, he's been steadily working for Charmaine ever since. You lost me a lucrative client, Mrs. Haverford."

"I preferred it when we were on a first-name basis."

"Even though you didn't know mine."

"An oversight," Annalise admitted, which felt different than an apology.

For the life of her, Shauna could not figure out what the woman was doing on her doorstep. She still managed a smile at the girl who stood just behind Annalise, a carbon copy of her mother with golden hair and big blue eyes. Mother and daughter were both dressed in preppy-looking skirts with white button-downs. Annalise's skirt was a pink-and-green-striped pattern, while her daughter wore a muted gingham design.

The girl must have been in school today, although they both looked as though they'd just stepped out of a *Southern Living* magazine spread. Zach and Timmy would have had those white shirts smeared with dirt or food in minutes.

In fact…

Shauna glanced down at her own paint-splattered overalls and long-sleeve beige shirt. She liked wearing overalls when she painted murals for clients. Lots of pockets for extra brushes and rags. But between her unofficial work uniform, her thick hair piled into a messy bun on top of her head and the fact that her feet were bare and the hem of her denims soaked, she felt like something the cat dragged in compared to Annalise.

“What are you doing here?” she blurted as discombobulation got the better of her.

“I believe we have an appointment,” Annalise said slowly.

“Mommy, I pooped, and the toilet won’t flush,” Zach shouted from the top of the stairs.

“Put down the lid and leave it,” she called back, then turned to their unexpected visitors. “We’re having a minor water leak issue.”

Annalise’s cornflower eyes widened. “I see.”

“Do you think he washed his hands?” the girl asked, her pert nose scrunching.

“Wash your hands,” Shauna yelled over her shoulder, then winked at the girl. “Actually, use hand sanitizer because we have no water. A reminder is always a good idea with boys.”

“My brother never washes his hands,” the girl reported.

“Not true,” Annalise said tersely then smiled again. It had turned into an expression more fittingly referred to as a grimace. “Perhaps I have the wrong address. I was supposed to tour a carriage house for rent.”

Right. Understanding dawned, although Shauna still couldn’t figure out why Annalise Haverford was interested in renting her apartment.

“This is the place. Boys, I’m going to give a tour of the apartment. Don’t start in the kitchen without me.”

“Where are my flippers?” Timmy asked as he appeared on the steps donning his swimsuit and goggles. He was the smaller of the boys, ribs visible on his slim frame.

“You don’t need flippers,” she told him. “Or goggles. Stay out of the kitchen until I get back. You and Zach can play in the yard.”

“Can we set up the sprinkler?”

"It's sixty degrees. No sprinkler." She stepped onto the porch and shut the door behind her. She loved her oversize porch with a wide swing on one side and comfy painted rocking chairs on the other. "Sorry about that. Busted pipe in the kitchen. An inch of water is exciting for young boys."

"Carriage house," Annalise said.

Shauna blinked. "Come again?"

"You said you were giving a tour of the apartment. It's a carriage house. That's how it was described on the rental site."

"Sure." Shauna shoved her feet into the clogs she'd left outside the front door and started down the porch steps. "The available unit is on the second floor of the carriage house. It's the original guest quarters. Two bedrooms and a smaller bonus room that could be used as an office or—"

"Another bedroom?" Annalise suggested.

"That would work, I suppose, although it's small and doesn't have a closet per se. I converted the workshop off the garage on the first floor to a second unit. That one is rented. Is this for a friend or family member?"

"It's for me," Annalise said, her voice almost a whisper. "And my children. We need a place to rent for a while."

Shauna startled but didn't break stride out of an inherent regard for people facing hard times. She didn't know Annalise Haverford well or particularly like her based on Annalise undermining Shauna, not to mention the woman's general reputation around town.

After spending most of her life as a have-not, Shauna had a keen distaste for women who lorded their social and financial status over those around them. She'd attended seven high schools in four years and had always been on the periphery of the cliques, both popular and more obscure. But she knew women like Annalise. The kind who judged others based on the brand of sneakers they wore—or as adults, the purses they carried. The cars they drove or whether their furniture matched.

There had been plenty of gossip, both confirmed and unfounded, around Magnolia when Annalise's husband, a well-known financial adviser, had been arrested for scheming his clients out of millions of dollars.

White-collar crime at that level was so foreign to Shauna that she hadn't paid much attention. In truth, she'd half blamed the people gullible enough to invest with him. She didn't trust anyone to take care of business other than herself.

She wasn't sure if that said much about her, but it was the way things often went for those who'd experienced legitimate insecurity in their lives.

She understood what real trouble looked like—the metallic taste it left in a person's mouth. It seemed far-fetched to believe Annalise might understand that.

However, the only other call she'd received on the apartment was from a group of recent high-school graduates who'd asked about putting a beer die table in the backyard. She hadn't even heard of the drinking game, but there was no doubt those young men weren't a fit.

She needed the extra income badly, especially considering what was waiting in her kitchen. At least she trusted a woman like Annalise to take care of the place.

"There's a swing set, Mommy." The relief in the girl's voice was evident as she pointed to the play structure Shauna's friend Declan had helped put together in the corner of the yard a few weeks earlier.

"That does not belong to us, Margo." Annalise glanced at Shauna. "We'll need to understand your rules for how tenants are allowed to access the property."

"Rules," Shauna repeated, turning the word over in her brain. Was she supposed to set guidelines for this woman to follow? Oh, how the mighty had fallen.

"Sweetie, you are welcome to use the swing set anytime. If you and your mom and brother move into the apartment—"

"Carriage house," Annalise interrupted.

"Carriage house," Shauna amended, keeping her gaze focused on Margo. "This is your home, and you can play in the yard or the driveway and have friends over whenever your mom says you can. Zach and Timmy would love to have a friend to play with so close." She winked at the girl. "If you can get over the fact that they're smelly boys and younger than you. I think you'd be able to boss them around with no problem. You have my permission."

If the girl took after her mother in any way, there was a good chance she already excelled at being bossy.

To her surprise, Margo bounced on her toes like she could barely contain her excitement. "I'll be real nice and help look after them and make sure they wash their hands."

"Then you're ahead of me on several counts. Do you want to check out the play structure while I give your mom a tour? There's a climbing wall and a slide on the other side."

"May I, Mommy?" Margo asked.

Annalise nodded. "Don't muss your clothes."

A bit of the girl's exuberance dimmed, but she agreed then ran toward the corner of the yard.

"She's a sweet kid," Shauna said as she led Annalise up the stairs.

"Very few people would describe my daughter as sweet. She was on her best behavior with you."

There was a thread of disbelief in the woman's tone.

That tiny glimmer of vulnerability told Shauna more than the local gossips ever could about Annalise Haverford's present state of mind.

She led the way up the stairs and into the bright, cheery space she'd just finished renovating and looked around with great pride. "Here it is."

She'd started work on the carriage house the moment she'd closed on the property a year earlier. Although plenty of projects needed attention in the main house, this had been her priority because of the difference the rental income could make in her circumstances.

Shauna hadn't had a permanent home for most of her childhood. Going forward from the gray, drizzly winter morning she'd awoken to her mom's final overdose, everything she'd owned in the world had fit into a battered backpack and beat-up suitcase with one broken buckle.

Now she was a landlord for two adorable apartments in a cozy neighborhood in the type of town she'd never imagined herself being a part of when she was younger. If only the people who'd made her believe she would never amount to anything could see her now.

"It's cute," Annalise said in the same tone she might use to describe a pile of dog yak as cute. "Smaller than it looked in the photos online."

There wasn't a chance in hell Shauna would be made to feel less by this woman. By anyone at this point in her life. She could do that well enough on her own.

"It's certainly not what you're used to, so you're welcome to look around," she said, gesturing to the hallway that led to the tiny bedrooms and office. "If it doesn't work—"

"I'll take it. The listing said a deposit plus first and last month's rent due upon signing the lease. Is that negotiable?"

Harsh spots of pink colored Annalise's cheeks, but she kept her chin high. "I'm a little short on cash at the moment."

Suddenly, Shauna doubted the wisdom of renting to this woman. Not because Annalise wouldn't be able to cover the rent. She'd figure out how to get by because that's what Southern steel magnolias had done for generations.

But Shauna was finding her footing in this town within the complicated social circles of mothers of school-age children. She might not be part of the in-crowd, but people seemed to like her well enough. Would renting to Annalise Haverford with her scandalous husband and besmirched reputation change that? Was it worth it?

"Mommy, come quick," Timmy shouted as he bounded up the steps and burst through the apartment door. "Zach is gonna fight a bad guy."

"What bad guy?" Shauna reached for her son.

"A stranger," Timmy said on a shaky breath. "He came to the door and—"

"I told you boys not to answer the door."

"I know, but Zach isn't a good listener. The bad guy asked for you. We told him to go away but he won't. He's big, Mommy. And scary. He looks like Uncle Declan only real mean. He put his foot in the door, so Zach couldn't close it. I ran out the back but—"

Shauna was already taking the steps two at a time. She knew only one man who fit that description, but it was impossible that he'd found her when she refused to believe he'd even try.

That didn't comfort her or slow her down as she ran up the driveway and around the porch.

"Get away from there," she shouted at the broad-shouldered giant who still had the power to weaken her knees, her usual concern for causing a scene her neighbors might witness forgotten in her panic.

"Shauna."

The deep voice pulsated through her like a drumbeat, the answering thrum of nerves as familiar to her as her own features in the mirror.

Just like the face of the man who walked down the porch steps and strode toward her.

She hadn't seen Flynn Murphy in nearly seven years, but her body—her heart—would have recognized him anywhere.

He was a difficult man to miss, towering over most people at six foot five inches of solid muscle, honed by over a decade in the military.

Declan, his brother and one of Shauna's dearest friends, had told her Flynn was now retired from the army, working as a cybersecurity contractor and data specialist for private firms around the country.

It made sense, she supposed, given his experience. His hair was a few inches longer than it had been, the ends nearly grazing his collar. She'd never seen him in dressy clothes and had to admit he wore the pressed trousers and crisp white button-down well.

His gray eyes reminded her of steel as he stared at her, hard and unforgiving.

That tense stare reminded her that it wasn't Flynn's right to forgive her for anything. She'd been the one wronged by him, left behind with no word or promise, her heart broken in two.

"You need to go," she said, and her voice was steady despite the emotions rushing through her. "We have nothing to say to each other."

"Mommy, do you know the stranger?" Zach asked from

the porch. Timmy had returned to the house through the back door and came to stand next to his twin.

"Go in the house, boys." She looked over Flynn's shoulder and offered her sons a reassuring smile. "I'll be right there."

"We wanna stay," Timmy said. His voice shook with anxiety. How in the world was it that Flynn had managed to scare her babies half to death just by his presence?

Because he was Flynn Murphy.

She used to adore his menacing personality because she believed it would protect her.

And he had, against everything and everyone except himself.

"In the house." She didn't often employ mom-tone, but Zach and Timmy knew better than to disobey her when she did.

They turned and headed inside, but she didn't allow herself to meet Flynn's gaze until the door shut behind them.

"Go," she said again.

He didn't move, but she could feel the tension mounting. "You might have nothing to say to me, Shauna." He inclined his head toward the house. "But it appears I have more than I imagined to say to you. Those boys look like me."

She locked her knees so they wouldn't buckle. So much for feeling safe. Just when she was getting comfortable in this town, her world came crashing down around her. She wanted to deny Flynn's words, but what was the point?

With their flaxen hair, pale blue eyes she knew would darken as they got older and the mischievous smiles each boy would flash to get themselves out of trouble, Zach and Timmy did resemble their father. They looked like Flynn.

"We're not having this conversation now, Flynn. You don't get to show up and have things go your way." Two blond heads appeared in the family-room window that overlooked the front yard, and she would not hash this out with her boys witnessing it.

Flynn took a small step toward her, maybe only an inch closer, but it felt like he'd invaded her space on every level. *Don't lose it in front of him,* she mentally told herself, and dug her fingernails into her palms in a feeble attempt to ground herself in something besides Flynn's overwhelming magnetism.

"I'm not leaving until—"

"You most certainly *are* leaving," a melodic voice said. A moment later, Annalise was at Shauna's side. She jabbed a finger with a chipped nail—Shauna wouldn't have expected that—toward Flynn. "I don't know who you are, mister, but you have no right to scare those boys and intimidate my friend here with all your…" She waved that finger up and down. "With all of you. You need to leave before we call the authorities."

"I haven't done anything," Flynn said through clenched teeth. His brow furrowed, and those soft lips that Shauna had loved against her skin drew into a terse line. "Not yet."

"You're trespassing," Annalise insisted. "I don't know what kind of cave you crawled out of, but that's against the law in Magnolia."

Flynn lifted a brow at Annalise. "Do you own this property?"

"Shauna owns this house. I'm her tenant." Annalise shot a glance at Shauna as if she'd known Shauna had been about to tell her she wouldn't rent the apartment to her. "Right?"

"My tenant and my friend." Shauna repeated Annalise's claim because when was the last time anyone but Declan had defended her? When was the last time she'd allowed it?

Now she took strength in Annalise's disdain for Flynn, and whether it was real or contrived didn't matter.

Flynn looked like he wanted to argue. He excelled at arguing but then shook his head. "I'll call you," he told Shauna.

"You don't have my number."

"I'll figure it out." He glanced at the house again. "Soon, Shauna. We will talk about what you never told me very soon."

Then he turned on his heel and stalked to the curb where a massive black pickup truck waited.

Of course that was the vehicle he drove.

"He's intense," Annalise said with a shaky laugh as she took a step away.

Shauna had the ridiculous urge to pull the woman, who was not her friend despite what they'd both said, back to her side.

"Among other things," she whispered. "Thank you for running him off. Most people would be too scared to go up against Flynn Murphy in a temper."

"Oh, darlin'." Annalise did a hair toss worthy of a supermodel. "If I let a pesky thing like fear keep me from taking action, I would have spent the past five months curled in a ball under the covers. Still, I might have run that giant man off for the moment, but you'll have to face him eventually."

"Eventually," Shauna agreed. "Thankfully, not right now." She offered Annalise a genuine smile. "Let's go in the house and sign your lease. I think the past few minutes have more than fulfilled your deposit."

CHAPTER THREE

"You can't do that." Meghan Banks swallowed around the disbelief and ensuing panic that gripped her chest. "I don't understand how or why this is happening."

Greg Wheeler, the principal of Magnolia Elementary, where she worked as the art teacher for students from kindergarten to sixth grade, offered a strained smile. "It was a shock to all of us when the school board announced there was no funding for certain extracurricular programs for next year. I'm sorry, Meghan. We won't be renewing your contract."

"No." She shook her head. "Art isn't extracurricular. It's part of their education, Greg. The kids need art." Meghan said the words with conviction like they would make a difference. "I need this job." That was the bottom line. "I just signed a lease on an apartment."

"I'm sure families will be interested in supplementing the primary curriculum with art classes. That woman who owns the gallery in town has been raising money to offer after-school classes and whatnot. You could maybe get a job with her?"

"I don't want to teach after-school classes and whatnot." Meghan took a breath. It wouldn't do her any good to freak out. Greg was young for an administrator, only a year older than Meghan, who'd celebrated her twenty-ninth birthday last week. Pushing thirty, she was alone with no family to speak of and potentially no job. Not exactly what she'd planned for her life.

Nope. Not going there. Too depressing. There was still hope to salvage the situation. She had to believe it was possible.

If only Grammy were still alive, Meghan would have somebody to work through this with or offer a sympathetic ear. Although Greg seemed to be saying the right words, she didn't get the impression he really cared.

She wanted to believe he did. "You said certain programs are being cut. How are you managing to fund the others?" she asked as she rose from behind her desk.

"That's not your concern." She noticed that he'd stopped making eye contact with her. Never a good sign.

She looked around the classroom, from the drawings on the wall to the colorful bins of art supplies to Picasso, the beta fish who lived in a small tank on the bookshelf. The kids would miss Picasso.

"We had to make some difficult choices about what we'll offer next year. This was the decision I…we…the board made."

"Is it because I wouldn't go out with you? Are you eliminating my job in retaliation?"

He'd seemed annoyed but not upset when she'd explained she wasn't interested in dating him, but maybe he'd held a grudge all these months. Greg bristled and adjusted his wire-rimmed glasses on his nose. He was a wiry man overall, from his narrow face to an almost underweight body for a man of his height.

Meghan was built solidly with a curvy figure that would have been envied back in Renaissance times. Not so much these days, but she liked her body and her strength. Right now, she wondered what would happen if she body slammed her boss to the ground and pinned him until he cried uncle or agreed to let her keep her job.

"Of course not. Don't be ridiculous. I'm offended that you even suggested that, Meghan. You should know better. We are professionals here. I'm a professional. I might not understand why you said no, but I respect your right to make a bad decision."

How comforting. But she shouldn't have mentioned anything. This wasn't going to help her cause, but he'd acted strange when she said no to a date. It was as if he felt she should have been grateful that he deigned to ask her out. Meghan had way bigger fish to fry than a disgruntled potential suitor. "What options do we have for keeping the art curriculum in the school next year? It's not just a program, Greg. It's an essential component in the development of our students."

"I understand why you see it that way."

"There is research that backs it up." She moved around the desk and picked up one of the self-portraits the fourth-graders had been working on earlier in the day. It was apparent how much time and effort the student had put into this drawing.

"Art instruction helps children with motor, language and social skills, decision-making, risk-taking and inventiveness. I could go on and on about the benefits."

"I don't think you need to get dramatic."

Meghan hadn't been dramatic a day in her life. The only role she played to a tee was one of a doormat.

"We'd be happy to have you return to the school in a volunteer capacity," Greg told her. "Several members of the PTO have already told us they'd be willing to take over some of the work and do crafting projects a couple of times a month with the different grades."

"An art teacher isn't somebody who simply manages craft projects."

"You should lose your judgmental attitude. It's not becoming."

What Meghan was becoming was more irate with every second.

"Could I have a few days before you tell the rest of the staff?" She needed time to regroup and come up with a plan. Surely she could come up with a plan.

Greg agreed with a frown. "Although it's not going to change anything," he told her. "You can't stop this, Meghs. The decision has been made, and I need your assurance that you'll support the district's stance when talking to parents and students."

As she resisted the urge to tell him he couldn't call her by her nickname, she tried to wrap her brain around what he was saying because it sounded like…

"Are you saying you expect me to tell people I support this decision? That I support being fired?"

"Laid off," he clarified. "Unfortunately, because you've only been in the district for a year, there isn't a severance package to speak of."

"It keeps getting better. You're firing me with no compensation, and I'm supposed to tell people I think it's peachy keen?"

"You choose the words you want to use, but we must present a united front. It's important. Obviously, if you're a team player, I'll be happy to write a recommendation letter."

"*If* I'm a team player," she repeated.

"You know what I mean."

"I do."

She had two months left working her dream job in her dream community and then no future to speak of. She didn't want to leave this town, partly because of the promise she'd made to her grandmother when it became clear the cancer was going to win the battle.

She'd told Grammy that she would stay in Magnolia, the town the older woman had lived in and loved for all of her ninety-two years. The place Meghan had visited for months each summer and on every extended school holiday—the only place Meghan had truly felt at home.

The area continued to grow, becoming more vibrant with each passing season, so maybe Meghan could get hired in a neighboring district. She closed her eyes and reminded herself not to give up yet. Her maternal grandmother had been a fighter, and somewhere deep inside, Meghan wanted to believe she took after Nadine Eilmes, who she'd adored with every ounce of her being.

She would figure out a solution one way or the other. Greg made a few more imbecilic remarks and scurried out of the classroom. She rolled her eyes as she thought about the fact that she'd considered going on a date with the man. What in the world had she been thinking? She might be approaching a world-record dry spell, but even she wasn't that desperate.

She quickly gathered her things and headed to her car for the evening. This morning, she'd loaded it with boxes from her grandmother's house to take to her new apartment. There wasn't anything of value left after her mother had sent the estate sale crew to do their business.

The house was nearly eighty years old and had once been elegant with crisp white paint and columns on the exterior of the Colonial-style structure. The bones remained solid, but the home required significant updates and far more of a financial investment than Meghan could dream of making to restore it to its former glory.

She'd put notes on the few pieces of furniture she wanted to take with her and then been shocked but somehow not surprised when the uptight woman handling the auction had told her she would have to pay for anything she wanted to remove from the house. Those had been her mother's terms, the woman had explained, looking down her nose at Meghan as if Denise Banks had labeled her daughter a freeloader.

Maybe Meghan should have expected it. After all, her mom hadn't been happy when her youngest daughter decided to move to Magnolia to care for Nadine in her last stage of life. But Meghan's grandmother had been everything to her, and despite how trying some of the moments had been toward the end, she wouldn't have traded it for anything.

She liked to believe that her grandmother had been the one to arrange the rental she'd found in some sort of angelic mission. The studio space was tiny but affordable, and Shauna Myer, Meghan's new landlord, had always been kind when they'd interacted at the school.

It wasn't as if such a beautiful, independent, Bohemian-looking mother would become Meghan's bestie. Still, she was a friendly face, and Meghan often felt challenged by dealing with adults due to her social anxiety.

She managed her panic with a series of breathing and calming exercises when things got overwhelming. But interacting with people other than her students didn't come naturally. She pulled down the driveway toward the parking space Shauna had told her was hers.

She climbed out of her car only to hear soft music and female voices coming from the back patio.

It was a perfect spring afternoon in the coastal North Carolina town with the scent of flowering trees making the air especially sweet. Although it was only midweek, she supposed she shouldn't be surprised that Shauna would have friends over for a happy-hour cocktail. Shauna probably had all kinds of friends.

Meghan purposely kept her eyes away from the patio as she unloaded her small sedan, then heard her name being called. For a moment, she thought she was conjuring the summons in her mind because she wanted friends.

"Meghan, come on over," Shauna called again.

Meghan's mouth went dry and her heartbeat accelerated as she placed the boxes on the ground and started toward the house.

Be normal, she told herself. She was saying hello to some women. That was what people did. It's what teachers did.

Meghan could manage back-to-school nights and seeing students around town. She was comfortable with kids and could handle talking to their parents when art was the topic—she was quick with a sincere compliment.

It didn't matter if the child was a budding van Gogh or relegated to drawing stick figures for their whole life. Meghan found the creativity and talent in every person, probably because that's what she most wanted for herself as a child.

She grounded herself in the feel of the cool grass underneath her ballet flats as she drew closer. But it felt like her heart might beat straight out of her chest when she realized it wasn't a group of women on the back porch.

Oh, no. This was much worse. It was Shauna and one other woman, Annalise Haverford. Annalise, who ran the very same PTO that Greg told her was stepping in to take over her role at the school.

Annalise's younger child, Margo, was adorable but had a mean streak as wide as the Mississippi River. The older one, Trey, was a basically sweet kid, but he'd been struggling since his father had been sent to jail.

Maybe they were all struggling, although Meghan had trouble mustering sympathy for a woman who'd deemed Meghan's life's work inconsequential.

"How's the move going?" Shauna asked as Meghan stepped onto the patio. The single mom looked effortlessly beautiful and artsy in her overalls and slim shirt.

"Fine. I'll have everything here by the end of the weekend."

"I should warn you," Shauna said with a shake of her head. "There's no water at the moment. A pipe burst in the kitchen, and I'm waiting for the plumbers. Annalise is keeping me company. You two must know each other from school."

"It's lovely to see you, Ms. Banks," Annalise said with a regal head bob. The sleek blonde must have been a beauty queen back in the day.

"Call me Meghan."

"You're going to be neighbors," Shauna said. Was it Meghan's imagination, or did her smile falter slightly?

Meghan blinked. "Excuse me?"

"I've rented the carriage house," Annalise explained. The way she said it made Meghan think she was referring to a Tuscan villa.

"The upstairs apartment?" Meghan clarified.

Shauna seemed to stifle a laugh. "The very one. We're having a drink to celebrate signing the lease. Or to calm my nerves. Hard to tell which exactly. Would you like a margarita?" She gestured to the pitcher that sat between them on the table.

"No." Meghan zeroed her gaze on Annalise. "Unfortunately, I don't know how long we'll be neighbors, but you might have guessed that already."

Annalise raised a brow. "I'm afraid I don't know what you're talking about. I want you as a neighbor, Ms. Banks. Meghan. I know you. I trust you. Do you have a problem with me specifically? Did someone you know invest with my husband? If so, I—"

"I got fired today," Meghan blurted. Greg had told her not to mention it to her coworkers. These women weren't that. "I'm finishing out spring semester, and then the art and music programs are being cut. I was told PTO members would take over my duties."

"That's ridiculous." Shauna straightened in her chair. A thick braid fell over one shoulder and her legs, which were curled underneath her, still seemed impossibly long in her overalls and ribbed shirt. "The kids love you. You're a licensed teacher. What's PTO got to do with this?"

"Craft projects apparently," Meghan said.

She noticed Annalise had gone pale, her glossy lips drawing into a thin line. She wore a knee-length skirt in a striped pattern with a tailored-white blouse and a pearl choker. Honestly, Annalise Haverford looked more professional than Meghan had a day in her life.

"I'm not involved with PTO activities any longer," Annalise said, her voice tight. "My presence at meetings disturbed some of the other parents."

"So you're not part of the group taking over my job?"

"Of course not. PTO is charged with raising money to support the school and helping with programs that enrich the educational experience. We aren't teachers."

"Neither am I after this year ends. At least not at Magnolia Elementary." Meghan dropped into a chair across from Shauna. "Maybe I will have that margarita."

"They can't do that to you," Shauna insisted. "Is it that new little twerpy principal? He looks like a ferret."

"I believe he had something to do with it," Meghan confirmed.

Shauna nudged Annalise. "We've got to fix this. You have to use your influence to help her keep her job."

"Me?" Annalise bit off a laugh. "I told you I got kicked out of PTO. That's a new low around here, especially given all the money I've raised over the years. I am in no position to be anyone's champion."

"Then I'll do it." Shauna poured a generous serving of margarita into one of the plastic glasses on the tray. "Art curriculums are important."

"Not to Principal Ferret," Meghan explained then grimaced. "That was mean. I'm never mean."

"I'm already rubbing off on you," Annalise said and clinked Meghan's cup with her own. "This cozy arrangement should be an adventure."

"My son just told me I needed more adventures," Shauna said with a smile.

"I don't think this is what he had in mind, darlin'." Annalise took a long drink.

It certainly wasn't what Meghan had expected either, but for better or worse, these two women gave her a sense of being a little less alone. And she'd take that feeling any way she could get it.

CHAPTER FOUR

"A FIGHT, TREY? Seriously?" Annalise smacked her open palm against the steering wheel as she turned onto the long gravel driveway that led to Whimsy Farm on Thursday afternoon.

She had an interview for a job, although she couldn't figure out for the life of her why a housekeeper position required the kind of background check she'd had to submit along with an in-person interview.

It was humiliating enough that her former cleaning lady had recommended her for the position.

Annalise Haverford as a maid. Wouldn't the knowledge land her mother on the fainting couch if Carolann ever discovered it? Financial instability was one thing; lowering herself to becoming household help was simply beyond the pale.

But this was no ordinary job due to the potential client. Country music superstar Walker Calloway had purchased the farm at the first of the year. Word on the street in design circles up and down the Carolina coast was that Walker was done with Nashville and planned to make North Carolina his home base.

Annalise had heard he'd been interviewing designers and architects to lead a complete overhaul of the main house.

Annalise hadn't done more than a few token projects in the past decade—she'd been too busy being a supportive wife and perfect mother. But if she could snag Walker Calloway as a client, what a comeback that would be. She'd prove to Everly Mae, her own mother and herself—if she were being honest—that she had something of value to add, other than her ability to put together an Instagram-worthy charcuterie board for a party of Jonathan's best clients.

Of course, those same clients were now happy to see her buried along with her husband's reputation, not that she blamed them. Jonathan had done horrible, despicable, criminal things, but she hadn't been a part of his crimes.

It would be easier to reinvent herself someplace else, to change her name and start over.

But Annalise had a stubborn streak that would make her salt of the earth Southern ancestors proud.

"It wasn't a big fight," Trey muttered.

"You and Beau Tinsdale were sent home. You hit him. Haverfords don't hit their friends."

"I'm sorry, okay. What are we doing out here anyway?" Trey asked, his knobby knee bouncing as he gazed out the window. "This is a farm."

"I'm aware of that. Your mother is getting a job at this farm."

He looked dubious. "You don't know how to work. Daddy always said your job was window dressing, whatever that is. I like ranch dressing."

"I prefer vinegar at this point," Annalise muttered.

She could remember Jonathan making jokes about how she spent her time, but she'd always assumed they were harmless. She and Jonathan had been a team. He'd picked her—bland, middle-class Annalise Fluk, with no pedigree to speak of, over the debutantes his mother would have preferred as his match.

In return for giving Annalise a prominent last name and

the social status her mother had always wanted for her, she'd made it her mission to be the perfect helpmate to Jonathan.

She was kind when it was called for and ruthless when she needed to be in order to advance their status.

Her body was trim and fit, and she never missed a manicure or went out in public without makeup. She'd even taken a class on ways to please a man in the bedroom. Online, of course. She would not have been caught dead talking about anything as tawdry as her sex life in public.

In the end, what had all of her efforts gotten her? She'd thought she would rule the town of Magnolia for all of her days. And she would have been a benevolent dictator eventually. Still, it took smarts and moxie to claim the title of society queen, even in a town that was as welcoming and inclusive as Magnolia.

If Annalise had her way, she would have ensured everyone knew their place. Only now, she was the one who had been taken down several pegs, if not a whole floor.

"Why would you want to work with horses? You don't even like horses. And why do I have to come with you when Margo doesn't?"

"Because Margo didn't get sent home early from school for fighting." It had been like a spike to her gut when Principal Ferret, as she now thought of him, called and told her Trey and Beau Tinsdale had been fighting on the playground. Luckily, she'd arrived before Everly Mae, so that was one confrontation she was able to avoid. Trey refused to speak about the altercation, and Annalise needed to get through this interview before dealing with her son.

One hurdle at a time these days.

"Margo fights plenty."

"Excuse me?"

"She just doesn't use her fists."

Annalise didn't know how to respond to that bombshell, so she did what had always worked best. She ignored it. It was amazing what a person could ignore when they set their mind to it.

"I want you to stay in the car while I have this interview. For the record, I'm not going to be working with horses. This is a house manager position." That was an elevated description, but Trey didn't question her.

"Does the person who lives here need some window dressing?"

She snorted. "That's an excellent question, honey, but I'm no longer in the market to be anyone's window dressing. I had plenty of that with your father."

"Daddy says—"

"I don't want to hear about what your daddy says." Annalise took a breath and forced a gentler tone. "I am going to help the nice man who lives here redecorate his house. It's a talent I have." Might as well send her intention out into the universe.

Trey didn't respond, and she wondered if he'd been shocked into silence at the thought of his mother being talented at anything other than ordering about the people around her and making reservations at the country club in town.

When she looked over, Trey stared out the window at the pasture on the other side of the wood fence. His face was a picture of wonder and delight.

When was the last time she'd seen her son look so relaxed? Tears stung her eyes at the thought that it might have been well before Jonathan's scandal broke.

"They have a lot of horses," she said, her foolish panic swirling at seeing several of them running along the fence line next to her car. There was no way for the horses to get to her. It wasn't like they would jump the fence and come at her vehicle with their giant terrifying hooves. Several of her children's friends took riding lessons, but not Trey and Margo.

Annalise didn't do horses.

"If I rode a horse, he would be the fastest ever."

"Yes, I'm certain that's true," Annalise agreed. Her son had started running the day he learned to walk. Trey was filled with energy, and from the time he was a small boy, she'd put him in a variety of activities to keep him busy and out of trouble. Thanks to her ex-husband, trouble had found them anyway, despite her best efforts.

"For today, you need to sit still," she said as she pulled to a stop in front of the stately old home. It was a classic two-story painted brick in the classic Georgian style that had great symmetry and balance with an archway above the front door. Rows of tall windows lined both the first and second floors.

But there was paint chipping in certain areas, and one of the shutters on an upstairs window had come off, giving the facade a lopsided look, like a grand dame who'd done a lousy job taking off her makeup and woken up the following day with her fake eyelashes in various locations they did not belong on her face. The flower bed in front of the porch was bright with tulips and lilac bushes, although the latter looked overgrown in places.

There was a magnolia tree blooming in the yard, much like the one on Shauna Myer's property with its goblet-like blooms in vivid pink weighing down the branches. For whatever reason—desperation most likely—Annalise considered it a good omen.

"Can I at least have your phone?" Trey asked.

She wanted to say no. Losing screen time privileges was

part of his punishment for the fight, but she also knew she was making a big ask of a ten-year-old boy to remain in the car for however long this interview took.

She hoped she'd be back soon. After all, how much time could it take to determine whether a person was capable of cleaning toilets? Not that she intended for her position to remain so menial.

Once she got her foot in the door, she'd find a way to impress Walker Calloway with her decorating skill. This was Annalise's big shot, and she wasn't going to mess it up. There was too much riding on it. She handed Trey the phone after rolling down the windows.

It was a beautiful afternoon, the kind of perfect early-spring weather she adored before the oppressive heat of summer fell like a heavy blanket over the town. Normally, she might be out working in her garden at this time of day. Everything was in bloom, and her fingers itched to take pruning shears to the tangled bushes that surrounded the front porch of the farmhouse.

Annalise liked a neat and orderly garden and this was anything but. She took a deep breath and said a few silent positive affirmations as she knocked on the door and waited for Walker Calloway to answer.

She wasn't much of a country music fan but had been listening to the Calloway Brothers, the super duo band he'd formed with his now deceased brother, in her car for the past couple of days. Except it wasn't Walker who answered the door.

The man who stood on the other side wasn't as hulking as the giant she'd chased off Shauna's property, but he was just as physically overwhelming. More so to Annalise.

Shauna's guy hadn't intimidated her with his brawn or bulk or angry glare. This rugged stranger made her immediately tongue-tied and unable to draw in a decent breath with his steady gaze the color of wet earth after a torrential downpour soaked it.

Torrents of attraction ripped through her, and she struggled to maintain her composure, something wholly foreign to Annalise. She couldn't remember ever reacting to a man this way. Every cell in her body sent up danger alerts.

Not quite every cell. One particular part of her anatomy sat up at attention, hoping Annalise was having the same effect on him as he was on her.

"No reporters," he said, his dark eyes flat as he stared at her. "You have five minutes to vacate this property before I call the police but only three until I get out my shotgun."

Okay, he was not having the same reaction as her. He wore a flannel shirt and faded jeans that sat low on his hips with scuffed boots. When had she developed a penchant for cowboys? She licked her dry lips and tried to focus.

"Good afternoon, sir, and I hope you're having a pleasant day as well. I have an appointment with Mr. Calloway."

The man's expression didn't change, but something flashed in his bitter-chocolate-colored eyes. She couldn't tell whether it was amusement or admiration. But either way, she liked it. She should not like anything about the gatekeeping stranger. It was imperative she get past him and regain her composure.

"You don't look like a maid," he said.

She couldn't quite place his accent. It wasn't Southern, although he certainly looked comfortable in those tight-fitting jeans he wore over muscled legs. What she wouldn't give for him to turn around.

She mentally shook her head. It didn't matter where he was from. It mattered that he let her into the house to see Walker.

"I'm Annalise Haverford," she said. "I'm interviewing for a house manager position. Who might you be—the butler?"

A grin split his face for a millisecond, and she caught a glimpse of straight white teeth. She would have preferred if he had some kind of nasty tobacco habit that turned his pearly whites dingy yellow. She couldn't abide bad oral hygiene.

"I'm Jack Grainger, Walker's…" One heavy brow lifted. "His ranch manager."

"I thought this was a farm. What's the difference?"

"I'm from Montana. Ranch manager sounds better than farm."

"Well, now, Mr. Grainger. I suppose you can call it whatever you want, as long as you step aside and let me in."

He didn't move. "You're not right for this job."

"For your information, I can clean a floor until it sparkles so brilliantly, the queen of England would be lucky to eat off it."

"Let me see your hands."

"Excuse me?"

"Your fingernails. I would like to see them."

Thinking of how she'd been humiliated by her raggedy nails during the recent run-in with Everly Mae, Annalise balled her hands into fists. "Why?"

"I don't believe you're here for the housekeeping position. I'm guessing your hands will prove that you don't do anything more taxing than using your fingernails to scroll social media. You're fancy, and housekeepers aren't generally fancy."

"What exactly do you think I'm doing here?"

"Looking for a story. There isn't one." He started to close the door, but she shoved her sneakered foot into it and thrust her hands toward him.

"I can tell you a lot of stories, Mr. Grainger. One about betrayal and having your world upended and being a single mother to two kids with very little in the way of prospects in a town that hates your guts. My former housekeeper, the one I can no longer afford, recommended me for this position. I'm highly qualified. Overqualified, in fact. I don't know what not-broken nails are going to prove to you, but here they are just the same."

He kept his gaze on hers, and she tried not to be unnerved by his scrutiny.

"I understand that Mr. Calloway has a story, but I'm not interested in the past. Yours or his, and I'm certainly looking to leave mine behind."

Her fingers trembled, but she ignored it.

Jack Grainger ignored her outstretched hands as he stepped back to allow her entry. She quickly glanced over her shoulder at the car to make sure Trey was still in the front seat. She would have waved, but the boy's attention was one hundred percent engrossed by the phone.

Suddenly she didn't want to follow Jack Grainger. She didn't want any of this, but needs must, she supposed.

He was speaking as he led her down a long hallway that smelled slightly musty. Annalise told herself not to look at his butt in the jeans, but she couldn't help peeking. It was better than she'd imagined.

"We need someone to come for light cleaning and food prep a few hours every day. Neither Walker or I cook for shit. The house is five thousand square feet, with four bedrooms and three baths. There's an office in the guesthouse out back. But Walker's using that—or will be using the space—as a recording studio. So it won't need to be cleaned."

"Has he changed anything since he moved in?" She

glanced around at the chintz furniture, most of which had gaudy floral patterns or some terrifying-looking bunnies in the case of one unfortunate overstuffed chair.

"He's getting to that eventually."

"Yes, well." She cleared her throat. "I also have a background in design, and I know most of the suppliers in this area."

Jack whirled on her so fast she stumbled back a step. His hand shot out and wrapped around her wrist to steady her. Without hesitation but not before noticing the feel of his calloused palm, she shook off the touch and righted herself.

"So that's your angle? Once again, Mrs. Haverford—"

"Not Mrs.," she corrected, letting the Southern seep into her tone because it made her sound confident even when she didn't feel it. "I am no longer anyone's wife, although you may call me Annalise."

"I'm not going to call you anything," Jack told her then continued walking forward. They made it to the kitchen, which was huge if outdated. Her mind began to whirl with the possibilities of replacing the yellowing maple cabinets and white appliances. "You're leaving."

"I can take care of this house. Connie told me Mr. Calloway wants someone discreet who he can trust." She pointed at herself. "I don't want anyone to know how low my circumstances have brought me, so not only will I not talk about Mr. Calloway, but I also won't even mention the capacity in which he employs me."

"He does *not* employ you," Jack countered. "I manage the staff on the farm, and I'm not hiring you. Along with the responsibilities inside the house, I've decided I need an employee who can also assist me in the barn. Now that spring is here, there's more work to be done."

"You want a maid-slash-farmhand?"

"It's not too much to ask." The look on his face suggested otherwise. "It would be full-time employment."

"With benefits?" she asked, then rolled her eyes when he barked out a laugh. "I'm not talking about a 401k or benefits of any other kind. Health insurance would be nice. Dental perhaps? You know regular visits for oral cleaning are important for good dental health."

"You're odd."

"I'm singular."

He snorted and tried to cover it with a cough. "You aren't a fit for the job."

"You're changing the description as we speak. Don't you think Mr. Calloway should be the one making that decision?"

Just then, there was a noise on the side of the wraparound porch. The door from the outside to the kitchen opened, and a young boy with an obvious black eye entered with Trey behind him.

"Gus, what are you doing?" Jack's voice was noticeably gentler than when he'd spoken to Annalise.

"Trey, I told you to stay in the car." Her stomach tightened as the boy, who looked about Trey's age but was on the scrawny side, touched a finger to his shiner. He had dark hair and pale skin with knobby elbows and knees. He wore a grubby T-shirt and athletic shorts, one of his socks pulled up to midcalf while the other sagged around his bony ankle.

Jack Grainger was forgotten for a moment as Annalise stepped forward and focused her attention on her son. "I was told you got in a fight with Beau Tinsdale. Please don't tell me there were more boys involved."

Trey refused to meet her gaze.

"You better spill it right now, mister, or your two weeks

of grounding will turn into a month. You'll miss the start of the Little League season."

"Mom, you have to let me play baseball. I'm the starting pitcher."

"I don't have to do anything if—"

"He rescued me," the other boy said, his voice squeaky, which fit him perfectly.

"I thought you said you tripped." Jack came to stand beside Annalise. "You told Walker and me that you tripped over your shoelaces."

"I did trip," the boy mumbled. "After the big bully—"

"That would be Beau, not me," Trey clarified.

Gus nodded. "He knocked me down, and I was trying to get back up and then he pushed me and I tripped. I wasn't lying. I tripped."

She could almost feel the tension rolling off Jack. "And Trey here helped you by punching out this Beau bully?"

To Annalise's surprise, Trey met Jack's gaze with a challenge sparking his blue eyes like they were on fire. "I know I'm not supposed to hit people. But Beau deserved it."

Before Annalise could remind her son that violence wasn't the way to handle a bully, the door to the pantry opened, and Walker Calloway stepped out. "You're hired, Ms. Haverford."

She should be used to strange happenings by now, but this interview was one for Ripley's Believe It or Not! over in Gatlinburg.

"Call me Annalise," she told him. "I'm a master at organization as well. Might save you from spending time in the pantry searching for…" She inclined her head. "What exactly were you doing in there, Mr. Calloway?"

"Call me Walker." One side of his full mouth tipped into a smile. The photos and videos she'd seen on the internet didn't do the man justice. Walker Calloway looked like he should be a poster on the wall of every country music fan under the age of a hundred and three.

He had thick hair a shade or two lighter than his the boy's, a chiseled jaw, straight nose and enviable cheekbones. He was tall and broad and had clearly earned his reputation as one of the most crush-worthy country stars. Walker was every bit as attractive as his friend Jack, but Annalise's body was strangely unaffected by his obvious charm and magnetism.

And she didn't think it had anything to do with the aura of sorrow surrounding him like a shroud.

Walker Calloway she could handle. Jack Grainger was another story entirely, one she refused to turn the page on no matter how enticing it might be.

"Looking for chips," he answered without missing a beat.

"Walker, it's not going to work with her."

Walker ignored Jack—quite a trick as far as Annalise was concerned—and approached Gus and Trey. "What's your name, son?"

"Jonathan Grant Haverford the third," her son replied. "I'm called Trey."

"Trey, I'd like to thank you for standing up for my nephew. I know the school and your mama have opinions on fighting, and they're not wrong, but I appreciate you stepping in when you saw a situation that warranted it. Gus could use some more friends in Magnolia."

"Me and Trey aren't friends," Gus reported with a sigh. "I don't got friends here."

Annalise noticed Walker's shoulders stiffen while Jack scrubbed a hand over his jaw and looked up to the ceiling like he was silently calling on some celestial creature to intervene.

Annalise was no angel, but Walker had offered her the job despite the bulldog's objections. She knew which side her bread was buttered.

"Trey can be your friend," she offered, giving her son a pointed look. She hadn't exactly encouraged him to make an effort with misfit-type kids in the past, but they would all need to adapt if their lives were going to get back on track.

"Can I see the horses?" her son asked, smooth as a baby's bottom.

She automatically started to deny him, but Gus nodded. "Jack'll take us to the barn. Right, Jack?"

Walker straightened, and a moment of silent communication passed between the two men that Annalise couldn't interpret.

"You bet, buddy. Uncle Walker can talk to Ms. Haverford about the details of her employment." He raised his hands, palms out like he was giving up. But she had a feeling a man like Jack wouldn't surrender so easily.

"It's going to be fine," Walker said as Jack walked past him.

"Oh, I know it is, Walk," Jack replied, darting a wary glance toward Annalise. "I'm going to damn well make sure of it."

CHAPTER FIVE

"I DON'T UNDERSTAND why he's here." Shauna thunked her head on the wood bar top at Champions, the local bar her friend Declan owned in downtown Magnolia.

"I don't understand most of what my brother does," Dec replied as he hand-dried a load of pint glasses he'd just taken from the dishwasher behind the bar.

Declan had come to the thriving coastal community shortly before Christmas to help Shauna when she'd been injured in a skydiving accident and unable to walk or drive for several weeks. They'd met as teenagers in foster care, and it had been Declan who'd introduced Shauna to Flynn, his older brother.

She'd been young then. Flynn Murphy had overwhelmed her senses and heart with his strength, bad-boy protective vibes and all that annoying sex appeal he exuded.

But she wasn't that girl any longer and understood that fairy tales didn't always have a happy ending.

"He won't stay," she said more to herself than Declan.

"I agree," her friend answered then waved as a couple of patrons entered the bar. It was one thirty on a Friday afternoon, so the establishment wasn't nearly as crowded as it would be in a few hours.

Declan's plan hadn't been to settle in Magnolia, but he'd fallen in love and decided to buy the bar he was helping to renovate. The space was now warm and inviting, with wood-paneled walls and a long oak bar with antique brass details running the length of one wall. The bar had comfy stools with leather upholstery, dart boards, shuffleboard and pool tables in the back, where locals and visitors to town gathered most weekends.

Shauna had stopped by after finishing up a mural on the dining room walls of one of her newest clients. It had been a struggle to put the finishing details on the idyllic scene she'd painted when her heart refused to settle and her hands wanted to tremble.

"He could do a world of damage while he's here," Declan continued. He placed the pint glasses under the bar and then leaned toward her. "He could hurt you again, Shauna. I don't want to see that."

"Flynn has no power over me anymore."

"He knows about the boys," Declan reminded her.

"I didn't confirm anything." A stupid argument because she knew she'd just delayed the inevitable with Annalise's help.

"Are you going to force him to take a DNA test? He will. Flynn will do anything to prove a point. You know how obstinate and relentless he can be."

And angry and curt but also protective and gentle and a man who made her feel like she was more precious than the air he breathed. At least until he walked away without looking back.

She laughed like this was some trifling joke. The alternative was bursting into gut-wrenching tears, and Shauna didn't have time for a breakdown.

"What does it matter? Flynn never wanted to be a father. He told me that straight up. No kids. No commitments. It's why I didn't bother telling him about Zach and Timmy in the first place. Nothing would have changed. It isn't going to now."

"It's changed because he's here." Declan sighed. "I wish I could have found a way to get him out of town before he realized you were here, too."

"It's fine, Dec. Like you said, once he wanted to find me, you couldn't have stopped him."

"Why now?"

Shauna wished she knew.

"What will you do if he wants to take an active role with the boys?"

Her stomach turned on itself, and she pressed a hand to it, willing the ache to stop. "As much as I don't want to face whatever comes next, he's their father."

"This will rock their worlds." Dec pointed at himself. His muscled frame was evident under his fitted black T-shirt. Declan might not be as tall or broad as his brother, but he was just as handsome and intimidating when he wanted to be. "They don't even know I'm their uncle."

"They already think of you like that. It will be thrilling to know it's true."

"Would it be thrilling to meet their father only to have him turn around and leave? That's a distinct possibility with Flynn."

"You keep asking questions I can't answer." She gave a little shake of her head and pushed back from the bar.

"Beth thinks you should have him legally sign away his rights as a father and not introduce them. She believes it will be better the boys never know rather than risk being hurt."

She swallowed as her chest constricted. "It feels stupid now, but I honestly believed this day would never come.

Flynn was so final when he walked away. I thought he was out of my life forever."

"Is that what you want?" Declan asked quietly.

There was no way for Dec to truly know how much Shauna had loved Flynn when she was younger. She'd never talked about their relationship in any detail. It was almost too much for her heart to manage. She couldn't explain the connection that bound them together. But he understood enough to realize there was more to it than she'd ever told him.

"I want to protect Zach and Timmy from being hurt by anyone, especially Flynn."

"Who's going to protect you?" His voice had gone hard. "If you need me to—"

"You have your own past with Flynn." She reached out and squeezed her friend's hand as she climbed off the bar stool. "I don't want my trouble to become yours, Dec. You've always been willing to take care of me, and I love you for it. But I'm not your responsibility. I can take care of myself."

He nodded like he believed her without question. If only she could believe it herself.

"Beth and I are here if you need anything. We're supposed to leave for two weeks in Nashville. If you want, I can stay instead."

Declan and Beth divided their time between Nashville and Magnolia while she was in school for her nurse-practitioner program. Shauna was happy to see her friend settled and in love. She would never impose on his life with Beth.

She smiled. "Look at you. Declan Murphy, the picture of domestic bliss. Go with Beth. I'll be fine and no doubt Flynn will be in and out of town like a hurricane. After a few days of gusts and damage, he'll move on. I'm an expert at cleaning up. It will be fine."

"Beth hates the word *fine*," Declan said with a frown. "She thinks it's what people say when they're too overwhelmed to admit the truth."

Shauna laughed. "Your fiancée is wise, my friend. Let's just say I survived Flynn crushing my heart into a million pieces once before. I'm going to be more careful with it this time around."

Another group of customers took seats at the bar. "Be with you in a second," Declan told them.

"I'll talk to you later." Shauna offered another smile and tried to ignore the way her cheeks ached.

"If there's anything you need, I'm here."

She appreciated his support, even though this was a battle she'd have to fight on her own.

Walking out of the bar, she turned in the direction of the hardware store, where she needed to pick up a few items to finish the final details for the kitchen repair. She'd also promised the twins they could plant a wildflower garden this spring and wanted to see what varieties of seeds Lily Dawes, who ran the local store her family had owned for several generations, would recommend.

Shauna pulled her sunglasses out of her purse just as a man stepped out of the alley next to Champions.

"Are you rallying the troops against me?" Flynn asked as his shadow fell over her.

Her sunglasses dropped to the ground as she startled and jumped back a step.

"Are you crazy?" she demanded , bending down to retrieve the sunglasses. "Damn it. One of the lenses popped out. I got these suckers on clearance, Flynn. What's wrong with you? Do you think it's acceptable to sneak up on people? Are you following me?"

He picked up the lens before she could and handed it to her. "I'm assuming those questions weren't rhetorical. No, I'm not crazy. I have the psychological assessments from my time in the military to prove it. I'm not sneaking anywhere. If I were trying to be stealthy, Shauna, you wouldn't know I was here. And I'm not following you. I was headed to Champions to check out Declan's new place when I saw you walk out."

"You could have simply waved and called hello."

He removed the mirrored sunglasses that covered his gray eyes. "Are you telling me you wouldn't turn and head in the opposite direction?"

She tipped her chin and shoved the broken sunglasses into her purse. "I'm on my way to the hardware store in this direction, so I wouldn't have scurried off." Lie. "I'm not afraid of you." Big fat lie.

"Good. I'll walk with you."

"I thought you were on the way to see Declan."

"He can wait."

"We have nothing to say to each other."

"Those two boys who look like me might disagree."

"I want you to sign papers relinquishing your right to them," she blurted. It hadn't even crossed her mind to make that request, but once Declan mentioned the idea, it seemed like an easy way out for all of them.

She slowed her steps at the sound of the low growl that came from Flynn. Declan made the same kind of noise when he was angry or frustrated, but it didn't skim across her nerves like a jolt of electricity.

"No."

"Why not?" She rounded on him a few steps from the

hardware store's entrance. There was no way she would get anything accomplished with Flynn prowling behind her.

"Because they're mine."

"Oh, no." It was simple enough to ignore her body's reaction to him and his overbearing possessiveness when her temper spiked. "You made it crystal clear you didn't want this. You said the actual words 'I don't want to be a father. I can't commit to you. I can't give you what you need, Shauna.'" She ticked off the ways he'd rejected her like it was a grocery list. "I remember everything you told me that day."

"I remember, too," he said, his voice so low she almost had to lean in to hear him. "But I didn't know, Shauna. I didn't know you were pregnant."

She threw up her hands. "I didn't know I was pregnant either. We had one night together when you came to town, Flynn. Do you think I did it on purpose? Because that's ridiculous. I hadn't thought about becoming a mother and certainly not a single mom to twin boys. Let's remember that you brought the condoms."

She squeezed shut her eyes when she realized her voice had risen and someone walking past did a double take. The last thing she needed was to become a topic of gossip when she'd just started to find her place in Magnolia. She would leave that to Annalise.

"I didn't try to find you and tell you about the pregnancy because you clearly didn't want to be found. That message came across loud and clear. I've made a good life for myself and my boys." She bit down on the inside of her cheek when her lips trembled with emotion. "They are mine, Flynn. You didn't want to be a father, and I respected that. You owe me the same courtesy."

"I'm not the same person I was back then," he told her as if that would make a difference.

"Neither am I."

His gaze gentled. "That much is clear. You're even more than you were before. More beautiful, more dazzling—"

"More sleep deprived," she said, shaking her head. The last thing anyone could say about her was that she dazzled. "You'd be amazed at how being a parent messes with your ability to get a good night's sleep."

"I'm ready to step in, and I don't plan to walk away this time. I want you to know that."

"I don't believe you. I can't let myself."

"Then you'll have to let me prove it."

"There's too much at stake," she whispered. It was hard to know whether she was talking about her boys or herself. Probably both.

"People don't change," she insisted. They'd both lived through enough to understand that. She wanted him to argue, but he continued to stare then lifted a hand and gently touched a finger to the birthmark on her left earlobe.

"My north star," he said like he was rediscovering something wondrous. When they were younger, he'd been fascinated by the tiny birthmarks that dotted her skin, spending hours tracing paths between them.

Shauna wasn't a vain woman. She didn't have extra time or energy to give a fig about her appearance but knew the past five years had aged her. She worked and worried and worked some more. While she'd never been someone people would describe as carefree, being solely responsible for her sons added a weight to her shoulders that made her feel old beyond her twenty-nine years.

What would it be like to share some of that responsibility with another person? She hadn't been dramatic when she told Flynn she thought he wouldn't stay, but she also knew that he wouldn't turn away from supporting his sons, even if it was only financially.

"No," she whispered. "I can't, Flynn. Not again."

"Let me be a father to my sons." He closed his eyes for a moment as if it pained him to make the request. "I'm not going to force myself into your life."

"You're not?" She couldn't help blurting out the question. Flynn was and had always been so domineering in his attitude and energy. Shauna had more faith in her own strength now but doubted whether she could genuinely keep him from doing whatever he wanted. That was before taking into account the legal factors. He had rights. She couldn't deny that.

"I did say those words. I walked away from you, and while I want to believe I've changed or maybe that I had it in me to step up all along, I don't know that for sure. I'm willing to try if you let me. Will you let me?"

She opened her mouth and then snapped it shut again. She knew how to deal with pushy Flynn and determined Flynn, but this gentler, conciliatory version of him threw her for all kinds of loops.

"I don't want Zach and Timmy to be hurt."

"We agree on that," he told her. "Do you really want me to sign away my rights as their father? I'll do it for you."

She drew in a breath and waved to a mom she recognized from the school who was walking past. The woman's eyes widened as she took in Flynn. A lot had changed over the years, but clearly not his effect on women. He didn't seem to understand what his physical presence did to people.

He'd always been so strong and capable, so the thought that he would be willing to give up being a father if it was what she wanted humbled her.

"I wanted you to be the bad guy," she admitted, unable to meet his gaze. "It was easier to focus on my anger with you than any other emotion. Because you walked away, it let me off the hook from tracking you down and telling you about the boys."

"My sons."

"*Our* sons," she countered. "Relinquishing your rights isn't necessary. You can meet them if you want, but we're going to take it slow, Flynn. They are my priority, and you can say all the words you want about changing or whatever epiphanies you've had in the last five years. I don't trust it. I don't trust you. I'm willing to let you in because it's the right thing to do, not what I want." She channeled her anger and the betrayal she'd let fester in her heart for all these years because it made her feel more in control. She needed all the help she could get. "Let me be clear, I don't want you in our lives."

"Got it. Crystal clear." He nodded.

She pointed a finger at him. "You know as well as I do how important stability is for a child. If this becomes too much for you to handle at any point, you have to be a grown-up. You can't just walk away, not from Zach and Timmy."

"I won't." He wrapped his hand around her finger, and she shuddered as awareness tingled through her, hot and intense. She quickly pulled away her hand.

"This is not about you and me. There is no—"

"I mishandled us in the past," he interrupted. "And you have every right to feel the way you do. The truth is, you scared me back then, Shauna. The way I felt with you, and the thought of being happy, scared the shit out of me. I'm not scared anymore."

She took a step away from him because his words pulled

her in like a magnet. Focusing her gaze on one of the nearby pots filled with colorful spring blooms, she drew a steadying breath. This charming town was her home. She'd chosen it as a place where she could raise her sons independently. Flynn would not lure her into trusting him again so easily. "I don't care. I don't want to hear it. This is a line I will not cross, Flynn Murphy. We are the past and if you want a future with your sons, you will respect that."

His eyes went flinty again, all trace of gentleness gone.

"I'm trying to give you what you need, Shauna, but it doesn't come easy for me to let somebody else tell me what I can and can't do, what I should or shouldn't feel."

"I know. But that's the way it is. You're strong. You've always been strong. Now I am, too."

He looked past her shoulder like he was taking in the picturesque main street for the first time. "This is a heck of a place you've chosen for yourself. Did you google towns that most closely resembled a Hallmark movie set when you decided to move here?"

She felt herself smile. Leave it to Flynn to understand her motivations. "Not specifically, but Magnolia made the top of several lists of the best small towns in which to raise a family."

"I just bet it did. I agree to your terms for now."

She didn't like that addendum but needed to end this conversation and emotionally regroup. "I need a little time to talk to the boys. Come to dinner tomorrow night."

A different woman walked past, gorgeous in a pair of slim jeans and flannel shirt, her blond hair gathered into an effortlessly messy topknot. She waved to Flynn but not Shauna.

"Hey, Flynn," she called. "Are you getting settled?"

He nodded. "Hey, Cameron. I am. Thank you."

"Let me know if there's anything you need."

"Will do." He smiled then returned his focus to Shauna again, his smile vanishing. "Dinner tomorrow night."

She raised a brow, annoyed at the pang of jealousy that went through her at the admiring way the woman had looked at him. "Unless you have other plans?" She refused to ask about the woman.

Heat sparked in his eyes. "She works the front desk at the Wildflower Inn, where I'm staying at the moment. No other plans, Shauna. I'll see you tomorrow."

They stood there for several seconds staring at each other, both unwilling to walk away first. Stupid, she told herself. She would not allow herself to be stupid when it came to this man.

"Six o'clock," she said. "Don't be late." Then she turned and walked into the hardware store. Once the door closed behind her, she glanced out the window.

Flynn remained where he was for a few long seconds before heading purposefully down the sidewalk. He walked like a man on a mission, and she got the impression she and her boys were it.

What had she gotten herself into?

CHAPTER SIX

MEGHAN WAS HALFWAY across the parking lot Friday afternoon when she heard someone call her name. Because the voice was unfamiliar, she ignored it.

Although Greg had promised her he wouldn't publicize the elimination of her position to the rest of the staff right away, that had been as much of a lie as most of what he'd said to her.

She'd had less than twenty-four hours to process losing her job before being inundated with well-meaning coworkers and parents exclaiming over the unfairness of the situation. Even worse, the school's longtime music teacher, who was also being let go at the end of the year, had promptly turned in her resignation and packed her bags, leaving the school with no one to head up the music curriculum for the next two months.

When Principal Wheeler had come bellyaching to Meghan, she'd suggested the PTO step in the way they were going to for the art department the following year.

Greg had shaken his head and said no one could take on the role on such short notice and until they could find a substitute teacher, Meghan would have to manage both. Meghan had been about to tell him exactly where he could shove that suggestion.

Then the first combined classroom of music and art students filed in. Her classroom had been crowded, but the kids seemed hopeful that she would make everything okay.

Magnolia Elementary hosted two big events during the school year, a holiday concert just before winter break and the year-end spring choral event, along with a corresponding art show.

They couldn't have one without the other. Well, they could, but it wouldn't be the same. She'd welcomed the fifth-graders to her classroom, and they'd gotten to work on brainstorming how to making both a success even without a designated music teacher.

It was hard to think of managing other people's problems when her own were so overwhelming, but by the end of the fifty-minute period the kids had reminded her about so many of the reasons she loved her job and how much she would miss it.

Fifth-graders could be problematic, but the students rallied around her, offering ideas for the event and suggestions for how she might keep her job. One of the boys encouraged her to set up a tent in the gymnasium to save on rent and eat leftovers from the cafeteria like she was at boarding school, only for teachers. Sadly, eating stale pizza every Friday was not a viable option.

"Ms. Banks?"

This time she stopped and turned because she recognized that voice. It was Gus Calloway, one of the sweetest students she taught. Her heart seemed to skip a beat when she took in the man walking next to him as he approached.

Even before Gus had started school in Magnolia, Meghan had been a fan of the Calloway Brothers.

She'd snagged tickets to one of their shows in Nashville a few years back, although Nash Calloway, Gus's father who'd died in the tour bus accident last December, had been her favorite.

Walker was the lead singer and front man of the band, but Nash brought humor and lightness to concerts and interviews. In a role reversal of the typical birth-order personalities, older-by-five-years Nash seemed not to take their fame so seriously.

Walker gave the impression of being hyperaware of their reputation and potential legacy within the hallowed halls of country music.

Meghan didn't typically like people who took themselves seriously. It reminded her too much of her neurosurgeon mother.

Not that being a country music star was anything like her mother's career in medicine.

"Hey, Gus," she said with a wave, trying to keep her focus on the present moment. Meghan had too much of a tendency to let her mind wander.

"Hi, Ms. Banks." The kid was adorable with his guileless eyes, mop of wavy brown hair and skinny frame. "You going home for the weekend?"

"I am." She frowned as she took in the bruise that still colored the boy's eye. She didn't believe for a second that Gus had received the injury from tripping over his own two feet in the midst of the scuffle like he'd told everyone. But she couldn't prove it, and since both Trey Haverford and Beau Tinsdale were also involved in the incident, Meghan figured she should leave well enough alone.

The last thing she needed was to go up against the two most powerful—and currently feuding—mothers at the school, even if one of them was about to become her upstairs neighbor.

"But you're not gonna quit and never come back like

Mrs. Batterly, right?" The boy looked genuinely concerned, which Meghan appreciated.

"I'm here until the end of the school year, Gus."

She took a breath and turned her attention to Walker. Meghan could feel the heat rising in her cheeks. She could thank her Irish grandmother for her fair skin and tendency to both flush with emotion and burn in the sun. The freckles that dotted her nose and cheeks as well.

If Walker Calloway noticed his effect on her, he didn't react. Heck, he was probably used to it. At the concert she'd attended, audience members had tossed at least a dozen pairs of panties onto the stage. Hers were far too practical for tossing, even if she'd been so inclined.

"I'm Meghan Banks, Gus's art teacher," she said, holding out a hand.

"I know." Walker did not shake her hand until his nephew nudged him.

She smiled and tried not to blush. The parking lot emptied fast for the weekend, but a few parents were still standing in small clusters around the perimeter. Although she knew Walker was the attraction, she didn't like the attention his proximity placed on her. "You must be Gus's uncle."

"Yeah. That's me."

"Uncle Walker plays guitar real good," Gus reported. "Piano, too. My daddy taught him how to play when they were little. Daddy was the big brother."

"We learned together," Walker said, meeting her eyes for a second before glancing at the ground. "Our father was a deacon at the local church, so my brother and I learned to sing in the Sunday choir."

"But Daddy was better than you," Gus said confidently, "because he was the best at everything."

"Yep, he was," Walker agreed without hesitation.

Meghan practically gasped at the look of pain that blasted from Walker's eyes at his nephew's words. It was as if a corresponding phantom ache reverberated through her. She could feel the deep well of this man's sorrow.

She took a step back like she could protect herself from his suffering.

"Uncle Walker's pretty good now." Gus smiled at her. "He's good enough to teach music at the school."

She swallowed then immediately choked on her own spit. "I don't understand, Gus."

"Uncle Walker can be the substitute teacher until the end of the year."

Nothing the boy was saying made sense, although she understood the words. She glanced from Gus's earnest face, his cheeks round and rosy despite how thin his body was, and shifted her gaze to Walker, who was still staring at the ground like he wanted it to open up and swallow him whole.

That made two of them.

"Oh, how sweet," she said, "but I'm sure your uncle Walker has other responsibilities. I know he has a job or career or however you describe being a musician. He has his own stuff to do."

His own stuff like making Grammy-winning albums and selling out stadiums around the country. She was pretty sure the Calloway Brothers had played at the Grand Ole Opry last year.

"I have time."

The words were spoken so quickly that she barely registered them. "Mr. Calloway—"

"Call me Walker."

"Walker," she repeated because she liked how his name felt on her tongue, a piece of candy that would melt in her mouth, tart and sweet at the same time. "Are you saying you want to be the Magnolia Elementary music teacher?"

"I said I would do it."

He did not look like someone who wanted to volunteer in any capacity, let alone make the kind of commitment it would take to see the students through the music program for the end of the year.

"You really want to do this? It's a nearly full-time position, and you'd be in charge of organizing the spring concert as well as the classroom time."

"I'm not saying I want to be a music teacher," he clarified. "I'm saying I'll do it because Gus wants me to."

"It's 'cuz I'm orphan now," Gus explained. "Uncle Walker and Jack will do almost anything for me because they feel really bad."

Meghan couldn't help the half laugh and part sob that escaped her throat but quickly schooled her features. She could feel Walker staring at her but kept her gaze focused on Gus. "You've been through a great tragedy, one far more devastating than anyone—let alone a boy your age—should have to endure. It makes sense that the adults who care about you want to try to help make things better."

"I know. Nothing makes it better, but you're the nicest teacher at this school, Ms. Banks. You're the only one who hasn't asked for Uncle Walker's phone number or tried to get an autograph from me."

"Really? I'm sorry, Gus. That's not right."

"It's okay." He shook his head. "Not everybody is a country music fan."

She rolled her lips together to keep from smiling again. The way the boy misunderstood her meaning was entertaining. Gus was an odd little duck, and from what he told her, he'd also struggled to make friends at his previous school.

He told her that his father and uncle always claimed that the other children weren't nice because they couldn't contain their jealousy over how cool Gus was.

But the boy knew that wasn't it. He'd been quiet in class, and it had taken some time for her to discover the quirky, playful kid underneath his uncertain exterior. Based on the way Walker was now staring at Gus and realizing he'd potentially been played, Meghan understood that Walker Calloway was wise to his nephew's tricks, even if it took him a minute or two to remember that.

"You're hired," she said before Walker could tell them both he'd changed his mind.

"You think you have me wrapped around your little finger," he said to his nephew, not bothering to respond to Meghan. "This is exactly what your father used to do. He'd go all innocent and earnest when trying to get me to do something he knew I didn't want to."

"Like when you sang that duet with the pop princess lady." Gus sounded positively gleeful now.

She remembered the song Gus was referring to. It had been the theme of the biggest summer blockbuster in theaters two years earlier.

"Your father had cowriting credits on that song," Walker told his nephew, "and it made us both a lot of money."

"You had to dance in the video," Gus shot back. "You're a good singer, Uncle Walker, but you can't dance."

When Meghan couldn't contain the laugh that bubbled up, Walker transferred his gaze to her. "You have something to say about my dancing?"

"I liked that song," she told him with great sincerity. "Everyone has talents, Mr. Calloway."

He raised a brow. "Walker."

"Okay, Walker. You have more than your fair share of

talents, even if dancing isn't one of them. I'm sure teaching music is higher on the list."

"I play music. I've never taught anybody anything. That was what my brother did. The boy is right."

She smiled, hoping to give them both confidence in his abilities. They needed a music teacher, although the idea of spending time with Walker Calloway sent ribbons of panic spiraling through her belly.

"Well, we're desperate, and you're a warm body. So as I said, you're hired." She shook her head. "Actually, I need to clear it with Principal Wheeler, but I'm sure he'll agree."

"That man is a goober," Walker said.

"That's not nice, Uncle Walker."

"I apologize for speaking ill of Principal Wheeler. When should I plan to start?"

"Monday is the first day of spring break," she reminded him.

"Spring break?"

"You've heard the term, I assume."

"I've played spring break parties in Daytona."

"Not the same type of break."

Gus burst into a fit of laughter that made him sound like a demented hyena. It wasn't the first time Meghan had heard it. The kid spent many of his lunch periods in her classroom, and he would crack himself up telling her silly knock-knock jokes.

But Walker was staring at him as if he'd never heard the sound—like it was something akin to the hallelujah chorus.

"You'll have a full week to prep and prepare," she told him. "I'll call Principal Wheeler tonight and confirm everything. You'll need to have a background check done by the district but given… you being you, I'm sure they'll make it work."

"Are you going away for spring break, Ms. Banks?" Walker asked.

The words were in the form of a question, but they sounded more like an accusation to Meghan.

She shook her head. "I'm moving into a new apartment this weekend, so I plan to take next week to get settled."

"Then you'll be available to help me prep and prepare, as you call it."

Definitely not a question, more a command. An interesting technique when so much of country music featured themes of women, trucks and drinking beer with like-minded laid-back buddies. Walker did not seem laid-back in the least.

And he wanted her help? Her knees went weak at the thought, which was ridiculous. This man was not for her, not even a little bit.

"Will you help Uncle Walker, Ms. Banks?" Gus asked. The kid was a lot more charming than his uncle.

"I'll do my best." She took her phone from her purse, opened it to contacts and handed the device to Walker. "If you put your number in here, I'll text you once I confirm the details with the school."

"I've had a lot of women ask for my number over the years," he said as he took the phone from her. "This is the first time in a while I've given it willingly."

"Uncle Walker likes skanks."

Gus shrugged when both Meghan and Walker gaped at him. "That's what Daddy used to say. I don't think you're a skank, Ms. Banks, even though I don't exactly know how to recognize one."

"With respect to your late father, *skank* is not a polite way to describe any woman." She bent down until she was eye to eye with Gus. "It's very nice of you to volunteer your uncle to help with the music program. I'm sure your daddy would be proud of you."

The boy nodded solemnly. "I miss him. You miss your grandma who just died, too, right?"

Meghan blinked back tears. She'd taken a week off when Grammy died, but most of her coworkers and students didn't like to bring up her loss. Discussing grief made people uncomfortable, so she appreciated Gus's openness. "I know this might not help much, but I believe the people we love stay with us in our hearts. Your father will always be with you."

She heard a noise that sounded like a scoff from Walker, but Gus seemed to agree with her words.

"I like thinking he's still with me."

Walker returned her phone to her when she straightened, his gaze unreadable. "I didn't realize you and Gus were so tight."

"He's special," she said simply.

Walker sighed and ruffled the boy's hair. "Yeah, he is." He studied her more closely. "He might not be the only one."

Wow. Would it be weird if she asked him to sing that line? The way Walker was looking at her and the fact that his deep voice made the little hairs on the back of her neck stand on end was a powerful combination.

This was business, she reminded herself.

"Yes, well. I have to go. I'm meeting my boyfriend." She wanted to smack herself upside the head. There she was with one of the hottest men she'd ever seen potentially flirting with her and she had to mention a fictitious boyfriend.

"Lucky guy," Walker murmured. "I look forward to hearing from you, Ms. Banks."

She forced another smile. "You can call me Meghan."

"Meghan," he said in that low, rumbly voice. "We'll talk soon."

"Yep. See ya, Gus." She quickly turned away before she did something embarrassing like throw herself at Walker, boring underpants and fake boyfriend be damned.

If only her grandmother could see her now.

CHAPTER SEVEN

SHAUNA PULLED THE pan of brownies out of the oven and turned to where Zach and Timmy sat at the kitchen table, grateful the contractor had been able to complete the work on the floor and install a new dishwasher quickly so their lives weren't disrupted for long.

"I think they look yummy," she told them, making her voice extra bubbly. "The butterscotch chips were a perfect addition."

Her boys stared like she was discussing a monster she'd discovered living under the bed instead of the dessert she'd baked for tonight. Zach and Timmy loved brownies and ice cream. They also enjoyed helping her in the kitchen, which was why she'd chosen to make the basic dessert.

It had been halfway through mixing the ingredients when she'd told them the stranger who'd shown up at their house was their father, and he'd be coming to dinner that evening to meet them.

Maybe she should have told them right away or possibly years ago about Flynn, but it was hard to explain they didn't have a father because he didn't want to know them.

It had seemed simpler to claim he wasn't a part of their lives and never would be and leave it at that. On some level, she'd realized she would eventually have to explain in more detail, but in all her wildest imaginings, the notion of Flynn doing something so ordinary as coming to dinner had never occurred to her.

"All this quiet and stillness from the two of you is freaking me out," she said, hoping to draw a smile from one of them. No such luck.

She'd had lasagna, salad and garlic bread, plus the brownies for dessert. Based on the mood of the twins, she was half-tempted to call Flynn and cancel until the boys could wrap their minds around the sudden change that would upend everything they knew.

She didn't try to reschedule because she could not put off this reckoning for the length of time she would have preferred, which was forever. She'd told him the truth—she hadn't shared the news of her pregnancy with him because she thought he wouldn't want to know.

He hadn't planned to be a father, but now that he wanted to get to know the boys, she couldn't deny him.

She'd kept them apart for nearly six years. What if believing him when he walked away that night and told her it was the end had been a mistake? Would it have changed how he felt if he'd known about her pregnancy?

Zach and Timmy were the best things that had ever happened to her. She hadn't known she was capable of the type of love she felt for her boys. That kind of unconditional devotion hadn't been a part of her life, not with her addicted mother or the various foster placements she'd had over the years.

All she'd wanted growing up was to belong, and it had taken becoming a mother to finally achieve that. She belonged to her boys, body and soul. Knowing her choice not to tell them about their father was causing them pain nearly brought her to her knees.

How could she make this better?

"We want Declan to be our dad," Zach said.

"He's not scary," Timmy added, then popped his thumb in his mouth before realizing what he'd done and taking it out again.

Her sweet younger son had stopped relying on his thumb to self-soothe when he was four. This was a nightmare.

"The good news is that Declan is your uncle." She removed the potholders and walked over to the table. "I'm sorry I didn't tell you any of this earlier. I didn't think Flynn—your father—was going to return. It seemed easier not to mention the details, but that was wrong. I should know by now you can't run away from the hard stuff. It will always find you."

"We could run away," Timmy suggested. His chin wobbled. "Go somewhere the bad guy can't find us."

"I like it here," Zach whined. "Can't we make him go away?"

"He's not the bad guy." Shauna couldn't have guessed her boys would be so vehemently opposed to getting to know their father. As a kid, all she'd wanted was to have a relationship with her dad, to have him swoop in and rescue her when things got rough with her mom.

But Timmy and Zach didn't need rescuing. They had a stable home, and she was a good mom. She'd created the family she'd always wanted, albeit without the dad.

"This is not your father's fault," she forced herself to say. "I didn't tell him about the two of you."

"But he kissed and hugged you then left," Zach reminded her.

And broke her heart into a million pieces, but young children couldn't possibly appreciate that.

"Nothing is going to happen to our family," she assured them, deeming it wise to ignore the kissing-and-hugging comment. Was that what they thought of how babies were made? “Flynn is going to have dinner with us. He’ll be in our home, and you can talk to him and show him your toys or school projects if you want. If not, that’s okay. He only wants to spend some time with you.”

Timmy, the more sensitive of the twins, suddenly burst into tears.

“Oh, sweetie, it’s okay.” Shauna leaned forward and kissed his forehead, feeling tears on her cheeks that matched his. She looked over at Zach. He always wanted to act like nothing bothered him—he got that from his dad—but was also crying.

The doorbell rang at that moment.

Of course it did.

What was she supposed to do? She couldn’t ignore Flynn.

She drew in a deep breath and made a decision. He wanted to be involved in his sons’ lives. Welp, buddy. Here was a chance for a crash course in parenthood.

She dashed a hand over her cheeks as she walked to the front door, but another round of tears was already stinging her eyes as she opened it.

“Holy crap. What happened?”

The tears came fast as she took in the shopping bags with footballs peeking out that Flynn held in each hand. He’d probably brought balls because that’s what dads did with their sons in television commercials and American lore. Hours spent in the backyard tossing balls.

Flynn had made an effort.

“It’s fine,” she said on a sob. “Come in. Dinner’s almost ready.”

“You don’t seem fine,” he said slowly.

When his gaze went past her and his eyes widened in

a look that could only be described as terrified, Shauna nearly laughed.

A moment later, Zach and Timmy each took one of her hands.

"Why are you all crying?" Flynn asked. "Do you always cry before dinner?"

To his credit, he didn't turn and flee. She wouldn't have blamed him if he had.

"It's an emotional time," she said as she stepped back, drawing her boys with her.

Flynn nodded as he stepped into the house, processing her words. He wore dark jeans and an olive green Henley that made his eyes pop. His chiseled jaw was clean-shaven, and the ends of his hair were still damp like he'd recently gotten out of the shower.

Shauna did not want to think about Flynn naked in the shower.

"We want Declan to be our daddy," Timmy blurted, then buried his face in Shauna's flowing peasant skirt. Embarrassment brought her right back to the present moment.

"I don't blame you," Flynn agreed. He didn't sound angry that his son would have preferred a different man for his father, but that shouldn't have surprised Shauna.

Flynn had always believed Dec to be the better of the Murphy brothers. Maybe that was why Flynn worked so hard to protect and care for his brother, even when there was no one to offer Flynn that same support.

"Timmy, that's not nice," she admonished. "Declan is your uncle, and he's a nice man. But so is your father."

Flynn raised a dubious brow.

"You're nice," she insisted. "At least, you can be when you make an effort. Speaking of effort, boys, it looks like Flynn—your dad—brought you some gifts."

"Call me Flynn," he said in that sandpaper-rough voice. "It will make all of us more comfortable."

Timmy continued to hide his face, but Zach wiped the back of his arm across his nose and peered at the bags. "I like basketball," he said.

Flynn nodded. "I brought one of those, too."

"Footballs, basketballs and a baseball for each of you."

"What about soccer?" Zach's blue eyes narrowed.

"I can go back for soccer."

"I bet you can't even play soccer," Zach said.

Shauna wanted to scold the boy for his churlish tone, but Flynn didn't seem to notice or mind.

"I was stationed in Germany for a year," he said. "I learned to play soccer—in Europe they call it football—while I was there. Are you two any good at sports?"

"They're in first grade," Shauna reminded him.

Zach shrugged. "I'm a fast runner and super strong, but Timmy can throw better."

"You get that coordination from me," Flynn told Timmy. "I've always been good at sports." He turned his attention to Zach. "We can improve your accuracy, and your brother will get stronger. Dec was a real wimp when he was little. Look at him now."

"Did you just call your son a wimp?" Shauna demanded, rolling her eyes. She didn't know why she felt peevish all of a sudden. Flynn was making more of an attempt with the boys than she'd expected, and at least everyone had stopped crying.

"No," Flynn said slowly. His mercurial gaze raked over her. "I called my brother a wimp. Timmy is small, but he's going to grow and get strong." He nodded at the boy, who'd inclined his head to study Flynn. "Do you know what's more important than being strong?"

Timmy shook his head and sniffed.

"Being smart and kind." He ran a hand through his hair. "I know your mom well enough to know she's raising you to be both."

Shauna swallowed back a soft groan. Direct hit to the heart.

"Why weren't you our dad before now?" Timmy asked, turning to more fully face Flynn but keeping hold of a fist-ful of fabric from Shauna's skirt.

"I've always been your dad," Flynn said. He placed the shopping bags on the ground in front of each boy. "My work and other circumstances kept me away, but that's changing."

"I'm hungry." Zach picked up his bag. "Mommy, can we eat dinner then go play ball? We need a basketball hoop for the driveway."

"Wash your hands," Shauna told the twins. "Your birth-day is coming up next month. We can discuss a basketball hoop."

"Awesome," the boys said in unison. They did that some-times, and Shauna never failed to be charmed by it. The twin bond was something special, and while she didn't always understand its nuances, she appreciated that her sons would always have someone who understood them at a cellular level.

She'd wanted that as a kid, a family with siblings—someone to share secrets and experiences.

They took their bags with them and headed to the tiny powder room on the main floor to wash their hands for dinner.

"When is their birthday?" Flynn asked quietly.

"May twentieth. They were born only two weeks early, which is great for twins. Neither of them had to stay extra in the NICU. That was one of my biggest fears when I was pregnant." She laughed and tugged on the end of her braid. "I had a lot of fears at that point. I still do."

"I'd like to help alleviate some of them," Flynn told her, reaching out to touch her hair.

She went still, then shrugged and stepped away. "You did better than I expected with the tears. Come back to the kitchen." Nerves stampeding through her chest, she led him through the house then pulled the lasagna from the warming drawer under the counter.

"I don't like crying."

She laughed softly. "I figured, but you didn't turn tail."

"Do you think so little of me, Shauna?"

How was she supposed to answer? She'd done her best not to think of Flynn in the past several years. It had become more complicated when Declan moved to town, a constant reminder of their shared past.

But her bond with Flynn had been different, more intense and overpowering in every way. As a foster-care kid, Shauna had learned to compartmentalize her feelings. That's what she wanted to continue doing with Flynn, but his looming presence and her reaction made it difficult on every level.

"I don't know what to think of you," she admitted. "Of any of this."

"It's one night. Dinner. We're trying it on for size."

"You brought father-son toys."

"Sporting equipment."

"Don't be obtuse. Everyone knows what a baseball mitt from your dad means."

"I didn't," Flynn said. "And I still learned to play ball. Dec and I tossed to each other bare-handed."

A good reminder, Shauna thought. Even if Flynn left or things went south, Timmy and Zach would not be alone.

They had each other, and she would never leave.

"Your brother is happy now. He and Beth are good together." She looked up to find Flynn studying her, his gaze unreadable.

"She's not the woman I would have expected him to fall for," he said after a moment.

"Maybe you don't know him that well anymore. It's been a while, Flynn. You can put the plates on the table," she told him.

"I do the forks," Zach announced, running over from the hallway.

"I do napkins," Timmy added, not to be outdone.

"You sit down together to eat?" Flynn seemed to find that a novelty.

"Every night," Zach confirmed. "You don't sit in a chair to eat?"

"Usually in front of the TV," Flynn answered, earning groans of jealousy from the twins.

Timmy grabbed napkins from a drawer. "Mommy never lets us watch television while we eat."

"Not even cereal in the morning." Zach let out a put-upon sigh. "We don't get our own iPads either. You could buy them for us for our birthday if you want."

"Zachary Michael Myer." Shauna placed her hands on her hips. "This is not how you behave when you meet someone new. You will not be getting an iPad for your birthday. The two of you can continue to use mine for screen time."

"He's not new," Zach shot back. "He's our dad."

"Don't sass your mom," Flynn said, distributing the plates. "If she says no iPad, that's the rule. She makes the rules."

Shauna blinked.

Zach didn't seem to be fazed at having another adult

correct him. Was it due to Flynn's naturally commanding demeanor or the fact that he was the boy's dad?

The twins climbed into their seats on either side of the table. Shauna brought over the lasagna while Flynn placed the salad and basket of garlic bread on the table.

He automatically took the seat at the head of the table, and her heart pinched at how right that felt. She didn't want it to feel right, but the truth was she'd never sat in that particular chair.

Shauna hadn't been raised in any way that resembled traditional, and as a single mom, she tried to make routine and ritual a natural part of their lives.

But there was a small, secret part of her—silly, she knew—that bought into the ideal of the American family. A mom and dad and maybe a golden retriever or Labrador bounding through the yard.

She knew better than to allow herself to give in to those sort of white-picket fantasies.

An awkward silence descended over their odd little group as she began to dish out lasagna portions.

Her boys usually never stopped talking, so she knew nerves must have taken over their initial enthusiasm about the gifts.

Flynn stared at his plate like it held the secrets of the universe, and she noticed his cheeks tinged with pink.

Was Flynn Murphy blushing because he also felt nervous?

She'd always known him to command every situation. This tiny sliver of vulnerability appealed to her more than it should.

"What's the strangest thing you ate when you were in the military?" she asked Flynn as she took a bite of lasagna.

"Guinea pig," he answered immediately.

The response elicited a round of disgusted cries from the twins. "My friend Emmett has a pet guinea pig named Snickers," Zach told him. "You ate Snickers."

"Not specifically your friend's guinea pig." Flynn flashed a rare—Shauna assumed—smile. "They are considered a delicacy in Ecuador. I was at a dinner with a local family, and it would have been rude not to partake in the meal. If it helps, I don't think they'd named the guinea pig."

"That's disgusting," Shauna told him. "What else?" Nothing was more fascinating to little boys than talking about gross food, and Flynn didn't disappoint.

He'd been in the army for over a decade so he had plenty of stories to share. Once he warmed up to the subject, he was a shockingly engaging storyteller. He weaved tales about his adventures in both the jungles of South America and Middle Eastern deserts.

As much as Shauna had tried to put Flynn out of her mind, he'd been there. Zach and Timmy looked like their father. When Flynn wrinkled his nose as he described a particularly vivid account of one of his fellow soldiers dealing with the effects of food poisoning, her boys mirrored the gesture perfectly. She was once again reminded that the man she'd once loved—who'd betrayed her more deeply than any other person she'd known—would always be a part of her life.

The trick would be keeping him from infiltrating her heart.

As Zach and Timmy warmed up to Flynn, their shyness dissipated. She listened as they peppered him with questions, mostly about his time as a soldier. They answered the questions he asked about their favorite foods, colors, hobbies and a myriad of other details.

The evening was better and so much worse than she could have imagined.

It had been naive to consider, even for a moment, that Zach and Timmy wouldn't like Flynn. Yes, he was intimidating and could be overbearing and slightly scary, but he was also the most intriguing person Shauna had ever met. The years had mellowed him somewhat, and the anger that had always seemed to be woven into his soul felt more restrained. It was as if he'd finally learned there were better ways to go through life than as a bulldozer intent on plowing through everything in his path.

They cleared the table, and the twins ran to get the mitts and baseballs out of their bags.

"Can we go play in the backyard?" Zach asked even as they were already moving toward the door.

"Sure," Shauna told them. "I'll bring your dessert to the patio."

Timmy approached Flynn and looked up at him with those giant, expressive eyes. "Will you play with us?"

A muscle ticked in Flynn's jaw. "You bet. I'm going to help your mom clean up, and then I'll join you."

The boys accepted that answer and headed out the door.

"I can handle this," Shauna said with a genuine smile. "You should—"

"I want their names changed," Flynn said.

She opened and closed her mouth several times. "What?"

"You called Zach by his full name, Zachary Michael Myer. My middle name is Michael."

"I'm aware." She felt her tension rebounding tenfold. "Zach has your middle name, and Timmy's is David."

"Declan's middle name. They should both have the last name Murphy. Their father's last name."

"You aren't listed on their birth certificate," she felt compelled to point out.

"Not by choice."

"You chose to walk away from me." She took a pint of vanilla ice cream from the freezer and slammed it on the counter. "What happened to 'You're in control, Shauna. You make the rules.'? You handing out demands doesn't feel like me being in control."

"Things have changed. I know them now."

"You had one dinner with them and bought some bribery gifts. It doesn't make you a dad."

"The gifts weren't bribery. They were icebreakers. And I'm already a dad."

"Not in the ways that count." She shook her head. "I don't want to fight with you, Flynn, but I will if I have to. Get to know your sons. Prove to them, and to me, that you'll stick around."

She squeezed shut her eyes and blew out a breath before meeting his gaze again. "I had too much false hope as a child. I wanted people to love me and choose me more than anything else. There were times I thought that was happening, but it never did. The pain has never left, and you caused even more when you rejected me. It's too soon to talk about changing names or anything permanent."

"I have legal rights."

"I'm their mother." She pointed to the table. "I can tell you where every scratch in the wood came from. I've devoted every moment to their well-being and happiness. That's what being a parent means to me. It's too soon for you to expect more than I'm willing to give. Go toss the ball with your kids, Flynn."

He growled low in his throat. "I want *more*." He took a step closer to her. "You know I'm not a patient man,

Shauna. I don't have many virtues, and that's at the bottom of the list."

"You have enough." She couldn't help reaching a hand up to cup his jaw. "Give me time, Flynn. Give the boys time. We all need that."

He leaned into her touch like a wild animal needing to be soothed, and she felt the spark of desire flame between them. Flynn was back in her life, and lord help her, he wasn't the only one who wanted more.

CHAPTER EIGHT

"ARE WE POOR?"

Annalise tried not to blanch as she thought about how to answer the question posed by her daughter.

They'd spent most of the day loading and unloading boxes and bags from their big, expansive, meticulously decorated house into the dime-sized apartment that was now their home.

The bank had seized most of the larger pieces of furniture, bought on credit, and Annalise had consigned many of the smaller valuable objects to a store in Charlotte. There was no way she'd have them on display any closer to home, although the truth was she could practically open her own shop just based on the useless flotsam and jetsam she'd collected over the years.

Things she used to consider the measure of her worth as if a Baccarat crystal vase offered legitimacy.

"We're rich in our devotion to each other," she told Margo.

"She means poor," Trey said from where he lounged on the sofa, one gangly leg thrown over the back.

"I *mean* we have been given an opportunity to learn the true definition of wealth," she insisted. "Trey, put down the device and help unpack the kitchen."

"I don't think I want to learn that lesson." Margo frowned as she looked around the cramped space. It seemed bigger when Annalise first toured and the apartment hadn't been filled with her stuff.

She still had way too much to fit comfortably.

There was a knock on the door, and it embarrassed Annalise that her first instinct was to tell her kids to stay quiet until whoever it was went away. As if they were in some sort of absurd horror movie.

It was a reaction learned during the past several months in her former home after Jonathan had been hauled away to jail. She'd come to expect a steady stream of unwanted callers, from angry former clients to business creditors to curious reporters looking for a quote from the wife left behind.

She'd put on a brave face for the kids, but when they were in school, she'd taken to dropping to the floor whenever the bell rang and scurrying to a corner until whoever was at the door gave up and went away.

She would no longer hide and scurry away. This was the first day of the rest of her life. Maybe she would find a cheap poster with that little ditty to hang on one of the empty walls. After all, she'd consigned most of their artwork.

Trey sat up on the sofa and Margo moved closer to him, both darting their concerned gazes to her.

"Let's see who's coming to visit," she said brightly. She wasn't going to raise children who were afraid to answer the door. She braced herself and opened it only to find her new landlord standing on the other side, flanked by her twin sons.

"We brought lemon bars," Shauna said slowly as she took in Annalise's wary gaze. "To welcome you. Is everything okay? Is there a problem with the apartment?"

"No problem at all." Annalise shook her head and let out the breath she hadn't realized she was holding. "Thank you. That was very kind."

The boys were looking past her with obvious curiosity.

"Why don't you all come in, and the children can get to know each other since they'll be neighbors? Trey and Margo, this is Mrs. Myer."

"You can call me Shauna."

Annalise raised an eyebrow. "They will call you Mrs. Myer because that's how they show respect."

"I'm not a Mrs."

"Ms. Myer?"

"How about Ms. Shauna?"

Interesting that the unconventional, free-spirited woman wasn't afraid to stand up for well…even something so small as how Annalise's children should refer to her. "That will do," Annalise responded.

"These are my sons Timmy and Zach," Shauna supplied. "They're excited to have the two of you here. We don't have a lot of kids their age on this block."

"We got balls," Zach announced.

Annalise heard Trey snicker.

"Footballs and baseballs and basketballs," Shauna clarified.

"Our new daddy gave them to us," Timmy offered shyly. "Well, he's not new. He's always been our daddy, but we didn't know about him before. He was a secret mommy kept and—"

"He wasn't exactly a secret," Shauna interrupted.

Annalise noticed the other woman's fingers tighten on the edge of the plate holding the lemon bars.

"Our mom's gonna be a maid tomorrow," Trey said. "That's a secret, too, but I don't know why. Dad always said there's nothing to be embarrassed about an honest day of work."

Annalise met Shauna's gaze and rolled her eyes. "That's rich," she muttered, "coming from my ex-husband."

"What did you say, Mommy?" Margo asked, too sweetly.

"Why don't the two of you go check out Zach and Timmy's balls?" she told her kids with a pointed glance at Trey. "Remember, you're supposed to be grounded from the screen."

The kid shoved his gaming console between the sofa cushions.

"We're gonna get a basketball hoop for our birthday next month," Zach said proudly. "Do you play basketball?"

"A little," Trey answered. "But baseball is my favorite."

"Did your dad teach you how to catch a ball and throw? Our dad is teaching us. He was here last night for dinner. I'm a lot better already. I can show you."

"Sure," Trey agreed. "Before my dad left, he was teaching me how to throw a curveball. I can show you that if you want."

"I want to learn," Timmy said.

"Me, too," Zach echoed.

"You want to come, Margo?" Trey asked his sister, then turned back to the twins. "She's a girl but has a really good arm."

Annalise felt tears prick the back of her eyes. She had no idea if Trey realized what he was doing by including his sister. Typically, Margo was booked with playdates and birthday parties. She was as much a social butterfly as her mother.

Many of those invitations had dried up in the months since the scandal broke, and Annalise had been accepting her daughter's flimsy excuses to explain away the change in her circle of friends until very recently.

"Yeah," Margo agreed. "I can show you how to swing the bat, too. Daddy taught Trey, but I watched and learned."

As the kids filed out, Annalise heard them talking on the way down the stairs.

"Where's your daddy now?" Zach asked. "Did he go on a business trip?"

"Sort of," Trey said. "He went to a big house."

"That's one way of describing it." Annalise took the tray of lemon bars from Shauna. "Thank you. You might not know it, but you arrived at the right time. We were engaged in a debate about whether or not we were poor."

Shauna shook her head. "I've been poor. This is not poor. This is a reduction in circumstances."

Annalise needed to hear that. "Are there other nice people like you hanging around the school?"

Shauna choked out a laugh. "Single mothers whose baby daddy just showed up and demanded to have a relationship with his kids? I might be one of a kind."

Annalise carried the dessert over to the counter of the postage-stamp-sized kitchen. "People who are genuinely nice and authentically friendly. I don't think I hung around many of those, although I might caution you about oversharing."

"I doubt I'm telling you anything that Timmy and Zach won't divulge to any stranger on the street. If my sons have their way, they'll be bringing their new—or at least new to them—father for show-and-tell."

"The giant?"

"Flynn is a large-ish human, but you didn't seem to have any trouble going toe-to-toe with him."

"Yet you invited him for dinner."

"Yes, and I'm here to welcome you to your new apartment, not burden you with my man problems like we're friends."

Annalise shrugged and tried to ignore the pang of longing that went through her. "I lost all my friends, or so-called friends, when my life imploded. I lost everything."

"You have your kids."

"Good point."

"And a whole lot of stuff to make fit in a two-bedroom apartment." Shauna glanced dubiously around the space.

"Don't forget the bonus room that now belongs to Trey." She drew in a breath. "My kids have a home. I'm going to make it a loving one. That's what's important."

"And it sounds like you've got a job?" Shauna wiggled her brows. "As a landlord, I like the idea of my tenants employed and able to pay rent."

"I'm not going to be a maid," Annalise insisted. "At least not for long."

"No judgment here." Shauna held out her hands. "I've done plenty of jobs that other people wouldn't value or respect. Your ex might not have taken his own advice, but he wasn't wrong. Honest work is nothing to be ashamed of."

"I'm an interior designer." Annalise figured if she said the words often enough, she might begin to believe them. "At least that's what I went to school for, and I was good at it. Jonathan didn't want me to work, so I quit, which was stupid."

"You didn't know."

"No excuse. No more excuses."

"So you're going to be a maid who redecorates as you clean?"

Before thinking about the appropriateness of the gesture, Annalise pretended to scratch her nose with her middle finger.

Shauna burst into a gleeful peel of laughter. "That does not seem very Southern. Aren't you supposed to bless my heart or something?"

"Also, bless your heart," Annalise conceded. "I took a job as Walker Calloway's house manager."

"Do you mean housekeeper?"

"I use the terms synonymously."

"As is your prerogative. So are you planning to date a reclusive country singer who is clearly messed up after his brother and half his band died in a tour bus accident?"

Annalise sniffed. "That's crass."

"That's the truth."

"No, I'm not planning to date him. He's not my type." Without warning, an image of Jack Grainger appeared in Annalise's mind, but she quickly put it aside. The craggy rancher-slash-farm-manager wasn't her type either, no matter what her body wanted her to believe.

"Walker Calloway bought Whimsy Farm, a beauty that needs updating. I'm going to be the designer who helps him."

"While cleaning his toilets on the side."

"It's a foot in the door that I wouldn't otherwise have, and I'm a meticulous cleaner. I figure I'll impress him with that and then as we're chatting like people do with their housekeepers, we can talk about my suggestions for the house. I have ideas for the garden, too."

"But you have no references."

"I have an impeccable eye for color and design, and I know all the best vendors." She grimaced. "I owe half of them money. Jonathan handled the bills and apparently wasn't paying most of them. We renovated the kitchen and master bath last year, and I'm not sure anyone received the full amount they were owed. I don't know how he managed to keep people quiet for so long."

"What was your husband doing with the money?"

Annalise shrugged, surprised that the question didn't

elicit the emotion it would have a month ago. "Mostly coke and redheads as far as I can tell."

"That's not a great combination."

"Not in the least."

"I have a couple of people I can introduce you to," Shauna said then clamped shut her mouth like she couldn't believe she'd offered.

"No takebacks," Annalise said quickly.

Shauna flashed a patient grin. "I actually know people who need help. I'm a painter. Although some of the work is basic residential stuff, I do a lot of decorative painting—murals and decorative finishes. A couple of my clients are interested in updating parts of their houses. They could use help with the designs."

"And you'd recommend me? Why? We're not friends."

"We might agree on that, but you shouldn't point out your difficulties with making friends to people trying to be friendly with you."

"You think people don't already notice my challenges?"

"Probably," Shauna agreed with a wry smile. "Maybe that's okay. I have to say I like you better dealing with reduced circumstances than when you were flashing your giant diamond around the school. You looked like you had a stick up your butt."

"It felt like I had a stick up my butt," Annalise admitted, unsure why she could be honest with this woman but appreciating it just the same. "The reason I'm able to pay rent, not to mention insurance and groceries and anything else, is because I sold that diamond. It wasn't worth as much as Jonathan led me to believe but it's going to cover a few months. I'll be selling most of my designer clothes and handbags, too."

Shauna's dark eyes widened. "That's going to be a big change."

"I'm okay with change at this point, and I'd appreciate any potential clients you could put me in contact with. Maybe if I have success with some smaller projects, it will make me seem more legitimate when I pitch Walker my ideas."

"You're so sure that's going to work. Your big game plan is landing a rich and famous client."

"Unless I come up with a better idea."

As Shauna studied her, Annalise tried not to fidget. She wasn't a fidgeter.

"You're pretty and put together. Blonde like Barbie. I'm sure you could find another rich husband. Isn't that what divorced women of your ilk do?"

"Many of them." Annalise didn't bother to deny it. "But I will never let a man control me or put myself in a position where anyone has authority over my life."

Shauna nodded slowly and went to the window that overlooked the backyard. "I understand that sentiment, although I've heard stories that you can have an actual partnership when you find the right person. A give-and-take. It can be healthy, which I know nothing about."

"Maybe that's true for some people," Annalise answered with a sniff. "I don't plan to test the theory. Are you interested in a partnership with the giant?"

"He's not a literal giant," Shauna insisted.

"It's more than his physical presence," Annalise told her. "He gives the impression of being a giant of a man in personality, too." She winked. "I imagine in all areas."

"We aren't friends, so we're not having that conversation," Shauna said. "But you're right about Flynn having a big personality. It annoys me that you're right. I don't know how to be with him and not lose myself. It's been years since I saw him and he hurt me. One dinner and my dumb heart wants to ignore everything that happened in the past."

"Hearts are dumb," Annalise agreed. "Female parts, too, if you know what I mean."

"Really dumb."

"Thank you," Annalise said again.

Shauna glanced over her shoulder as she headed for the door. "For the lemon bars?"

"For making me feel normal and not totally alone even if I'm trash at making friends. Talking to you makes me believe I can do this. I'm going to drop my kids off to school on Monday, head to Whimsy Farm and knock Walker Calloway's socks off."

"Except Monday is the start of spring break."

Annalise felt her mouth drop open. One step forward, five miles back. "How could I have forgotten spring break?"

"I'll watch your kids," Shauna told her. "My boys will enjoy having them here, and I've taken the week off."

"I can't ask you to do that."

"You didn't ask. I offered, and I'm sure there will be a time you can pay me back."

"I owe a lot of people a lot of things," Annalise murmured even as she nodded. Because truly what choice did she have other than to accept Shauna's help? It wasn't easy to take assistance from anyone, let alone a woman she barely knew. She preferred being in the position of granting favors, but until she figured that out, she would gratefully accept this one.

CHAPTER NINE

SHAUNA DIDN'T HEAR from Flynn for three days after their dinner, not that she was counting the time that ticked by.

She'd expected her boys to ask her to call him or track him down at the Wildflower Inn, where he'd told her he was staying. It seemed odd to think of rough-around-the-edges Flynn at the adorable, welcoming boutique hotel that sat in the fancy part of town about ten minutes from Shauna's house.

Neither Zach nor Timmy mentioned anything, although she caught them glancing out the front window when they thought she wasn't looking and they'd become seemingly obsessed with improving their ball-handling skills.

What if Flynn didn't come back?

She wasn't sure why she even cared and cautioned herself not to bother thinking about him. But the wonder and worry wouldn't stop.

From the moment Shauna was placed in her first foster home, she'd done her best to be the sweetest, most compliant kid in every situation. At first, she'd known things were temporary. Her mother died of an overdose when Shauna was eleven, and her greatest hope had been to be adopted by another family.

She wanted to belong and desperately wished for a home and a permanent place in the world.

It was hard for an older kid in the system, even one who made an effort to be perfect. After a while, she tried to stop caring and wishing for more. But she never quite got the hang of detaching.

Part of her remained vulnerable to hope. And hope was a dangerous emotion, so she'd come to rely on herself and no one else.

Sure, she could do favors for other people, the way she was doing for Annalise. If Annalise helped her in return, that was fine. That was payback. But wanting and wishing for something more with Flynn or allowing herself to depend on him felt different, and she couldn't open herself to being hurt.

She certainly did not want her children ever to feel the vague sense of insecurity that still plagued her.

Of course, she was overreacting at this moment. Flynn would show up again because once he set his mind to something, there was no changing it. He'd set his mind on getting to know his sons.

But they weren't going to do it on his terms. He couldn't gallivant in and out of their lives like a fun uncle. Being a dad came with responsibilities. If he wanted this, he would have to step up in all the ways.

She walked into the backyard and waved to the twins and Annalise's kids. She wasn't sure how Trey and Margo would act when their mother wasn't around. The two of them were quite lovely now that she was getting to know them. Shauna had been judged plenty of times on how she looked or the type of clothes she wore or the circumstances of her life that she couldn't control.

So she should have known better than to do the same with Trey and Margo, as well as their mother, but the truth was if the Haverfords' situation hadn't changed because of what their father had done, they would never have crossed paths.

Annalise ran in different circles than Shauna, and so did her kids. But she got the sense that her new tenant, despite her prickly outward behavior and the way she'd previously acted, found the change in her life somewhat freeing. Perhaps her kids did as well. It was a lot of pressure to be the top dog when everyone was constantly vying to take over the position.

She admired the fort the kids were building in the back corner of the property with old drop cloths and chairs from the patio, then headed into the garage to continue working on the vintage dresser she was redoing.

She'd found the piece listed for free online and was repainting it with the hope of selling it and making a tidy profit. Usually her schedule didn't allow for even the idea of a side hustle, but spring break week gave her some much-needed time off.

With the boys getting bigger and their activities starting to cost more, Shauna wanted to do anything she could to bring in extra income.

Meghan's car was gone from the parking space she'd been allotted in the driveway, so Shauna knew she wouldn't disturb her new first-floor tenant.

She'd brought lemon bars to Meghan when she moved in yesterday, just as she had to Annalise.

The young art teacher surprised Shauna by taking the tray of dessert and quickly closing the door in Shauna's face, looking absolutely terrified. Or possibly nervous? But why?

It was funny because she would have expected Annalise to be harder to get to know, but the single mom seemed desperate for human contact. As friendly as Shauna had found Meghan during school hours, she seemed to want to keep to herself, at least for now.

Shauna didn't take offense. She imagined the woman was processing a lot between her grandmother's death and having to move out of her family home, to the uncertainty about her job and future in the town.

Shauna was planning to use the money she received in rent and put it into a college savings account for the twins. So how was it that she'd managed to find two tenants who had uncertain incomes?

She almost laughed at the irony given her background and financial insecurities, but she still had a good feeling about both of them. She began to hum along to her favorite Taylor Swift playlist as she got her painting supplies ready.

She'd just dipped her brush into the base color when Zach's voice rang out from the yard.

"He's here, Mommy. He came back."

Shauna swallowed as her heart did a funny little dance inside her chest. She knew exactly who *he* was and wasn't sure whether to be relieved or annoyed by the relief she heard in Zach's voice as he announced Flynn's arrival.

She walked out of the garage and squinted against the bright sunlight. Flynn stood at the edge of the grass wearing jeans, boots and a worn gray T-shirt that looked so soft she wanted to burrow her face against it.

His muscles bulged under the thin fabric, and the corner of a tattoo she didn't recognize peeked out from the edge of his left sleeve.

Do not be curious about that tattoo, she warned herself. Her body paid no attention.

"You want to meet our new neighbors?" Zach asked Flynn as he and Timmy drew closer.

Flynn lifted the mirrored sunglasses off his face and glanced toward Trey and Margo, who openly stared. Shauna downplayed Flynn's size, but Annalise was right. The man did have a massive presence.

"Sure," he said and Shauna let out a little puff of breath. She'd half feared he would tell his sons he didn't want to meet their friends. He hadn't exactly been known for his social skills back in the day, but he claimed to be different now. Maybe the army had—if not softened him, then at least managed to round out a few of his sharper edges.

"Meet Margo and Trey. They're poor now, so they have to live with us," Timmy announced.

She needed to talk with her kids about oversharing the same way she'd had the conversation with Annalise. Neither of the Haverford kids seemed to take offense.

"I'm Flynn."

"He's our dad," Timmy explained. "The one we didn't know about until a few days ago."

"Their dad went to live in a big house," Zach explained.

Shauna noticed Trey's jaw tighten while Margo stared at the grass surrounding her feet. Grass that needed to be mowed.

"My dad spent some time there, too," Flynn told the kids. "You'll be okay."

The boy visibly relaxed.

"He's going to get out real soon," Margo said, "and then we won't be poor anymore. I don't like being poor."

"Me neither," Flynn agreed.

Shauna stifled a laugh. It was a strange conversation for an adult to have with four misfit kids, but it seemed to be working for all of them. Flynn didn't make it weird for the pair who'd had their life upended. None of them were bothered by the fact that he was clearly so out of his element in dealing with children.

"What took you so long to come see us after Mommy made you dinner?" Timmy asked, echoing Shauna's thoughts.

Flynn frowned at her then looked at the boy. "It was a couple of days. I didn't realize that was a long time."

"Mommy got hurt and was in the hospital, and Declan came to stay. Uncle Declan," Timmy corrected himself. "Mommy called every night, but she was only gone for a little bit. We didn't even have time to miss her."

"We didn't miss you either." Zach kicked at the grass. "On account of we hardly know you."

Shauna knew her son was lying, and she had a feeling Flynn realized it as well.

But he didn't comment. Instead, he just nodded again. "Well, I was getting things figured out so we can get to know each other better. That's what I want. Is that what you want?"

Both boys nodded.

"It's a deal then. I'm going to talk to your mom for a few minutes. Hey, Trey," he called as the four kids turned to head back to the fort. "Let me know if you have any questions about having a parent in the big house. I'll answer what I can, and I'll be straight with you."

The boy nodded. "Your dad is cool," he said to the twins as they headed across the lawn.

"What are you doing?" she demanded once she felt sure the kids were far enough away that they wouldn't be able to hear them. "We don't hear from you after dinner, and now you show up with no warming in the middle of the day. What's the deal, Flynn?"

He blinked, and to her surprise, there were no bright sparks of temper in his gray-green eyes. He looked genuinely flummoxed. "Like I told the boys, I was arranging things to be here on a long-term basis."

"And we—they—are just supposed to trust you? I'm supposed to trust that you'll live up to your word?"

"Yes, Shauna. When have I ever not lived up to my word?"

"Remember that I grew up in foster care, the same as you." She poked a finger into his chest, not at all surprised that it felt like prodding a cement wall. "People make all kinds of promises. Words mean nothing."

"You thought I wasn't coming back?"

"No. Yes. I didn't know what to think. The point is that kids need stability. I might not have gotten it, and you and Declan might not have gotten it, but my boys know that they are the most important thing in my life and my heart. They're curious about their father and interested in getting to know you, but I will *not* have them hurt."

"I'm not going to hurt them." His voice was so steady and sure it made her stomach do somersaults. And then he added, "I'm not going to hurt you either."

She couldn't meet his gaze any longer. She whirled and walked toward the garage, trying to gather her emotions like they were marbles spilled on the ground, scattering in all directions.

She'd just reached the garage when she felt his hand on her arm, firm yet gentle. And she knew that if she pulled away, he'd let her go.

The Flynn she'd known before would have held on, too tightly maybe. Their connection had always been too intense for either of them to trust when they had no basis for that in their lives.

"It's hard to believe in anyone but myself." She shook her head slowly. "It was bad enough before, but now there's too much at risk."

"Shauna, I rented a house. I've been getting furniture for it—bedrooms for Zach and Timmy." She turned, wrenching her arm from his grasp. "Bedrooms?" she demanded. "They have a bedroom. They live here with me."

He held up his hands, palms out. "I know. I'm not trying to take them, but they are my sons. Even if you don't want me to be a part of your life, I'm going to be a part of theirs. That might mean a sleepover. Don't you want a break? You look like you need a break."

She gaped at him and felt her chin tremble. Here was a man who sent her blood racing because of how good he looked in an old T-shirt, and he'd told her to her face that she looked like a haggard mess.

At least, that's how she interpreted his words.

"I don't know how to do this," she whispered.

Flynn flashed a strained smile. "Me neither, obviously."

"I'd like you to text or call before you come over. Why are you here right now anyway?"

"I thought I could take the boys for ice cream. There's a grand opening sign on a storefront next to the downtown bakery. It seemed like it could be a good neutral outing. You can come too if you want. And their friends."

"What if the kids were busy? What if I had plans to take them another time? Are you going to disappear again if you don't get your way?"

She wasn't being fair and had a feeling they both knew it, but Flynn didn't rise to the bait. "Shauna, the boys are my priority now."

"How can that be? You came to town without knowing them. Not even knowing they existed. Suddenly you're going to change your whole life for them?"

"Isn't that what you did when you got pregnant?"

"That was different." She chewed on her lower lip.

"How?"

"I don't know, but it was."

"I'm sorry," he said, dragging a hand through his hair. "I should have called or texted."

"You rented a house in Magnolia?"

He nodded. "I saw the sign when I went for a run the morning after our dinner. It's only about half a block from the hotel."

"You rented a house in the same neighborhood as the Wildflower Inn?"

"It seemed like a good neighborhood. Is it not?"

"It's excellent. It's where the rich people in town live. Trey and Margo lived there before things changed for them. Are you rich?"

He looked almost embarrassed by the question. "I do okay. Private security pays pretty well, and I can work from almost anywhere with a few trips thrown in to visit clients. I'm going to support the boys."

"You're upending your life, and I don't even truly understand why you came to Magnolia in the first place."

"To see Declan," Flynn answered immediately, and disappointment speared through her. "And you. A lot of the reason was to see you. It's past time, Shauna. Things were bad between us, and we can't go back. There were some good times but also so many things I'd fix if I could."

"We can't go back," she repeated, more because she needed to hear it again than to convince him.

"I know, but we can go forward for the boys' sake." He held out a hand. "I'd like to call a truce."

"A truce." She placed her fingers in his grip. She would do anything for her boys, even make a deal with the devil she knew.

CHAPTER TEN

MEGHAN KNOCKED ON the door of Walker Calloway's house the Wednesday morning of spring break week, and immediately second-guessed every aspect of her life. From why she was there offering to help him come up with lesson plans to the sensible ballerina flats she'd worn to visit a farm to her whole college experience and why she decided to be an art teacher in the first place instead of something that was more secure and paid better like her mother had wanted her to.

It was difficult to contain her swirling thoughts once they began to spiral. Things were going downhill when she could acknowledge the wisdom in her mother's preachy advice.

She opened the flap of her satchel and started to pull out the water bottle she'd packed there, only to realize the lid on the stainless steel container hadn't been shut all the way. Now her planner and all of her papers were sopping wet.

She lifted the bag away from her body, only to see a circle of wetness quickly expanding on the front of her tan pants. Who wore tailored tan pants on an off day in the first place? It looked like her hip had peed itself. How perfect.

Unfortunately, she didn't have time to beat the hasty retreat she wished for because the door opened and Annalise Haverford stared at her, wearing jeans and a fitted black T-shirt under a floral-patterned apron. Meghan barely had a chance to wonder why her new neighbor looked like she was playing house at Whimsy Farm because the woman's cool perusal and slight pursing of her lips made her anxiety kick up a notch or twenty.

"Meghan?"

"Annalise?"

"What are you doing here, and why is there a wet spot on your pants?"

Annalise didn't exactly sound like Meghan's mother. She was only a few years older than Meghan, and while Denise Banks had grown up in Magnolia, she'd moved to Philadelphia for college and done her best to lose her Southern accent.

Annalise couldn't lose that slow drawl if she buried it six feet under.

"I have an appointment with Walker," she said, straightening her shoulders and then inclining her head. "Did you have an appointment with Walker as well?" Or was it possible the two gorgeous specimens of physical perfection were dating? Annalise didn't seem like Walker's type, but what did Meghan know?

"I haven't seen him all week," Annalise admitted, her mouth tightening further.

"Then why are you here?"

The elegant blonde's chin lifted. "I'm his new housekeeper, although I prefer house manager."

That gave context to the apron, although Annalise still looked more put together outfitted for the role of housekeeper than Meghan felt having dressed for a professional meeting.

"Why don't you come in? If he's expecting you, maybe he'll make an appearance. I'm sure he's out in the music studio. That's where he spends most of his time when he's not stalking around the property. I'm not sure what he's doing, but I'd love a chance to speak with him. You might be my chance."

As if uncomfortable with revealing even that weakness, Annalise dropped her gaze. She studied Meghan's bag more closely. "You're dripping."

"My water bottle spilled."

"Let's clean it up." Annalise led Meghan through the house, which was not what she would have expected from a country music chart-topper. It looked like her grandmother's house, which had most recently been updated to add a push-button landline phone instead of a rotary dial.

"What kind of appointment do you have with Walker?" Annalise asked casually. Nothing Annalise did was casual as far as Meghan could tell.

"He's going to be the new music teacher, or more specifically, the substitute for the rest of the year."

"Are you joking?" Annalise spun on her heel to face Meghan, looking vaguely feral. "Tell me Everly Mae did not coordinate that. She'll be golden at the school in perpetuity for that kind of mastermind move."

Meghan shook her head. "I did. At least, his nephew did and approached me about it. I'm not sure Walker wanted to do it, but he doesn't seem to be able to say no to anything Gus requests."

"He's a funny little kid."

"Gus is special." Meghan wasn't sure why she felt the need to defend the child. "He's sweet and funny and smart, and he's been through a lot."

"I do not deny any of that. I like him. He keeps me company, follows me around when he's not tagging after that inhospitable farm manager Walker employs."

"You said he was funny," Meghan felt compelled to point

out as they entered the equally dated kitchen. “People called me funny and did not mean it as a compliment.”

“He’s unique,” Annalise clarified, “and I mean in a good way. I know he’s had a rough time. I was thinking of bringing Trey out so they could play. It’s spring break week, and all that poor kid has done is helped me dust and scrub floors.”

“I’m sure he’d like that, but maybe leave Margo at home.” Meghan immediately regretted the words. “The house smells very clean. You must be doing a good job.”

“Why should I leave my daughter at home?” Annalise’s voice had dropped several notches.

“Because she might not want to play with the boys.”

“She’s been playing with Shauna’s boys just fine this week. Maybe you haven’t noticed because you keep yourself shut up in that apartment all the livelong day.”

“Yeah, that’s probably it. I didn’t realize.”

Annalise moved forward so suddenly that Meghan instinctively clutched her bag tighter and then pushed it away when cold wetness seeped through her shirt to her belly.

“Tell me what you meant.” Annalise took the bag from her and placed it on a towel she’d unfolded on the counter. “Teachers don’t speak about children randomly or make mistakes. At least not teachers like you—good ones.”

“You think I’m a good teacher?”

“What are you avoiding telling me about my daughter?”

“She’s a mean girl.” What did Meghan have to lose at this point? “I think she gets it from you.”

Annalise’s eyes narrowed. “I don’t want her to be a mean girl,” she said after a moment then sighed. “Does everyone at the school hate me?”

“Do you care?”

"Surprisingly, I find that I do. You know I've worked tirelessly to raise money for various charities in this town."

"I know. You never let anyone forget it. It's none of my business," Meghan said, "but you give the impression of having spent life riding around on your high horse."

To her surprise, Annalise's lips twitched. "Right now, I do a lot riding around on a donkey and feeling like a horse's ass."

"Do your friends know you're cleaning houses?"

"I prefer to think of it as managing Mr. Calloway's property."

"With loads of bleach and a scrub brush, by the smell of things."

"It doesn't matter because I don't have friends anymore." Annalise seemed to contemplate her own words. "Maybe I never did. Another aspect of my life I didn't realize I cared about."

Meghan considered that. She'd never been great at making friends. Her social anxiety and introverted nature kept her from relaxing around people. But she'd understood how it made her different and envied the Annalises of the world.

To think she had something in common with the self-proclaimed ringleader of the school's mom pack gave her pause.

Then made a tiny spark of satisfaction glow in her chest.

"I'm sorry you're losing your job," Annalise said. "I don't regret not being involved in PTO at this point, but I wish there were some way I could help you. You're a good teacher, and despite what that nit-wit principal believes, art and music are important for the school."

"I'll find another job," Meghan said, even though she had no idea what or how.

"*Nit-wit* is a fairly kind way to describe the person who

decided to ax your position in the first place." Walker Calloway strode into the kitchen like he owned the place.

Well, he *did* own the place.

"I'm thinking about having a word with that principal. Gus is upset about this change, and my nephew doesn't need anything else in his life to upset him." His dark eyes flared with intensity, almost burning Meghan.

She swallowed and tried not to fidget under his scrutiny. "Many of the kids want the art and music programs to continue."

"I don't care about many of them."

Annalise stifled a laugh, and Walker flicked his gaze to hers. Was it Meghan's imagination, or did his features lose some of their ferocity?

"My kids want music and art," the other woman said with a shrug. "Heck, other than PE, art is the only subject my son even enjoys. He's not much for the recorder."

"They still play recorders? I remember learning 'Three Blind Mice' when I was in third grade. By that point, Nash had already mastered the piano and guitar. I had a lot of catching up to do."

"You managed okay," Meghan said, unsure why she felt the need to offer some words of comfort. They sounded lame. "Does Gus play?"

Walker shook his head. "Nash talked about teaching him but things have been crazy busy the last couple of years. He never got that far. The house looks good," he told Annalise. "Smells good, too. Way better than it did before."

"Thank you." Annalise looked genuinely pleased by the praise, which also surprised Meghan.

"Did you rearrange the furniture in the family room?"

"I thought it flowed better with a few tweaks. I can move it back if you'd like."

"It's fine." He grabbed a can of sparkling water from the refrigerator. "I think things are good in the house until next week. Plan on helping Jack in the barn the next couple of days."

Annalise's mouth tightened, but she nodded. "I'll head out there now if there's nothing else either of you needs."

What kind of strange turn of events was it that Annalise would be asking Meghan if there was anything she needed?

"No, thanks. Apparently, I've got lesson plans to create," Walker said.

"I'm fine." Meghan's voice was an embarrassing squeak.

Annalise gave her a funny look and then exited the room, leaving Meghan and Walker alone.

She immediately wanted to call the other woman back. "Where's Gus?" she asked.

"In the barn with Jack. He likes the goats."

"You have goats?"

"It's a farm."

"Right."

Walker flashed a quick grin. "To be fair, all the animals came with the property. Horses, goats, chickens, five cats and two herding dogs. Mostly they herd Gus."

"I bet he likes that."

"He likes the animals." He took a step closer, and she noticed that his eyes had gentled slightly. His whole demeanor appeared more relaxed. He wore cargo pants and a loose-fitting flannel shirt, but he was just as appealing as when he was in those butt-hugging jeans. "He likes you, too. A lot."

"I'm on the same level in his estimation as farm animals." Meghan chuckled nervously. "That's more appreciation than I've had from a man in ages." She felt color spike in her cheeks and wished she could take back the words.

"Men are stupid," Walker said simply.

"You're a man." She made the comment as if he didn't realize it.

"I've been stupid about a lot of things, women included."

Was he giving her a warning? She was being silly. A man like Walker wouldn't give Meghan a second look in any sort of romantic way. More than likely, he was trying to smooth over her awkward comment.

How could she feel so at ease and confident in the classroom but like such a doofus when it came to talking with adults?

"As long as you do a good job with the music classes, I don't care how stupid you are in other areas of your life."

Walker's thick brows drew together. "Okay. That's fair."

Also another ridiculously stupid thing to say. "We should get started on your lesson plans," she told him, sounding like an old-fashioned schoolmarm.

If Walker noticed, he was enough of a gentleman not to mention it. Of course he noticed. Everybody noticed Meghan's social struggles.

Everyone other than the kids she taught.

"Let's go to my music studio. I have instruments there, so we can discuss what might work for the different grades. How many grades are there, by the way?"

"Kindergarten and then grades one through six, two rounds in each. Depending on the schedule, you'll have two or three music classes each day. Art classes happen during your off periods. We have a shared space."

"So you and I will spend a lot of time together?"

"We don't necessarily have to. It's not a requirement." Meghan realized she sounded even more inept than usual and tried to bail out. "I mean, we could see each other if you want. I have nothing against spending time together, but don't feel like you have to be with me."

Oh, my god. Was it possible for Meghan to find a way to sew her mouth shut so she would stop making a fool of herself in front of this man?

"Did you and the previous music teacher spend time together?"

"Joanie had been at the school for a lot of years. Her kids are grown now. She has grandkids, so she spent most weekends with them."

"You've only been at the elementary school a year."

"Yes. I moved to Magnolia to take care of my grandmother. She had cancer."

"I'm sorry. I hope she gets better."

"She died a month ago."

"I'm sorry," he repeated.

"I'm glad I got to be there with her at the end. She meant the world to me."

Meghan followed Walker to a path leading to a small shed behind the main house. It was painted the same pale yellow color on the outside but looked fresher like it had been given some recent attention.

Walker paused with his hand on the door. "I'm sorry about your grandmother. Obviously, the two of you were close if you came here to take care of her. Was it your mother's mother or your dad's?"

"My mom's mom. I spent summers with her growing up because my parents worked long hours. They wanted me out of their hair."

He gestured for her to enter the shed. "My mom hated summer breaks when my brother and I were underfoot. She would kick us out in the morning with strict instructions not to return until dinner."

"What did you do?"

"We lived in the country so there were plenty of things

to keep us busy. We built forts and raised hell with the neighbors."

"I wasn't much of a hell-raiser," Meghan said.

"I'm shocked to hear that."

She looked at him and liked the twinkle she saw in his maple-syrup-colored eyes. He was teasing her. Meghan wasn't the type of woman used to being teased by a man, at least not in the way Walker was doing it. His words felt like flirting instead of him making fun of her in some way.

She wouldn't let herself get distracted by a bit of kindness. He was famous and probably used to making small talk with people from all different backgrounds.

"This is an incredible space," she said, turning her attention back to the shed's interior. She wasn't sure what she'd expected.

Based on the house, it had been more like her grandmother's attic, stuffed full of broken ladder-back chairs and boxes of old Christmas decorations.

The shed had been recently renovated, probably taken down to the studs. The walls were covered with what looked like reclaimed wood, giving it a cozy feel. At least a dozen guitars were hanging on the walls. Two pianos, plus a keyboard and an upright piano were situated around the room. A comfy-looking couch sat on the far side of the room. The space was bigger than it looked from the outside.

Meghan was immediately both smitten and jealous. "I would give anything to have an area like this for art. It's amazing. Did you use a local decorator to help you with the design?"

"No decorator," Walker told her.

"You did this?"

He laughed softly. "I can't take credit for it either. Jack conceived this space. It was the first thing he did when we moved to Whimsy Farm."

"Jack, your farm manager?"

"Jack has been with me since the start of my career. He was our manager and publicist, like the third Calloway brother, even though we're not related by blood. He was Nash's best friend and became mine as well. I had two older brothers looking out for me." His Adam's apple bobbed as he swallowed. "Now only one."

Meghan had been on the receiving end of more than her share of sympathy after her grandmother's death, so she didn't appreciate when people who didn't understand loss offered empty platitudes.

If she had a nickel for every time someone told her Grammy was in a better place, she wouldn't have to worry about not having a job next year. She could live off those nickels, but Meghan had taken little comfort in the words. She'd been so empty inside and knew Walker Calloway understood that kind of desolation.

It was hard to believe that someone idolized by so many people would feel alone. She imagined he had plenty of friends to share his thoughts and memories with.

But Meghan recognized the emptiness in him because it mirrored her own.

"They say time heals all wounds, but to me, it just feels like I'm fading along with her memory, except here I am."

He looked surprised by her words. "I don't have the luxury to fade away because I have Gus to take care of." He ran a hand through his thick hair, curling at the ends and needing a trim.

It had been shorter when she'd seen the band in concert. He'd seemed controlled and contained like he planned every hip wiggle and wink to the crowd.

This version of Walker felt less tame, and she was surprised how much she liked it.

"Since we have lesson plans to create, we'll ensure you

impress him with your teaching ability. You'll make him proud, Walker."

"I don't deserve that. Not many people know this, but Nash didn't want to do that show in Minnesota," he said, his face somber. "It was three days before Christmas. He was ready to be home in Nashville with Gus. I insisted on it. We'd gotten into a financial bind and needed the money that gig would bring in. I arranged for the bus that took us to the venue. If it wasn't for me, he'd be here."

Meghan stared at Walker, unable to look away. His eyes had gone molten, his pupils so dilated she could barely make out the maple-colored irises.

"No one but me knows this, but a year ago I was supposed to come down to Magnolia and take my grandmother to her appointment for a mammogram, but one of my girlfriends got tickets to a music festival in Nashville."

"The Honeybee Festival?" he guessed, mentioning the same show where she'd seen him play.

She nodded. "I asked Gran to reschedule the appointment because I didn't want to miss the show. Then she forgot about it, and I forgot about it. By the time she saw the doctor, the cancer had spread. Maybe if I had taken her in the first place, they would have caught it early, and she'd still be here."

Walker shook his head. "You can't put yourself through that sort of mental anguish. I don't know you well, Meghan, but I have no doubt you loved your grandmother. Her death isn't your fault."

She swallowed around the emotions choking her, unaware until this moment what it would mean to hear those words.

"I could say the same thing about you and your brother." She smoothed a hand over the damp spot on her pants. Having left her bag in the kitchen, she had nothing to act as a shield against the way Walker's gaze affected her.

The moment felt strangely intimate as they stared at each other, but she didn't turn away.

"You could," he admitted finally. "Although I wouldn't believe you."

"For Gus's sake, at least consider that you might not be the bad guy you want to believe." Who was this woman willing to challenge a handsome, powerful man when her knees practically knocked together with nerves? Meghan didn't recognize herself, but she liked this version.

"I'll consider it," Walker conceded with a nod.

"I appreciate that. Now let's start working on your lesson plans."

His mouth twitched. "That was a horrible transition, but I appreciate it. I don't think I can take any more deep thoughts today."

"Do you know 'The Paw Patch' song?" she asked with her own smile. "It was one of the previous teacher's favorites."

"Um… I don't think so."

She winked. "Then we are done with deep thoughts, and you are in for a treat."

His lips widened into a grin, and Meghan tried to steady her heart as they got down to business.

CHAPTER ELEVEN

FRIDAY MORNING, Annalise had just placed her hand on the doorknob to the kitchen entrance of Walker's farmhouse when she realized she'd left her phone in the car.

Nerves were making her discombobulated. Today was the day she had no more excuses for avoiding working in the barn with Jack.

She'd managed it for as long as she could. Even though Walker had told her on Wednesday afternoon she could begin helping Jack, Annalise had kept herself busy inside the house yesterday, polishing silver, laundering sheets and blankets from the linen closet and using wood soap on the kitchen cabinets. She didn't take direction well, which was an issue, but these past few days made her even more confident that redecorating and redesigning the farmhouse would allow her to establish the business she dreamed of—if she could convince Walker to give her a chance.

She had so many ideas and had begun collecting fabric swatches and creating an inspiration board late at night and in the early morning hours before she came to work.

But she'd found a note on her car windshield when she'd left the house the previous day. "I'll see you at 7:30 sharp" had been written in bold script signed with only a *J*.

There was no question about who that *J* belonged to.

It was just after seven, and she'd decided to arrive a few

minutes early to make a fresh pot of coffee in Walker's kitchen and prepare breakfast.

Maybe if Walker saw how valuable she was inside the house, he wouldn't banish her to the barn.

Annalise wasn't exactly an expert at preparing breakfast for her own two kids. They'd always relied on the housekeeper. It embarrassed her that she'd usually stayed upstairs until she heard Connie and the kids talking.

Annalise's mother had been persnickety about caring for her house, and Annalise's efforts never seemed to meet those exacting standards.

This job, humble though it was, gave her a strange sense of satisfaction at her abilities.

She walked around the corner of the wraparound porch to see the back door of her car open and a small figure emerge.

"Jonathan Grant Haverford," she yelled, forgetting the early hour, her voice pitched high in disbelief.

Her son, who did not have a future in cat burglary, froze for a moment and then dropped to the ground like she wouldn't notice him flat on his belly, scooting under the car.

Annalise strode forward, grateful not to have an audience for this little scene. Her nerve endings snapped with temper.

She nudged Trey's jeans-clad leg with her boot. "Get out from under there and explain what you're doing. You're supposed to be at home with your sister."

"I wanted to see the horses." Trey climbed out from under the car and dusted off his yellow shirt, his tone surprisingly defiant for a boy in big trouble.

"You should have asked me to bring you out here. Did you ride all the way with no seat belt?"

He started to roll his eyes and then apparently thought

better of it. "Mom, you drive like a grandma. It isn't as if anything's going to happen."

"You don't know what's going to happen," she insisted, wanting to pull her lanky son into her arms for a hug as much as she wanted to throttle him. "Except for one guarantee. You can rest assured there will be no fun in your future. First a fight and now this. Did you think I wouldn't notice?"

"You work in the house. I was going to the barn. I planned to hide until no one was around. I want to see that horse with the star on his forehead again."

"For your information, I'm working in the barn today. I imagine Shauna would have noticed if you didn't make an appearance this morning."

"Margo was gonna tell her I was sick."

"You roped your sister into this deception as well?"

Trey kicked the toe of his grimy sneaker against the gravel. "You said you were getting off early today to take us to the beach, so we didn't think—"

"I see you brought reinforcements."

Annalise should have realized Jack was approaching. Not because she could hear his footfalls, which were preternaturally quiet for a man of his size. But moments earlier, a shiver had passed through.

Her grandmother would have told Annalise to toss a pinch of salt over her shoulder to ward off evil spirits, but Annalise knew her body's annoying awareness of Jack Grainger caused it.

"This is a mistake. I'm taking him home," Annalise muttered. "He snuck into my car this morning and—"

"You didn't notice he was there?" Jack asked with a laugh.

"I'm real good at hiding." Trey needed a haircut. His bangs swooped across his face so he had to continuously flip his head to see, like some kind of teen pop sensation. "I snuck in the back seat while Mom was in the shower this morning and covered myself with a blanket. I didn't move at all."

He sounded proud of his deception. "I even had a straw to breathe through to stay hidden. I saw that in a movie."

"I didn't notice," Annalise admitted quietly. "My mind was on other things this morning."

She made the mistake of meeting Jack's gaze at that moment. One thick brow lifted as if he knew exactly what kind of thoughts had distracted her that morning. Thoughts of him, primarily.

"I was going to make coffee and prepare some breakfast for Gus before—"

"You never make me and Margo breakfast," Trey said.

"You are not currently in a position to complain about my skills at mothering, young man. Not with this stunt."

"I apologize," she said to Jack, wondering if her voice often sounded so prim and uptight. "I'm going to run my son home and return as soon as possible."

"Or you can let him stay." Jack shrugged. "You're the mother so it's up to you."

"I wanted to see the horses. I love horses."

"Then maybe you should learn what it takes to care for them. I can always use extra muscle around the barn."

Annalise started to laugh then noticed that Trey suddenly stood up straighter, puffing out his chest as if to display said muscles.

"Mom, can I please stay? I'm sorry I upset you."

"But you aren't sorry you stowed away?" she clarified.

He shook his head with another hair toss. Annalise would be making an appointment with the barber today. "I don't want to hang out with Margo and the twins again."

She swallowed. Trey had been a good sport this week, and according to Shauna, her sons adored him. But it was a change for her popular, outgoing boy to always hang around the house.

Margo had received a couple of invitations to friends' houses and outings with girls from her class. Apparently, the way Trey had stuck up for Gus Calloway against the Tinsdale boy had impacted his friendships.

"That's a generous offer from Mr. Grainger," she said.

"Call me Jack."

"I'll work real hard, Mr. Jack."

Jack winked. "I know you will, son. You may also regret tricking your mama when I'm through with you."

"No, I won't. I mean, I regret tricking her, but I'm here now. I want to see the horses so badly."

"You'll earn that privilege if you work hard," Jack told him, then quickly added, "but only if your mom agrees."

"Please," Trey said, throwing his arms around Annalise. She couldn't remember the last time her son had voluntarily hugged her, let alone in front of someone, and it didn't matter if this was a manipulation of her emotions. She loved feeling him pressed against her.

"You'll do everything Mr. Jack tells you, and there will be no riding."

"Come on," Trey whined, looking up at her with pleading eyes. "Mr. Jack, tell her. Horses like being ridden."

"Some of them," Jack agreed.

"Like the one with the star on his forehead."

Jack made a face. "Not Orion. His previous owner didn't treat him well, so he's skittish. We're working on training him."

"I bet he'd like me."

"No riding." Annalise breathed through the familiar

panic that gripped her as she thought about the accident she'd had as a girl.

Jack nodded, and if he noticed her distress, he didn't mention it. "Definitely not Orion. He's not the right horse for an inexperienced rider."

"I want experience," Trey said.

Annalise clenched her fists in front of her. "You will listen to Mr. Jack and me. Trey, this is nonnegotiable. Do not push me."

The boy let out a heavy sigh, and Jack studied her. "Are you going to be okay helping out in the barn?" he asked.

"Yes," she answered without hesitation. If Annalise had learned one thing about herself over the past several months, it was that she could handle a lot more than she'd ever expected or anyone had given her credit for. She didn't have to ride a horse. She just needed to scoop hay and clean up poop. It wasn't the most humiliating thing she'd done recently.

"I'm going to make that pot of coffee, and then I'll see the two of you in the barn."

Jack's brows furrowed, and she wondered how he managed to communicate so precisely with only the slightest facial movements. She wasn't used to having anyone read her so easily, let alone a man.

Jonathan hadn't paid enough attention, seeing her as nothing more than an extension of himself.

As she walked into the house, Jack continued to consume her thoughts. There was no ring on his finger, yet she wondered if he had a girlfriend.

She imagined he would be popular with women. Annalise could see him with a beautiful cowgirl—wavy hair, sun-kissed skin and all the confidence in the world. Basically, someone the exact opposite of Annalise, who faked her way through every part of her life, including the bedroom.

No more faking. There was too high a price to pay on the other end, chipping away at her soul.

She made coffee and put out the yogurt and berries, as well as the granola she'd made the day before.

She should try that recipe for her kids. She wasn't sure what stopped her other than more insecurity. She knew her skills couldn't compare to the homemade muffins and waffles that Connie used to prepare.

Shauna was equally as domestically gifted. Her lemon bars had been annoyingly delicious. At dinner last night, Margo shared how their new neighbor taught her how to make homemade icing, just like the kind on the televised baking shows she loved to watch.

Annalise had been in a fog since Jonathan's arrest, numbly going through the motions of caring for her kids while she tried to stitch together the frayed edges of their lives. But it was more than edges. There were gaping holes in the fabric of her existence that she needed to somehow patch.

It was time she did more than survive. She needed to learn how to thrive and show her kids by example they could overcome any challenge.

With a new sense of purpose, she walked toward the barn and told herself this was just another challenge. She wouldn't let Jack Grainger see her fear. Luckily, he wasn't around when she arrived.

"Mr. Jack got called out to a meeting," Trey reported.

"What kind of a meeting?"

"He didn't say. Told me to start on the stalls and that you could reorganize the tack room if this work was beneath you."

"No honest work is beneath me." She said the words for herself as much as for Trey. "We'll knock out the stalls together."

The smile he gave her nearly stole her breath. "Thanks for not making me go home, Mom. I'm sorry I upset you."

"We must be honest with each other, Trey. It's you, me and your sister now. If we're not honest, things are going to be even harder."

Trey made a face. "They've been pretty hard already."

"That's true, but the struggles won't last. It's going to get better, son. I promise."

"Do you still love Dad?"

Annalise opened her mouth to immediately answer that she loved her children's father. Then she thought about what she'd just told her son regarding the importance of honesty.

"I care about your dad," she said, choosing her words with care. "Because he's your dad. But he betrayed a lot of people, me included. I don't know that I can forgive him for that."

"Is it okay if I love him?" her son asked, his voice tiny. She remembered that for all his confidence and bravado, he was a kid who didn't want to disappoint either of his parents.

Annalise knew how that felt down to her bones. She couldn't control Jonathan's relationship with Trey and Margo, but she was determined to take more care with hers.

"Of course it is. You can even love him and be angry with him at the same time. You can be sad he's gone and still wish for something different."

She tried to offer a smile that didn't wobble at the corners. "If you want to talk about it with me or anybody else, you are welcome to explore your feelings. He'll be gone for a while, so we'll have to figure out things on our own. Despite all the bad things he did, I know he loves you. That isn't going to change."

"I don't want to be like him." Trey picked up a nearby shovel. "He always told me I was a chip off the old block, but I don't want to do bad things, Mommy. I don't want to go to jail."

The "Mommy" gutted her. She couldn't remember the last time he'd called her that. "You're doing good things already, like defending Gus. It wasn't easy, and I know you're paying a price. Sometimes there are difficult aspects to doing the right thing, as unfair as that is."

"Will you let me ride a horse if I do the right thing?"

She laughed despite the emotion bubbling up inside her. "I'll think about it, which is as honest as I can be. Right now, we need to get to mucking those stalls so that Jack doesn't think we're the kind of privileged soft people who don't know how to do a day's work."

He nodded. "I'm tough because that's what boys have to be. But you and Margo are kind of soft, especially your booby area. They're like pillows."

She laughed again. "Margo and I can be tough, but I'll take that as a compliment," she told him, reaching out to ruffle his hair.

She was in the stall in the back of the barn when Jack returned. She heard him giving Trey instructions, but he didn't seek her out.

Annalise was annoyed to be disappointed by that and dug into the task of cleaning stalls with more gusto. Sweat was beading on her forehead and dripping down her back when Trey came and found her a while later.

"Mr. Jack had to run to town. He told me I should feed the horses out in the pasture, and you could cut off early or rest on the porch if you want to."

She felt her eyes narrow. "So you keep working, but I stop early? Does he think I can't handle it?"

Trey shrugged, unperturbed by her indignation. "He

said after I'm done in the pasture, we can both quit. I told him we were going to the beach."

"Do you think he's mad about that?"

"He didn't seem to mind."

"I'm going to organize the tack room," she said, forcing a smile. It wasn't her son's fault that Jack was irritating as all get out. Why would he think she'd need a rest after a couple hours of physical labor?

Yes, her arms were burning and she might have trouble lowering herself onto the toilet tomorrow due to the ache in her backside, but he didn't know that. For all Jack Grainger knew, she was one of those CrossFit fanatics who could toss tires and muck stalls for days on end.

Trey went about feeding the animals, and she entered the tack room. It wasn't in bad shape, but she quickly found a better system and worked on organizing the labeled equipment to match the names she'd seen on the stalls.

"Hey, Mom, come quick," Trey called just as she hung the final bridle on its hook. "Now, Mom. Hurry!"

A dozen terrifying images flashed through Annalise's mind as she rushed from the barn toward the enclosed pasture that bordered the structure. She had good reason, at least in her mind, for her terror of horses. The urgency in Trey's voice brought back too many memories of… She stopped short at the scene in front of her.

"He likes me," her son announced happily, smiling as a giant animal with a star on its forehead loomed over him, either nuzzling Trey's head or getting ready to take a massive bite out of him.

Blood roared through her head, but Annalise did her best to retain her composure and not let her panic show. Animals could sense fear, and she was pee-her-pants terrified at the moment. "Trey, you need to get back," she said, her voice just above a whisper. "Jack said that horse is wild. He could hurt you."

"His breath tickles. And Mr. Jack said Orion is skittish. He's not going to hurt me."

"You don't know that. He could rear up or—"

"The boy is safe enough with Orion, especially during feeding time."

With a start, she glanced to see Jack suddenly at her side. "Why are you always sneaking up on me?" she demanded.

It looked like he was trying to suppress a smile. "I wasn't trying to sneak."

She had to believe him. With the pounding in her head, a marching band could have approached, and Annalise wasn't sure she would have heard.

"Mr. Jack, he likes me."

"He sure does," Jack agreed. "You're doing good with him—with all the chores on your checklist."

He glanced at Annalise. "You both did well today. The tack room looks amazing. I'm expecting *Southern Living* magazine to arrive for the photo shoot at any moment."

"You're not quite magazine ready, but I'll get you there." Annalise tried not to yelp out a warning when Trey dropped a kiss on Orion's nose. "I'm trying to retain my composure for the sake of my son, but can you guarantee that giant beast isn't going to trample him?"

"I take it you had a negative experience with a horse at some point. I don't mean to pry, but you're kind of freaking out over nothing."

She sniffed. "Unlike seemingly every other young girl in the world, I was always afraid of horses. Any sort of large animal terrifies me," she admitted, although she'd recently discovered that was the least of her long list of fears.

"My mother insisted on riding lessons because that's

what girls from wealthy families did. We needed to look the part." She kept an eye on Trey both to ease her worry and because it was easier than seeing the judgment she expected to find in Jack's gaze. "It didn't turn out well. I was thrown and nearly trampled on my first day in the ring. Scared me to pieces. Mom tried to force me to get back on to prove I had what it took to the audience of other mothers and daughters."

"You didn't have anything to prove." Jack's voice was flinty, and she didn't know whether that was good or bad.

"It was the one and only time I defied my mother. Maybe she'd been right to push me, but I couldn't do it. Not with so many friends watching and my fear and weakness on full display."

"I don't think fear is a weakness," Jack said. "Everyone is afraid of something."

She turned to him at that moment, unable to resist. "I find that hard to believe where you're concerned. What are you afraid of, Jack?"

She expected him to give a glib answer akin to Indiana Jones and his fear of snakes. That would have been endearing but not nearly the emotional punch his response landed on her.

"I'm afraid I won't be able to save Walker from the grief of losing his brother. I'm terrified we'll all get sucked into that vortex, and I will have failed the people who mean the most to me in the world."

Annalise sucked in a breath and waved to Trey as Orion followed him across the pasture. "What makes you think it's your responsibility to save them?"

"Because I should have died instead of Nash," he answered like it was the most obvious thing in the world.

His response elicited more questions, like how could he

believe he deserved to die in place of his friend? Before she could ask, Gus came running from the house.

"Hi, Trey," he called, wiping the back of his arm across his mouth like a napkin. He wore saggy sweatpants and a too-small Calloway Brothers T-shirt and worn flip-flops. "I didn't know you were here. My daddy rescued Orion from a man who was mean to him. He doesn't like very many people."

"Hey, Gus." Trey turned with a wave as the horse galloped toward the other end of the pasture.

Gus marched up to Jack. "Orion likes Trey," he said with wide-eyed wonder. It must be a bigger deal than Annalise realized. Despite lingering anxiety, her heart warmed at the idea of her son having some sort of connection with the troubled horse.

"I see that, buddy." Jack smiled gently at Gus.

"We should go," Annalise told Trey as he joined them. "Thank Mr. Jack for allowing you to help."

"Thank you, sir," Trey said without hesitation.

"Have you been here all morning?" Gus asked. "I wish I would have known. Do you want to stay and hang out? Probably not. You've probably got plans with your real friends."

Annalise's heart clenched for the awkward kid, and she silently prayed her son would handle this moment with more maturity than she'd modeled for him.

"My mom is taking me and my sister to the beach," Trey reported. "The water's too cold for swimming, but it's still fun."

Annalise felt Jack shift uncomfortably next to her, but he didn't jump in to smooth over the awkward interaction between the boys so she stayed silent as well.

"Yeah, sounds like fun," Gus agreed with a sigh.

Trey shoved a lock a hair out of his face. "You could come if you want."

"I want." Gus looked like he was going to explode from happiness.

"I mean, if it's okay with you, Mom," Trey quickly amended. "Sorry, I forgot to ask first."

The fact that her son was asking at all made her want to explode with happiness right along with Gus. She smiled at both boys. "I'd love to have Gus join us. Do you need to ask your uncle?"

Gus's mouth pinched into a thin line. "He went out as soon as I got up. I don't know when he'll be back."

"You can go to the beach," Jack said. "Listen to Ms. Haverford and wear sunscreen."

Annalise stifled a groan. She must be out of her mind that Jack's sunscreen warning made her knees go weak. Heaven forbid she ever see the man empty a dishwasher—it could cause her to spontaneously combust.

"I will, Jack. I promise." Gus bounced on his toes like he couldn't quite contain his excitement. "I need to get dressed. You want to come with me? I can show you pictures of my daddy riding Orion."

"Sure," Trey said, surprising Annalise once again.

He climbed through the split-rail fence, and the two boys headed toward the house. Trey's gaze continued to stray to the horse pasture while Gus waved his hands as he spoke.

She glanced at Jack, who was frowning as he watched Orion munching grass on the far side of the pasture. Tension radiated from him, and she crossed her arms over her chest.

"I'll keep him safe if that's what you're worried about," she said.

He turned toward her and shook his head. "Walker was

supposed to take Gus boating today as a spring-break treat. I guess it was a rough night."

Annalise raised an eyebrow. "He seems to have a lot of those."

When she'd been the one employing a housekeeper, she'd never considered the details the woman might pick up about the fabric of Annalise's life. After less than a week of working for Walker Calloway, it had already become clear that he was a man dealing with more than his share of demons.

"Too often," Jack agreed.

She couldn't help but wonder about Jack's demons and the toll it must take to put his own healing aside to make other people his priority.

She liked that about him. She liked a lot of things about him.

Her breath caught in her throat when he reached out and grazed a finger across her cheek.

"You had a smudge," he said simply.

Dirt. Of course, that was it. Jack probably dated women who were young, gorgeous and uncomplicated. None of those applied to Annalise, and she'd do well to remember that. He wasn't her type, even if she had been interested in dating again. Which she wasn't. She took a step back, putting much-needed space between them. "I'm going to make sure the kitchen is clean before we go. We'll have Gus back by dinnertime."

He nodded, and she wondered if she'd imagined the way his dark eyes had sparked moments earlier. "That'll be just fine."

"Fine," Annalise repeated and turned away, knowing she was anything but fine.

CHAPTER TWELVE

"You don't have to do this."

"I want to," Flynn answered. "I wouldn't be here if I didn't want to."

Shauna sniffed and wrapped her arms tightly around her waist as she and Flynn walked toward the elementary school entrance the following week. It was her morning to volunteer in the twins' classroom, a time she cherished and made a point of carving out once a month. She wished she could commit more often, but because she stuck to a strict work schedule during the hours when her boys were at school, there wasn't that luxury. Zach had mentioned the volunteer hour to Flynn when he'd been over for dinner the previous night. Before either of her boys could ask, he'd offered to come with her. The twins had been so excited. There was no way she could deny any of them. Flynn had been making a regular effort, and she couldn't deny that even her heart fluttered at the idea of him becoming a permanent fixture in the daily structure of their lives.

Some nights he came by—texting or calling first—to play catch with them and Trey in the backyard. Other evenings, he simply called or FaceTimed. He told her he didn't want to infringe too much on her routine, and it was a challenge to reconcile her mind to this considerably gentler version of the hot-tempered man she'd known.

But there was no denying his appeal, and she wasn't the only one who noticed.

Annalise and Meghan spent time with Shauna on her front porch each evening, rotating who brought drinks and snacks, sometimes alcoholic and just as often a thermos of chamomile tea to share. Both of her new friends—if she could call them that—liked to tease her about Flynn. She could tolerate their good-natured ribbing more than the appreciative glances Flynn received from women whenever they were out in public together.

Even the school secretary, who was older than dirt, batted her heavily mascaraed eyelashes when Shauna approached the front desk with Flynn at her side.

"Hello, Mrs. Newberry. This is Flynn Murphy. He'll be volunteering with me today."

"You must be related to that handsome Declan," Mrs. Newberry said with a wink.

"My younger brother." Flynn shocked Shauna by winking and flashing a disarming smile. "Not as handsome either."

The secretary tittered, her eyelashes quivering so hard it looked like they were trying to take flight. "When Declan volunteered with us last winter, we all thought there might be a spark of romance between the two of them, but now I see—"

"Could we sign in and get the hall passes?" Shauna asked with a firm nod.

"I'm sure the class will be so excited to meet you," Mrs. Newberry told Flynn as she scrawled their names on the sticker badges. "I feel for the children who don't have both parents as part of their lives." She glanced at Shauna, who refused to make eye contact. "It's a tough row to hoe."

"It is," Flynn agreed.

"Their classroom is at the end of the hall." Shauna signed them both in on the register and took the visitor badges.

"Have a good day, Mrs. Newberry." She tried not to let annoyance seep into her tone. Surely the woman meant well, and well-meaning people were part of the deal in small-town living.

"You too, dear. I'll ensure any lingering gossip about you and that handsome man who showed up when you had your accident is put to rest."

Shauna gave a thumbs-up over her shoulder as she walked away. "Slow news day here in Magnolia," she said with a self-conscious laugh.

"She's talking about my brother, right?"

"Your brother who we both know is madly in love with Beth Carlyle."

"People thought there was something between you and Dec?"

She couldn't get a read on how Flynn felt about that. Unlike hers, his voice gave nothing away.

"You know how talk goes. Dec and I have never been anything but friends." Shauna put a little pep in her step. She wanted this conversation to end posthaste. "He stuck by me when—"

"I left?"

Instead of answering—because what was the point of rehashing the past?—she opened the door to the classroom. Eighteen pairs of eyes looked up at them. "Hello, Ms. Bronson," she said, noticing that Zach and Timmy were smiling broadly.

"Hi, hi," the younger woman chirped, then glanced at Flynn. "Welcome. Zach and Timmy told me we'd have an extra set of hands today. The more, the merrier."

Shauna wished she could agree. "What can we do to help?"

"The Thursday folders are ready to stuff in the back of

the room. In a few minutes, we'll be breaking into small groups. I'll lead the reading group at the front table. Shauna, you can help with today's math worksheet."

The woman gave Flynn a shaky smile. "I'm sorry, I didn't catch your name." No one could deny Flynn's effect on women. If they weren't flirting with him, most were scared to pieces by his rugged physical presence.

"Flynn Murphy," he said.

That seemed to put Ms. Bronson at ease. "Declan's brother?"

Flynn gave a tight nod.

"Wonderful. He was so great with—"

"I'm not good with kids," Flynn interrupted.

Shauna thought about stepping in to smooth things over but resisted the urge. He wanted to be involved and would have to figure out how to make that work.

The teacher's cornflower blue eyes widened. "Oh. Well then, why don't we have you sit in the free play area when we break into small groups? You won't have to do much unless a student needs help or has a question. If they can rely on you, I'll be able to concentrate on my reading group."

"No distractions." Flynn saluted the teacher. "Roger that."

In return, Ms. Bronson lifted a hand like she might salute him and then offered a limp wave.

"We're not going into battle," Shauna reminded him as she led the way to the back of the classroom where the student folders were kept.

"I understand. It's just that my skin is all tingly like I'm heading into enemy territory."

She bit back a grin and tried to ignore her own tingling skin. Zach and Timmy both waved but stayed in their seats. Her sons were clearly proud of having both parents volunteering.

The school secretary's words pinged through Shauna's head. Had people felt sorry for her sons all their lives because they didn't have a father?

Shauna had worked her butt off to be everything her boys could need. Yet just by being there, Flynn filled a hole she hadn't realized was gaping open.

She suddenly felt like she'd tucked her skirt into her underpants before leaving a public restroom. From the front, everything appeared normal. But people were laughing behind her back, or worse, feeling sorry for her and the twins. She forced herself to put those thoughts out of her head. They wouldn't serve her little family or even Flynn.

Yes, she blamed him for walking away in the first place, but she could have reached out at any point during the years and hadn't. She'd convinced herself she was protecting her boys but realized she'd done them a great disservice.

Regret left a bitter taste in her mouth.

"Is stuffing folders that bad?" Flynn asked as he folded himself into a tiny chair at the table in the back of the room. "You look like we've been tasked with picking maggots out of spoiled meat."

"Gross." She made a face and took the seat next to him. "It's nothing. I'm thinking about a problem I have at one of my job sites."

"You can tell me about it if you want." Flynn grabbed a stack of papers and began loading them in the green folders the kids brought home once a week. "I'm pretty good at solving problems."

He was even better at creating them, at least where her heart was concerned.

She should be used to Flynn surprising her, so she tried to take it stride that he did great at volunteering in stride. He and Declan were similar in looks and straight-shooter manners, but Flynn had never possessed the gentle side his brother did, even though Dec tried to hide it.

Maybe Flynn had been hiding even more than Shauna realized because he was patient with the kids and engaging in his own gruff-with-a-side-of-teddy-bear manner.

Oh, the man was dangerous. By the time they walked out of the school an hour later, the fleshy part of Shauna's palm under her thumb was aching and bruised from her pinching it over and over.

"That went well," she said, internally rolling her eyes at how fake the enthusiasm in her tone sounded. "I'll text you later about soccer practice. I'm sure the boys would love for you to drop them off instead of me."

Without a word, Flynn reached for her hand. She tried to pull away, but he held fast. His jaw set as he examined the damage she'd inflicted on herself.

"What's going on?" He ran a finger over the swollen skin. "Don't tell me nothing because I know what this means."

She swallowed and shook her head. "It's not like that, Flynn. I don't self-harm as a coping mechanism anymore." It shamed her that she'd ever craved the release cutting had given her, but she'd worked tirelessly with the help of therapy and by adopting healthier coping mechanisms to leave that shame in her past. "I haven't for nearly a decade."

"Then what's the deal?" He lifted her hand into the air. "This might not be the same damage the edge of a razor blade could cause, but you hurt yourself. I have a feeling it's because of me." She wanted to lash out even though that wasn't her usual personality. She wanted to claim he had no power over her, but it wasn't true and honesty went hand in hand with healing for Shauna.

"I don't know," she admitted. "You overwhelm me.

Sometimes I'm not sure how to handle it. I've worked to have control of every part of my life. That's how I like it. You show up and change everything. You don't even have to try."

She tugged her hand out of his grasp. The sun was high in the brilliant blue sky, and she could hear the happy sounds of children on the playground. All Shauna wanted to do was sink to her knees and cry.

"The twins adore you," she said, willing her chin not to tremble. "Their classmates are fascinated by you. I'm singing, dancing and making homemade muffins and elaborate food crafts for every school party. You just have to be you." She closed her hand into a fist. "This was a mistake."

They both knew she was talking about more than the bruises on her palm.

"You don't have to try with me," he said, his tone sincere. "You shouldn't feel like you need to try to with anyone, but you can't believe I care about cupcakes or your too-bright smile or phony friendliness."

"I'm not a phony."

"You know what I mean. For the record, I'm busting a gut to try. This is more effort than I've ever given in my life. I'm trying to do the right thing. I'm trying not to run away when all those rug rats are staring at me like they can't decide whether I'm the boogeyman or going to break into a Shrek-style dance."

She smiled and rolled her lips to hide it. "With some green spray paint, you'd make a decent Shrek."

He laughed. "This isn't easy, and you might not want to hear it, but we're a team, Shauna. We have to be for the sake of our sons. I don't want to make this hard on you. I never wanted to hurt you."

"But you did. Badly, Flynn."

"I hated myself for it every day. I appreciate you giving me another chance, but I need to know you'll be able to handle it."

"I will." She nodded. "I still see a counselor regularly. The only good thing that came from that awful night was them sending me to a therapist. It's where I first started to heal. Maybe you think I'm weak because I need help—"

"I've seen a therapist for the past three years."

Shauna knew she looked startled as shock rolled through her.

Flynn shrugged. "I came back because I feel like I'm healthy enough to handle it. I wasn't before. It was a darker place than either you or Dec realized. If I had stayed, there's no doubt I would have taken you down with me."

Shauna did her best to take this stunning revelation in stride. Flynn Murphy was in therapy, working on himself and getting in touch with his emotions.

She had to get a hold of herself because that was about the sexiest thing she'd ever heard. He must have read the change in her because his irises darkened like a storm cloud blowing in from the horizon. He leaned in until his shadow fell over her, but it didn't feel dark or scary.

A strange sense of anticipation swept over her, like being handed a tall glass of lemonade on a hot day. Shauna was ready for that first refreshing sip.

She closed her eyes but wasn't surprised when his lips met hers, part exploration and part question. As an answer, her hands lifted to either side of his face, his stubble rough against her skin. She was moments away from inclining her head to kiss him more fully when the sound of the bell ringing from the school had her jumping away.

"That was a mistake," she said, irritated with how breathless she sounded.

"No." The one syllable was spoken in such a low tone she barely heard it. Then she met his gaze, and her heart spun like it was on a wild merry-go-round at the intensity she saw there. "Nothing that feels so good could be a mistake, Shauna. Kissing you is like drinking sunshine."

She nearly melted on the spot. "You're a poet now, too?"

"Just a man trying to make things better, and not just with Zach and Timmy. I need you to understand—"

"Hey, neighbor," a voice called.

Shauna turned to see Annalise moving toward them; her face a calm mask even as curiosity burned in her blue eyes. The elegant former mean mom lifted her designer sunglasses onto the top of her head. "Am I interrupting something?"

"We were just heading out from volunteering with the boys," Shauna said instead of answering the question directly.

"I'm impressed you're involved, given everything else you do."

Shauna searched Annalise's face, wondering if the woman was patronizing her but was shocked to see a flash of respect in the woman's cool gaze.

"Thank you," Shauna murmured.

"She's impressive in all ways." Flynn gave Annalise a terse nod and turned his attention to Shauna. "Text me about soccer practice."

He walked away, and Annalise stepped in front of Shauna. "Did I legitimately catch you kissing your baby daddy in the elementary school parking lot? Girl, we should have started hanging out a long time ago. You would have taken the attention off me."

Shauna's cheeks burned. "Nobody saw us."

Annalise laughed as she gestured toward the school windows. “I’m on my way to a PTO meeting in the band room, which happens to face the front of the building. I guarantee someone saw it. You’ll be lucky if no one posts photos on the Magnoliaships page on Instagram.”

“What is Magnoliaships?”

“Relationships,” Annalise explained with a wink. “The moms around here pretend like they’re too sophisticated for gossip, but that page has a couple thousand followers.”

“How is that a thing for adults?”

“What kind of rock are you living under? It’s a sign of the times.”

Shauna groaned. “Then I hope no one took a picture.”

“Is Flynn Murphy a good kisser?”

Shauna did her best not to grin. “You don’t think I’m going to kiss and tell.”

“I certainly hope so.” Annalise wiggled her perfectly arched brows. “While you’re deciding whether to climb down off your paragon-of-virtue horse, come with me to a PTO meeting.”

“Are you joking?”

“You were the one who told me that all parents are members of PTO.”

Shauna scoffed. “That doesn’t mean I want to hang out with those vultures. They send out a signup sheet for volunteering. I sign up. I do my part. I stay out of their way. I used to stay out of your way.”

“Now I need backup.”

“You don’t need backup. You’re like Teddy Roosevelt carrying a big stick.”

Annalise waved to two mothers walking past. Neither returned the gesture.

“I should have brought a stick to whomp some stupid people over the heads,” Annalise said with an eye roll.

Shauna chuckled. "You better hope nobody gets that on video."

"Right?" Annalise looked pleased that Shauna understood her joke. "Come with me."

"Why are you even here?"

"They're meeting about next year's art and music programs. I'm going to propose a fundraiser."

"Save Ms. Banks?"

"Exactly." Annalise's serene smile wasn't fooling Shauna. "I've been kicked off almost every charity board in the county and several in Raleigh. They can't kick me out of PTO, and my idea is a good one."

"What's your idea?"

"A spring concert fundraiser headlined by a famous country music star."

"Did Walker Calloway agree to perform?"

Annalise made a face. "Not yet, but he's going to, and I won't even need to do the convincing. You should see the way he looks at our little Meghan."

Shauna shook her head. "She's a grown woman who doesn't need to pimp herself out to a famous country music star to save her job."

"Needs and wants are two different things. She wants to save her job, and this might be the best way to do it. We need to support her. I need you to support me."

Shauna started to back away. She didn't make waves or get involved because that was how she got people to like her. It also meant she never stood up for herself, even when she was left behind.

"Come on," Annalise coaxed. "It will be fun."

"Do you think so?"

"No, but I think it's past time I use my power and reputation—such as they are at this point—for good. How much worse can it get for me?"

Annalise flipped her hair over one shoulder like she hadn't a care in the world.

Shauna had too many cares. She'd taken on too much over the years doing what was expected and what people wanted. She did what she thought would keep her safe and had been left anyway.

If toeing the line didn't mean safety, what was the point of doing it? She thought about Flynn's kiss and felt out of control. Maybe she could learn a thing or two from Annalise.

"I'll go in with you," she said before she thought better of it.

"Yes!" Annalise linked their arms and practically dragged Shauna toward the building. "Will you be the Thelma to my Louise or should I be Thelma and you're Louise? Which one hooked up with Brad Pitt because Flynn is—"

"No Thelma. No Louise. Definitely no Brad Pitt. I'm doing this for Meghan. She's a good person and deserves support against those PTO bullies."

"Is that a bit of bite from Mother Love?"

"I have bite," Shauna said, straightening her shoulders as she followed Annalise into the school. "I grew up in foster care. I can hold my own against any queen bee that comes our way."

"Then you're my new favorite ride-or-die. Let's take care of business."

"I think the meeting has already started, Annalise," the secretary said, shaking her head. "You probably shouldn't—"

Annalise offered Mrs. Newberry a smile that would

make honey seem sour in comparison. "No worries. I know the way." She squeezed Shauna's hand. "We've got this."

"I'm Thelma," Shauna said as she opened the door to the band room. At this moment, she felt braver than she had her whole life. She could get used to feeling brave.

CHAPTER THIRTEEN

MEGHAN SLAMMED ON her car's brakes, turning into Shauna's driveway with more force than was warranted. Drawing in a breath, she commanded herself to calm down. Children lived here. Despite how angry she felt at the mothers of those children, there was no need to risk harming someone with her reckless driving.

Stomping up to her apartment and screaming into a pillow was tempting. That was her preferred coping mechanism for emotions that weren't polite. As a child, she'd eventually learned to bury the feelings her mother found unbecoming. She could make the best of any situation life handed her.

Meghan had spent years crafting a protective shell around her heart, but something about her Grammy's death had broken through the work she'd done. It felt like she was shoving her finger into a dam that was going to inevitably crack wide open.

With that in mind, instead of retreating to her apartment to hide or eat her feelings—another favorite pastime—Meghan stalked toward the front porch where she'd seen Shauna and Annalise sitting.

Although she was becoming more comfortable with her new friends, the two of them were still reasonably terrifying. They were polar opposites in personality, but it was like that old-school Wonder Twins cartoon she'd watched at her grandmother's house. Together, they made a more powerful force than either of them could on their own.

"Are you here to celebrate?" Shauna asked as Meghan walked up the steps. "We're both having sparkling water tonight."

Annalise grimaced. "I'm working in the barn tomorrow, and I need my wits about me."

"But there's wine in the fridge," Shauna reported, "if you want a glass."

"How could you do this to me?" Meghan demanded, hands on hips as she confronted the women. "I can't face Walker or my colleagues. I might as well pack up my desk and scurry out of town."

"Calm down," Annalise said like she was speaking to a child, which only infuriated Meghan more.

"I can't be calm. Who is going to hire me after this silly stunt backfires?"

Shauna looked genuinely confused. "What stunt?"

"The fundraiser," Meghan shouted, then gulped in air. She probably needed to take hold of her emotions, although it felt good to let them fly. "How could you pitch a school fundraiser with Walker as the main draw? He teaches at the school, ladies. It's bound to be awkward when he finds out."

Annalise shook her head. "I'm sure he'll do it. He seems to like you."

"He doesn't perform anymore."

Shauna sat up a little straighter. "What are you talking about?"

"He hasn't been on stage since the bus accident."

"That's a coincidence." Annalise sounded confident, but Meghan saw her fingers drumming a nervous beat on her pale pink jeans. "He's been busy taking care of his nephew. It's not like he's got some issue with returning to the stage."

"It's exactly like that," Meghan said. "He told me the other day going over lesson plans in his studio. He wasn't even sure he'd be able to play a few notes for the students."

"The students?" Annalise's air of casual assurance fell away. "You're exaggerating."

"I never exaggerate. On the other hand, you have oversold your capacity to make this fundraiser happen and my ability to convince Walker to participate."

"I didn't think it would be a problem," Annalise admitted with a sigh.

"How about that wine?" Shauna asked. "We all might need it."

Meghan shook her head. "Not tonight. I plan to eat ice cream out of the carton for dinner and pretend this fiasco never happened."

"All is not lost." Annalise's eyes narrowed as she gazed out at the front yard. Meghan could almost see the wheels spinning in her mind. "I might remind you, Meghan, we're trying to help."

"This is *not* the kind of help I need."

"You need a job, and this fundraiser will ensure you keep the one you have."

"There's no concert without Walker, and he's not doing it."

"You'll never know unless you ask him," Shauna pointed out.

"I'm not asking him anything."

Annalise patted the seat next to her on the porch swing. "Have a seat."

Meghan thought about turning tail, but she still liked these women even though she was angry. And she believed they'd been trying to help her.

She sat on the swing, surprised when Annalise took her hand. "One of the biggest stars in country music agreed to teach elementary school music classes to help you. I think there's a good chance he'd be willing to do this."

"She's right," Shauna said, "and you should have seen her go up against Everly Mae and her PTO minions. She was a perfect Louise, as much as I hate to admit it."

"I couldn't have done it," Annalise said, grinning, "without Thelma at my side."

Meghan snorted. "Since when did the two of you decide you were Magnolia's answer to a female-empowerment duo?"

"Just this afternoon," Annalise said. "But we'd be happy to rewrite the script and make a trio."

"You've lost your darn mind, Annalise. Maybe you're so interested in besting the women who kicked you out of your kingdom that you aren't thinking straight."

Meghan pointed toward Shauna. "And apparently, you aren't either."

"We are in full command of our mental capacities," Annalise assured her. "For all her earth mother sensibilities, Shauna is a formidable wing woman. She has bite."

"We think you have teeth, as well," Shauna told Meghan. "You just need to be willing to use them."

Annalise's gaze sharpened with determination. "The three of us can take a bite out of this town."

Meghan was hardly able to keep up with the conversation, which wasn't new to her. In her own family, she'd always been a few steps behind her more gregarious and clever siblings.

She liked to take a few minutes to think about her words before she spoke them. That's why she gravitated toward drawing—there was no need to rush through it. She could take as long as she needed to put the vision that she had in her head onto paper.

"Walker will be at school again tomorrow for his classes. What will he think when he hasn't agreed to it?" She pressed two fingers to her forehead, where a dull pounding had started. "What will he think of me?"

"We told the PTO mavens they weren't allowed to mention his involvement until we finalized it," Annalise explained like it was that simple.

"When has being told not to share ever stopped a Southern woman from spreading the latest news?"

"Good point," the sophisticated blonde conceded. "You better get over there and talk to Mr. Calloway tonight."

"Why me?" Meghan demanded. She planted her feet on the porch, itching to bolt away from the expectations she could feel from her two friends. The swing swayed in a lopsided rhythm. "You committed to him, and you're the one who works for him."

"Yes, but you work *with* him, and he likes you. I don't just mean as a colleague."

Meghan felt her face heat; at the same time, warmth pooled in her belly at the thought of Walker's intense gaze. "Why would a man like Walker be interested in somebody like me? I'm not fishing for compliments," Meghan clarified quietly. "I just don't see a world where that could happen."

"Then you don't give yourself enough credit," Shauna said.

Meghan laughed, although it wasn't funny. "I give myself exactly the right kind of credit. I know who I am, and I'm okay with that. Calloway would disturb that peace. I've worked hard for my peace."

"You like your job," Annalise reminded her. "Or so I thought. If we secure Walker as the headline act—"

"The only act," Shauna clarified. "Why would we need anyone else?"

Annalise nodded. "Good point. This will change your life, Meghan."

"Will he be expected to sing for my supper every year?" Meghan sighed at the humiliating thought.

"I've considered that. If we can cover the salaries and budget for the art and music programs for the next year, that gives us time to apply for grants and additional funding. There's money out there. We'll find it if you want to continue teaching at Magnolia Elementary."

"I do," Meghan said without hesitation. She might be annoyed by her neighbors but couldn't deny this was beginning to sound like a brilliant idea. "And I appreciate you taking an interest in my career."

"That's what friends are for." Annalise sounded like she genuinely meant the words. "Will you ask Walker?"

Meghan blew out a breath and tried not to let fear overtake her. "Yes. I'll do it."

"Maybe…" Shauna cleared her throat. "You want to put on a dress that isn't stained. I can't tell if it's a paint splatter across your middle or ketchup."

"Ketchup," Meghan confirmed, glancing down at the splotch of faded condiment. She'd tried to wash it off and then had forgotten it was there. "The cafeteria served Tater Tots today. I love Tater Tots drenched in ketchup."

"Doesn't everyone love Tots?" Shauna asked with a smile.

"I haven't let a Tater Tot cross my lips in decades." Annalise closed her eyes for a moment. "I can still remember their greasy goodness."

Meghan laughed. "That's why you look like you, and I look like this." Her curves didn't bother her, and not because the body positivity movement encouraged people to accept themselves.

Meghan had been body positive long before it became trendy, much to her mother's chagrin. For years, Denise

Banks had tried to shame, cajole and bribe her youngest into losing weight. Meghan might not be able to control much in her life, but she governed how she felt about herself. Her mom could make all the insinuations and outright comments she wanted about how Meghan would have more self-esteem and less anxiety if she were thin. Meghan knew weight wasn't the answer to her issues. Despite everything, she liked her body just fine.

"You can give him a call now," Shauna suggested.

"I can't ask him for this kind of favor over the phone," Meghan countered. "He might not even answer my call."

Annalise rolled her eyes. "Why wouldn't he answer?"

Meghan bit the inside of her cheek instead of blurting that she was the kind of person others routinely ignored. Neither one of these gorgeous-in-different-ways women could appreciate that.

"You can spring it on him tomorrow morning when he gets to school." Annalise took a long drink of her sparkling water. "That's how my ex-husband got me to agree to many things I didn't want to do. He would ask me publicly, giving me no chance to decline without embarrassing him or myself."

"Walker has stepped back from performing in public due to the trauma of a tragedy that killed his brother and several members of his band," Meghan reminded Annalise. "Do you honestly think that potential shame in front of a bunch of elementary school students will sway him one way or the other?"

"The expectation of those kids, including Gus, might," Annalise answered without hesitation. "He's a good guy. He won't want to disappoint them. He's a good guy, Meghan," she repeated as if Meghan needed to hear the words.

Maybe she did. Perhaps it was time she claimed something for herself or made an effort on her own behalf. She'd let life pass her by on numerous occasions because failure felt like too high a price to pay, but she'd failed anyway. She was a failure as far as her family was concerned because she didn't have the drive and material success they took for granted. Now she was failing to keep her job.

What did she have to lose?

She hopped off the porch swing like it had just bit her in the back end. "I'm going right now."

"After you put on clean clothes," Shauna suggested with an encouraging smile.

Meghan grimaced as she glanced down at the ketchup stain again. "Clean clothes, then I'm being brave."

"Go, girl." Annalise clapped her hands. "Way to take a stand and save your own butt."

Shauna pumped a fist in the air. "Who needs Thelma and Louise? Team Front Porch Club to the rescue. Call us after he agrees."

"I will." Meghan swallowed back her anxiety the same way she'd stuffed down her dreams for many years. Finally, she was ready to rescue herself.

As Meghan climbed the steps to Whimsy Farm's main house, her initial burst of courage deserted her. She remained committed to not letting fear stop her the way it had so many times previously in her life.

"You can do it." She said the words out loud to give them more power. "You've done harder things than ask Walker Calloway for this favor. You are braver than you know. Nothing is going to stop you."

"I like your conviction," a quiet voice said as she lifted her hand to ring the doorbell.

She let out a yelp and turned to see Walker lounging in

a rocker situated in a shaded corner of the porch. How had she not noticed him when she got out of the car?

"Should I agree with whatever you're about to ask without hearing it? Based on your conviction, I have no choice but to consent to your request."

"We all have choices," Meghan answered as she approached him. It was nearing sunset, and the sky beyond the property had started to turn pink and orange.

If she'd been a photographer, she would have shot him, bathed in golden light as he sat forward, for the cover of some glossy magazine. He wore faded jeans with a slim-fitting denim shirt tucked into the waistband. His leather belt and square-toed boots looked deceptively broken in. She wondered if he'd paid extra for that.

"As you heard," she said with as much of a laugh as she could muster, "I'm choosing to be brave despite my nerves and now my humiliation at you overhearing my pathetic attempt at a pep talk."

"There's nothing pathetic about you, Meghan." Walker gestured to the chair next to him. "Have a seat so we can talk"

Right. That's what she needed to do. She needed to talk and convince him just as she told herself she would. Only the more time she spent with Walker, the more tongue-tied she seemed to get in his presence.

"Where's Gus?" she asked as she sat.

"He and Jack are doing their after-dinner chores in the barn."

"How'd you get out of chores? Too famous for that?"

His mouth tipped into a hint of a smile. "I was on kitchen cleanup duty."

"You guys have a good system going. It sounds like you and Jack are making the best of a tough situation."

"I guess." Walker shrugged one big shoulder. "Jack is

trying and pulling me along for the ride. He's the most stubborn man you'll ever meet. He refuses to let me sulk in private, no matter how much I insist that's what I want. But you're not here to discuss my issues. You want something from me."

He sounded both wary and weary at that moment, and she opened her mouth to deny his claim, then closed it again. She did want something from him. She *needed* it.

"The students like you," she told him. "Maybe even more than the moms now hovering around our classrooms like you."

He mock shivered. "I've no interest in the moms around the school right now."

Meghan swallowed. It was silly to think he might be interested in her instead. Walker had dated several high-profile women in the past few years. She'd spent an embarrassing amount of time on the internet scrolling through pictures of him and his former girlfriends.

They were pretty, skinny and blonde, mostly models or actresses with a singer or two thrown in for good measure.

Walker had a type, and she wasn't it. That didn't matter. She needed him to help her keep her job, not date her.

"Annalise wants to coordinate an event to raise money for the music and art programs at the school. She's already sold PTO and the district administrators on the idea."

"You'll get to keep your job? That's good. The kids like you, too. You're a great teacher."

"Thanks." She licked her lips and then felt color stain her cheeks as she noticed Walker's gaze focused on her mouth. "There's only one catch." She offered what she hoped was the same encouraging smile Shauna had given her earlier. "She wants to do a benefit concert."

Walker didn't react, but she felt the change in him. He knew what she was asking.

"I'll make some calls if you want," he said, pretending he didn't. "I can see who's available. If you give me the date, maybe we can pull in somebody big to headline—"

"I want you." She drew in a breath at the way his expression sharpened. "To sing at the concert. I'm sure you realize that's what I'm asking. You're invested in this community because you live here. Because Gus will benefit."

He'd been gently rocking back and forth but stopped suddenly. He leaned forward again and placed his hands on his knees. She got the impression he was struggling not to clench his fists. Not to get up and stalk away from her for having the audacity to make the request of him.

"I know it's a big ask, and your time is valuable. But—"

"As you know, the first time I picked up a guitar since the accident that killed my brother was when you were here to go through the lesson plan. I'm not planning to make music again."

Meghan frowned. "You have that beautiful studio with all the instruments and sound equipment."

"That was Jack's doing. He wanted to set things up to entice me to play. I told you he was stubborn."

"I thought you spent most of your time out there."

"Not playing. I owe the record company another album. The band owes them. Nobody seems to care that the band is nothing without Nash."

"They want you to record it on your own? The Calloway Brother band. That's cold."

"They want a Walker Calloway album."

"You don't want to give it to them?"

"I can't. I'm nothing without Nash."

"I know you miss him, but that isn't true. I've seen you play."

"With Nash," he corrected.

"I watched you in concert. You're talented on your own. Hot, too, which doesn't hurt."

He barked out a laugh. "It doesn't hurt?"

"You know what I mean." Suddenly Meghan's nerves fell away. It turned out she wasn't the only one who needed to be brave. "I can accept you telling me no, and I appreciate the offer to reach out to your friends. But don't let your grief and sorrow over losing your brother silence you. Obviously, I didn't know Nash, but I can't imagine he would want that. It would break my grandmother's heart if she thought I was turning my back on my creativity. Maybe being a teacher isn't as glamorous and exciting as your career, but it's the same principle."

Walker raised a brow, heat sparking in his usually gentle eyes. She'd touched a nerve. "Are you sure? I've always heard that those who can, do and those who can't, teach."

"Is that why you're in the classroom now?" she shot back.

He shook his head. "I'm sorry. I shouldn't have said that. I don't mean it. If it weren't for teachers, the world would be a darker place than it already is."

"There's nothing derogatory you can say to me that someone in my family hasn't already said. Most of the criticism came from my mom. I don't care if it takes everyone in this town hearing me give myself a pep talk. I'm not going to stop. I know I have something of value to add. I've had a lot of people try to convince me otherwise."

"We had a lot of people tell us we'd never make it." Walker nodded. "I probably would have given up without Nash."

"It sounds to me like you *have* given up. I hope that changes," she told him and then stood and looked out to the front of the property as she heard Gus call her name. "That boy doesn't have his father anymore, and it's a tragedy. He has you, Walker. If you aren't willing to be brave for yourself, maybe you can be brave for him. I'll talk to Annalise and see what she thinks about a different headliner and get back to you with the date."

"I think you're braver than you give yourself credit for, Meghan." He brushed her fingers with his as he came to stand next to her.

She had little time to register the sparks that zoomed through her at his touch. Gus had made his way to the top of the porch.

"Ms. Banks, I galloped on Stargazer tonight."

Meghan saw Walker's gaze flick to Jack.

"He was perfectly safe," the other man said, clearly reading Walker's mind.

"Nothing is perfectly safe," Walker muttered.

"What are you doing here, Ms. Banks?" Gus asked.

"I had some school business to discuss with your uncle," she told the boy with a smile, "but I should be going now."

"Ms. Banks asked me to perform in a benefit concert that will help the school raise money to keep the art and music programs going," Walker told his nephew. Meghan was shocked he'd revealed so much. She felt even more shocked when Walker continued, "Do you think that's a good idea, Gussie?"

"Yes," the boy exclaimed at the same time Jack shook his head no. Unaware of the thunderclouds of temper coming off the adult standing behind him, Gus clapped his hands. "That'd be awesome, Uncle Walker."

"You have to get in the studio," Jack insisted. "You owe them an album, Walker."

"I don't have songs for a new album, Jack."

"You don't need new songs for a concert," Gus told him. "You can sing the songs you and Daddy wrote."

"Then that's what I'll do."

Meghan tried but knew she failed to hide her shock. "I thought you said—"

"I'll do your concert." Walker shrugged.

Jack shook his head. "A benefit concert. The record company isn't going to like it. They've been patient so far."

"We'll talk about this later, Jack. Or maybe we won't because I've made my decision."

"Annalise will be thrilled to hear it," Meghan said.

"Annalise?" Jack's voice was a low growl. "Tell me this was not the housekeeper's idea."

"Oh, she's more than a housekeeper," Meghan said. "She is a force of nature."

She smiled at the look of consternation on Jack's striking features. She had a feeling he was well aware that Annalise Haverford was a force to be reckoned with.

"I'll see you tomorrow," she told Gus and Walker. One of the world's most popular country music stars had agreed to participate in the fundraiser that would save her job. She'd convinced him to do it. "Have a good night."

Jack tipped his hat because he was a gentleman, then turned on his heel and stomped away because he was an angry gentleman.

"You're going to be okay, Walker."

"None of us are okay," he said after Gus entered the house. "But we'll manage."

"I hope you do," Meghan told him and then hurried from the porch before her newfound bravery made her do something stupid.

CHAPTER FOURTEEN

THE NEXT FEW weeks passed in a whirl of activity for Annalise. Between her work at Whimsy Farm and the preparations for the school fundraiser, it almost felt like things were back to normal in her life.

Except now, she was trying to manage things without being a raging bitch to the people around her. She had no idea how she'd gotten away with treating people as though they were less than her for so long. There were still those in town who wanted to hold her accountable for Jonathan's crimes, but she was determined to prove she was different from her villainous husband—changed from how she acted for years.

She was learning to be kinder, although it didn't always come naturally, especially when the women she'd considered her friends, like Everly Mae, seemed determined to thwart her at every turn.

The first hurdle had been getting a permit for the concert. It had shocked her when the request was denied, but then she remembered that Everly Mae's long-suffering husband, Tobias, was on the town council.

Meghan had been the one who'd solved the issue. She'd asked one of the moms from school, Avery Atwell, who handled marketing and events for the town, to intervene with Magnolia's mayor, Malcolm Grimes.

Annalise had tried to befriend Avery when the woman

had first arrived in town. She was blonde and beautiful and had the shine of big-city polish that Annalise once admired. To her chagrin, Avery'd wanted nothing to do with her, and the woman's stepdaughter, Violet, quickly became Margo's nemesis at the elementary school.

Annalise was ashamed to remember how she'd planned birthday parties and other social activities for girls in Margo's class and excluded Violet, but that was how Annalise had been raised. Her mother taught her from a young age that anyone who threatened her dominance within the social structure needed to be eradicated like a weed in a garden.

Would Annalise ever make up for the rotten things she'd done and could she truly change her daughter's personality at this point? Margo did not seem to appreciate the new kinder, gentler version of her mother.

They stood between two cars at the edge of the parking lot behind the dance studio in town.

"I won't do it," Margo said, stomping a ballet-slippered foot. "You can't make me. Violet is *not* my friend. You were the one who told me she's a nobody. Her dad is a firefighter. That's not important."

Annalise could feel her skin turning hot and blotchy, which sadly could not be blamed on the bright afternoon sunlight as she thought about the myriad of hateful things she'd told her daughter and son over the years.

The awful thoughts and judgments she'd made about other people, almost all of them having more to do with her own insecurity and immaturity than being grounded in truth.

"Firefighters are essential, Margo, especially if your house is on fire." She crouched down in front of her daughter. "I haven't been a nice person, sweetheart, but I'm trying to change."

Her daughter furrowed her feathery brows. Annalise longed to smooth the upset from her daughter, no matter what had caused it.

"Because now that we're poor, you have to be?"

"Because I should have been all along. Kindness matters, Margs. Way more than I realized." She took the girl's hands and squeezed. "I made a lot of mistakes—"

"Like Daddy?"

Oh, no. Annalise tucked a stray lock of hair out of her face. She badly needed a trip to the salon, but that was nowhere in her future. "Your father did some bad things, and he will be in prison for a long time. My mistakes weren't like his, but I still want to do better. I want to help you do better, too. The first lesson for us is the value of treating people with kindness and respect. All people."

"Violet doesn't like me any more than I like her."

"Have you tried being nice?"

Margo shook her head.

"She invited you for a playdate after dance class," Annalise reminded her daughter. "I think that means Violet is trying. Could you try, too?"

"Am I a bad person like Daddy?" Margo asked, her voice barely above a whisper.

"Honey." Annalise wrapped her arms around Margo's thin shoulders and felt the girl sag against her. Annalise hadn't grown up with an affectionate mother, and she'd been much the same way with her children before everything went off the rails in their lives.

She hated that neither of her kids was particularly comfortable with being hugged. That was changing slowly. They were all changing, for the better, she hoped. "You are a beautiful girl both inside and out. I know you have a big heart. You have to let people see it."

Margo pulled back and pressed one finger to Annalise's chest. "Just like you do?"

"Yes," Annalise agreed. "We're going to learn to make this work together." She hugged her daughter again and blinked back tears.

She looked up to the blue sky overhead. The green leaves of the trees that lined the sidewalks of Main Street seemed to dance in the warm spring breeze. It wasn't too late for either of them, she reminded herself. It was never too late.

"I'll be nice to Violet." Margo slipped her hand into Annalise's as they approached the building. "I can't promise I'll like it."

"Fair enough."

Sometimes Annalise struggled with the change from mean girl to decent person. It didn't make her proud, but snark and snobbery were finely honed defense mechanisms at this point.

Being kind wasn't only modifying her actions toward others. It was transforming how she viewed herself on the inside. It opened her up to care in ways that made her feel vulnerable. Vulnerability was a state she'd left behind in her childhood because she didn't like being hurt or disappointed.

Her mother had allowed for no perceived weakness and being vulnerable was a flaw.

Or maybe it was a strength because she liked herself a lot more these days.

She wanted Margo to feel the same way and not be scared of being hurt.

As they entered the studio, Margo swayed closer to Annalise, which was new. Usually, her daughter marched into the class and took her place in the center of the group of girls. Now she hung back. Was it Annalise's imagination, or did Margo's two best friends move closer together so there wouldn't be space for her at the barre?

Annalise had trouble turning the other cheek. She squeezed her daughter's hand, hoping to imbue the girl with as much confidence as she could.

Violet Atwell stepped forward and gave an almost comically indignant side-eye to the other girls. "There's room over here, Margo," she called.

Margo dropped Annalise's hand like it was on fire and ran toward the girl who minutes earlier she wasn't sure she could be nice to.

Annalise swallowed around the ball of emotion lodged in her throat. She waited until Margo was settled between Violet and another girl, then turned to make her escape.

Vulnerability was a real kick in the teeth.

"She'll be okay."

Annalise glanced toward Josie Trumbell, the longtime owner of Josie's School of Dance. The pretty brunette had never been anything but kind and supportive, even though neither Annalise nor her daughter had given the dance instructor the respect she deserved.

"I want her to be better than okay," Annalise said quietly. "But it's a start."

She could feel the eyes of the other mothers on her. She had no place with them anymore and had no desire to return to her old life.

That didn't make the transition to a new one more straightforward.

"How are you doing?" Josie asked, her voice gentle.

For a moment, Annalise imagined it was her mother asking the question. But Carolann Fluk didn't care how her daughter felt as long as Annalise projected an air of confidence. The same kind of confidence as a great white shark in the water.

"I'm trying to do better," Annalise answered honestly. "I apologize for my past behavior."

"Dance moms have a reputation to live down to," Josie said with a laugh. "You aren't the worst I've encountered over the years."

"I suppose that's a comfort."

"I'll take care of your girl when she's here. She's safe with me."

Safe. Annalise knew Josie wasn't talking about physical safety. She meant she'd protect Margo, even though the girl had done nothing to deserve it.

That was the thing about people who were genuinely kind on the inside. They did the right thing even when they weren't getting anything in return.

"She's going home with Violet after class."

"Avery mentioned that when she dropped off Violet." Josie nodded. "We'll take care of her."

Annalise smiled, although it felt brittle, and walked toward the door. She could see Everly Mae waving but took her sunglasses out of her purse, covered her eyes and kept moving.

Once in her car, she turned up the radio and sang along as she headed to Whimsy Farm to pick up Trey, who'd had a sleepover with Gus the previous night. It was an odd-couple friendship, but her son didn't seem to care about what it meant for his place in the social hierarchy.

Gus brought out a side in Trey that Annalise rarely saw—a softer, more creative version of her son. It showed her how much she'd let her ex-husband control the way Trey was raised and the values they instilled in him.

Not that she disliked his involvement in sports, but she'd

discovered that Trey liked drawing almost as much as he enjoyed throwing a ball.

Most nights, he'd head down to Meghan's apartment after dinner and the two of them would draw and paint together. Her neighbor and unexpected friend assured Annalise that she loved spending time with kid outside the classroom.

Jack also seemed to like Trey, certainly better than he liked Annalise.

Ever since Walker had agreed to headline the benefit concert, his farm manager had avoided Annalise like she'd personally convinced Walker to sell his soul to the devil.

She didn't understand, mainly since it seemed apparent that Walker had said yes because he liked Meghan.

Meghan didn't realize that, but Annalise figured the sweet art teacher needed time to get used to the idea. Annalise wasn't going to play matchmaker. She was an utter failure at relationships. Besides, she had designs on Walker, at least designs on his house.

She got out of the car in front and started up the porch steps when she heard the sound of shouting.

Her stomach dropped to her toes when she realized the noise was coming from the small indoor arena connected to the barn. She ran forward, mouth suddenly dry. There was no chance her son would be riding a horse, despite how obsessed he'd become with Orion.

Trey knew how she felt about horses.

The scent of hay and leather spiraled through her as she moved into the barn. She'd gotten used to the enormous animals as she helped Jack take care of them.

She could even enjoy petting the soft head of one of the particularly gentle horses, like Stargazer. But she wouldn't ride one.

She didn't want Trey riding one.

Yet there was her son, trotting around the arena on Orion, no less. Jack had the horse on a lead as it made a wide circle.

"Hi, Ms. Haverford," Gus called. He was sitting on one of the large wooden crates at the side of the arena. "Trey is real good for a beginner."

Her son seemed to notice her at that point, and he turned in the saddle. Jack noticed her, too, and she saw his shoulders go rigid.

The horse must have picked up on her nerves and the change in mood. His legs shot out as he gave a little jolt.

It wouldn't have been a big deal, or so she assumed, if Trey hadn't been looking over his shoulder and not paying attention.

When the horse did a mini-buck, Trey lost his balance and slid off the saddle. For a terrifying moment, Annalise thought his foot had gotten caught in the stirrup, the same way hers had when she'd had her incident as a kid.

But Trey fell to the dusty ground with a thud as the horse pranced for a few seconds and then slowly calmed down.

She opened her mouth to scream, but no sound came out as she ran toward Trey's still form.

Jack was kneeling next to the boy before she got to them.

"Breathe," he told Trey. "Slowly, son." He'd gathered the boy in his arms.

"Get away from him," Annalise whisper-shouted as she slid to her knees on the other side of Trey.

"He's okay, sweetheart." Jack's voice curled across her senses, and it pained her to admit how much it did to settle her nerves.

She gasped as the horse Trey had been riding appeared behind Jack and nudged his shoulder. "You got the air knocked out of you, kid," Jack said. "You're going to be fine."

Annalise was spitting fire and angry at her son, Jack and the whole damn situation. Interestingly, her temper didn't stretch wide enough to include the horse. The animal was doing what animals do, which was to be unpredictable and dangerous.

Trey sat up of his own accord. Jack released him but stayed close.

"Orion, that was badly done. Gus, can you grab the reins, please?"

"I'm fine." Trey's thin chest rose and fell in a steadier breath. "Can I get on and try again?" Trey directed the question to Jack as if his mother wasn't sitting right there.

"Absolutely not," Annalise told him. The boy's chest was still rising and falling in uneven gasps of breath.

"Come on, Mom. It isn't that big of a deal. Remember when I got hit by a baseball last season? I was covering second base, and it knocked the wind out of me even more than this."

"This could have been worse," Annalise insisted, heart stammering in her chest.

Gus came running over. "My dad once read a book about a boy who threw a baseball that hit his friend's mom and killed her."

"That boy was Owen Meaney. A fictional character. Also, not the right time to share," Jack told Gus with a wince.

"I'm saying baseballs can be as dangerous as horses."

"Tell that to Superman," Annalise muttered, thinking of the actor who'd been paralyzed in a riding accident.

Jack returned to Trey. "Do you want to help Gus put Orion back in the stall and then give him fresh hay?" He glanced at Gus. "You and Trey can get a glass of orange juice in the house and pack up his things. His mama and I will be along in a minute."

Annalise was ready to leave right now, but after two weeks of being all but brushed aside and ignored by Jack Grainger, she also itched for a fight.

Turning the other cheek was a hard business, and she had a lot of pent-up frustration.

If Jack thought he would lecture her the way Jonathan used to, telling her how best to parent a boy…well, the man could just shut his handsome mouth.

"Is that okay, Mom?" Trey clearly read her agitation. He leaned in and gave her a small hug. She knew he intended to placate her, and damn if the kid wasn't a master at emotional manipulation.

She took his chin between her thumb and pointer finger and lifted it, so he was forced to look into her eyes. "I make the rules in this family, Trey. You know the rules about horseback riding."

"I wanted to try it. You saw me. I'm already getting better. Jack is a good teacher, Mom. I'm safe with him."

The words cut across Annalise's chest like the crack of a whip. Her children hadn't been safe with their father. He'd left them swinging in the breeze and paying the price for his dirty deeds.

It embarrassed her to think that she'd chosen him or allowed her mother to pick him for her.

"I love you, buddy," she said instead of arguing. "But I make the rules."

She dropped a quick kiss on his forehead and then watched as he took the lead rope from Gus. The two of them headed out of the arena with the now calm horse following. Annalise watched them for a moment, gathering her wits and emotions even though it felt as though they were spread across the barn like a million little puffs of dandelion fluff.

She could feel Jack's presence behind her, the heat of him, and the sound of his even breathing.

He didn't rush her or make excuses or tell her she was an overprotective helicopter mother.

She waited another beat to see if he would start in like Jonathan. He remained silent, so she slowly turned.

"I'm sorry, Annalise."

She blinked. "For what?"

"The boys told me you said it was okay for Trey to ride. I would never have put him on that horse without your permission." Jack cleared his throat. "Although he was right. Trey is safe with me."

"He didn't look safe when he was thrown to the ground."

"Tell me about your experience."

She released a shaky breath. That hadn't been the response she'd expected. She'd thought he would fight or offer a bevy of lame excuses for why Jack knew best. She did not expect him to cut quite so quickly to the heart of the matter.

"My mama wanted me to ride when I was younger. I went to a private school outside of Charlotte, even though my parents were middle class and could barely afford it. But I was their only child, and my mother had big aspirations for me."

She smiled, although it felt brittle. "When you have big aspirations in the South, they involve the right schools."

Jack inclined his head. "I don't have much experience with the right schools or people, but I know what you mean."

"I came to horseback riding late compared to the other girls. It's not an activity for people without money unless you're on a working farm, and we had a tract house in a nondescript neighborhood. The kind of neighborhood where none of my friends were invited over if—"

"Yeah. I get you on that one as well."

"I've always been afraid of animals. I got bit by the dog next door when I was a toddler, and horses have big teeth."

"They don't often use them."

"But they've got them."

One side of his mouth curved. "They do."

"If I'd been a better beauty queen, I would not have been forced to ride." She rubbed a hand over the back of her neck where her skin pricked. "But I was a horrible competitor."

"I find that hard to believe." Jack rocked back on his heels, studying her. "How could anyone else win a beauty competition with you in the mix?"

She opened her mouth and shut it again because he sounded genuinely dumbfounded.

"There are lots of pretty girls in pageants. I was nothing special."

"I don't believe that. Anyone can see you're special."

Just when she thought she had Jack Grainger pegged, he forced her to view him differently.

"It doesn't matter why I was bad at pageants, but I was. My mom decided I should ride horses instead. The right kind of people rode horses. She didn't care if I was afraid. According to her, I could overcome fear if I was dedicated enough. But riding isn't cheap."

"At least in the way you're talking about. Your parents must have made quite the sacrifice."

Annalise suddenly felt like she had bile coursing through her veins like a river after a heavy spring rain.

"My mother made friends with the riding instructor," she told Jack, allowing one brow to lift ever so slightly. "She was good at making friends with men to get what she wanted. My father was even better at looking the other way."

She saw Jack's chest expand as he processed the meaning of those words. She appreciated that he didn't reply, just waited for her to continue.

"Unfortunately for both of us, I had more fear than dedication. I wanted to please her. I tried. The horses felt my fear. Heck, every animal within a hundred-mile radius probably felt my fear. I made it through a week of lessons and had an accident. I was riding around the ring and the horse spooked—a car backfiring maybe. The horse reared up, and I fell. Only my instructor had been paying more attention to my mother than me when he adjusted the stirrups. My foot got stuck."

"Tell me the horse didn't drag you," Jack said, shaking his head.

"I probably would have been okay, just banged up, but he turned at a jump in the arena. I hit my head on the corner of a rock at the base of it. I was in a coma for a week."

"Damn, Annalise. Does Trey know what happened to you? He only told me you don't like horses."

"I don't like to revisit that. It was humiliating. It was life-threatening. I recovered, and something good came of it."

"Your mother gave you a break?"

"The family who owned the riding club also owned the country club in our town. They gave my family a lifetime membership. I think they were afraid of a lawsuit, but I didn't have to ride horses anymore. I played tennis and swam with the other girls. I became a lifeguard and the leader of the pack of teenagers who lounged poolside all summer. I couldn't ride a horse, but I can apply tanning oil like it's my job."

"That's an odd job for a Southern belle."

"It led to others, but…"

"No horses?"

Annalise reached up to rub a smudge of dirt from Jack's face as he'd done for her that first day in the pasture. "I told myself I wouldn't live in fear anymore."

"If it makes you feel any better, you had me fooled. I knew you didn't like horses, but the fear was well hidden."

"I know." She flashed a smile. "Hiding emotions is one of my few talents."

"You're too hard on yourself."

"Says the man who's been avoiding me for the past two weeks because I'm trying to save an elementary school art teacher's job. I'm too hard on myself? That's rich coming from you."

"Walker needs to record an album." Jack ran a hand through his thick hair, and she tried not to look at how his bicep muscles bunched. "The executives were giving him time to process the grief, but if he feels well enough to headline a benefit concert, I can't hide him anymore."

"Buy him out of the contract," she suggested.

"It's not that easy, but that's not your problem either." His dark eyes held on her, and she could hear a quiet whinny from one of the stalls. At this moment, it didn't scare her. "You've done a good job here, Annalise. You're also a good mom. Trey is a great kid, but..."

"He should be riding a horse?"

"He shouldn't learn to be afraid. I don't think you want that for him."

"I don't. I don't want it for either of my children." Her breath seemed to catch in her throat as his gaze settled on her mouth. "Or for me."

"You're the bravest person I know." He leaned in and kissed her like she was precious to him. His lips were far softer than she would have imagined for a man who seemed to be all hard angles and planes. He didn't touch her anywhere else, but she could feel the connection to her core.

She felt brave and wild, and Annalise forced herself to pull away because, more than bravery, she needed control.

There was no control for her with Jack.

"I've got to go." She nodded and pressed two fingers to her mouth.

"I know," Jack said calmly. His gaze looked anything but calm.

"Thank you for keeping Trey safe, Jack. I do trust you." And before he could answer, she fled. It wasn't a brave move, but it kept her in control.

CHAPTER FIFTEEN

SHAUNA STOOD ON the sidelines of the twins' soccer game the following Saturday and tried to ignore the stares from the other parents.

She was flanked on either side by Flynn and Declan. Separately, the Murphy brothers were hard to ignore but together…

"Wow, the testosterone is pretty thick in this little corner of the sidelines," Beth Carlyle said as she came up and threw an arm around Shauna's shoulder. "Are you getting enough air over here?"

Shauna and Beth, the daughter of her neighbor May, had become friends at Christmas, around the same time Beth and Declan first met. They were an unlikely pairing on the surface, but Shauna knew her childhood friend was deeply devoted to the woman he'd fallen in love with last winter when he came to Magnolia to help with the boys.

Dec made a show of sniffing the air. "It smells like Flynn is still using the same cheap drugstore cologne he favored when we were teenagers."

"I don't need cologne," Flynn said, his tree-trunk arms crossed over his chest. "I've got pheromones."

There was a beat of silence, and then Beth burst out laughing. "Declan talks about you plenty." She pointed a finger at Flynn. "But he didn't mention your wicked sense of humor."

"It's because he's jealous," Flynn answered.

"In your dreams, bro," Declan told him.

After giving Shauna another squeeze, Beth wrapped an arm around Declan's waist and rested her head against his arm. "Oh, Timmy nearly scored a goal. Go, Timmy," she shouted, then waved as both boys looked in their direction. "Go, Zach!" But she yawned as soon as the boys' focus returned to the game.

"You need a nap," Declan told her. "You're working too hard."

"I just came off a twelve-hour shift at the hospital. I need a foot rub," she countered.

Dec placed a gentle kiss on the top of her head. "I can help with that."

"You two are so cute it almost makes me want to barf," Shauna announced with a laugh that she hoped didn't sound forced.

She could feel Flynn studying her and did her best not to look at him for fear of what he might be able to read in her eyes. She didn't want to feel jealous of Declan and Beth.

Both of them had been through a lot and deserved the happiness they'd found together. Shauna reminded herself that she had found her own sort of happiness with her boys in this town she loved.

She was making a home and friends in the place where she belonged, something she'd only dreamed of as a kid. So what if she'd never had anyone to massage her feet?

She could buy a foot massager. She could take care of herself. She certainly didn't want Flynn Murphy in that role.

They were managing well together, and he'd effortlessly become a regular part of the boys' lives. She'd also noticed the changes he'd told her about. He seemed less angry and more patient.

Timmy and Zach absolutely adored having their father involved in their lives, and Shauna did her best not to feel guilty for not making it happen earlier.

She hadn't been ready. Maybe Flynn hadn't been ready. It was still difficult for her to trust that he wouldn't walk away. She'd had so many people in her life disappoint her when she allowed herself to care about them. She couldn't risk that with Flynn.

When the soccer game ended, Declan and Beth hugged the boys and then headed toward their cars, hands joined like two people comfortable in their love for each other. Shauna pressed her hand to her chest to ease the wistful ache radiating from her heart.

"Mommy, when can we go to Miss May's house?" Zach asked as they walked toward the parking lot next to the field.

The boys were spending the night at her neighbor's house, which they did each month. Beth's mother, May, had befriended Shauna immediately when she'd arrived in town. Then May suffered a stroke just before Thanksgiving, and her three daughters reconnected as they helped her recover.

Shauna reminded herself that it was okay to accept help from other people. These monthly sleepovers were a huge help by giving her a night off.

Beth's youngest sister, Trinity, was also living with May, along with her four-month-old baby. Shauna would be just a couple of doors down alone at home, so she knew her kids would be fine.

"Trinity wants you to come over and make homemade pizza for dinner. Once we get home, both of you need showers and to clean your room so you can head over."

"No shower," Zach yelled.

At the same time, Timmy asked, "Do we have to clean the room?"

"Yes to both," Flynn answered before Shauna could. "Your mother said so."

Shauna was so used to the boys trying to negotiate her rules around cleanliness—both personal hygiene and their rooms—that it surprised her when they didn't argue with Flynn.

"It's not fair that they listen to you more than they listen to me," she said as the boys loaded their stuff into her car and then climbed in. "But I appreciate you backing me."

"What are your plans for tonight?"

She thought about it. "Probably a bowl of cereal and some embarrassing reality TV. Maybe if I'm feeling energized after that, I might whip out a dust cloth."

"Come over for dinner," Flynn said. He wore a long-sleeve hoodie, jeans and sneakers but looked as handsome as if he'd walked off the set of a magazine photo shoot.

"Is that an invitation or a command?" she asked.

"Would you please come to dinner tonight?"

"Just the two of us," she murmured. "I'm not sure that's the best idea."

"It's dinner, Shauna. That's all."

"Do you cook?"

He shrugged. "I can do better than a bowl of cereal."

"Okay," she agreed because suddenly she didn't care to be alone. More than not wanting to be alone, she yearned to spend time with Flynn. It was stupid and reckless for her heart. "We can review what I know about the boys' calendar for the summer and how you might want to be involved."

It seemed safe to talk about their sons.

"I want to be involved in any way you'll let me," Flynn

told her. He lifted a hand and moved one finger slowly across her jaw.

The touch felt strangely intimate, especially given that they were standing in a parking lot.

"I'll see you tonight, Shauna."

"Can I bring anything?"

"This is your night off. I'll take care of everything."

She nodded and tried to ignore the fuzzy feeling that bubbled up in her chest at the thought of spending an evening with Flynn. The good thing about being a single mom to twins was that she had very little time for self-reflection.

She and the boys made it home without any squabbling, but there was an incident with the soap in the shower, and then they argued over who'd been the one to leave LEGOs scattered across the floor of their room.

By the time she'd gotten their duffel bags packed and dropped them at May's house, she was so out of sorts that she thought about canceling dinner with Flynn.

Except she really couldn't blame her nerves on her rambunctious boys. They were more a result of the thought of time alone with Flynn.

She couldn't deny the attraction they shared, even if she wanted to believe the connection that bound her to him was in the past.

He'd been nothing but a perfect gentleman since arriving in Magnolia. It seemed beyond mortifying that she might accidentally reveal how much he still affected her.

She also knew that not going would betray just as much, and she wanted to believe she could handle it.

All she had to do was remind herself about the heartbreak she'd felt when he'd left her behind after their night together.

After dropping the boys off, she took a quick shower but

purposely did not shave her legs. There was no reason she needed smooth skin, and this felt like a safeguard so she wouldn't let things get out of control.

Even if she'd owned nice panties, she would not have chosen them. Lucky for her, everything in her dresser drawers was of the plain cotton variety.

Okay, she needed to stop thinking about underpants and Flynn simultaneously. That was doing little for her nerves. They were getting together in order to work on successfully co-parenting, nothing more.

Her body didn't agree. By the time she parked in his driveway, her stomach swooped like a seagull gliding along the wind currents. It felt like a tornado was coming, and she might be stuck in the middle of it.

Flynn opened the door before she even got to it.

"Were you expecting someone else?" she asked. "You look surprised to see me."

"I thought you might cancel," he said.

Was it her imagination or was Flynn blushing? She didn't know if it made her feel better or worse that she wasn't the only one struggling with their past.

"We have a whole list of summer activities to get through," she told him. "Assuming you're staying. Tell me you didn't invite me over here to give the news in person that you're already leaving town."

"I guess I deserve your lack of faith," he said, blowing out a long breath. "But I don't like it. Come on in, Shauna. Let's have dinner, and then we can pull out our respective calendars."

She followed him into the house, noting that it smelled like him. Not drugstore cologne, despite Declan's teasing. Flynn smelled clean, a little spicy, and male like the poster child for effortless masculine appeal.

She hadn't been in his rental house before now and couldn't help gawking at how perfect it was. As she'd told him, this was Magnolia's more upscale side with hundred-year-old homes that boasted beautiful gardens and crisp green lawns.

Houses in her area were well-loved but more eclectic, often a work in progress for young families or longtime residents with homes that needed updating.

"Did this house come furnished?" She traced a hand over the back of a tufted leather sofa.

He gave her a funny look. "Everything you see is mine."

"You have good taste," she murmured. Expensive taste, she added silently. The house was filled with furniture that combined elements of both modern and traditional styles.

Leather couches, thick rugs and tables made of burnished wood.

Expensive.

"How'd you get the stuff here this fast? Do you have a friend who owns a furniture business?"

"I have a friend with a moving business. A guy I knew in the army. I hired his company to pack up my place in Virginia and get everything down here. I wanted the boys to feel at home when they came over."

He held up a hand before she could respond. "I know it's not like your home, but it was something I could give them."

Shauna found herself growing light-headed. She didn't know how to handle Flynn like this.

"Tell me you don't have a pool in the back. Because I think they'll ditch me for this house if it came with a pool."

"No pool, but I had a hot tub at my other place."

"They would like a hot tub."

"It was the first thing I bought when I left the army and found a permanent home. Declan and I were obsessed with hot tubs and pools when we were little. I have residual pain from a few injuries during my time in the service. It helps a lot."

She wanted to ask about his injuries but didn't want to admit how curious she was about them. About him.

It was stupid, but she could convince herself it was vital for her to know who Flynn was now. Not for herself but because of her children.

"Would you like a glass of wine?" he asked.

"Sure." He followed her toward the back of the house. "Were the injuries the reason you got out of the army?"

"They contributed, but mostly it was time. I didn't need it the way I once did."

"I never thanked you," she said.

"We don't have to do this."

"Even that night when you came back. I thought we'd have more time at that point, so it didn't seem important."

"I didn't want to revisit the past then, and I still don't," he told her.

"It needs to be said, Flynn."

The night in question had been the worst in Shauna's life, and that was saying something. Although the situation in the foster home where she'd been placed along with Declan hadn't been ideal, she'd liked making a friend. Flynn had aged out of the system by then, but he tried to be a part of his brother's life as much as he could.

And he'd immediately been stitched into the fabric of Shauna's heart. She hadn't known what to do with the connection that pulsed between him, but when the boyfriend of her foster family's daughter attacked her and brutally beat Declan, who tried to intervene, any choice about a future with Flynn was taken from her hands when he'd walked in on the scene.

She could still picture Flynn, bloody and scarred as she pulled him off the limp body of the man who'd tried to hurt her. Even with the rage coursing through Flynn at that moment, she hadn't feared him. In her soul, she knew he wouldn't hurt her. Not physically anyway.

"I need to say thank you for saving me that night. If it weren't for you, he would have hurt Declan and me more than he did. He would have…"

"You don't have to say it."

"He would have raped me."

His fist clenched around the beer bottle he'd taken out of the fridge. "I wanted to kill him," he said softly. "Sometimes I wish that I had."

Their foster father had a friend in the court system and had worked out a deal for Flynn. Face charges or enlist. Declan had been in the hospital when his brother left for the military.

"Don't say that. The army wouldn't have been an option for you if he'd died."

"I still hate that you were hurt. I hate that Declan was involved." He took a long drink of beer. "Most of all, I hate that I had to leave. I wanted to stay, but I was no good for you then. I was no good for anybody."

"As much as I wanted you to stay, I must admit that Uncle Sam did a bang-up job with you."

"In a strange way, things worked out for both of us."

He checked the oven, and she was hit with the powerful scent of garlic and butter.

"I want it to be different for Timmy and Zach. And for us. Maybe I didn't know exactly why I was coming to find you, but now I do."

"The boys," she said softly. She needed to remember that

Flynn had put down the start of roots in Magnolia because of the boys. Not her.

People didn't stay for her. Declan would have left if he hadn't met Beth. Someday even her boys would leave, which hurt her heart more than she could say.

She drew in a deep breath. Someday wasn't now. "What did you make?"

"Chicken marsala."

"Italian. I'm impressed."

"Another one of my friends is from a big Italian family. His mom invited me to stay when I was on leave since I didn't have anyone to return to."

She wanted to argue that he'd had her, but nope. He'd made his choice just like everyone she cared about did eventually.

"Tell me about your friends," she said, sipping her wine. "I understand the man you were, but I want to know the man you've become."

Shauna relaxed as Flynn spoke. He was surprisingly willing to answer any and all of her questions.

She chopped vegetables for the salad and cut the crusty bread he'd bought from the local bakery in downtown Magnolia into thick slices. She told him about her life since the boys, although it was far less exciting than his. Flynn seemed to hang on every word. He had dozens of questions about the twins and their personalities. Who had walked first? What they were scared of and her hopes and dreams for them.

Shauna had never shared her dreams for the boys, even with May Carlyle, who felt like the mother she'd never had. She'd almost been too afraid to put them into words.

She'd met too many kids in foster care who'd had their dreams crushed repeatedly until they stopped dreaming.

Shauna never truly knew what to wish for in the first place because the things she wanted in her life—love, security, sheets that smelled like fresh laundry—seemed so small and pathetic in the grand scheme.

But even those tiny dreams had been a challenge for her to make come true. So she mostly kept her dreams to herself. Flynn had no desire to judge her. He was somebody who might care about Zach and Timmy in the same way she did. Maybe a mother's love couldn't be replicated, but once Flynn gave her the chance to open up, she did so willingly. Conversation flowed easily, and she realized that Flynn truly had changed during his time away.

She reminded herself that those changes didn't impact her other than being able to trust him more with their sons. Trust didn't come easily for Shauna.

"This is what it might have been like," she said as they finished cleaning up the kitchen after dinner, only realizing she'd spoken the words out loud when Flynn turned to face her more fully.

"Do you mean if you and I had been raised in normal houses?"

Her eyes drifted closed as happy images floated through her mind. She opened them again and wiped at an invisible spot on the counter. "We might have met and gone on dates like regular people. We would have functioned without the weight of emotional baggage as a burden."

She wondered how he'd respond to her words, the secret reflections of her heart.

"I used to think about that all the time." He put down the dish towel he'd been holding and moved closer to her. "There were long nights in the barracks and the field when exhaustion wouldn't let me fall asleep. I'd imagine how things could have been different."

"You did?" His answer shocked her and eased the invisible tension that gripped her chest like a vise.

"Yeah. We would have gone to prom, and I'd have gotten you the most obnoxious corsage you've ever seen. We would have danced—"

"You're a horrible dancer," she reminded him.

He conceded that fact with a smile and touched his thumb to her bottom lip. Awareness zinged through her. "You could have laughed at me. We would have laughed at a lot of things, Shauna. There would have been so much joy."

She blinked as tears filled her eyes. "I've experienced joy, Flynn. Zach and Timmy brought it to me. I'm sorry I didn't tell you about them. I thought I was doing the right thing, but it was selfish."

"You don't owe me an apology." His tone was rough. "I long ago stopped imagining a life where our childhoods had been different."

She tried not to be hurt by that. It made sense. He'd moved on.

"You and I became who we are because of our parents," he said. "My personality might leave a lot to be desired, but you're perfect."

"Hardly," she said with a laugh.

"Just the way you are," he continued as if she hadn't spoken. Then he leaned in and kissed her. His tongue licked the top of her lip, and she closed her eyes on a sigh. He pulled her in tighter, the heat of him warming her even as goose bumps erupted along her skin. She opened to him, their tongues melding as she wound her arms around his neck. This was perfect and…wrong.

"I should go," she said as she pulled back, willing her ragged breathing back to a normal rhythm.

"You could stay," he told her. He didn't sound as affected by the kiss as she felt, but his eyes had gone dark, filled with all the desire his voice masked. "I'd like you to stay tonight."

She couldn't take her gaze from him.

She needed to leave. Flynn Murphy was dangerous to her heart. But while she tried to find the strength to walk away, he leaned in and trailed gentle kisses against her jaw and down her neck.

She could lie and say she didn't remember the last time she'd felt something so wonderful. But she remembered—it was the last time she'd been with this man.

"Will you stay?" he asked against her skin, his voice low and gentle.

No, the rational part of her brain insisted.

"Yes," she whispered because no matter what the future brought, she wanted this moment with this man.

So when he took her hand and led her toward his bedroom, she followed without hesitation.

CHAPTER SIXTEEN

THE FOLLOWING WEEK, Meghan stood next to the bifold door that separated her classroom from the music room in the elementary school. She listened to Walker's deep voice leading students in a soulful rendition of "If I Had a Hammer."

She peeked in, and it came as no surprise that even the wiggliest of the kids in the second-grade class participated and listened with rapt attention to their new music teacher. Walker's talent and charisma were a gift. He made even the most basic lessons feel special and did a bang-up job of making Meghan feel special as well.

Often when they had corresponding free periods, he would come into her room to talk or sit at the chair on the other side of her desk while they both worked.

He seemed to value her opinion on every subject they discussed, and she couldn't quite get used to someone of his fame and fortune being interested in what she had to say.

Who was she kidding? His fame has less to do with it than his inherent appeal and that sexy half smile he flashed like a badge. When their gazes met, she felt her stomach tie in knots, like she was a schoolgirl with a crush on the most popular boy in her grade.

Walker was also popular with the other staff members. He had a way of putting everyone at ease and didn't seem to mind the barrage of questions from his new coworkers about topics ranging from what he ate on the road to sleeping on a tour bus to meeting Willie Nelson.

The curious moms made him less comfortable, but he handled them gracefully. Meghan had never seen so many parents request teacher conferences from a music teacher.

"Am I interrupting something?"

She felt her face flame as she turned to face Greg Wheeler and didn't appreciate being caught daydreaming about Walker.

"Just making sure things are going okay next door. Walker was a little nervous about the lesson for today."

Greg rolled his eyes. "Yes, I'm sure the famous country music star was just a barrel of nerves when thinking about talking to a roomful of elementary school kids. He can handle playing a sold-out stadium show, but ankle biters are a tough crowd."

Greg made a show of inclining his head as if listening more intently to Walker's lesson. "Is that 'Here Comes the Sun' by The Beatles?"

Meghan nodded.

"It's an improvement from 'Three Blind Mice' on the recorder."

"How can I help you?" Meghan asked, taking a step forward. She didn't appreciate his condescension and felt strangely protective of Walker, the last man on earth who would need her in his corner.

"I suppose any performing, no matter how big or small, could be a struggle for Walker given his issues."

That wasn't an answer to Meghan's question, and the insinuation irritated her.

"He isn't struggling," she countered. "The kids love him, and the other teachers and parents do, too."

"Trust me, I've noticed," Greg said, his voice tight. "Everybody loves Walker."

Meghan didn't like the sharp glint in Greg's pale gaze as his eyes narrowed on the door between the classrooms.

She didn't like anything about Principal Ferret at the moment. How had she ever considered going on a date with him? Crippling anxiety might hinder her social life, but even she had standards.

The bell rang, signaling the end of the school day, and she hoped Walker would be distracted by a parent or another faculty member before saying goodbye to her and taking Gus home.

There was something about Greg's demeanor right now that Meghan didn't like or trust. She made a point of keeping her distance from Walker during staff meetings or anytime Greg was around. She got the feeling seeing her friendship with the school's most popular substitute teacher grated on the principal's nerves.

"Everything I've read and heard leads me to believe the guy had a breakdown after his brother's death. He completely swore off music."

"The accident was a tragic loss. Of course it affected him."

"So maybe he should be paying us for his time at the school. It's like he's getting therapy."

"You know he's donating his salary," Meghan pointed out then realized she'd said the wrong thing when Greg's beady eyes flashed with anger.

"A prince among men," he conceded. "But we've hit a snag with this fundraiser you're hoping will save your position."

"A rather large snag," Everly Mae Tinsdale confirmed as she sashayed into the room on a cloud of too-sweet perfume. Meghan's mouth flooded with bile.

Not for the first time, she wondered how she'd lumped Annalise into the same category as Everly Mae. How had the two women been friends when they were nothing alike at their core?

Meghan should know better than to judge a book by its cover. She'd certainly been misjudged often enough. The more she got to know Annalise, the more Meghan liked and respected the other woman.

She couldn't imagine circumstances that would allow her to see a soft side of Everly Mae.

"Annalise will handle it." Meghan tipped up her chin. "I'm sure it's a big loss not having her as involved with PTO, but she's still committed to doing what's right for the children at this school. She has a big heart and a talent for raising money."

Everly Mae gave her the sort of smile a tiger might bestow on its prey just before the beast pounced. "Annalise can't handle this issue." She sounded much too cheerful about it. "The permit to hold the concert in the town square has been denied. Again. For good."

Meghan shook her head. "That's not possible. Annalise talked to Avery Atwell, who got Mayor Grimes to agree to help with the permit."

"Malcolm Grimes is the mayor, not the king of Magnolia." Everly Mae sniffed. "Town council decides on permits, and they've denied it."

Meghan's heart plummeted to her toes. Without a place to set up for the concert, there was no point in moving forward with plans for a fundraiser.

"I don't understand why you're doing this." She looked between Everly Mae and Greg. "This will save the school's music and art program. Why wouldn't you want that?"

"This school will still have music and art," Greg said like it was a foregone conclusion. "We are a community, and our success isn't built on one person, one program or one team. It's frankly conceited of you to think you are so irreplaceable. It's about the students, Meghan, not you or your ego."

Meghan had first heard the term *gaslighting* on social media and hadn't quite understood the idea of abuse in the form of a person sowing self-doubt and confusion in their victim's mind. Still, the idea had struck a chord, reminding her of conversations with her mother when Meghan's feelings had been dismissed or the facts of a situation had been twisted to suit her mom's narrative.

She thought about it again as Greg gave her a chastising stare and suddenly wondered why she was fighting so hard to work for this man. Even if she wanted to stay in Magnolia, she had no real ties to this town despite her connection to her grandmother. She could find a job in a neighboring district or maybe even waitressing. Anything where she wasn't treated so shabbily.

"Bless your heart, Meghan." Everly Mae pursed her coral-hued lips. "This truly isn't about you. As Mr. Wheeler says, we will make the music and art programs special at this school, with or without you. The truth of the matter is Annalise Haverford has no power here anymore."

She pointed an elegant finger at Meghan. "Perhaps unknowingly, you hitched your cart to the wrong horse. I will not allow her to overshadow my efforts in taking care of the PTO in her stead. A school fundraiser that will draw national attention? Somebody's biting off more than they can chew in taking that on. I'm sure you understand. I know some initial publicity has already been done in this haphazard event planning, but you'll have to cancel it. Annalise will have to ensure that everyone knows you were dragged along on her tattered coattails. Walker Calloway as well. He didn't know any better, poor man."

"I appreciate your concern for me," a deep voice said from the door leading to the hallway.

Meghan glanced at the nearly closed partition between

the two rooms. She had expected Walker to show up from there and hated him witnessing the lecture from Everly Mae and her fake kindness. The woman's voice was as sickeningly sweet as her perfume.

It made Meghan nauseous.

Walker stepped farther into the room. "I can handle my own reputation. Luckily, I also own land where we can host the event."

Meghan figured the look of shock on her face must mirror the one on Everly Mae's.

"You're going to let a bunch of strangers trample around the grounds at Whimsy Farm?" Everly Mae sputtered. "You can't be serious."

"I made a commitment to this school, and I plan to honor that. I'm sure you can appreciate commitment."

"If you want to contribute to the school," Everly Mae cooed, "we can find a better use of your time and talent. We have many ideas for—"

"I'm doing the concert. Do either of you have a problem with that?" He looked between Greg and Everly Mae. "Because if you put a stop to it, trust me, it will not be Annalise who is left with egg on her face. I'll make it known far and wide that the school administration and parent leadership rejected my generous offer."

"We're not rejecting anything," Greg said quickly. "It was an unfortunate turn of events that the council denied the permit for the use of the town square."

"Or any land the town owns," Meghan clarified because with Walker standing there, she suddenly felt braver than she normally did.

"Any land," Greg confirmed reluctantly. "Obviously, your willingness to use your private land changes the situation."

Everly Mae crossed her arms over her chest. "You'll also carry the risk of injury or accidents during the event. You know how unfortunate accidents can be, Mr. Walker."

Meghan, who was not prone to violent thoughts, wanted to punch the woman.

"I am aware of how quickly accidents can happen," Walker said, his eyes stony as he stared down Everly Mae. "I assume since you harbor such grave safety concerns that you won't be attending the event."

"I'm PTO president," Everly Mae said. "Any money raised for the school goes through my organization."

"Annalise is still copresident on the books," Meghan offered. "She told me so, and her name is also on the bank account. She can manage the donations."

"Is that wise?" Everly Mae scoffed, pink crawling up her neck like an army of ants. "It was an oversight on…our secretary's part to not remove Annalise. I'm certain we can agree that we don't want anyone with the last name Haverford given access to anything of value that might be stolen."

"You know she works for me," Walker said, his voice low.

Alarm bells went off in Meghan's brain at the fire that flashed in Everly Mae's eyes. She was reminded of that scene in the dinosaur island movie when the velociraptor studied its prey moments before striking. That predator had the same look.

"Annalise is helping Walker redecorate Whimsy Farm," she blurted.

Walker gave her a funny look.

"I'd heard that a design company out of Charlotte was on the short-list for that job," Everly Mae said.

"It's not important for this conversation." Meghan looked at Greg. "The benefit concert is back on, right?"

"It would seem so," Principal Ferret agreed.

The door between the classrooms opened, and Gus ran in.

"Hey, Uncle Walker, I got an A on my math test."

"That's great, kid."

Gus gave a curious glance to the principal and Everly Mae.

"Well done, Gus," Greg said, his weaselly face pinched. He ushered a fuming Everly Mae out of the classroom.

Meghan wasn't sure what to say or how to react to Walker's gesture.

"Thank you," she said, meeting his gaze because that seemed like a good place to start.

His smile made her knees go weak. "You're welcome."

"Can we go get an ice cream to celebrate?" Gus tugged on Walker's hand.

"I think there's something in all those parenting blogs Jack had me read about not rewarding kids with food."

Gus's big brown eyes rolled to the ceiling. "Then don't think of it as a reward. It can be a treat, and Miss Banks can come with us. You'll be treating her, too."

"No need to include me," Meghan protested, "but I highly recommend the cookies and cream if you're going to Sunnyside Bakery."

"That settles it," Walker said. "I suppose we're going for ice cream. We'd love to have you join us, Ms. Banks. We can talk more about this new development for the fundraiser."

"What's the development?" Gus asked, adjusting the strap on his backpack.

"We're going to be having the concert at Whimsy Farm."

The boy's eyes widened. "That's cool."

Meghan shook her head. "It's too much to ask you to perform and host the fundraiser."

"You didn't ask," Walker reminded her. "I offered."

"Let's get ice cream," Gus repeated because apparently the thought of his uncle doing a concert on their property didn't hold his attention as much as the thought of an ice cream cone.

"Why don't you drive with us?" Walker suggested. "I can drop you off here after."

They were friends, she reminded herself, and they were planning a fundraiser together. This didn't mean anything. Gus was with them.

Still, her anxiety spiked, leaving little trails of panic sizzling down her spine.

She fidgeted but nodded. "That would be lovely. Thank you."

"Come on. Pleeease." Gus tugged on his uncle's hand when she and Walker continued to stare at each other before at last moving toward the door.

They climbed into Walker's truck, and her nerves subsided as they drove the few minutes to downtown.

Gus babbled on about his day, taking some pressure off her to make conversation, although it shouldn't be difficult.

She'd been hanging out with Walker nearly every day at school. Yet being in his giant truck felt different than being together in the classroom. He parked near the bakery, and Meghan did her best to act like it was perfectly normal for her to be seen in downtown Magnolia, sharing ice cream with a country music heartthrob.

She had to hand it to the folks in Magnolia. No one made a big fuss over Walker, although she caught a few curious glances in her direction. It was as if people understood he was trying to create a new life for his nephew, and they wanted to respect him and give him the normalcy he so obviously craved.

They talked about random subjects like the weather and Gus's favorite color—lavender. Then Walker cleared his throat, and in an almost tentative tone, explained his plans for a stage set up on his property. "My brother coordinated something like this on his thirtieth birthday. He owned land outside of Nashville, and we did a benefit concert for a children's hospital."

"We had ATVs and a giant trampoline and a zipline." Gus sucked a drop of ice cream off his hand. "Uncle Walker, can we get a zipline?"

"You remember spending time at the cabin?"

Meghan's breath caught at the look of torment on Walker's face.

"That seems like so long ago," he murmured.

"Yeah, I remember." Gus shrugged like it was no big deal. "Daddy always laughed more when we were at the cabin." He glanced toward the front window. "Margo's outside with her friends. Can I go talk to her?"

"Yes, and bring a napkin," Walker advised. "You need to eat that ice cream faster, dude."

"Working on it," Gus said as he licked around the edge of the cone.

"Are you worried about him forgetting his father?" Meghan asked when the boy was out of earshot.

Walker stabbed at his scoop of cookies and cream with a spoon. "Sometimes. Mostly I'm worried that I won't do right by Gus."

"You already are."

"Because Jack forces me to," Walker admitted with a laugh.

"He's not happy about this benefit concert. Why?" Meghan took a tiny bite of her strawberry. She was almost too wound up to force down any kind of food.

"Because the record company wants me in the studio. I

told them I'm staying in Magnolia with Gus and taking a break from music. Jack thinks the publicity from the concert will upset the apple cart."

"Why is another record so important?"

He laughed. "Because it's what I do. That and touring. The tours are where big money is for bands, but that's off the table. Gus needs time to recover before I ask him to handle one of the two people he has left in life going on the road again."

Meghan wasn't sure Gus was the one who needed time.

"Can't you get out of your contract with the record company? Pay them back or however it works."

Walker ran a hand over his jaw and glanced toward the front of the bakery. The space was cozy and welcoming with pale yellow walls, wrought-iron tables and local artwork. The pastry case was always filled with delicious options. "My brother was a talented musician, an amazing father and one of the best men I've ever known."

He met Meghan's gaze again. "He was also a gambling addict. I didn't know. Even Jack didn't realize the extent of it, and Jack knew everything. But Nash had a secret life, and he burned through a lot of money. It makes me sick to my stomach to think of how much."

"That was his money, not yours."

"He had access to my accounts and we shared a financial adviser who was more a drinking buddy than a trusted source of sage money advice. I know it sounds stupid, but he was my big brother. I trusted him with everything—my money and my life."

"That's a powerful kind of love," Meghan murmured.

"Nobody knows how bad it is—no one but Jack. Things started coming out after Nash's death. Jack let go of everybody on the team. We stripped down to basics again. There were some nasty characters my brother had been keeping company with, and we needed to make a clean break."

"That's why you came to Magnolia?"

"Jack also figured it would be easier for Gus to start someplace new. He didn't have many friends in Tennessee, both because he struggles socially and because we took him on the road with us whenever we could. He missed his entire second-grade year while we toured. Nash hired a tutor. At the time, neither of us thought about how living on a tour bus might not be the best thing for a little kid. We hadn't had a solid upbringing, so it seemed like an adventure. I didn't realize it then, but I think my brother had a bit of a Peter Pan complex."

Meghan raised a brow. "It hasn't just been parenting blogs you've been reading lately. That sounds like deep introspection."

His eyes crinkled at the corners. "I like talking to you, Ms. Banks."

"Meghan," she corrected.

"It's a hard habit to break with teachers, you know?"

She did know, but she didn't like it. If Walker thought of her as Ms. Banks, his nephew's art teacher, that meant he didn't think of her as a woman. She shouldn't care. She shouldn't want him to think of her in that way but couldn't seem to stop it.

"I like that you can talk to me." She dabbed at one corner of her mouth with a napkin.

"You missed a spot." He reached out and pressed his thumb to the other side, then pulled it away and sucked the tip into his mouth.

Meghan worried she might be drooling in response.

"You know you can talk to me, too," he said.

"I talk to you plenty."

"There are plenty of things you aren't sharing. Deep-introspection-type things. I'd like to know you, Meghan."

Her mouth went dry, and she pushed away from the table. "We should be going. The bakery is getting crowded, and somebody will want this table."

Walker's lips twitched, but he rose, long limbed and effortlessly sexy. He was not a man with whom she planned to share her deepest secrets. He liked her now. He'd find her pathetic if he knew who she was, just like her mother and siblings did.

"We didn't actually talk much about details for the concert. I know this will put a lot more work on you."

He took the empty ice cream cup from her—she'd managed to finish it after all—and his fingers brushed her skin. He had calluses on the pads from playing guitar. For a moment, she wondered what those calluses would feel like trailing over her bare skin.

Nerves of a different kind than she recognized bubbled up inside her, but Walker didn't seem to notice. He threw their trash into a nearby can and then turned back to her.

"I think what you mean to say is this will put more work on Jack and Annalise. I'm not worried about it. Jack is the most organized person I've ever met."

He held up a hand when she would have argued. "At least until I met Annalise. What was all that business about her decorating my house?"

Meghan bit down on her lower lip. "I know she's cleaning and taking care of things for you, but I don't think she'd want Everly Mae or some women from PTO to know about that. She has a background in design."

"Makes sense. She's always rearranging things."

"So if you're looking at hiring somebody to help you with the house..."

"I am."

"You should consider Annalise."

Meghan was surprised Annalise hadn't done more to sell Walker on her services. She seemed so confident. Meghan knew she desperately wanted a career in interior design. "You're a loyal friend. I hope she returns the favor."

Meghan wasn't sure Annalise considered her a friend, and it made Meghan's heart hurt. She could relate to Gus. She was awkward in social situations and struggled even as an adult to make friends.

"Let's grab my nephew," Walker said, "and we should get you back to school." His phone rang again.

"Somebody wants to get a hold of you." It was the third time since they'd sat down at the bakery that his phone had buzzed.

He shrugged. "Just a friend I've lost touch with, trying to reconnect."

Meghan couldn't help herself. She glanced at the phone screen, which was still ringing, and saw the image of a woman before Walker quickly sent the call to voice mail.

He probably had lots of old friends who wanted to get a hold of him, but he chose to talk to her, which meant something. Or she wanted it to. Wanting and wishing and hoping—those were Meghan's familiar companions.

CHAPTER SEVENTEEN

"WE NEED MORE Porta Potties." Annalise and Jack sat at the yellow Formica table with a blue flower pattern in his tiny kitchen the following day. Instead of getting together in Walker's expensive kitchen, Jack had insisted that they conduct their business in his apartment above the barn.

It was clean and cozy, reminding her of her current living circumstances, which she liked more than she'd expected.

There was something to be said for being a minimalist.

"Don't you think most guys will head into the trees to take a leak?"

She sputtered out a laugh. "Well, they will if there's a huge line because we don't have enough Porta Potties. I don't think that should be the plan."

"Men like peeing in the great outdoors," Jack told her.

She raised a brow. "Be that as it may."

"Okay, we'll double the number of Porta Potties, but that's going to cut into the net profits for the school."

Annalise input a few numbers on the spreadsheet. "If things go the way we planned, we'll still have plenty of money for salaries and supplies at the elementary school. Plus money to set aside for the following year so we can pay a grant writer to ensure more funding."

Jack smiled. "You have this all figured out. I imagine the organizations you used to work with are struggling without you."

A gaping pit of regret opened in Annalise's stomach, a tiny sliver of vulnerability but deep and terrifying, nonetheless. "I don't think anyone cared about me enough to be overly concerned about my absence. Plenty of well-meaning women in this town and throughout the South are taught from a young age to lend a hand, organizing potlucks and fundraisers. As the saying goes, we're a dime a dozen."

Since her divorce, Annalise had found that self-deprecation was an excellent defense mechanism, but to her surprise, Jack didn't join her in laughing.

"You are singular," he said matter-of-factly. "I can't imagine anyone like you. You might not realize it, but I'm sure you've been missed. Hell, you've only been working at the farm a couple of weeks, and you'd be sorely missed around here."

"Oh." That one syllable escaped on a tremulous puff of air. Wasn't that a lovely thought, even though she doubted it was true?

"You didn't know me before the scandal broke. You wouldn't have liked me very much." She laughed to cover how rattled she felt. "Sometimes I'm not sure you like me now."

"I like you."

"That's a comfort, I suppose. Looking back on it, I don't like the person I was during my marriage."

"Do you miss him?" Jack pushed back from the table, crossing his arms over his chest like he was curious about the answer but didn't want to hear her admit the one he expected.

"No. Embarrassingly, I don't miss Jonathan. I don't even miss the financial security I thought we had. I realize it was based on other people being robbed, and it certainly was no Peter and Paul situation."

"Your husband must have been a spectacular con man to take in so many people."

"Ex," she reminded him. "So much of what we think we know about life is an illusion. People see what we want them to believe—what they're shown or told without bothering to look behind the curtain. I appreciate what I've found in the shadows even when it seems like the darkness could swallow me whole."

"I know that feeling," Jack said, and the sense of connection between them was like an electric current. It made all the hairs on the back of her neck stand on end.

"One thing I do regret," she said, wanting to change the subject before she did something silly like launching herself across the table and fusing her mouth to his, "is disappointing my mother. It's ridiculous because she isn't the kind of mom I want her to be. But I don't like letting her down. She also doesn't let me forget how badly I've failed."

Jack uncrossed his arms and laced them behind his neck, leaning back in the chair until it balanced on two legs. Jonathan had aggressively corrected Trey when he tried to sit in exactly that same way. An arbitrary infraction for her husband to harp on, given what she now knew of his benchmark for good behavior, which was dirtier than the grimiest gutter.

"Family is a complicated thing," he said.

"My mother is straightforward," Annalise countered. "She wanted me to be a perfect dutiful wife, no matter what. If I can give anything to my children, it will be the gift of allowing them to become whoever they were meant to be."

"Intentions are important." Jack sighed. "My own experience taught me that I'm not meant for family life."

"But you're so good with Gus."

"Gus is different."

"You're good with Trey, too."

"Trey is Gus's friend. That makes him special."

Those words warmed her heart. "How old are you, Jack?"

"Thirty-seven."

"Not exactly past your prime." She inclined her head. "You could still have a family."

"Nash Calloway died in my arms, and the last thing he did was elicit a promise from me to look after his son and brother."

Annalise felt her jaw go slack.

Jack blew out a slow breath. "I didn't mean to share them, but it changed everything. Walker and Gus are my responsibility."

"You can take care of them and still want something for yourself."

"Wanting doesn't do much except remind me of how my life is lacking. The ways I'm lacking."

"I don't believe you." She made a show of letting her gaze trail over him like it was a joke. Like her heart and body weren't equally consumed by him. "I imagine you're popular with the ladies."

He cocked one thick brow. "I haven't had any complaints, but I'm also clear about the parameters. I'm a rough man, Annalise. I have scars on my back from a dad who was too fond of the belt and calluses on my hands from working in the barn and pastures."

"Some women don't mind calluses," she said softly, feeling compassion for Jack's past even as she imagined how it would feel like to have his hands on her.

"A number of them don't mind rough either," he acknowledged. "Maybe Nash did me a favor. I don't have to worry about my future. It's tied to this farm and the remaining Calloway men. I might be good for an adventurous romp between the sheets, but that's about it."

She barked out a nervous laugh and raised her palm to her heated cheek. "Maybe that's enough for some women."

She wasn't certain what he read in her gaze, but his chair scraped across the scuffed wood floor as he rose. Then he walked around the table and reached for her.

He placed a hand on either arm and hauled her up and against him. Her breasts were pressed to the soft fabric of his chambray shirt, and it felt like there was nothing between them based on the need burning through her.

Her toes curled, and her knees went weak. She darted out her tongue and licked her dry lips. Jack's eyes blazed as they zeroed in on that motion. For a moment, it looked like he was in physical pain.

"Would it be enough for you?" he whispered, his minty breath fanning across her jaw.

She wasn't sure and highly doubted it. Annalise had never let herself simply enjoy without consequence. There always had to be a reason, a motive, a way to get ahead.

When was the last time she'd let herself do something for pure pleasure? It had been so long, she barely recognized what made her happy.

Jack made her knees weak, and right now, that was enough. The way her stomach dipped and her breasts tingled as he stared at her was more sensation than she'd experienced in forever.

More. She wanted more.

So instead of answering with words—what could she say without giving away too much?—she lifted her face and brushed her lips across his.

It was chaste as kisses went, but the fact that she'd initiated it meant something to Annalise. She'd been taught to defer to a man in all things, even physical pleasure.

It had been foolish to accept that as her fate, as if she didn't have a right to go after what she wanted.

Jack.

For a man who seemed ready to take charge in any situation, he was deliciously patient when it came to kissing. It was as if he understood some of the pleasure at this moment for her was derived from the fact that she had control.

He angled his head to give her better access to his mouth but otherwise allowed Annalise to set the pace. She deepened the kiss, and the sensation of the current pulsing between them was overwhelming, sending heat spiraling through her.

She memorized his taste like she was savoring the unexpected treat of a favorite childhood candy. In the future, when she tasted a mix of mint and sugar, it would remind her of Jack.

At this moment, he was weaving his way into the fabric of her being with nothing more than a kiss. She pulled back to look at him, curious if he was as affected as her.

To her astonishment, he looked even more shaken. His strong cheekbones were tinged with pink. His eyes blazed but were also a bit hazy like he might have forgotten his own name.

She liked the thought of causing that kind of reaction in a man and in this man in particular.

"Does that answer your question?" she asked.

"It answers one and inspires a host of others." He leaned in and pressed open-mouthed kisses to the underside of her jaw. "More specifically, how much time do you have, Annalise?"

"In the grand scheme of things?" She barely recognized the teasing note in her voice.

Jack nipped at the corner of her mouth. "In the grand scheme of the next hour anyway."

"What a relief."

He pulled back and frowned.

She tried to control her smile. "I thought you were going to say in the next five minutes. We'd have a bit of a disagreement if that were the case."

"Mmm. I'm sure we'll have plenty of disagreements," he told her, using his thumb and forefinger to open the first button on her floral-patterned cardigan. "But they won't be about whether I have enough time to satisfy you. Let there be no doubt about that."

She had no doubt.

"Tell me you have time right now." He dipped one finger inside her collar, tracing it along her throat.

Yes, this man would do amazing things with his callused hands and she wanted to experience every one.

"I'll *make* time," she said.

"Even better."

Instead of claiming her mouth again, he scooped her into his arms.

"Jack, I'm too old for this. I can walk to a bedroom."

"I can carry you just as easily."

She drew her tongue along his throat, groaning in pleasure at the hint of salt on his skin.

He lost his footing for a second. "Now if you're gonna do that..." His chest rumbled with a laugh. "We'll likely end up in a messy pile on the kitchen floor."

"We need a bed."

"Debatable." He kicked open the bedroom door. "We're

going to begin there, but I have plans for you that may involve a variety of surfaces."

He gave her bottom a little squeeze. "A variety of positions."

"Oh," she breathed. It was something she hadn't expected to hear so soon after her divorce, but she liked it. She liked it very much.

He drew back the thick duvet and lowered her onto sheets that she would have sworn were high-thread-count Egyptian cotton by their softness.

Jack might be a simple man in some respects, but evidently appreciated quality. She hoped she wouldn't disappoint him.

"You're thinking," he said as he smoothed the hair away from her face.

"I'm always thinking." She tried for a flirty smile, but it felt a little wobbly at the edges. "Right now, I'm thinking about you naked."

"Liar." He leaned down and kissed her, slow and deep, as if he wanted to reassure her.

It worked because her doubts couldn't hold a candle to the pleasure that Jack's mouth against hers produced.

"But we'll go with that, as long as we go together."

Annalise lifted to a sitting position and began to undo the rest of the buttons on her sweater. She wanted to appear confident. It wasn't as if she were insecure about her body. She'd worked out religiously during her marriage and since the divorce…well, the truth was she could probably stand to gain a few pounds at this point.

"You're beautiful," he said as he stripped, much more efficiently than her. She couldn't imagine Jack Grainger being self-conscious a second of his life.

And there was no reason for him to be. His chest was

hard planes and lean muscle. A scar just below his ribs marred the perfection of his burnished-gold skin. She wanted to know the story behind each mark.

She wanted too much from Jack already.

"Compliments make me uncomfortable," she said, not bothering with one of her usual brash comebacks. If Jack was going to choose her, she wanted him to know exactly who he was getting. The real Annalise. The woman she was only beginning to discover.

His gaze skimmed over her like a caress. "You'll get used to it, sweetheart. Because I'm not shutting up." The desire in his whiskey-hued eyes trapped her as sure as a hunter's snare.

It felt powerful to be wanted by this man.

For a moment, she questioned the wisdom of getting involved with Jack. It would complicate her already chaotic life.

But when he joined her on the bed, his body fitting to hers like he'd been built to hold her, Annalise stopped thinking and worrying. There would be time for that later. Right now, she concentrated on the electric shock waves of pleasure Jack's touch produced.

She loved the feeling of his weight on her and lost herself to all the ways her secret fantasies—and some she hadn't even imagined—were coming true in Jack's arms.

CHAPTER EIGHTEEN

Shauna carried a second pitcher of margaritas to the front porch the following night.

"Being your neighbor is going to make me fat," Annalise said as she scooped a chip into the chunky guacamole Shauna had placed on a small table between the chairs.

"I'm going to get even fatter than I already am," Meghan blurted before Shauna could answer.

She stared at the younger woman in shock, noticing Annalise had paused with the chip midway to her mouth and was also staring.

"I was joking," Annalise said, "and you clearly aren't fat. You should not be concerned in the least about your weight. It's the most ridiculous thing I've heard in a while, and my entire existence borders on preposterous."

Sometimes when Annalise spoke, Shauna forgot they were now friends and was intimidated by the cultured blonde's inherently snobbish demeanor. Annalise had a way of looking down her nose that made a person worry they'd tucked their skirt into their underpants and were flashing their private bits to the world.

Shauna placed the margarita pitcher on the table and surreptitiously touched a hand to her bottom to make sure her skirt was in the right place.

It didn't seem that Annalise meant to be terrifying. It

came naturally to her; she was much kinder and a better friend than Shauna imagined.

"I *was* joking," Meghan insisted.

"You weren't joking, and we don't want to hear that kind of talk. You are beautiful exactly the way you are."

"Say it again for the people in the back," Shauna agreed, pouring each of them another drink. "Who messed with your confidence so badly?"

"My mother," Meghan answered without hesitation or emotion.

"Wow."

"She *tried* to mess with it. I'm fine with who I am."

"You can do better than fine," Shauna told her.

Meghan rolled her eyes. "That's easy for you to say, nibbling on the corner of a chip like one of those wild pony girls."

Shauna blinked while Annalise looked at her curiously. "I'm not familiar with the term *wild pony girl*. Is that like a buffalo gal?"

"I've never ridden a horse in my life." Shauna lifted her hands, feeling the need to say the words even if she wasn't sure why she was defending herself.

"You both fit the bill," Meghan said, looking somewhat sheepish. "Although it's my term for a certain type of woman. A wild pony girl is beautiful and effortless without even realizing it. She has long legs, thick hair cascading everywhere and total confidence. She's nothing like me."

"Stop." Shauna shook her head. "You have your own style. You know who you are and don't need to saddle up for any of it. For the record, very little in life is effortless. It's an optical illusion."

She held up a hand when Meghan would have argued. "I'm a single mom with no family support structure. Until a couple of years ago, I was living paycheck to paycheck, stretching every dollar to save for a house. It's a wonder the whole fabric of my life didn't rip apart at the seams."

Annalise tipped her glass in Meghan's direction. "Let go of whatever arbitrary standards your mother held you to. Trust me. It isn't worth trying to live up to them."

Meghan sighed. "Honestly, I thought I had released them. I guess all that screaming into my pillow didn't work."

"The past has a way of popping up at the most annoying times," Shauna said, thinking of her demons. As much as the boys enjoyed having Flynn around, his presence threatened to unleash feelings that she'd thought were locked away.

"Does this sudden preoccupation with pony girls have anything to do with Walker?" Annalise asked with a knowing smile. "I can guarantee that man likes you just as you are."

"No need to compare yourself to a horse," Shauna added with a laugh.

Meghan shook her head but didn't join in the joke, which bothered Shauna. "Walker and I are just friends. I'd be setting myself up for disappointment if I pretended otherwise."

"I don't know about that," Annalise mused. "Plus, you might have a whole bunch of fun on this side of the disappointment. I'm coming to realize fun is underrated."

Shauna sat forward as she studied Annalise. She seemed more relaxed, and not just as a result of the margaritas, although they didn't hurt.

"Something's different about you," she said to Annalise.

"No." Annalise's denial felt forced. "I want Meghan to understand that none of us is totally what we seem on the outside. As you said, Shauna, it's not effortless. It would be nice if we could see ourselves the way the rest of the world did."

"Not denying that," Shauna said slowly, still scrutinizing the woman. "But you're not the same."

"I'm letting my hair go back to its natural color." Annalise tugged on the long ends.

"I'm not talking about your hair. You seem less like you have a stick up your butt."

Annalise let out a derisive sniff. "I never had a stick up my butt."

"You seem relaxed," Meghan said over her salted rim.

"Satisfied," Shauna agreed. "Like you've had great sex recently. How is that possible?"

Annalise rolled her eyes. "I can't believe—"

Meghan gasped, drawing their attention. "Jack," she whispered, sounding scandalized.

"You two need to lay off the margaritas." Annalise had slipped back to her heavy Southern drawl. Shauna suspected the thick accent might be her tell. "Why would you think that?"

"You're not denying it." Shauna pointed the corner of a chip at Annalise.

"Do I need to deny such a ridiculous suggestion?"

"Not if it's true," Shauna answered.

Meghan had gone from looking scandalized to intrigued. "I knew it. It's the whole Sam and Diane thing."

Shauna couldn't help being distracted by the random comparison. "Do you mean Jack and Diane from the song? 'Two American kids growing up—'"

Meghan shook her head. "Sam and Diane from that show *Cheers*. My grammy loved it."

"Never heard of it," Annalise muttered.

"Cheers," Meghan repeated. "The bar in Boston where everybody knows your name."

"Gotcha," Shauna said.

Annalise nodded. "Yeah, I know what you're talking about now, but I don't go to bars."

Shauna wondered exactly what was in the tequila she'd used to make the margaritas. She hadn't been this confused by a conversation—or had so much fun simply hanging out—in forever. "What does that have to do with—"

"The main characters, Sam and Diane, were always at each other's throats, like you and Jack. But there was also a whole mess of sexual tension mixed in."

"Like you and Jack," Shauna added.

Annalise frowned at her empty margarita glass but placed it on the table instead of pouring a refill. "Can we change the subject?"

"You're still not denying it." Shauna punched a finger in the air and then demanded, "Tell us you didn't have sex with Jack Grainger."

Annalise scoffed, and for a moment, Shauna thought they'd gotten it wrong.

Then Annalise dropped her head into her hands, pale hair falling like a curtain around her face. "It was an itch we both had to scratch to get it out of our systems."

Shauna noticed Annalise's graceful fingers trembling slightly. "Is he out of your system?"

Annalise closed her eyes and scrunched up her face as if she were in pain. "Not in the least."

"How did it happen?" Meghan asked. "When did it happen? I mean, I know how—the mechanics of how it happened. Like with Sam and Diane. They first did it in season—"

"Okay, enough about TV shows," Shauna announced.

"All three of us have been relying too heavily on just getting by. This is real and fun and I want all the juicy details."

"I can't give you juicy details."

"Of course you can. That's what girlfriends do."

"Are you going to give us juicy details about Flynn?"

Shauna felt her eyes go wide. "How did you know?"

Meghan made a sound that was a cross between a yelp and a yodel. "You have juicy details, too? Everybody has juicy details but me."

"Because you won't make a move on Walker," Annalise said. "But we'll deal with that in due time." She turned to Shauna. "You slept with Flynn? Your baby daddy. The love of your life."

"I never told you he was the love of my life." Shauna took a big gulp of her margarita. "I haven't admitted anything."

"Yeah, you kind of did," Meghan said.

"I'm not giving details. We were scratching an itch, just like you and Jack."

Annalise flashed a knowing look. "How'd that go for you?"

"It's like I'm covered in poison ivy welts. I want to scratch all day long."

There was silence on the porch in response, and Annalise said, "I think poison ivy might get a bad reputation."

Shauna burst out laughing. "Poison ivy doesn't get a bad reputation."

"But it feels so good when you scratch." Annalise flashed a Mona Lisa grin.

"You're making me want poison ivy," Meghan said. "That's not right."

Shauna pointed at Annalise. "I think you should talk more, and I should talk less."

"Why?" Annalise narrowed her eyes.

"This all started with you. I wouldn't have said a word if you hadn't been sitting over there looking loose-limbed and satisfied."

"Are you satisfied, Shauna?" Meghan asked. "Flynn's intimidating, but he looks like he knows his way around a woman's body."

"Oh, he knows his way," Shauna agreed. "My body is satisfied. My heart and mind are anxious. If things don't work out with Jack, Annalise can walk away."

"There's nothing to work out," Annalise protested. The light had started to wane, and it bathed the sophisticated mother of two in golden light. That light didn't hide her discomfiture at the suggestion of feelings between her and Jack Grainer. Shauna didn't push it because she didn't want the same scrutiny in response. "It was purely physical. He doesn't want anything more. Neither do I."

"Sure, sure," Shauna agreed. "Flynn will be part of my life going forward. At least I think he will if he doesn't take off again." She slumped forward and held her head in her hands. It was easier to talk to the floor than to make eye contact with her friends. "I slept with a man I don't completely trust. One who will break my heart if I'm not careful. He could hurt my boys, and I'd have to kill him."

"I'll bring the shovel if it gets to that point," Annalise said, drawing Shauna's gaze.

Meghan pointed a chip in her direction. "I've got a shovel, too."

Shauna laughed. "I appreciate both offers, but I hope I'm not going to have to bury a body." She pressed her hand to her forehead. "It was a terrible mistake."

Meghan choked on the chip she'd just swallowed. "Did you tell Flynn that?"

"No, because I was loose-limbed and satisfied at the

time. Now that I have more clarity on the situation, I'm determined it can't happen again. Are you and Jack going to happen again?"

Annalise shrugged. "No. Maybe. Probably. I sure hope so. It was that good."

"Pour me another margarita." Meghan's voice was a plaintive whine. "I don't need juicy details. I can imagine them based on the tone of your voice."

"It's everything you can imagine and more." The enigmatic smile returned to Annalise's face.

"Hey, Mom."

All three women startled when Trey came around the corner of the house.

"The twins want to make s'mores."

Annalise's grin broadened. "The twins do?"

He rolled his eyes. "Well, I wouldn't say no to a s'more."

"Is your homework finished?"

"Yep."

"Do you promise to take a shower as soon as the s'more making is done?"

"Also yep."

Annalise sat back in her chair. "If it's okay with Shauna, it's okay with me."

Shauna nodded. "Fine with me."

The boy pumped his fist in the air. It wasn't only Jack who had elicited a change in Annalise. She was more relaxed with Trey and Margo and treated Shauna like a real friend.

"Grab the supplies from our kitchen," Annalise told her son. He ran toward the back of the house, shouting for the other kids.

"You've got s'more supplies?" Shauna raised a dubious brow. "Marshmallows leave people sticky."

She knew Annalise wasn't a fan of any sort of mess.

"I'll deal with sticky." Annalise stuck out her tongue in a playful gesture. "Right now, I'm going to give you a run for your money in the mom-of-the-year category."

"There's root beer in the fridge." Trey had appeared again at the corner of the front yard, huffing mightily. "Can we make floats, too?"

"Your teeth will rot away, but we might as well go for the gusto," Annalise said and they all laughed—even the boy—because there was no heat to her admonishment. She was teasing her son, and the new sort of sweetness in their interaction was obvious. It made Shauna's heart happy.

"I'll grab the s'more skewers and meet you out back," Shauna told them.

"I'll clean up everything here," Meghan offered. Annalise stepped off the porch and put an arm around her son as they headed toward the garage apartment.

Shauna turned to Meghan. "You are beautiful, and you don't want poison ivy."

Meghan drained the last of the margarita and then toasted her empty glass. "I'm nowhere near ivy of any kind, so it doesn't matter."

Shauna knew how hard it was to shrug off deep-seated beliefs about oneself. After all, she had no reason to worry that everyone she cared about in her life would eventually leave her, but the fear remained.

That was what happened when Shauna opened her heart.

As much as she wanted Meghan to see herself in a different light, the advice went two ways. She knew her friends would tell her she was a nice person, worthy of love and a good mother.

It wasn't as if she doubted the love she felt for her boys. It was bigger than she could have imagined, and she was trying to build a stable home yet lacked confidence in her ability.

But what if she suddenly went off the rails the way her mother had when she'd been a kid? What if the people she loved now rejected her?

That's why it would be easier if being with Flynn was nothing more than scratching an itch. That's why she needed to protect herself from being hurt by him. She tried to shrug off those worries as they watched the kids roast s'mores.

The boys were happy in their home and had friends—not just at school but also at the Haverfords. It made Shauna's throat clog with joyful tears to watch Zach and Timmy laugh and be kids without a care in the world. She'd never had that opportunity.

As most parents understood, the mood in a house ruled by soon-to-be six-year-olds could change in an instant. Or, in Shauna's case, it might change overnight.

The twins woke the next morning grumpy and arguing. She had a killer tequila headache that reminded her why she usually limited herself to one drink and restricted how much sugar her boys ingested.

She finally got them settled at the table, each with a plate of scrambled eggs, wheat toast and blueberries on the side when the doorbell rang.

Flynn stood on the other side, holding a box from Sunnyside Bakery.

"Who wants doughnuts?" he yelled before she could stop him.

Immediately, Zach and Timmy came running. They went from zero to out of control in less than ten seconds. Flynn looked stunned as the boys rushed forward, clamoring for doughnuts.

"A half each," she said, her pronouncement met with big-time moaning and groaning. "You need a healthy breakfast before school. Your brain won't function with all that sugar."

She leveled a glare at Flynn. "We don't have doughnuts for breakfast on weekdays."

"I didn't know."

"You should have asked," she snapped back. "Timmy, grab a knife from the utensil drawer, and I'll slice a doughnut."

The boys ignored her as they carried the box toward the kitchen, arguing over what flavors and who chose first.

"I'm not joking," she called as she followed, turning her back on Flynn. She figured he would stay, but that wasn't her concern at the moment. Her concern was making sure she didn't drop off her already rambunctious boys to school on a massive sugar high.

"Dad brought the doughnuts," Zach said, moving them out of the way when she tried to grab the box. "He gets to say how many we can have, not you. You're not the only boss now."

Shauna had a fairly even temper, but her son's words made her see red. She was angrier at Flynn and herself. She should have made the rules clear. Although this was uncharted territory, she'd never had to share parenting duties.

"You do not speak to your mother that way," Flynn interrupted, his voice booming so that all movement and noise completely stopped as she and her boys froze.

"You brought the doughnuts," Timmy said softly. His voice trembled. He backed away from the table then turned and fled up the stairs.

"I'm gonna brush my teeth." Zach eyed the doughnut box like it was filled with raw Brussel sprouts. "I had enough breakfast." Shauna was silent as he took his plate and cup to the sink.

"I'll finish cleaning up," she told him. "Go check on your brother."

She crossed her arms over her chest and rounded on Flynn. "What's wrong with you?"

"With me?" Flynn jabbed a finger into his chest then pointed it at her. "I was supporting you."

"By getting the boys riled up when we need to get to school then scaring the crap out of them? Nice support, Flynn."

"I didn't know doughnuts were off limits." He held up his hands. "Geez, Shauna. You would have thought I'd offered them a line of coke."

"Keep your voice down," she said on a hiss of breath. "We don't joke about drugs in this house."

"I wasn't trying to…" He let out a low growl. "There's another rule you should have clued me in on."

"No offense," she said as she picked up Timmy's abandoned plate, "but you aren't my top priority. I'm doing my best to raise these boys right. On my own."

"You're not on your own anymore."

Oh, how she wanted that to be true. Even though Flynn had made no promises, she had already opened herself to the possibilities of the future.

She should know better.

"They aren't used to someone shouting at them. It's not my way."

"Because you're a better person than me," he supplied. "A better parent. No one is arguing that."

"It's also not the point I'm trying to make."

"What's the point, Shauna? I don't know where my place is in your life. You allow me bits and pieces, but it's not enough. I want more."

She heard a crash from upstairs.

"It's okay, Mom," Zach yelled down. "Nothing got broken."

"You need to go," she told Flynn.

"My kids just ran away because, as you so generously put it, I scared the crap out of them. Don't I get a chance to smooth things over?"

She checked her watch. "You have exactly four minutes before we need to be out the door."

"I don't know how to smooth things over because they shouldn't talk back to you."

"Kids talk back."

"I got my butt kicked when I talked back. Declan, too."

"I'm not taking my parenting cues from how you were raised. You shouldn't either."

"That's all I've got."

"Go watch a few episodes of *Full House*," she suggested.

"Excuse me?"

"I'm joking, Flynn. Sort of." She gave a sharp shake of her head. This was new territory for both of them; maybe she could handle it better if he didn't set her heart racing. It would be easier to kick him out.

Maybe that would be easiest, but it wasn't the type of mother she wanted to be.

When the twins were born, she'd made a vow to always do her best. She might not have known much about being a good parent but believed that if she had set that intention, everything else could be managed.

Using Flynn's mistake to her advantage definitely was

not her best. In fact, she felt small and petty just considering it.

"Would you please finish cleaning up in here?" She gestured to the leftover fruit on the cutting board on the counter. "I'll check on the boys, and you can drive them to school. It will give you a chance to smooth things over."

"Don't you want to be there to make sure I don't screw up again?"

Yes.

"No. I trust you, Flynn." At least she wanted to.

"Thank you," he said softly and took a step forward like he might reach for her. She moved away. "Those boys are my family now, Shauna. I appreciate you seeing that, too."

She nodded and headed up the stairs, ignoring the fire that burned in her chest. Because she wanted to be included in Flynn's definition of family. And her pathetic need for love was bound to get her into more trouble.

CHAPTER NINETEEN

IT WASN'T EXACTLY a surprise to Meghan that the whole of Magnolia seemed to buzz with excitement over the upcoming concert. On any given weekend, the town bustled with activities to entertain locals and visitors, from festivals to art shows to seasonal markets.

Nothing that compared to an event featuring a bona fide star had ever hit the streets of Magnolia. The excitement felt almost palpable. However, she hadn't foreseen the number of people who seemed genuinely happy that the music department and art programs were being saved.

Parents she'd never met made a point of approaching her. Several of them had sheepishly admitted they'd wanted to pitch in with ideas to help keep the teachers but hadn't known how.

She'd become an expert at referring well-meaning community members to the volunteer spreadsheet Shauna had created. Meghan had honestly thought she was unique in her fear of branching out and trying new things or taking risks. Now she realized she wasn't even unique in that respect.

Plenty of people were afraid to stand up for something they believed in, fearing they might be judged or publicly fail. It made her appreciate Shauna and Annalise all the more. Two people who'd been through enough to be well within their rights to only want to take care of their own lives. But they didn't.

They were taking action and—

"Excuse me," a soft voice said as Meghan walked toward the hardware store downtown.

She turned to see a tall, graceful blonde with an amiable smile standing a few paces behind her.

"You're Meghan Banks, correct?"

She nodded.

"I'm Carrie Reed Scott. I don't think we've met."

Meghan swallowed. "I'm a big fan of your work," she told the local Magnolia artist. "Your dad, too, of course. I know he's famous around here, but your art is so…well… it feels personal."

"My paintings are personal." Carrie nodded, blushing softly like the compliment truly meant something to her. "I appreciate you recognizing that."

Meghan had known of Carrie and her famous father long before moving to Magnolia. Back when she'd come to visit her grandmother, they'd gone downtown, which hadn't been much to speak of at the time, but Grammy had liked to take her by Niall Reed's art gallery. The man was a famous painter and had several decades of wild commercial success for his overly sentimental depictions of coastal life.

There were collections of women in straw hats and prairie dresses holding the hands of children carrying bunches of wildflowers. Meghan hadn't exactly been able to relate to the sensibilities he portrayed, although looking back, she understood the appeal. Niall Reed's paintings had made her long for a life she'd never known, one where mothers adored their children.

She hadn't given him much thought. Upon returning to the town, she'd learned he'd died and his three daughters—all from different mothers—had reunited to claim an inheritance and were doing their best to revitalize Magnolia.

It's part of why she'd agreed to her grandmother's deathbed request that she make her life there. If the town continued to grow and thrive with more young people coming in, maybe she could be at the forefront of it. Perhaps Meghan could belong in a way she never had.

"Is there something I can help you with? Would you like tickets for the benefit concert?"

She heard the hum of a mower across the street in the town square and breathed in the scent of freshly cut grass. Spring had fully arrived, the days growing longer with local merchants setting up displays on the sidewalk and tourist activity picking up. There would be a massive influx for the fundraiser, and she couldn't help being intimidated by the thought of so many people coming together for her sake.

"We'll get tickets," Carrie assured her. "My husband, Dylan, is a huge Calloway Brothers fan, so he's excited to see Walker live. I wanted to talk to you about a more personal matter. I've been meaning to reach out, and I apologize that I haven't. To be honest, Meghan, I owe you a huge apology."

Meghan blinked. "I don't know how that's possible. We've never met."

"We're both artists. When I took over my father's gallery, I made a commitment to support art and artists in this community."

"You have an amazing selection." Carrie's gallery was about a block and half down the street, and Meghan often stopped in on Saturday mornings to browse the offerings. "I love how you share details about each artist and why you chose to display their work." Meghan wrinkled her nose. "Coming from a teacher, I also appreciate you offering merchandise at different price points. I've purchased a few birthday gifts from the gallery."

"Yet we've never met." Carrie frowned. "How is that possible?"

"Until I lost my job and my two friends decided to organize the fundraiser to save it, I wasn't exactly well-known outside the classroom."

"I suppose that's true," Carrie agreed.

Meghan tried to ignore the stab to her pride. She knew she wasn't memorable. Her association with Walker gave her some recognition, but Carrie's words made her wonder if the people who'd recently approached her were being genuine in their concern. Did they care about the program, or were they interested in supporting her because she might offer an in with Walker?

Maybe she was no better. She'd used her relationship with Gus to entice his uncle to help. Her palms started to itch like they did when an anxiety attack was coming on. Meghan could overthink the most straightforward things until she was swirling the drain in a deluge of confusion and panic.

"Are you okay?" Carrie asked, her tone gentle.

The concern sounded genuine, and Meghan detested the part of her personality that made her doubt and second-guess. She forced a smile. "I'm fine. I don't think you have anything to apologize for. I'm not a working artist."

"Maybe not, but you're more important. You're a teacher. We wouldn't have some great artists through history without a teacher or mentor somewhere in their past who made them believe in themselves and helped them love art. You show kids that art can be an outlet when things are tough."

Meghan nodded. "That's why I chose to teach. Not exactly as an outlet, but I enjoy introducing kids to the art world, even more than creating my own pieces. Although I still dabble from time to time."

"What's your preferred medium?" Carrie asked.

"Oil pastels," Meghan said, heart aching at the thought of the set her grandmother had purchased for her last Christmas. She'd been using them recently when she and Trey painted together and knew Grammy would have liked that.

"You should show your work in the gallery. We can give you a whole room or host an opening, maybe in conjunction with the fundraiser. Let people get to know you as an artist in your own right."

"No, thank you," Meghan said with a laugh. She touched her hand to her throat, which tightened at the memory of the few times she'd participated in art shows. "Another piece of why I became a teacher is that displaying my art and opening myself up to judgment… I was not a fan."

"I understand," Carrie said, and Meghan got the impression the other woman really did.

It seemed hard to believe because Carrie was quickly developing an impressive reputation that surpassed her famous father's—critically as well as commercially.

"My daughter is a baby," Carrie said. "I have a stepson, but he was in high school when he moved to Magnolia, so I didn't have any reason to be involved in the elementary school community. That was a mistake. I should have reached out to you long before now. We're starting to organize classes at the gallery, different from the sip-and-paint events I dabbled in when I took over running it. That was to keep the lights on. Now that we're financially secure, I want to offer anyone who wants it a chance to experience the creative process. Have you heard they're in talks to build a new Magnolia community center?"

"I'd read that." Meghan wasn't sure what it had to do with her.

"One component of the project will be an art school, and

I'd like your help running the children's section. I know you have a full-time career, and I've seen enough of what Annalise Haverford can do for an organization when she sets her mind to it. Job security won't be an issue if she's in your corner. But maybe you'd like to supplement your work or simply sit on the board at the community center?"

"I'm just an art teacher," Meghan said, automatically feeling stupid for what that statement revealed about her opinion of herself. Shauna and Annalise would have been all over her for devaluing her ability to contribute.

Carrie only smiled, which told Meghan even more. "I know we're basically strangers," she told Meghan. "But we might have more in common than either of us realize. I'm not making assumptions about your past, but I know what it's like to grow up feeling like you aren't good enough. It's easier to hide your light because if you reveal it, that opens you to judgment. The scariest thing is that people might think as poorly of you as you do yourself."

Meghan wanted to argue that she didn't think poorly of herself. She was a realist who understood her limitations. But were they actual obstacles or only made substantial by her mind? Had she built her life around them to have an excuse to hide?

"You believe I have something to offer outside of the classroom?" Her stomach fluttered at the idea.

"I do," Carrie said. "If you're willing to put yourself out there and find a place to belong. It's not easy, but the effort is worth the reward. Think about it, and let's talk in more detail."

Meghan nodded. "I appreciate your faith, whether or not I deserve it."

"There's only one way to find out if you do."

Meghan's hands continued to tingle, the sensation wing-ing from her fingertips to her toes. It didn't feel like nerves anymore. It felt like excitement.

"I hope I live up to your expectations." She also hoped she didn't sound foolish by admitting her lack of self-confidence.

Carrie squeezed Meghan's arm. "You will, and perhaps along the way, gain the same faith in yourself."

Meghan hoped so. They exchanged numbers, then said goodbye. She started toward the hardware store again with a warm glow filling her chest.

A crowd was gathering out front with a few people snapping photos and she wondered if Walker was there. Most of the Sunnyside Bakery customers had respected his privacy the other day and she hoped he wasn't having it intruded upon now.

She'd met Lily Dawes, who ran the store, and couldn't imagine that woman allowing any customer to be harassed, even in a good-natured way. Meghan's heart plummeted to her feet when she realized it wasn't Walker drawing the crowd.

Danielle Griggs stood in the center of a group of adoring fans, clearly not concerned for her privacy as she smiled and posed for pictures and selfies. Dani, a country starlet whose popularity rivaled Walker's, was even more beautiful in person than she appeared in press photos and music videos. She was a tiny slip of a woman with an enviable amount of cleavage on display in her form-fitting sundress. The hem was only a few inches lower than her adorable backside, and she wore a turquoise necklace and matching cowboy boots.

Not exactly a wild pony girl by Meghan's definition but stunning in her own way. Honey-colored hair fell down her back like she was a fairy-tale princess come to life, and her voice was just as angelic.

Meghan had never been a huge fan, even though Dani might be the most popular female performer in country music. She also happened to be Walker's ex-girlfriend, and the duet they'd recorded while dating still received an inordinate amount of airplay.

Who Walker dated was none of Meghan's business, but she'd been curious. Rumors had swirled for months before the accident that killed his brother about an impending engagement, and the press had a field day with reports of Walker and Dani's breakup after the tragedy.

Meghan started to turn and head in the other direction, but a heavy hand landed on her shoulder.

"Meghan Banks." The gravelly voice belonged to Malcolm Grimes, Magnolia's longtime mayor.

"Hello, Mr. Grimes."

He was a stately older gentleman with dark skin and a wide smile. As was his style, he wore a crisp button-down, khaki trousers and a bow tie with a brimmed straw hat.

"Call me Mayor Mal." He glanced at the crowd, then back to her and gave an approving click of his tongue. "Your fundraiser is drawing a swarm of attention to our fair town."

"I'm glad, but I don't think Danielle Griggs is here because of me."

"Not entirely," he agreed, "but she mentioned a potential role in the concert while she's staying with Walker."

Staying with Walker. Ugh. Probably in his bed. Meghan wondered if Annalise had known about this and conveniently chose not to mention it.

She understood why her friend might think the knowledge of Walker's beautiful girlfriend—ex or otherwise—coming for a visit would upset Meghan. Yet just a few days earlier, Annalise and Shauna had encouraged Meghan to share her feelings with the man. Thank God she hadn't. How embarrassing would that have been?

"Would you like to meet her?" the mayor asked. "She's real happy to pose for pictures and the like."

"Not today." Meghan took an automatic step back. "I don't want to prevent some of her real fans from having their moment." She swallowed back a tiny squawk of alarm when Danielle waved in their direction.

"Excuse me, folks," the singer announced in a silvery voice. "The elementary school's beloved art teacher has joined our informal gathering. Come and take a picture with me, Meghan."

Why did Danielle Griggs know her name? Meghan shook her head. "That isn't necessary—"

"I insist."

Meghan did a double take. Danielle's voice remained sweet and melodic, but there was a sharp undertone to it.

"I don't think she's used to being told no," Malcolm said with a deep chuckle.

"Apparently not." Meghan's anxiety ratcheted up several notches as she was propelled toward the gorgeous star.

She felt like an ogre standing next to Dani, especially when she heard the click of a dozen cameras. The fourth-graders were making clay castles in this unit, so she was wearing an old denim shirt and ratty tan cargo pants, both washable and easily relegated to the chore bin if they got ruined. Not that she was a fashionista on an average day, but if she'd known she was going to be getting her picture taken, she would have made a little effort—maybe dabbed on some lipstick.

Out of the corner of her eye, she saw Danielle's plump mouth sparkling as she smiled at the crowd. Her lips actually shimmered—what a trick.

"I'm going to send these photos to Avery for the town's Instagram and Facebook pages."

Meghan couldn't tell who'd made the announcement but shook her head. "That's not necessary."

"Of course you can." Danielle winked. "As I said, Walker and I haven't finalized the details of my participation, but I love a good charity case."

Meghan choked back a gasp.

"A charity concert," Dani amended quickly, but Meghan was pretty sure Danielle had said exactly what she meant the first time.

She had not imagined the woman's underlying hostility, although she still couldn't figure out why it was aimed at her.

"Be sure to tag me," Dani reminded the crowd.

"I don't want—"

Danielle pulled Meghan more tightly against her slim frame. For a wisp of a woman, she had a solid hold. "Come on now. Don't be shy. It's for a good cause. We're making all this fuss over you, after all."

Meghan hoped her smile didn't look as strained as it felt. She didn't like being the center of attention. The fundraiser was about the art and music programs at the school, not her personally. Did Danielle Griggs understand that?

A few more people snapped photos. The small crowd began to disperse when it became clear Danielle wanted to have a private conversation with Meghan.

Mayor Mal mouthed "good luck" before walking away.

"So you and Walker are friends?" Dani waved to the last of the fans, then linked her arm with Meghan's and began to stroll down the sidewalk as if the cameras were still following.

"I'm his nephew's teacher," Meghan clarified. "That's how we met."

Danielle paused and released her once they were away from prying eyes. "But you're the reason Walker agreed to do the concert." She looked Meghan up and down as if taking stock of a sack of potatoes.

"It wasn't exactly me who—"

"I heard he was doing it because he likes you."

"Did Walker tell you that?"

Danielle scrunched up her powdered nose. "Walker would have to take my calls for me to hear it from him."

"Oh." Meghan's brain whirled as she tried to process that bit of information. "I thought you were visiting because—"

"I'm here because if Walker performs again, he engages with his former life. Unfortunately, after the accident, it felt as though everything he associated with his brother was left behind." She flashed a brittle smile. "Old friends included."

"I'm sure he's coping as best as he can."

"Mmm. Walker is special. I'm *sure* you realize that."

"He's a good uncle," Meghan answered. What else could she say? Of course she knew Walker was special, just like Dani was special. Unlike ordinary Meghan.

"I feel loads better now that we've had this little talk," Danielle revealed. "Maybe Jack had it wrong. Maybe Walker is doing this because of his adorable nephew. Kind of weird but cute."

Meghan wanted to react, but she was too busy trying not to have her feelings hurt by the idea that Jack had been talking about her. Not that he owed her anything.

Walker didn't either, for that matter. But it wasn't only Annalise and Shauna who Meghan felt had become her friends. She liked Walker, of course, but she also liked Jack quite a bit. He had a hard shell, but she'd thought he was hiding a teddy-bear heart underneath.

Maybe she'd been wrong. She wondered if Annalise would care. Probably not if it ensured Danielle Griggs's participation in the concert. No doubt they'd sell out with only Walker but adding Dani to the bill guaranteed more press coverage.

"It was nice to meet you, Maggie."

"Meghan."

"Yeah. I need to go now. Walker is expecting me." The woman studied Meghan more intently as if trying to gauge Meghan's reaction to her words.

A benefit to handling a lifetime of anxiety and insecurity was that Meghan could keep a straight face through almost anything. She'd long ago learned to hold it together in public so she could fall apart in the privacy of her own home. Today would be no different.

"Nice to meet you. I'm a big fan," she lied, then watched Danielle Griggs sashay down the sidewalk in the opposite direction.

CHAPTER TWENTY

THE NEXT MORNING, Annalise stood in Walker's kitchen, grinding her teeth so aggressively, she thought they might turn to dust.

How the mighty had fallen, she thought as she watched Danielle Griggs frown at the breakfast placed before her moments earlier. Or maybe "pride goeth before a fall" was more apt to describe this situation.

In her former life, Annalise had mistakenly believed financial security and social influence justified her overinflated sense of pride. Now it felt like she'd plummeted into a farcical alternate reality, proving she was as common as her humble beginnings.

"Still not right," Danielle said, her mouth pulled into a tight moue. "I can't possibly eat eggs that are so rubbery. And would you be a dear and cut the melon into smaller slices? My teeth are sensitive."

"You told me the previous two batches of eggs were too runny." Annalise picked up the plate, sorely tempted to dump the scrambled lot onto Dani's overly processed head of golden hair.

When Meghan had told Annalise and Shauna the previous evening that Walker's ex-girlfriend was in town, Annalise hadn't given it much thought.

Danielle Griggs's name had come up when she and Jack started the initial planning for the benefit concert, and Jack had made it clear that the country music starlet would not be invited as a guest for the event.

Annalise had assured Meghan that if the woman was in town and looking to cause trouble, Jack could be relied on to handle it.

He was a man who could be trusted. His word was gold. Annalise was more like gold crepe paper, tissue thin and easily shredded.

Dani had come down minutes after Annalise arrived at Whimsy Farm. Jack was nowhere to be found and Walker had not returned from dropping Gus at school.

If Annalise didn't know better, she would guess the two men were avoiding the house and the inevitable interaction between Dani and Annalise.

With good reason.

Dani had immediately started issuing orders and making demands. A specific breakfast order, details on how she took her coffee, complaints about the linens on her bed and the house's temperature, as well as the products she expected Annalise to procure for the guest bathroom.

Annalise decided she would display the new leaf she'd turned over and kill the little diva with kindness.

She might not possess that much kindness.

Walker walked into the kitchen, offering Annalise a sheepish wave. "You two have met, I take it."

"Would you like some eggs?" Annalise pointed to the trio of plates sitting on the counter. "There are plenty to choose from."

"Why are there so many?" Walker looked honestly baffled, and Annalise saw Danielle shift in her seat. If she wasn't mistaken, the pixie-sized blonde tugged at her V-neck silk pajama shirt to display her ample assets better. Annalise could understand how Walker might be distracted. Even she was having a hard time looking away.

"Exactly," Dani piped up since Annalise hadn't answered right away. "I know you like a clean house, Walker. The help in Magnolia doesn't meet the standards that Rosie set back in Nashville. Maybe she'd be interested in relocating?"

Annalise didn't rise to the bait, assuming Rosie was Walker's former housekeeper. Annalise might be humiliated by her fall from the upper echelons of small-town society, but she worked hard and was proud of a job well done.

She pulled the now-half-empty carton of eggs from the refrigerator. "Goldilocks over there is picky about the consistency of her eggs. We're going on scramble number four."

"I have a discerning palate," Danielle protested, batting her eyelashes at Walker.

"Would you like to cut her melon into smaller pieces?" Annalise handed Walker, whose mouth had thinned into a tight line, a knife from the block on the counter. "Her tiny teeth can't handle the bigger sections."

"No more eggs." He shook his head as he took the knife. "Dani, cut your own damn fruit and make your own breakfast if you have an issue. I'm not running a bed and breakfast. Annalise doesn't work for you."

"She works for you," Dani said, closing her fist around the knife and pointing it in Annalise's direction. "She's your housekeeper, and I'm a guest in your house."

"An uninvited guest," Walker clarified. "I apologize, Annalise." He took a plate of eggs and sat at the island instead of joining Dani at the kitchen table. "These eggs are wonderful."

She smiled despite her residual anger at Danielle Griggs. "I'm sure they're cold."

"Still wonderful." He turned to Dani. "Annalise is managing this house so she can become familiar with the place and how we live."

"Why would she need to be familiar with how you live?"

"Because she's going to direct the redesign of the interior. I wanted to get Gus settled before we started construction, but he likes it in Magnolia. Since we're going to stay here full-time, I want the house updated and better suited for us."

"I thought she was organizing the fundraiser."

"Along with Jack." Walker nodded.

"Hello, Dani."

Annalise nearly dropped the eggs she was returning to the refrigerator at the sound of Jack's deep voice. She turned to watch as he purposefully closed the back door. The man did everything with care and an attention to detail that made Annalise's knees go weak just thinking about it.

"Jack." Dani rolled her eyes. "Nice to see you still living off the Calloway coattails."

"You look well, Danielle," Jack said smoothly even though his eyes had hardened to granite. Despite her annoyance that he hadn't warned her about country-music Goldilocks arriving for a visit, Annalise suddenly felt defensive on his behalf. "When are you leaving?"

A laugh burst from Annalise's throat that she tried to cover with a cough.

"Not going to get rid of me so easily this time, Jackie-boy." Danielle picked up her phone and held it aloft. "Take a look at the Magnolia town Facebook page. Isn't this adorable? There's a photo of me with Walker's mousy little—"

She chuckled as if she'd made a joke. "Well, not exactly little, although the camera adds ten pounds. But the mousy art teacher you all are so intent on rescuing."

Meghan hadn't mentioned a photo op to Annalise. That wasn't good.

Jack moved toward the table and swiped the phone from Dani's manicured fingers. "Why the hell does this post say you are one of the special guests at the benefit concert?"

Walker made a sound that sounded somewhere between a groan and a growl. "Not happening, Dani."

"Look at the post, boys. It's got over a thousand likes and has been shared hundreds of times. Our adoring public wants to see us together again, Walker."

"Not a snowball's chance in hell," Jack muttered.

Danielle's icy blue eyes narrowed. "I wasn't talking to you, Jack."

He snorted. "You should have talked to me before you staged a ridiculous publicity stunt, Dani. Good lord, Meghan looks like she's afraid you might eat her alive."

"Were you rude to her?" Walker demanded, and there was an edge to his voice Annalise hadn't heard before.

Dani sat up straighter, clearly picking up on it as well. Annalise wanted to warn Walker to back off. She knew how women like Danielle Griggs operated. She'd been one back in the day.

If Dani thought that Walker cared about Meghan as more than just Gus's teacher, she'd go after the other woman like a tiger stalking a baby deer. The kind of innocent fawn that still had spots, sweet and defenseless.

"I'm never rude," Dani said, pushing back from the table and rising to her feet. "Unlike the two of you. I came all this way to discuss how best I can contribute to your worthwhile cause. Now I hear you don't want me involved." She pressed a hand to her chest. "It cuts deeply. I'll respect your decision, but I'm disappointed, Walker."

"You'll get over it," Jack told her.

“Yes, but will the fans?”

Annalise understood what it meant when people used the phrase “hear a pin drop.” That’s how it had been when Jonathan first told her and the kids that he was in a bit of hot water with the authorities.

The coward had chosen to share the news with Trey and Margo at the same time he told Annalise, rightly figuring that she wouldn’t cause a scene that would upset their children.

Danielle Griggs didn’t have that luxury with these two men.

“This has nothing to do with you, Dani.” Walker moved until he stood directly in front of the other woman.

Annalise felt as though she were witnessing something she shouldn’t, something private.

“There is nothing between us anymore.”

Dani’s smile remained fixed, but her fists clenched at her sides. “I can help. Tell me you aren’t going to allow this worthwhile cause to suffer because we have a few unresolved disagreements in our past.”

“Disagreements.” Walker spit out the word like it was bile in his mouth.

“I’m sorry, Walker. For all of it.” Either the woman was a brilliant actress or she actually meant it. The apology sounded sincere, even if Annalise didn’t understand it. She also wasn’t a top-notch judge of character.

“Okay,” Walker said simply.

“I think—” Jack began, but Walker held up a hand.

“This is on me, Jack,” he said without turning. “One song, Dani.”

“It has to be ‘When Stars Collide,’” she answered immediately. “You know that.”

Annalise was surprised Danielle didn’t push for an extended set. She had at least a dozen top ten hits, and several had crossed over to the pop charts. Annalise wasn't the biggest fan, but it was hard to avoid hearing Danielle Griggs's raspy soprano.

Her summer anthem "Good Girl, Bad Reputation" had been played everywhere last year.

Annalise recognized the gleam in Dani's gaze as she studied Walker. This had nothing to do with Dani wanting to court the publicity the concert would generate. That was small potatoes for a star of her magnitude. It was just as clear that Dani believed performing their Grammy-nominated duet from a couple of years earlier might give her the access to her former flame she clearly wanted.

Annalise realized she was holding her breath. Walker was laid-back in most situations, but she knew he still harbored deep demons from his brother's death. Jack worried about Walker's participation in the concert, his first as a solo artist.

Annalise wanted to be sensitive, but she also needed him to deliver a stellar performance. Meghan's future and the opportunity to repair much of Annalise's reputation were riding on it.

For all she knew, Dani could irritate him enough that he'd walk away. Where would they be if that happened?

"You can have your duet," he said after a weighted moment, "but that's all. Don't fool yourself into believing it means something about us."

"It's going to be enough that we're together again on stage," Dani assured him. "We're better together, Walker."

Jack muttered a curse that would have made a sailor blush, but Danielle was completely focused on Walker. The music industry wasn't for the faint of heart, and this moment made it abundantly clear why Danielle Griggs was such a success.

She had plenty of talent but even more nerve. In another

situation, Annalise would admire her, but at the moment all she could only think of was how this would affect Walker and Meghan.

Dani's smile turned sweet once again. "I have a few engagements on my schedule over the next several weeks, but I'm happy to postpone them so we can rehearse. I can help in other areas with logistics or marketing. Whatever you need, I'm here for you."

Annalise wanted to retch.

"We don't need your help," Jack said, his tone so icy it made a shiver run along Annalise's spine.

"Still not talking to you, Jack."

"That's fine because I only need you to listen." He rapped two fingers on the tile countertop. "Pack your bags and go, Dani."

"We'll do a run-through of the song this morning," Walker said, ignoring the two sniping at each other like this wasn't his first rodeo.

"Then we'll see you the weekend of the concert," he clarified after Dani let out a little yelp of excitement. "If we need to go over something in the meantime, we can do a video conference."

"Or you can come to Nashville and stay with me for a few days," Dani suggested. "We could write and—"

"Don't push me, Danielle. It will not end well for either of us."

Dani immediately nodded. "This is going to be great. A reunion of sorts."

"Not of any sort," Jack muttered.

Walker ran a hand through his hair, and Annalise could see how much it was taking out of him to be the mature one in this situation. "Let's head out to the studio. We'll get this over with so you can be on your way."

Annalise thought Dani might argue again and plead her case to stay, but she must have understood Walker had reached his limit.

"That sounds perfect," the other woman agreed, then flicked a glance at her empty coffee mug and the small bowl of fruit that still sat on the table.

"Can you take care of this mess?" she asked Annalise with a sickeningly sugary smile. "While you're thinking about redecorating and such, of course."

Annalise wanted to lash out, but that wasn't her place right now. Walker had done her a favor with the interior design comment and helped her save a bit of face when, in fact, they hadn't discussed any such thing. She had no idea if they actually would.

"I'll take care of everything. Can I get you anything else, Walker?" She wished there were a way to let him know how much she appreciated what he was doing without revealing her gratitude to Danielle.

Walker shook his head then walked out the back door, Dani babbling as she trailed along.

Jack had moved to the bay window on the other side of the table. His arm rested on the pane overhead, muscles bunching under the soft fabric of his Western shirt as he stared out to the bright, sunshiny day.

The temperatures were steadily rising, with a balmy spring giving way to the heat and humidity that would spend the summer resting over the town like a blanket.

"She's something else," Annalise said as she picked up the fruit bowl and coffee cup.

"Something vile and sly," Jack clarified. "I knew this was a horrible idea. The whole thing is a mistake."

"At least," Annalise felt compelled to point out, "it's only one song, and she wasn't wrong about the fans. They're going to eat it up."

"It's not about the fans. I could give a rat's ass about the fans right now."

"Managers probably aren't supposed to say or even think that."

Jack turned to face her, his brown eyes blazing with molten anger. "You have no idea the sort of trouble this could cause Walker."

There was something in his tone that set her temper on edge. She'd too quickly been lulled into believing that she and Jack were on the same page. That could be just the mind-blowing sex talking. Perhaps it showed that Annalise had learned nothing from Jonathan's betrayal. She shouldn't trust men so easily.

"You seem particularly hot and bothered by the thought of Danielle Griggs exerting her female wiles over Walker. He's a grown man, Jack. I'm sure he can handle it."

She was certain of no such thing, but now wasn't the time for uncertainty. "Is it possible you doth protest too much because there's some history between you and Goldilocks?"

If life were a cartoon reel, smoke would have swirled from Jack's ears. Annalise wasn't sure why she'd decided to poke at him other than her own heart was pricked by his reaction to Dani.

She'd foolishly let him into her heart when it was stupid to believe she had a future at this man's side. He'd given her no indication he wanted that. Jack had made his priorities clear, and she wasn't one of them.

"My only history with Danielle Griggs was cleaning up the messes she left in her wake and making sure she didn't pull both Nash and Walker under. You can joke about her penchant for Goldilocks indecision, but that woman is a human riptide."

Alarm bells went off in Annalise's brain. "What does that mean?"

His broad chest expanded with a slow breath. "During the time Dani was dating Walker, she had an affair with Nash."

"Oh, no." Annalise grimaced. "I assume Walker knew about it."

"Yes. It happened shortly after 'When Stars Collide' hit number one on the country chart." He closed his eyes as if reliving the painful memory. "Nash was my best friend, and Walker idolized his older brother. But Nash Calloway was not a perfect man."

"No one is perfect."

"Nash had more than his share of issues, and Walker felt responsible for some of them. Nash spent his childhood shielding Walker from their father's temper. You wouldn't know it if you'd met him. Nash was the kind of guy who could light up a room, but he had a darker side. He didn't care one whit about Dani. He took her to his bed because he was jealous of Walker's success outside the band."

"I believe you, but it's difficult to fathom." Annalise shook her head. "That is not the impression Walker gives of his adored big brother."

"Walker refuses to admit the kind of man Nash was," Jack said quietly. "It's hard to tell if he even has it straight in his own mind. I know he misses his brother, but since Nash's death, Walker has turned him into a saint—the best father, brother, and most talented musician. Nash was good at all those things but far from perfect. I'm afraid having Dani around is going to mess with Walker in a bad way."

"The fact that she's wormed her way into this benefit

concert doesn't sit well with me," Annalise admitted. "But you can't keep him in this bubble forever. You were the one who had a problem with the concert because it was distracting him from the real business of writing songs to fill his contractual obligations with the record company."

"Yeah. What's your point?"

"Magnolia is small potatoes compared to what Walker's going to face once he rejoins the country music world on a larger scale."

He studied her for a long moment, his eyes gentling ever so slightly. "It's not fair, you know?"

"There are a lot of things that aren't fair," she said with a cluck of her tongue. "What in particular are you referring to in this case?"

"You," he said, then cupped her cheek with one hand. "I'm referring to the fact that you're both beautiful and scary smart. You truly are a force of nature, Annalise Haverford."

His words soothed her previous anger like rubbing aloe on a sunburn. "You are, too. You just do the casual routine better than me."

"I've been the heavy from the first moment I met Nash. I was the straight man to his natural-born charmer. He used to say I could suck the fun out of any situation."

"I doubt that's true."

"It is, and I'm not sure it could be any other way. I ruined a marriage with my inability to trust." He pressed his forehead to hers. "I don't know what this is between us, but I don't want to ruin you."

"I'm not planning on letting you," she said even though part of her doubted whether she could stop it. Her feelings for Jack were a runaway train, and she was just trying not to lose purchase.

"I'm going to hold you to that, sweetheart," he told her and gently kissed her. The sweetness of it affected her almost as much as his slow, passionate kisses.

"You know what today is, right?" he asked as he eased away.

"Not really." She pretended to be ignorant of what he was talking about. "Dani's arrival threw me off my game. I have work to do now—"

"Your first riding lesson." His lips twitched. "I know you didn't forget."

"Maybe we should take a rain check."

"Stargazer is saddled and waiting for you. She's ready to go."

Annalise's stomach felt like a ton of bricks were weighing it down. "I'm not sure, Jack. Isn't it enough I'm letting Trey take riding lessons? He's the one who's horse crazy."

"You don't have to be afraid."

She made a face. "Of course I do. That fear keeps me safe."

"It keeps you in an invisible cage."

"Hey, Pot." She pantomimed holding a phone to her ear. "This is Kettle calling."

His grin widened as he took her hand and brushed a kiss over her knuckles. "You can do this, darlin'."

She wanted to make Jack proud. She wanted to make Trey proud and prove that she was stronger than the fears that ruled her life.

"I'll be at your side," he promised.

"Okay," she said before she lost her nerve. "Let me finish cleaning up. I'll meet you in the barn."

He nodded and kissed her again, and his touch gave her confidence. But she wasn't the only one who needed it.

"I'll be at your side during the fundraiser. I'm here for

you, Jack. For Walker and Gus, too. I don't know how much Walker can handle, but I believe with all my heart that the best way for you to support him is to let him figure it out."

He walked to the door and then turned to her. "I'm not good at relinquishing control, but I trust you, Annalise. You can trust me, too. We'll take care of each other."

The door shut behind him before she could answer, which was a blessing because his words brought tears to her eyes.

She knew what it was like to feel that every moment was a solitary battle, and she wanted something different for Jack. Just like she wanted something different for herself. Maybe together they could find it.

CHAPTER TWENTY-ONE

TWO HOURS LATER, Shauna offered Annalise a grateful smile. “Thanks for coming when I called.” She held up her left arm, the wrist now wrapped in a bubble-gum-pink cast. “I think I’m going to win the award for the clumsiest person in Magnolia.”

“I’m happy you called me,” Annalise said. “You’re lucky it’s only a sprain.”

“I don’t feel lucky,” Shauna muttered.

It had started as normal as any other weekday. She’d dropped the boys at school and then headed to the house where she was working on a mural for one dining room wall. She was satisfied with the progress, as was her client, and Shauna made the mistake of giving herself a mental pat on the back for managing her life so expertly despite Flynn’s exploding into it.

As if she’d summoned a different sort of crash, things went to hell minutes later. Her client’s goofy golden retriever had decided to chase a stray cat from the garden into the house like the animal had just stolen the dog’s favorite chew toy. The animals tore through the dining room, and the cat bounded up the stepladder Shauna balanced on as if Shauna would keep it safe.

The dog slammed into the bottom of the ladder, sending them to the floor. Shauna had been so busy trying to save the cat that she hadn’t noticed how she was landing.

She'd gone down on her left side, her wrist taking the brunt of the impact. Pain shot through her arm so swift and stabbing, it nearly made her nauseous.

Her client had been mortified and effusively apologetic as she'd driven Shauna to the ER. The older woman cried while Shauna gritted her teeth against the burning sensation in her arm. It hadn't hurt as badly as when she'd broken her leg skydiving last year, which seemed like a positive sign.

The woman had offered to stay, but Shauna sent her on her way to track down the stray—and unquestionably traumatized—cat, who was now hiding somewhere in the house.

The dog was locked safely in the laundry room, which upset the woman nearly as much as the accident. Frankly, Shauna didn't want to deal with it.

She'd thought about calling Declan, but he'd already spent more time than was fair helping her while she recovered from the skydiving injury.

Flynn was an obvious choice, but something stopped her from dialing his number.

She didn't want him to see her in this vulnerable position, so she'd called Annalise, honestly unsure whether the woman would even respond.

They were friends, but the kind of friends who shared a drink on the front porch or banded together for a good cause like saving Meghan's job. Were they close enough to be each other's emergency contact?

Annalise arrived within twenty minutes of Shauna reaching out, but as Shauna studied her friend, she wondered if something besides kindness had motivated Annalise to drop everything.

"I hope I didn't interrupt something important you were doing."

"Not at all." A blush crept up Annalise's neck and cheeks, and she studied the poster on the back of the exam room's door like it held all the secrets of the universe.

"Oh, my gosh." Shauna sat forward, carefully keeping her left arm raised at the elbow as the nurse had instructed. "Were you with Jack? Was there some morning delight going on?"

Annalise released a scandalized wheeze. "Nothing was delightful about my morning."

"You look guilty," Shauna insisted.

"What would I have to be guilty about?"

"I don't know. That's why I'm asking. Come on, Anna-banana, distract me from my pain. Be my Florence Nightingale."

"Do not call me that." Annalise's lips twitched, and some of the tension seemed to drain from her shoulders. "And enough with the dramatics. There's no big scandal involved. Jack was going to give me a riding lesson today."

Shauna frowned at the unexpected answer. "Is that code for something sexual? Riding lessons could mean—"

Annalise threw up her hands in exasperation. "It means exactly what it sounds like. Riding a horse."

"Do you remember that kitschy country song?" Shauna asked, tapping a finger to her chin. "Something along the lines of saving a horse and riding a cowboy. I think Jack fits the bill."

"What kind of drugs did they give you in here?" Annalise demanded with a startled laugh.

Shauna grinned in response. "This is all me, friend. Thank you again for coming and taking my mind off what an idiot I am. First my leg and now the wrist, although according to the doctor, I should be out of the cast in a week or so. Luckily, it's not my dominant hand."

"Are you planning to keep working?"

"I have to keep working. I lost so much income while I was recuperating over the holidays and that was with Declan taking over some of my projects. He's got his hands full with the bar and Beth, not that I would ask him. I'm tired of being dependent on people."

"I don't think your friends consider it dependent," Annalise told her. "I like that you called me. It was kind of a reverse rescue. Jack thinks I should learn to ride as a way to bond with Trey, and I'm a chicken."

"What's your deal with horses anyway? You're not afraid of anything."

"It turns out I've been fooling everybody, even you. I'm afraid of horses and love and failing my children and disappointing anybody who comes to rely on me and not standing up for myself." Annalise ticked off the list on fingers that were now neatly trimmed and devoid of polish. Shauna liked them better that way.

"Name a fear," Annalise said, lowering her hand, "and I bet I've made a home for it in my heart."

Shauna felt her gut clench. "This might sound unsympathetic, but it gives me great comfort when you reveal that you're human and not perfect."

"Are you joking? Compared to you, I'm a troll."

Shauna felt her eyes go wide, the residual ache in her wrist forgotten for the moment. "What on earth are you talking about?"

"You're everybody's favorite mother. You taught my daughter she could bake something other than store-bought cookie dough. You made my son actually like eating vegetables. He requested broccoli for dinner the other night. Who asks for broccoli?"

"It's good when you roast it in olive oil."

"You're genuinely kind and infinitely talented. If anyone has reason to feel intimidated, it's me." Annalise flipped a lock of thick hair behind her shoulder. "If you weren't clumsy as all get out and weirdly injury-prone, you'd be perfect."

Shauna bit the inside of her cheek, and when she didn't laugh at the joke Annalise was trying to make, the other woman shook her head. "What's wrong? What did I say? Did I offend you? It was supposed to be a—"

"I spent years of my childhood feeling inconvenient and out of place. I wanted to do the right thing so badly. I thought if I were perfect, somebody would want me forever. They never did. All I felt was weak and fragile. Now look at me." She glared at the cast. "I've done my best to make myself independent, so my boys would be proud. Yet I still wind up broken and needing help. Maybe that's just who I am."

"First, you're sprained, not broken." Annalise shook her head. "And if we're going to have a mutual admiration society for our strengths and acknowledge our weaknesses, then we're also going to bolster each other's spirits. That's what friends do."

Shauna sniffed and tried to take comfort in Annalise's odd pep talk. "We're real friends?"

"Real friends. As soon as you're discharged, we're going to the grocery. I'll teach you to pick out the tastiest items from the frozen food section that can be made with only one hand."

Shauna laughed. "That's helpful, I guess."

"Totally," Annalise confirmed in her Southern lilt. "Your boys will love me for opening up their culinary options, and you'll be able to handle it on your own."

Shauna nodded. "I want to handle things," she said quietly, unsure if that was the whole truth. It would be nice to have someone to depend on besides a friend—somebody who belonged to her. No matter how often she'd been rejected, it felt as though she hadn't been able to let go of the deep-seated need to belong.

She expected to see the doctor when the door burst open, but Flynn charged through instead.

"Why the hell didn't you call me?" he demanded.

"You know we're in a hospital," Annalise said, rising from her seat. "Shouting is generally frowned upon unless a person is in severe pain or pushing out a baby."

Shauna winced as he glared at her friend. Once again, Annalise didn't back down the way most people would in the face of Flynn's ire.

The two of them engaged in a standoff, then Annalise let out a slight sound of…well, understanding.

"So we're on the same page."

"Neither of you spoke," Shauna murmured, dumbfounded by whatever silent communication she was witnessing.

"Yes," Annalise conceded, "but we understand each other. You don't need me. I'll just head over to the grocery and pick up those items. You probably want to get home and nap or whatever."

"Whatever?" Did she think Shauna and Flynn were going to get it on with her casted arm in the way?

Flynn was practically twitching with anger. It seemed more likely that she'd be on the receiving end of a tongue lashing, but she knew for certain he'd never physically hurt her. As big and tough and angry as he could be, Shauna felt completely safe with Flynn Murphy.

She might be the only person on the planet to make that claim. He didn't look safe right now. He looked pissed as hell.

"I thought you said we were friends," she told Annalise, straightening on the exam table. "What kind of friendship move is this?"

"You're in good hands." Annalise lifted one of Flynn's giant paw-like hands. "You'll take care of her, right?"

Flynn grunted in response.

"You can't ditch me with him. You're the person I called. My ICE."

Flynn lifted a brow in question.

"In case of emergency," Annalise explained.

"I can be your ICE," he said.

Although his voice held no emotion, Shauna felt the words reverberate deep into her soul.

"I'm here if you need me," Annalise promised, "but you two have got this under control. Besides, we didn't even get into the fact that Walker Calloway's country Barbie ex-girlfriend is now going to be part of the benefit concert."

"Danielle Griggs?" Shauna gaped. "You need to stay. We need to talk. Flynn, I'm sorry but—"

He growled low in his throat.

"We'll talk later," Annalise insisted.

"I take back what I said about thinking you weren't afraid."

Annalise smiled and raised her hand in a wave as the door shut behind her.

Before Flynn could start in on whatever he wanted to say, the nurse returned. She went over the instructions and handed Shauna a printed copy.

"Is this your ride?" The nurse's sculpted brows lifted to her hairline.

"Not the one I'd planned on," Shauna told the woman.

"I'm her ICE," Flynn said simply.

Whether the nurse understood his meaning or was cowed by his menacing presence, Shauna couldn't say.

"Are you going to ride away with her on a motorcycle?"

One corner of his mouth…it wasn't exactly a smile… but it might have been a slight movement or maybe it was a figment of Shauna's imagination. "Not today. I brought my truck."

"Good," the nurse said, then turned to Shauna. "The pharmacists will tell you this, but you shouldn't drive while taking prescription pain medication."

"I'm good with over-the-counter," Shauna assured her.

"Just remember, you don't have anything to prove. If you need pain medication—"

"I have two little boys. I don't need pain medication. I need to be able to take care of them."

Flynn stepped forward. "I can take care of them."

This time it was Shauna who wanted to growl.

The nurse looked between them and smiled as she completed the paperwork.

"You have an appointment for a follow-up in one week."

"Will I definitely get the cast off then?"

"We'll see how the wrist is healing, but it's possible. Take care of her," she said to Flynn then touched his arm. "Whoa." She patted him with a bit more enthusiasm. "Somebody's been hitting the gym." She chuckled at her own joke.

Flynn kept his gaze on Shauna.

"Thank you for everything," Shauna said to the nurse.

"Have a good rest of your day. I'm guessing you will." The woman laughed again and then walked out of the room.

Shauna shifted her feet over the side of the exam table and stood. Flynn immediately reached for her good arm, but she shrugged away from his touch.

"I'm okay. This is a minor injury and inconvenience. It could have been worse."

"It's bad enough."

"How did you know I was here?"

"Your client called her husband, who happens to be a plumber doing some work at the bar. Declan called me. He couldn't leave, and Beth is in Nashville this week for classes, so I came. I would have come no matter what."

"Don't you have work?"

"It can wait. Why didn't you call me?" he asked again.

"I don't need to be rescued." Shauna grabbed her purse and pushed past him. "It barely even warranted a trip to the hospital."

"That's not what the woman whose dog nearly killed you told her husband."

"The dog didn't care about me. He was trying to kill a cat. Did she say what happened to the cat?" Shauna kept her gaze straight ahead as she walked down the hallway.

"Who gives a damn about the cat? I'm worried about what could have happened to you."

"I'm fine." Shauna kept her voice low because she didn't want to draw attention to herself. God, she hated drawing attention to herself. Here was another thing that would mark her as someone who found trouble or was found by trouble.

"Why are you being like this?" Flynn demanded.

"Why are you being like this?" she countered. "Where's your truck?" She'd walked out of the air-conditioned hospital into the heat of midday. The hospital was located about ten miles outside of town in an area that was quickly being developed for both commercial and residential use. The trees surrounding it weren't like the old oaks that dominated her neighborhood, but they'd take root and find their place.

Just like she had.

"It's over there."

He pointed to a section marked Reserved, and she huffed out a snort. "I don't think you're allowed to park there."

"It was the closest spot I could find. I wasn't concerned about the rules or restrictions of the parking lot."

"Of course not."

"Shauna, I was worried. Doesn't that count for something?"

She didn't bother to answer and moved toward his vehicle, needing the emotional space as much as a physical distance. He hadn't locked the doors, so she climbed in and kept her gaze straight ahead, breathing steadily even though her heart pounded like an erratic drumbeat.

"I'm going to stay at the house tonight," he said as he started the car.

"No."

"You need help."

"I have Meghan and Annalise in the carriage house if I need anything. But I won't." She didn't want to need help.

"Why can you rely on my brother but not me?" Flynn demanded as he pulled out of the parking space, punching the gas pedal.

"Declan has always been there for me."

"That's not fair."

"Life isn't fair. Do you think it was easy for me to accept Dec's help?" She rolled her eyes. "You don't know me at all, Flynn. I don't want to need you or your brother or anybody. When I rely on people—when I need them and let them in—I end up hurt. I've been hurt too many times."

"Did Declan hurt you? Because if he did, I will kill—"

"This isn't about Declan." She slammed her uninjured hand against the dashboard, the swirling tumult of feelings she couldn't seem to stop demanding an outlet. "This isn't even about you. My life doesn't revolve around you, Flynn."

"I never said it did." He sounded legitimately shocked by her statement. "I never thought that."

Maybe she was a better actress than she'd realized if he genuinely had no idea about his impact on her even when he wasn't an active part of her life.

Their sons reminded her of him in so many ways, but it was more than that. Even without the connection of shared DNA, Flynn was a part of her, as sure as if he ran through her veins. She couldn't stop it any more than she could stop breathing.

And she'd tried. But just like holding her breath in a bathtub of water, eventually she would break the surface, sputtering and gasping, her chest burning with the need for oxygen.

She didn't know how to let him go; physical separation was the only thing keeping her safe. Right now, she wasn't safe. She was terrified.

Not only from the fall off the ladder but because she wanted to rely on this man. In some ways, she had no choice. The accident today reminded her that being a single mother without a family to call on was a precarious position.

She was one accident, one fall away, from being in real trouble. When she'd broken her leg, she'd been able to blame herself and push aside the worry. She'd let one of her clients convince her to go skydiving. It had been an immature decision, but she'd been enamored by the idea of doing something for herself.

The boys were in school, and it felt exciting and precious to play hooky from work and have an adventure. Shauna had never been one for adventures, clearly with good reason. She'd learned her lesson. She no longer made selfish choices, yet she was in trouble again anyway.

"I don't understand, and you're not doing a great job of explaining it to me."

"I don't owe you an explanation. I don't owe you anything."

"Shauna, I'm not the enemy."

A sob broke from her throat, making her feel weak and embarrassed. "It's easier if you are. The alternative is..." She shook her head. "You're so capable. You're confident, and you live your life with no apologies. Until I became a mother, I felt like my existence was to blame for so many bad outcomes. If it hadn't been for me, then maybe my mom wouldn't have been so stressed out. Maybe she wouldn't have been desperate enough to take those pills. Maybe she would have stayed a carefree party girl like before I was born."

"You weren't responsible for your mother's overdose. You know that."

"I wasn't enough to make her want to live. I couldn't make those foster families want to adopt me permanently."

"You know how rare that is."

"But it happens. Kids in foster care get adopted. Just not me. Never me. Nobody picked me. Even Zach and Timmy didn't have a choice. They didn't pick me as their mother, but I'm what they got. So I'm bound and determined they will never regret having me for a mother the way I did mine."

She dragged in a shaky breath. "What kind of role model am I if I keep screwing up and getting hurt and needing help?"

"You're human." Flynn pulled to the side of the road and threw the truck into Park. He turned and took her uninjured hand, gently tracing his thumb on the edge of the cast. "You can be strong and human at the same time. I'm not always as confident as you seem to think. Like I said, my feelings for you scare the hell out of me, but I pick you."

"No. You left me." She hated the bitterness in her tone. She wanted his rejection not to matter. But it did matter. It always had. There were defining moments in her life. The day the police officer had scooped her up when her mother's body was removed from their small apartment.

Those terrifying minutes when that scumbag put his hands on her in violence. Declan and Flynn came to her rescue but watching Flynn leave shortly after was another defining moment. Her rational mind knew there had been no other option, but her heart felt the abandonment as another instance when she didn't measure up.

"You aren't here because you picked me," she reminded him. "I don't fault you for that. It's admirable that you're stepping up now that you know about the twins. But let's not pretend you made a choice to stay because of me."

"I came back for you."

"You came to see your brother."

"Because he would help me reconnect with you."

She wiped a hand across her cheek. "Don't pretend you couldn't find me on your own, Flynn. I know what you do. You could find a needle in a haystack. If you'd wanted to find me at any point, you could have."

"I didn't deserve to come back to you, Shauna. I wanted to hear from Dec that I did. Maybe it's stupid, but I'm trying. I need you to let me."

"You can sleep on the couch," she told him. "For one night."

"Okay," he agreed immediately. "Will you let me take care of you and the boys?"

"That's a big ask."

"Letting me in isn't going to push you out."

With that one sentence, he cut through to the heart of her insecurity—when the boys got to know their father, they'd prefer him to her. If people had a choice, even her own sons, they would always choose someone else.

And Shauna would be left alone.

Why wouldn't two rambunctious active boys choose Flynn? He looked like a superhero, and no matter how much she tried not to be, she was fragile. Not just physically. Her biggest weakness was her deep desire for love and the fathomless doubt that she deserved it.

"You know I need you as much, if not more, than you need me." Flynn released her hand and pulled onto the road again. It was as if he understood she needed a break from his focus.

"What do you need me for?"

"I don't know how to be a father. You're not the only one who's screwed up from things that happened long ago. Things both of us would rather forget. What if I can't control my temper? What if I'm like my dad? What if I use my hands in anger?"

"You're not. You wouldn't."

"I've done it before," he countered. His knuckles turned white as he gripped the steering wheel. "I had a career in the army as a result."

"That night wasn't about you. You were protecting me."

"It was about me. I would have killed him if they didn't pull me off him. Even now, I don't regret it. Not just because of what he tried to do to you. It felt good to have an outlet for my rage."

"You told me you're not that same person."

"Maybe I lied. Maybe that angry kid is still inside me.

Before they took us from him, my dad went off for the littlest reasons. Literal spilled milk would push him into a tirade. He broke my mom's nose because she put too much salt in a chicken casserole. That's who I come from. That's my role model."

"You aren't your father."

"You aren't your mother either."

She wanted to argue that it wasn't the same comparison, but she also wanted to believe him. "I need you to do something for me after you drop me at home."

"Sure, anything. What do you need? Groceries? A foot massage?"

She laughed. "You give foot massages?"

"I can try. How hard could it be?"

"Let's put a pin in that and focus. I'm going to give you the address of my client, and I need you to find the cat."

He muttered a curse. "I'm sure the cat is fine. It likely went off to clean its private bits after nearly getting you killed."

"I need to know."

She waited and watched as Flynn blew out a breath.

"Fine. Text me the address, and I'll find the damn cat."

"You'll make sure it's okay? That it finds a home, and the dog can't get to it anymore? Please, Flynn."

Flynn nodded. "I'll take care of the cat, sweetheart."

She sat back in her seat and felt something in her heart lurch. She didn't know why this meant so much, but it did. The fact that Flynn wasn't arguing also meant something.

She smiled. "We'll test your foot massage skills later," she told him, reaching out to squeeze his fingers. He wrapped his hand around hers, and she didn't pull away.

CHAPTER TWENTY-TWO

WITH TWO WEEKS to go until the benefit, along with the corresponding student concert and art show, Meghan felt she shouldn't have time for her jumbled thoughts and worries. Only she couldn't seem to stop them. Most of her troubled musings came not from thinking about the fundraiser or the attention it brought her, but she couldn't seem to push aside her feelings for Walker.

Danielle Griggs's visit to town confirmed it was ridiculous to think he might be interested in Meghan as more than his current coteacher. Yet that's exactly what she'd allowed herself to do.

Although Annalise and Shauna tried to convince her they saw a spark in Walker's honeyed eyes when he looked at Meghan, she knew it was nothing more than him being a nice guy because she'd helped his nephew.

It was difficult to ignore her crush when she spent time with the object of her affection almost daily. The more time she spent with Walker, the more she liked him. Not because he was famous or irritatingly handsome, although both were true.

It was how he worked with the kids and embraced his role as a teacher like he loved every moment leading rain stick percussion sessions and off-key choruses. She knew it wouldn't last. Greg had already posted the music teacher opening for the following year. Thanks to the attention from the benefit, there'd been a flood of applications.

"Are you still with us, Meghs?" Annalise waved two fingers in front of her. They were sitting, along with Shauna, at the Whimsy Farm dining room table, waiting for Walker, Jack, Carrie Reed Scott and Avery Atwell to arrive at the meeting.

"Maybe my mom was right about me all along," Meghan said, then shook her head, embarrassed that she'd allowed the words to slip from her mouth. "Never mind. Ignore me. It's been a strange few weeks."

"For all of us," Shauna agreed, touching a finger to the splint that now stabilized her wrist. "We're not ignoring that comment unless your mom said you're kind, generous and talented."

Meghan rolled her eyes. Her silly complaint felt even more trivial because she knew the story of Shauna losing her mother to a drug overdose and spending years in the foster care system. Meghan's troubles were nothing in comparison.

But her friends were looking at her, clearly waiting for an explanation, so she did her best not to fidget.

"My mom said I was too scared to live up to my potential. She's a brain surgeon so she had high expectations. Making her proud came easy to my older siblings. My sister is also a doctor, my brother runs a multinational tech company and I'm an art teacher who doesn't like the thought of the spotlight. My grandmother was the only person who thought I had value to add to the world. Now she's gone."

"She's not the only one." Annalise lifted the three-ring binder she was using to keep track of the event's details. "We're putting together the biggest event this town has seen to save your job. If that isn't faith, I don't know what is."

"It's about saving the art and music programs," Meghan insisted. "Not me in particular."

Shauna scoffed. "We're doing it for *you*."

Meghan threw up her hands. "I don't even know if I'm worth all of this trouble. I like being a wallflower."

"Honey, nobody likes being a wallflower," Annalise said with a shake of her golden hair. If Meghan tried to execute that hair toss, she'd look like she'd just been stung by a bee.

"There's an uncomfortable spotlight on me. People have expectations." She shuddered as she said the word. "I've spent a lifetime disappointing anyone who expected something from me. Why will this be any different?"

"You're already doing the job," Annalise reminded her. "Better than anybody I've seen. This is why we want to go to bat for you. *You* not just the position."

Shauna nodded. "It's why Carrie wants your help with the community center. You have plenty to offer."

"I wish I could believe the two of you. I wish I could see myself the way other people do. I don't know if I'm worth it." She breathed out a groan. "Now I sound like I'm fishing for compliments."

"You're allowed to want compliments and to be recognized for your contributions," Shauna said gently. "No matter whether it's saving lives in a hospital or molding lives in the classroom. Both have value. You have value."

"Anyone up for getting a tattoo so I can remember?" Meghan joked, blinking back tears at the sudden swell of emotion in her chest.

"We all know what it's like to have self-doubt," Annalise assured her. "Some of us are better at masking it than others. You are who you are without apologies. Your authenticity is your strength."

Meghan tried to smile. "My mom wouldn't see it that way."

"I spent too many years living to make my mom happy." Annalise smiled, but it looked wooden. "One, it never worked. Even worse, it made me unhappy and unsure who

I wanted to be. You're ahead of me in that department and perfect the way you are."

"You don't think I'm wasting my life teaching elementary school and owning an assortment of elastic waistband pants so I don't have to worry if I've had too much bread?"

"Everyone should have too much bread in a day." Shauna laughed.

"You only have to be you," Annalise promised. "The students like you. We like you."

"Walker likes you," Shauna added.

"This isn't about Walker."

"Does it have anything to do with his ex-girlfriend?" Shauna asked.

"This is the problem with having friends," Meghan said, holding up one finger. "My secrets aren't safe."

"They're safe with us." Shauna patted her hand.

"I've seen how Walker acts around Dani." Annalise grimaced. "Trust me. He's not interested in Danielle Griggs."

"It doesn't matter." Meghan tried to convince her heart of that. She didn't want to talk about her feelings for Walker when she didn't understand them. "You guys are right, and it's annoying. I'm going to try to take your advice."

"We give excellent advice," Shauna said. "And a lot of it. What advice are you specifically taking?"

All three of them laughed.

"I'm going to focus on being me and doing the things that feel right, even if they scare me."

"That a girl," Annalise said. "Three cheers to being scared but authentic."

They heard voices from the front of the house, then Walker, Jack, Avery and Carrie appeared in the doorway.

"Sorry we're late," Carrie said.

"I forgot I was a snack mom for Violet's soccer game today," Avery said with a sigh.

Meghan noticed the woman throw a pointed look toward Annalise. "I'm sure you would have brought in homemade something or other. But the Brave Bears will have to suffice with some convenience-store granola bars."

Meghan waited for Annalise to snap back. Although Margo and Violet had recently put aside their differences and become friends, the same couldn't necessarily be said for Avery and Annalise. She also knew women like the person Annalise had been before the divorce loved when someone else's weakness was exposed and they could revel in it.

"Did you get the kind with the little teddy bear on the box?" Annalise asked. "I've become quite the connoisseur of store-bought snacks. My housekeeper did a hundred percent of my baking and crafting. We all know she's gone with the wind. For the record, the teddy bears pair well with a nice pinot grigio."

There was a beat of silence, then a broad smile from Avery. "I went with juice boxes and bears for the soccer game, but I'm going to remember that if there are leftovers."

Annalise glanced at Meghan as the others took their seats. "Terrified but authentic," she whispered. "That's the tattoo I'm picking."

Meghan tried to appear confident and unconcerned with the attention this event would place on her.

Equally, she did her best not to make eye contact with Walker. Acting confident in the face of fear was one thing but making a complete fool of herself was quite another. She didn't relish the latter.

It was getting harder to keep her unrequited adoration out of her gaze. The meeting was productive, and to her surprise, the ideas she suggested were considered with just as much weight as the others, as if she belonged at the table.

The hour and a half they spent reviewing timelines, logistics and details went by in a flash, and she realized her nerves had finally settled.

She could do this. She could act normal with Walker. She did it every day at school. This was no different. But as she started for the door to walk out with her friends, he placed a hand on her arm.

"Do you have a minute?" The smile he flashed was almost uncertain. Was it possible she wasn't alone in her nerves?

Shauna gave an exaggerated nod behind his shoulder when Meghan stayed silent.

"Sure," Meghan managed, her mouth suddenly dry.

"I wanted to run something by you." He drew back his hand, and she wanted to reach for him again. His touch burned in the most delicious way.

"Okay."

"It's in my studio."

"We'll see you back at the house," Annalise called as she herded the others toward the front door.

Meghan had driven over, so it wasn't a big deal, and only Jack seemed to find it curious that Walker wanted her to stay.

Meghan forced breath in and out of her lungs as she followed Walker out the door and toward the studio building.

She hadn't been there since her first visit to the farm to discuss lesson plans. It felt like a lifetime ago, although in reality, it had been only a few weeks. She'd been nervous and intimidated by the man and a little bit starstruck, if she was being completely honest.

Those initial emotions paled in comparison to what she felt now. She struggled to control her feelings. Of course she had a crush on Walker Calloway. Most women at the school did—married or single—the men also gravitated toward him. He was a magnetic personality—comfortable being the center of attention. He drew admirers into his orbit without even trying.

Her crush was nothing special.

More importantly, *she* was nothing special.

"What's going on?" she asked as she looked around the space. "Tell me this has nothing to do with the third-graders burping through that last lesson."

He chuckled, the sound like warm honey, sweet and rich. "I wrote a new song." He ran a hand through his hair as his gaze met hers, then tracked away. "Several, in fact."

"That's amazing." She studied him more closely. "New material is a good thing, right?"

He didn't exactly look happy about it. His mouth had pulled into a taut line, and his eyes darted around the room.

"Have a seat, and I'll try to explain. I know you have plenty to deal with, and it's selfish to burden you with my troubles, but I consider you a friend. I need a friend at the moment."

She was both elated and disappointed at his words. A *friend*. Walker had friend-zoned her.

So much for a spark in his eye. It was probably spring pollen.

At the same time, she loved the idea that he'd turned to her. She considered him a friend as well, although she wanted more.

She put aside her yearnings as she took a seat on the plush leather sofa that sat under a window looking out on the Whimsy Farm pasture.

"You could never be a burden," she told him, hoping her voice didn't reveal more than what she wanted.

"You're a sweetheart." He lowered himself onto the stool across from her.

If he used the word *swell* to describe her, Meghan might lose her mind. But she smiled. Annalise wasn't the only one who could employ a mask to disguise her true feelings.

"What's going on, Walker? Why don't you look happy about finding inspiration again? Is it Nash?"

He met her gaze, vulnerability and relief shining in their depths. "I knew you'd understand."

"I'm not sure I do. I think your brother would be happy to know you're writing again."

"It was always the two of us making music," Walker said quietly. "From start to finish. We wrote the lyrics and composed melodies together. That's how it had always been, and in my mind, I gave Nash all the credit. Even more, since he's been gone. I thought he had the magic. I performed in his reflection, but the light belonged to him."

"You have your own light," she said gently.

He grabbed his guitar and began tuning it like he needed an excuse to avoid looking at her. "It sounds hokey, but yeah, that's what I'm discovering. The new songs are good. At least, I think they're good. Maybe the best I've ever written." He pressed three fingers to the strings and the room went silent. "I plan to play them at the benefit concert."

Meghan sucked in a breath. "Wow, that would be huge. It will satisfy Jack and the record company."

"If I do this, I won't be able to avoid recording any longer."

"Maybe it's time to stop avoiding it?"

One corner of his mouth curved. "You could be right. Can I play one for you?"

"I'd love that." Meghan wanted to hear him sing and

play but couldn't help the tiny stab of disappointment that pierced her heart.

She wasn't sure why he was bringing her to the studio, but a secret part of her wished he would reveal that he had romantic feelings. Instead, he'd outright told her he thought of her as a friend. Why did she continue to feel this strange connection shimmering between them like the sunrise making the ocean waves sparkle?

His cheeks were colored pink as he focused on his instrument, although it was difficult to believe Walker would be nervous about singing for her.

He began to play a few gentle chords. She'd always been a sucker for a good ballad, and immediately the notes made goose bumps erupt over her skin.

She kept the smile on her face even though her heart was hurling itself against her rib cage. He crooned soft words about a woman and a sunrise like he'd pulled the images and sentiment directly from her heart.

If Meghan hadn't already been half in love with Walker, this moment would have pushed her over the edge. She understood all those women and their tossed panties. He had a gift, a magnetism that went beyond anything she'd ever experienced.

He glanced at her several times during the performance. One line, in particular, stood out and made Meghan's blood heat.

"'She doesn't know she's beautiful, but she takes my breath away.'"

Breathing was supposed to be one of those functions that the body just took care of, but Meghan had to remind herself to draw air in and out of her lungs.

She wasn't about to assume she'd inspired the song, although every line and note seemed to encapsulate and encompass her feelings about the unexpected connection with this man.

Both the discovery and wonder of the emotions, plus the idea that the object of her affection felt the same way, tempted and terrified her.

He sang about a sky full of pink and gold, finding courage within and without. Annalise's words came back to her. Being afraid and going after what she wanted anyway.

When he finished, Meghan felt hypnotized by Walker's voice, so it took a few moments to regain her composure. The last chord reverberated through the room with its perfect acoustics; all she could do was stare at him.

His brows furrowed as he studied her. "Are you going to say something? Was I wrong? Is it too much…too sappy? Does it—"

"It's perfect," she whispered. Acting despite her fear, she stood and took a step forward. She bent toward him and cupped his face in her hands. His eyes widened in surprise, and she nearly pulled back. There was taking action despite fear and then there was reckless stupidity.

Meghan was pretty sure she was moving into the territory of the biggest mistake of her life. Before she could talk herself out of it, she counted backward from five…quickly like she was a rocket ship ready for takeoff. And when she hit Go, she pressed her mouth to Walker's.

The lips that had formed those beautiful words were soft and firm simultaneously. She could feel his shock. It was an awkward kiss as kisses went. Meghan was anxious and wound too tight and not experienced at making the first move.

As her grandmother used to say, in for a penny, in for a pound. If this were the only kiss she and Walker Calloway ever shared, she'd make it one to remember.

She angled her head and deepened the kiss. He put aside the guitar and lifted his hands to grip her wrists. He didn't push her away. He held her fast, his tongue tracing the seam of her lips. Suddenly, like an annoying alarm waking her from a blissful dream, she heard voices. One of them belonged to Gus.

She wrenched away from Walker and stumbled back, plopping down on the sofa again just as the door to the studio opened.

Walker's nephew, along with Jack, entered. "Hey, Ms. Banks," Gus said. "Jack said you were out here. One of the cows had a baby last night. Remember I told you she was pregnant?"

"Yeah, Gus." Meghan cleared her throat because her voice sounded husky, even to her ears. She saw Jack's eyebrows rise and wondered how much her face revealed. She glanced at Walker, whose focus was on the guitar strings.

Coward.

She willed him to look at her. She wanted to know if the kiss had affected him the way it did her, but he revealed nothing.

"Can you come now and see? What are you doing, Uncle Walker?"

"Just going over some things for the concert." Walker lifted a hand but not his gaze. "I think we're done here."

Done. Meghan swallowed. "Right," she agreed and stood, smoothing a hand over her skirt. She tried to ignore how her eyes burned and that her lower lip wanted to tremble as she followed Gus out of the studio.

CHAPTER TWENTY-THREE

ANNALISE FELT HAPPIER than she had in months, maybe even years. It didn't matter that she was coordinating last-minute details around the clock to ensure every aspect of the fundraiser went off without a hitch. She had a purpose and not just one that would end when the last note was played and the money collected.

Since Walker had agreed to let her take the lead on redoing his house, the affiliation with someone of his star power had opened doors she hadn't even imagined walking through. She was well on her way to forming solid relationships with furniture makers, contractors and other professionals throughout the region.

She'd worried she would have a difficult time because Everly Mae and her cronies had done their best to sabotage and bad-mouth Annalise up and down the coast. As it turned out, her leftover mean-girl posse was no match for the recognition vendors would receive through having their names and brands associated with Walker.

She owed him a considerable debt and had a feeling she owed Jack even more. Despite wanting to make a home in Magnolia for Gus, once Walker started writing music again, he had a single-minded focus on his craft. It was Jack who she met with to go over the concepts for the redesign. He was taking care of the house and farm, just as he was the fundraiser. It surprised her what a good partnership they seemed to have.

Once she'd gained his trust, she learned Jack was a man of great integrity and damn good taste. The more time she spent with him, the deeper her feelings grew. It was more than their physical connection. She would never have dreamed she could consider opening her heart to love again after the way Jonathan's betrayal wrecked her life. Jack made her want to believe in second chances.

Annalise wasn't sure whether it was more of a challenge to trust Jack or herself. Oddly, her friendship with Meghan and Shauna not only provided some welcome companionship, but it also helped heal her heart.

Her mother wasn't speaking to her after learning of the changes Annalise had made to her life—a transformation that involved embracing kindness, generosity and not relying on attitude or financial status—but Annalise liked the person she was becoming. She couldn't remember ever being able to say that about herself.

"Mommy, me and Violet got the chairs arranged like you wanted them. Can we go see the baby goats?"

Margo ran up to Annalise as she made the request, and Annalise had to smother a gasp of shock at the state of her once girlie and dirt-averse daughter.

Margo wore cut-off shorts and a pink T-shirt that had a stain of dried something or other on it. There was a smear of powdered sugar on her cheek, and Annalise had a feeling Jack had sneaked the girls a doughnut when she wasn't looking.

Margo's hair was back in a simple ponytail that matched Violet's and would have been unheard-of months ago. For a long time, those two girls had engaged in a silent war over who could best the other on the intricate braids they wore to school.

"We'll come back and help more after we give the goats

and horses some treats," Violet assured Annalise as she came to stand next to Margo, wrapping an arm around her waist.

Margo rested her head on her new best friend's shoulder like it was the most natural thing in the world.

"Sure," Annalise said around the lump of emotion that expanded in her chest, stealing her breath. Her daughter was a dirty, stained, happy little girl, and while they were still coming to grips with the changes wrought by Jonathan's criminal dealings, Annalise finally felt confident they would all flourish in their new life.

"Ask your brother if he needs help with the other animals," she instructed her daughter.

Trey was becoming a fixture at Whimsy Farm, shadowing Jack as he and Gus pitched in wherever they could after school and on weekends.

"I will," Margo said, and the girls ran off.

"You look like you've seen a ghost," Jack told her as he approached from the house. He drew a hand around the back of her neck and pulled her forward for a kiss like it was the most natural thing in the world.

Annalise almost let herself be swept away by the pleasure of it and the crisp, clean scent that enveloped him no matter how long he spent working in the barn or the pasture.

Then she remembered her children were in the barn and took a quick step away from him.

"How long are you going to make me your dirty secret?" He sounded both amused and frustrated. He'd been pushing her to join him for an actual date, but she wasn't ready to go public with whatever was between them.

"You aren't a secret," she said even though they both knew it was a lie. "But I like getting dirty with you."

His gaze gentled as he squeezed her hand. "Will you dance with me Saturday night?"

"I think we'll both be too busy working," she said, trying to sound casual.

"I can't imagine being too busy to wrap my arms around you."

Warmth flooded through her.

"But tell me about the look in your eyes."

She sighed and glanced toward the barn. "It wasn't a ghost. My daughter looks so happy and relaxed now. I hadn't realized that was missing from her life—from all our lives. I've done my children a terrible disservice."

"You have amazing kids. That's because of, not despite, you," Jack assured her. "Parents are allowed to make mistakes."

She was about to lean in and kiss him again when she heard the sound of cars coming down the driveway.

She muttered a curse when she recognized Everly Mae's Mercedes along with several other PTO board members.

"Did you know they were coming?" she asked.

Jack shook his head and grimaced. "If I'd known, I would have made myself scarce."

"Might as well face them head-on," she said, although she wished she'd put on some makeup this morning. She gave herself a mental head shake.

No, she didn't need a mask or armor. She was working on being satisfied with who she was all the time, not just with her friends.

She felt Jack's fingers brush her hand as Everly Mae climbed out of the Mercedes and adjusted her tortoiseshell sunglasses while she surveyed the property. Annalise wasn't sure what the other woman saw or even what she was looking for, but none of the women could complain when Walker had offered his land as a venue.

They'd limited the number of tickets and had sold out minutes after the online site went live. She took another step away from Jack and heard his beleaguered sigh. She wanted to explain she wasn't trying to keep him a secret or maintain a particular facade with these women.

Annalise was doing him a favor. Everly Mae had arrived with her whole posse in tow, which meant she came with a purpose. No doubt that purpose would include trying to undermine or humiliate her.

She was protecting Jack from an association with her and her tarnished reputation. She wanted to believe Jack understood she hadn't been involved in Jonathan's schemes and that she was no longer the same person. But doubts and fears were like that old video game where the frog had to cross the road. When she navigated one level, another traffic-laden highway would be there for her to travel with the potential to be splattered.

She didn't like the thought of that splatter hitting Jack. She ran a hand through her hair and squared her shoulders as the women approached.

"Coming to lend a hand?" she asked.

"As a matter of fact," Everly Mae said, "we've come to talk to you about the role you've taken in this event."

"Her role?" Jack interjected. "Do you mean the fact that Annalise has almost single-handedly coordinated the event? This concert will raise enough money to pay two teacher salaries and expand the curriculum for your school's art and music programs. You came here to thank her, right?"

Everly Mae lifted the sunglasses to the top of her head and gaped at Jack. Annalise stifled a laugh.

As much as she appreciated him coming to her defense,

he didn't know how school politics worked. He couldn't possibly understand how cutthroat things could be even when the stakes were minimal.

Trey and Margo were in a good place. Her kids had made friends who seemed to care about them. One false step on her part could affect their newfound stability.

She liked to think she had also matured, even though right now she wanted to kick Everly Mae's shin, pull her hair and get into a good old-fashioned catfight to finish things off once and for all.

But this wasn't the Real Housewives of Wherever, and she was no longer a housewife. She was a single, independent working woman and could handle whatever Everly Mae threw at her.

"Why don't you go check on the kids in the barn?" she asked Jack.

"I think I'll stay here," he said, crossing his arms over his chest. "I'm Walker's manager and in charge of the farm, so I have a vested interest in what she has say."

"What needs to be said," Everly Mae clarified. "The members of the PTO board have met with the school board. Concerns have been raised about Annalise's involvement because the Haverford name is synonymous with her husband's—"

"Ex," Annalise interrupted.

Everly Mae tsked as if that pesky detail didn't signify. "No one wants to see a cloud over this event. Questions are being raised about the safekeeping of the donations because of who's in charge."

Despite wanting to deny the other woman the satisfaction of a reaction, Annalise gasped. "Tell me you aren't insinuating I would skim money from the donations or ticket sales."

"It's not me." Everly Mae lifted her hands in a show of fake supplication, but she might as well have stabbed a knife into Annalise's heart. "I'm the messenger. People came to me because they know that we were friends." She sniffed delicately. "We are still friends of a sort, although it's difficult under the circumstances to remain friends with someone I can't trust. I've explained to the school board that I still care about you, Annalise. I know you want to do what's right."

As her body went cold with a resigned sort of humiliation, Annalise glanced at the other women, who looked both smug and uncomfortable, a strange combination.

"Everyone knows you're having money troubles." Everly Mae spoke quietly, although the words landed with the power of an explosion. "The school board thinks it would be better if you didn't take such a high-profile role the night of the concert."

Annalise wanted to scream, to claw at her own throat and let out the guttural cry that threatened to overtake her.

She wished she could implore one of the women flanking Everly Mae to call off this ridiculous attack, but it was her own fault.

She didn't have many allies in town or among the other mothers. She'd been an awful person to a lot of people, and most of them weren't as willing to forgive her as Avery Atwell.

"That's ridiculous," Jack spit out.

"She's right." As the piercing numbness seeped through Annalise, she answered her former friend's avaricious glare with a nod. "The school board is right."

"I don't believe for a second that anyone on the board—"

"I don't need a prominent role." She shrugged, feeling

powerless over the past and present. "We're saving the art and music programs. Who gets credit isn't important."

Everly Mae's eyes gleamed. "I'll introduce Walker Calloway, the purpose of the event and all the good it will do for the community. After all, I'm the leader of the PTO. Our organization will manage the funds since we have the nonprofit designation."

Jack shook his head, and Annalise could feel the disappointment in his gaze as he looked at her. "Are you going to allow her to pressure you this way?"

"No one is forcing me," Annalise said. "Apparently, you don't know me as well as you thought, Jack. Everyone in Magnolia understands that I make my own decisions and always put myself first."

That was the person people expected her to be, and it was a shockingly easy crutch to fall back on, even if the shoe no longer fit, like her foot had grown along with her heart. As she'd anticipated, Everly Mae gave a slight nod of satisfaction. Annalise was falling into line. In contrast, Jack's gaze went stony, his features hard like they were made of granite.

She wished her heart were forged from rock at this moment. It felt like it was cracking into a million pieces just when she'd managed to patch it all together again.

Maybe this was her inevitable comeuppance for believing things could change—that she could become someone different—a person she liked, worthy of love and respect.

Too big for her britches, her mother would have said.

"If the school board wants me to step down, it's fine. Frankly, with my busy design schedule for Walker and the referrals flooding in at the moment, I have more than enough to keep me busy. Work that benefits me personally and not just the elementary school. Bigger fish to fry and all that."

The glint in Everly Mae's eyes dimmed slightly. She clearly did not want to believe that Annalise could somehow end up triumphant.

Annalise probably shouldn't have mentioned the work with Walker. It was in the infancy stages, and even a hint of her success would be like waving a red flag in front of a bull as far as Everly Mae was concerned.

In the grand scheme of this defeat, that was small potatoes. More devastating was the fear she'd ruined her burgeoning relationship with Jack with just a few unfortunate sentences.

"I'll drop off the binder to you later and email everything I have on my computer," she told Everly Mae. "Jack can also fill you in on the logistics for the night of the concert."

Most of the work was done, so she figured Everly Mae would gladly take credit for the efforts Annalise had put into the event.

"It's better this way," the woman said with a self-satisfied smile.

Jack said nothing and refused to meet Annalise's gaze when she turned to him.

"I'm going to collect the children," she announced.

He gave a terse nod but didn't respond, and her throat burned with unshed tears. Silly. It was too soon for her to feel the way she did about him and safer to end things now before they were more involved.

She no longer craved the crown that designated her queen of the shallow social scene in this small town. She desperately wanted to reinvent her life, take care of her children and be happy.

Happiness seemed out of reach at the moment, especially when she'd rolled over and exposed her vulnerable underbelly at the first sign of a threat from Everly Mae.

She expected her children to stand up for themselves and others and do the right thing. Shame bored a hole right through her gut at the thought of what a shabby role model she was being. She should tell Everly Mae to take a hike and not back down to the woman's ludicrous insinuations and demands. She should not be forced to continue paying for her husband's crimes with the theoretical pound of flesh people seemed to expect from her at every turn.

But she didn't.

Instead, she tried to meet Jack's gaze one more time—to wordlessly explain that this was for the best. It was how it had to be.

But he refused to make eye contact. He wanted her to be someone she wasn't ready to become quite yet. With a regal nod to the women, Annalise plastered a bright, fake, painful smile on her face and walked away without looking back.

CHAPTER TWENTY-FOUR

SHAUNA WOKE EARLY the morning of Zach and Timmy's sixth birthday. The first hint of the late-spring sun hadn't yet peeked through the blinds of her bedroom window. But her heart raced as if she'd mainlined a motherlode of caffeine.

She gripped the soft cotton sheets like they were the only thing tethering her to the earth, wishing she could blame her turbulent emotions on worry about Annalise. The other woman was once the closest thing Shauna had to an enemy but now felt like the bosom friend she'd always longed for.

Annalise was devastated about being pressured to relinquish her involvement in the benefit. Yet when Shauna had pressed her to talk about her feelings and the rift with Jack, Annalise shut down. Her mask of detachment remained firmly in place, and Shauna didn't know how to break through those emotional walls. She wasn't sure she had the capacity given her self-doubt, which squeezed her confidence to a breaking point.

Her feelings for Flynn were becoming difficult to ignore. She was losing her heart to him all over again and hated to think how the emotional fallout could impact her boys if Flynn broke her heart as he had years ago.

A week earlier, he'd made an offhand comment about taking the boys fishing for their birthday. Zach and Timmy latched on to the idea with even more exuberance than was standard for spirited elementary-age boys. They'd insisted that since their birthday fell on a Saturday, fishing was the activity of choice and had begged Shauna to join in the fun.

She'd tried to decline gracefully, but there was no denying Zach and Timmy once they got their minds set on something.

Their excitement elicited a promise from Flynn to take it up a notch—the plan had morphed from a morning spent fishing at a local park to a full-day boating adventure on the open water. She couldn't let her kids go on the ocean without her to watch over them, even though she was the accident-prone member of the family.

Thankfully, her wrist had healed without incident. She wasn't sure how much more she could take of Flynn looking after her. Not that he did a lousy job of it. In fact, the opposite was true.

He was kind, attentive and grateful for the opportunity to play a more active role in all their lives. Shauna was falling hard and fast, and it scared her to pieces.

She'd always planned birthdays on her own and reliving the day her two sons were born was a bittersweet anniversary.

Each year, she was reminded that she had no one to truly share the milestones with, but Flynn was changing that. Despite her doubts, she wanted to believe they'd both changed enough to be a real family.

Panic made her pop out of bed like a pinball launched into an arcade game at the thought. There was plenty to do to keep her worries at bay. Chocolate chip pancakes with maple sausage and fresh squeezed orange juice to start and then a lunch packed of their favorite sandwiches. Peanut butter and honey for Zach and turkey and cheese with a light mayo spread for Timmy.

Both of them liked the crust cut off and busying herself with those routine tasks grounded her a little. It wasn't long before she heard the toilet flush and water running in the sink above her.

Shauna smiled at the influence Margo Haverford was having on the boys. The girl had been clear with the twins that washing hands needed to happen after every trip to the bathroom, whether they were making a liquid or solid deposit.

Shauna was hosting a pizza party later with Annalise's kids and Gus Calloway on the guest list. May and Trinity Carlyle were also coming, along with Magnolia's police chief and his adorable daughter, who lived next door to May.

She hoped to find a minute that she and Meghan could talk Annalise into reconsidering her decision not to speak at the concert tomorrow night. At first, Annalise had refused to attend, but Walker demanded she be there.

Shauna understood that people still had conflicted feelings about the woman because of her prior reputation and how badly her husband's fraud had impacted the community. But she deserved a second chance. Shauna planned to ensure she got it and not let Everly Mae steal the credit for Annalise's hard work.

There was a knock at the door. At the same time, footfalls thundered down the stairs. "Daddy's here!" Zach called.

Butterflies danced across Shauna's midsection. When had Flynn become Daddy? She hadn't heard either of the boys call him that before, although it made sense. He was their father and things were progressing in their relationship better than she had hoped. Truly, she didn't mind hearing the word *Daddy*, but she couldn't release the fear that they'd all be hurt if Flynn walked away. How was a man who mainly conversed in monosyllables so easy to love?

"Daddy! Daddy! Daddy!" they chorused, and the grin that split Flynn's handsome face allowed her heart to settle.

It clearly made him very happy that they had formally recognized his role in their lives. He looked toward her, and for a moment, he was so boyishly handsome and jubilant that it stole her breath.

They had their experience as orphans in common. His situation was even sadder than hers. He had no blueprint for being a father and no role model to pattern his behavior after. Yet he was doing better than she could have imagined.

"Happy birthday to my handsome sons," Flynn said as if he wanted to claim them in the same way they had him. "What's on the plan today? Driving lessons? You guys are old enough to get your licenses, right?"

Both boys dissolved into fits of giggles.

"We're going fishing, Daddy," Timmy reminded him. "We're not old enough to drive." Flynn tousled the younger twin's unruly mop of hair. "Well, maybe you're big enough to sit on my lap and help steer the boat."

They responded as if he'd just offered them a treasure chest of gold and priceless jewels.

"Can we, Mommy?" Timmy asked, turning and running for the kitchen.

"Yes, but come and give me a birthday hug first." The boys rushed over to fling themselves into her arms. If Flynn were bothered by the fact that they'd asked her permission for something he'd told them they could do, he didn't show it. Shauna knew there would come a day when he would expect to make decisions for their care on his own.

Maybe not with anything significant, but it would still be an adjustment. She guided each of his interactions with the twins. She gave him menu ideas for when they went to his place without her, and he followed her instructions on everything from bedtime to a snack schedule without question.

She liked having that kind of control. It would be difficult to share, but that was an issue for a different day. Today she would let Flynn take the lead.

The boys endured her birthday kisses, then talked nonstop to Flynn as they ate breakfast, peppering him with questions about the boat and fishing.

Such a classic activity for a father to experience with his sons, and while Shauna had trouble sharing their excitement, she appreciated it just the same.

"So you rented this boat from the marina south of town?" she asked when they were buckled into his truck and on the way. "You're sure it's safe to take out on the ocean?"

He lowered his sunglasses and gave her a dubious stare. "Do you think I would put you and the boys at risk?"

"No," she answered immediately. "It's just…"

"Mommy can't swim good," Zach announced from the back seat.

"And she's scared of water," Timmy added for good measure.

Shauna felt her cheeks flame with embarrassment. "I can swim," she assured Flynn. "I took lessons along with the boys."

Zach leaned forward. "She was the last one to put her face in the water."

"But I did it," Shauna reminded her son. "Besides, we're fishing today. Not swimming."

"Except if the boat sinks, and then we gotta swim so we don't drown." Timmy said the words matter-of-factly, but they sent a cold shiver tingling along Shauna's spine.

Flynn reached over the console and took her hand. "The boat is safe, and there will be plenty of time for swimming another day. I talked to Cam Arlinghaus, one of the local captains. He gave me directions to several inlets with calm water. This summer we'll plan plenty of other trips that include swimming."

"If the boat you rented turns out to be safe and it's available." Shauna's hand felt stiff and clammy with Flynn's larger one wrapped around it.

He flashed a sheepish grin. "I bought a boat."

"What?" she demanded at the same time Zach and Timmy took turns shouting their approval. A whole new round of animated questions ensued.

"Can we name it?"

"Is it big?"

"Does it got a giant motor?"

"What color is it?"

"How do you know how to drive a boat?"

"Yeah, let's start with that one." Shauna held up a hand to silence her boys. As if they sensed her rising panic, both of them miraculously went quiet. "Where did you learn to drive a boat?"

Flynn shrugged. "It's just something I picked up. I like fishing. It's relaxing. Being out on the water for a few hours makes life's cares disappear."

"I can understand that." Shauna nodded. "Because you're probably too busy worrying about having a mini-*Titanic* moment to worry over dryland problems."

"Not exactly."

"What would make you buy a boat?"

He glanced in the rearview mirror. "I thought Zach and Timmy would like it."

They shouted their agreement.

"How about a theme-park season pass while you were at it?" Shauna muttered, suddenly bitter that he could afford a boat on a whim when she felt lucky to make her car payment each month.

"I'm not a theme-park type of guy," he answered like she was serious.

"Yeah. I get that."

He raised a brow. "Are you okay?"

"Sure," she lied and turned up the volume on the radio. Zach and Timmy sang along with the Kidz Bop playlist pumping through the truck's state-of-the-art speakers.

"Are you mad about the boat? I wanted a way to connect with them. I thought it would be fun."

"It will be fun. You'll be the fun parent." She laughed, trying to let go of her resentment. "You should be proud of yourself, Flynn."

He kept his mouth shut but made a sound of incredulity low in his throat. Shauna needed to focus on something positive because she didn't like how her jealousy caused her heart to burn with irrational doubts.

"It's true. You overcame so much. You're obviously successful and rich enough to buy a boat, rent a gorgeous house and—"

"Do you need money, Shauna? I know I have a financial responsibility beyond what I spend when the boys are with me. If you're in a bind, just say the word."

She jerked away her hand and gripped her throat where a scream demanded an escape.

A bind? Her whole life constituted a bind. She was a single mom without a college degree working for herself. The rental income helped each month, but she'd maxed out her recently paid-off credit card to cover the kitchen repair and a new dishwasher. One step forward, five steps back seemed to be the theme of her life.

While she agreed that Flynn had—as he called it—a financial responsibility, she bristled at the thought of taking money from him. She didn't want to be dependent on anyone. There were too many leftover bruises from a childhood wanting so badly to rely on the people in her life.

She'd given her heart freely because she thought that was the way to ensure love. But life had kicked her in the teeth enough times to understand that it was just as often a path to heartache.

A body could heal, but invisible bruises were often the ones that did the most damage.

"This isn't about money, Flynn. I'm fine," she answered, then thought about Declan, Beth and her rule against using the word *fine* because she claimed it was a cover for whatever a person didn't want to share.

Flynn didn't know that and took her at her word. "Good. If that changes, let me know. I'm here for you, and the boat isn't a big deal."

"If you say so," she agreed.

He nodded, drumming his fingers on the steering wheel in an uncharacteristically nervous gesture. "Anyway, I'm glad it came up. We need to talk about…stuff."

She could guess what stuff he meant but wasn't ready to go there. "Today let's have fun with the birthday celebration, okay?"

His hands stopped their movement, but he still seemed tense. Finally, he let out a long breath. "Okay," he promised, his tone gentle.

Big, strong, angry Flynn Murphy was doing his best to be the man she wanted him to be.

And that need rocked her like a ship stuck in a squall

that could splinter a hull in seconds. Why did the man have to be so irresistible?

With a sigh, she straightened her shoulders, turned down the music and shifted to glance into the back seat.

"How many fish do you think we're going to catch today?"

"A million," Zach shouted.

"A gazillion million," Timmy said with a bright smile.

Flynn smiled. "No pressure. Do you know what the secret is to catching fish?"

The boys shook their heads and sat forward to listen intently.

"You have to whisper to them," Flynn revealed. "We must be quiet and patient and give them time to find the hook. Then we'll reel them in with no problem."

"Okay," both boys whispered in response.

Shauna felt sorry for those unsuspecting fish.

Her grin wobbled at the edges. This day was everything she hadn't allowed herself to hope for. She couldn't help the emotions leaking out of the corners of her eye. There was no way to keep the explosive mix of happiness and fear contained, at least until they pulled into the marina parking lot.

Then her forgotten nerves about being on a boat on the ocean took over. She managed to keep her smile fixed as they unloaded the cooler and bags of towels and fishing equipment from the back of Flynn's truck.

He gave the boys some cash and sent them toward the old bait shack on the hill. They seemed surprised and thrilled to be given such a grown-up task.

Shauna didn't protest, but when they bounded away asked, "Are you sure you should send them on their own?"

"Cam is waiting for them. He'll help guide the purchases.

I thought they'd get a kick out of actively participating in the preparations."

"You're right," she agreed, her voice trembling.

"Hey." He drew her to the far side of the hulking SUV parked next to his truck and cupped her face in his hands. "It's going to be okay."

She wanted to believe him, and not just about today's excursion.

"The weather is perfect, so the water will be smooth as glass. It will be like skimming across a cloud. I'll take care of you, Shauna. All of you."

It was silly to read more into his words. He was talking about their safety on the boat, but even that was something. It eased her troubled mind and heart.

"I know you will."

He kissed her, and she breathed him in, both familiar from when they were younger and new because of the man he'd become.

She wanted to trust their undeniable connection and thought about Annalise's advice. Take action despite the fear. If Shauna didn't open herself up to happiness, there would be no room for it to make a home in her life.

She kissed him back and before her doubts could stop her, said against his mouth, "I love you, Flynn."

A tremor of some emotion she couldn't identify pulsed through him, and she thought she'd gone too far, too fast.

He didn't respond with the same words but held her closer like he'd never let her go.

"I'll take care of you," he repeated, and she wanted to believe that was enough.

CHAPTER TWENTY-FIVE

"I CAN'T BELIEVE Everly Mae Tinsdale has the nerve to take credit for saving my job when the two of you have done all the work. That woman is the absolute worst." Meghan peeked around the side of the barn to the open field quickly filling with excited fans in advance of the concert, which was due to start in an hour. "Also, why are you two hiding?"

She glanced from Shauna to Annalise, neither of whom would make eye contact with her, then studied her friends more closely.

"All three of us are hiding," Annalise murmured.

Meghan nodded. "I know my reason."

"You laid a fat one on Walker Calloway," Shauna said with a forced smile.

"Not how I would describe the kiss, but that was the basic gist." Something was off. Meghan just needed to figure out what. She'd been preoccupied not only with what Walker thought of her but also with working out last-minute details for the event.

"My issue is obvious. What's going on with the two of you?" She'd spent her available mental energy on keeping herself from being overwhelmed by anxiety but now realized she wasn't the only one struggling.

"I'm fine," Annalise said. "I'm not even sure why I came today. You don't need me."

"Of course we do," Meghan retorted.

"Are you fishing for a compliment?" Shauna asked. "It's not like you to back down, especially from the likes of Everly Mae."

"Stop." Annalise ran a trembling hand through her hair, which boasted an inch of dark roots contrasting with her blond highlight. Meghan realized Annalise had stopped wearing makeup and carrying her designer purses. Things really were changing around Magnolia, not all of it for the better.

"I got a lecture on that from Jack," Annalise muttered. "I don't need one from you, too."

"Whoa, there." Shauna held out her hands, palms up. "Not looking for a catfight."

"Of course not," Annalise snapped. "You'll keep the peace at all costs."

"It's a better option than being a bitch just for the sake of it."

Meghan put a steadying hand on each of their arms before the conversation devolved any further. These women meant the world to her, and she wasn't going to let them implode. "Let's remember we're on each other's sides first and foremost."

She wasn't used to taking a stand, but Shauna and Annalise had taught her a lot about fighting for her convictions. She believed in the power of their friendship.

"Most likely this is a bump in the road with Jack," she said to Annalise, who grumbled in response.

"There is no road with Jack."

"There could be if you want it. The man is crazy about you."

"More likely, he thinks I'm crazy. Maybe I am. I should have known it wouldn't be easy to reinvent myself."

"But you are reinventing yourself," Meghan insisted.

"The only way to guarantee success in any area of your life is to keep men out of it," Shauna told them.

"Spill it." Meghan wagged a finger in Shauna's face. "You seem completely freaked out."

"You have no idea," Shauna murmured, and Meghan could see an emotion best described as abject terror in her friend's gaze.

"Something happened."

"What happened?" Annalise asked, blinking as if to clear her head. "Shauna, are you okay? You don't look okay."

A horn beeped from the long line of cars driving onto the property, startling all three of them.

Shauna shook her head. "It's nothing. We can wait until tomorrow to talk more. People are going to be looking for Meghan. Walker—"

"Tell us," Meghan said, squeezing Shauna's hand. The timing and location for a serious heart-to-heart weren't ideal. They were huddled against the side of the barn like teenage girls ditching class to sneak a smoke outside of school. But sometimes kids had the right of it. Nothing was more important than connecting with the people they cared about. "Everything else can wait."

"Let Everly Mae and her minions do the heavy lifting for a few minutes." Annalise wrinkled her adorable nose. "It's the least they deserve."

"I told Flynn I love him," Shauna said then pressed a finger to the corner of her eye. "Are anyone else's allergies going wild? The pollen count must be through the roof right now."

"Yeah," Annalise agreed while Meghan worked to come up with an appropriate response. "I've also been dealing with allergies. Pollen is everywhere."

Shauna offered a watery smile. "You used to be a better liar."

"What did he say?" Meghan asked when she found her voice. "And you do mean 'in love' not 'love like a brother for the sake of our kids.'"

"Not at all like a brother," Shauna confirmed. "He hugged me and said he'll take care of the boys and me."

"I'm going to kill him," Annalise answered immediately. "Doesn't matter that he's big and tough. I'll take him down."

"It's fine," Shauna said. "I knew better than to let myself fall for him again. This is my fault. I let myself believe in the fairy-tale ending when I know that's not my story."

"You don't know that. You deserve that ending if it's what you want," Meghan said. "I don't know what's going on in Flynn's handsome head, but he looks at you like you're everything to him."

"He told me once he's not built for love," Shauna admitted. "You know the old saying, when people show you who they are, believe them."

Annalise let out a delicate snort. "I believe Flynn Murphy is an idiot if he doesn't love you in return. Hell, Shauna, I'm half in love with you. You're damn near perfect."

"Remember our talk about masks?" Shauna's chin trembled, and she looked out across to the stage. "I try to appear perfect because of how broken I feel on the inside. It was okay in the moment, but since then, my doubts about being worthy of love have camped out in my heart like they mean to stay. Flynn knows me better than anyone. Even if he could fall in love, why would he pick someone with my past?"

She bit down on her lower lip and met Meghan's understanding gaze. "No one has ever picked me."

"We did," Meghan countered. "We're all damaged in

our own way. You've had more than your portion to overcome, Shauna. But you've done it. Maybe you were broken at some point, but now you're patched together and the result is even better."

"What about me? Pep talk me next," Annalise said with an enthusiasm that made the trio laugh. "I need someone to tell me that I'm going to be okay. Be my Glinda the Good Witch and bestow your wisdom. Am I better broken?"

"You aren't broken." Meghan reached out to hug her friend, surprised at how tightly Annalise held on. "People say it's because of the darkness that we notice the light. You're shining brightly," Meghan assured her friend. "You are the light guiding Trey and Margo as well. Don't let anyone—especially yourself—extinguish it."

Meghan had faith in the words, although of the three of them she had no business giving advice.

She wasn't shining brightly or ushering others into the light. Instead, she'd gone and stupidly fallen for a star when she should have known better. Ordinary people like her belonged with their feet flat on the earth, but maybe that made her uniquely qualified to help her brilliant friends.

As unlikely of an ally as Annalise might be, she'd done so much for Meghan. A few words of encouragement were the least she could offer in return.

"Don't let people like Everly Mae steal your light. Your kids need you to guide their way."

Annalise nodded, her eyes shining with gratitude, and Shauna joined them for a three-way hug. "We've taught you well, Padawan," Annalise said. "The student has become the master."

"Okay, now." Shauna laughed. "That might be enough wisdom for today. I think it's time we stop hiding."

"Nobody puts the three of us in the corner," Annalise agreed.

Shauna rolled her eyes with a laugh, and Meghan grinned, her heart lighter than it had been moments ago. She'd done it. She'd been the one to help get her friends through a difficult moment. Grammy would have been proud.

"You guys are the best," Shauna said, and for once, Meghan believed it.

When she caught a glimpse of Walker as she made her way through the gathering crowd, she didn't look away or try to avoid him.

He smiled and waved, and she did the same, wondering if her fears and doubts were all for nothing. Her heart yearned for that to be the case.

Once the concert began, she didn't have time for wondering or worrying about her place in Walker's life. She was too busy singing and dancing along with the rest of his adoring fans.

After an awkward introduction by Everly Mae, Walker kicked off the set with one of the Calloway Brothers' early hits, and the crowd went wild. It had been difficult, but based on the energy he exuded, no one would guess Walker had taken a break or endured a loss that brought him to his knees.

His voice was strong and sexy as he hit the gravelly low notes in several songs. He welcomed the audience and thanked them for their support of the school. Meghan had made it clear the focus of the event should stay on the art and music programs, which would hopefully flourish no matter who was in charge.

She didn't plan on relinquishing her position anytime soon but had scheduled a meeting with Carrie to begin the process of becoming more involved in the local art scene over summer break. There was no telling where it might lead, but it felt right.

"Even I have a crush on him now," Shauna said as she came to stand next to Meghan. Walker had moved on to a few songs from the Calloway Brothers' final album. Her palms tingled thinking about when he would debut his new music.

"He's amazing," Meghan agreed with a smile then fidgeted when a few people in front of them turned to stare before starting to sing along again.

"That was weird," she said to Annalise over the music. "I don't know those people."

Shauna elbowed her playfully. "I think it's because Walker keeps looking at you. They're probably wondering about the cutie who caught his attention."

"He doesn't keep looking at me," Meghan protested just as Walker finished a song and made obvious eye contact with her.

"Yeah, he does."

Meghan's face heated as warmth spread through her.

"I'd like to take a minute and try out something new," Walker said into the microphone. "For years, my brother and I wrote music together. When we lost Nash, I thought I'd lost music as well. Recently I've discovered my inspiration again."

"Oh, wow. He's looking right at you." Shauna grabbed Meghan's hand. "That is hot."

It was also undeniable. As the music began, it felt like everyone standing between Meghan and Walker disappeared. The notes coming from his guitar strings were an invisible cord that drew her toward him.

This was a different song than the one he'd played for

her in the studio. The emotion in his voice snared her like a siren song. He sang about loss, redemption and discovering his future in the light of a woman's eyes.

Was it possible Meghan was the woman he sang about? It seemed unlikely even though her heart wanted to believe it.

When Shauna squeezed her hand at the start of the second verse, Meghan forced herself to glance around at the crowd. They seemed just as enthralled as she felt, and she reminded herself that Walker was a professional. Captivating audiences was his bread and butter. There was a good chance many of the female concertgoers wanted to believe they could be the woman who inspired such a heartfelt, dazzling love song.

Only the women in the audience didn't know him like Meghan did. They hadn't spent hours talking and laughing together. She knew she'd shocked him with the kiss. She'd surprised herself with her boldness. Maybe this was his way of telling her he felt the same connection she did.

She'd given her friends plenty of advice about being their own light. Now Walker was singing about a light in the darkness. She'd spent too long hiding and letting fear get the best of her.

She vowed to herself that she would do more than kiss Walker. When the concert was over and the crowd left, she would share how she felt and hoped beyond hope that he might return the sentiment.

As the final notes ended, there were several moments of hushed, almost reverent silence.

Meghan heard a horse whinny from the direction of the barn, and she knew in her soul it was Orion voicing his approval. The crowd erupted into wild applause.

The enthusiastic group in front of Meghan and Shauna

were jumping up and down, so she lost sight of Walker for a moment as she was jostled and worked to right herself.

The shouting and clapping seemed to grow exponentially louder, and when she was able to see the stage again, Danielle Griggs was halfway across it.

The country music starlet wore a sparkling silver sheath dress with her blond hair falling in glossy waves down her back. Walker was waving and scanning the crowd—could he be searching for Meghan? He was clearly unaware of Dani's approach until she was upon him.

Meghan could only imagine the emotions that must be warring within him after playing the song he'd written on his own and the reception it had received.

But her emotions were the ones that felt out of control as Danielle turned him toward her and pressed a long kiss to his mouth. She seemed to stumble on her high heels, just as Meghan had lost her footing moments earlier, and Walker's arms went around her tiny waist.

"What the hell is she doing?" Shauna shouted into Meghan's ear, attempting to be heard over the catcalls and whistles around them. The crowd loved Dani and Walker together.

Meghan hadn't fully realized she'd lost her heart to the man until she felt it shattering inside her chest.

It was another few seconds before Walker pulled away from Dani, his features stunned. Then he seemed to remember the audience watching the spectacle.

Was it Meghan's imagination or did he try to subtly pull away from the bejeweled barnacle plastered to his side?

"Isn't he amazing?" Danielle said into the microphone, and the crowd responded with another enthusiastic round of cheers.

"Thank you all," Walker said as he leaned forward. His

gaze crashed into Meghan's just as Dani planted a smacking kiss on his cheek.

"I've got to get out of here," Meghan said to Shauna, dropping her gaze to the now-trampled grass in front of her. She could feel the tears coming and wasn't sure she'd be able to stop them.

"Of course you do." Shauna took Meghan's hand and led her toward the crowd's edge.

"I'm thrilled to be here with y'all tonight." Dani's voice was like fingernails on a chalkboard to Meghan's frayed nerves and aching heart. "And even more thrilled to be back with Walker and so in—"

"What she means…" Walker interrupted before the crowd drowned out his voice with their shouting.

What did she mean? Meghan wondered. What did any of this mean?

"Do y'all want to hear 'When Stars Collide'?" Danielle asked before Walker could finish his sentence.

The crowd roared once more, and Meghan realized it didn't matter what he'd been about to explain.

This moment showed her beyond a shadow of a doubt that she and Walker Calloway were never meant to be.

There was a reason posters came down from bedroom walls when teenage girls grew up. She might have encouraged her friends to let their light shine, but sometimes stars were in the sky for a reason. And those bound to earth shouldn't expect to mingle with celestial beings.

It was past time for Meghan to grow up and take control of the life she had. A life that would never involve Walker in the way her heart hoped.

CHAPTER TWENTY-SIX

ANNALISE COULDN'T FIGURE out how everything that had been falling into place a few days earlier was now crumbling to pieces.

An hour after the concert ended, she was busy helping with cleanup. The event had been a success, and she tried to ignore the bitterness she felt that Everly Mae had taken all the credit. Annalise didn't need public accolades any longer, even if she sometimes still wanted them. She'd done what she set out to do and had changed her life in the process. Although Jack was nowhere to be seen, lots of people were pitching in to make the work go faster, from Margo and Trey to Carrie and her husband, Dylan Scott, to Trinity Carlyle, Shauna and the twins.

Meghan had left after much convincing when it became clear how upset she was over Dani and Walker's onstage kiss. Annalise hadn't realized how fast and hard her sweet, kindhearted friend had fallen for Walker. Not that she blamed Meghan. Walker's appeal was undeniable, so his renewed relationship with Danielle Griggs had come as a shock to everyone.

Annalise had quickly come to despise the petite blonde stuck to Walker's side like she was made of glue. For his part, Walker barely appeared to notice Dani had latched on to him. He seemed happy and relieved that the concert had gone well and the response to his new songs had been so positive.

It broke Annalise's heart a tiny bit that Meghan had been so easily set aside. It was exactly what Meghan had feared and struggled to overcome in her past. Annalise wondered if any of them could truly leave behind their demons. Would they carry them along like passengers on the road of life?

Shauna was moving toward the future with the most positivity. She and Flynn worked together dismantling sections of the stage while their sons helped where they could.

While Shauna was still bothered by the fact that Flynn hadn't been able to tell her he loved her in return, the man's actions spoke loud enough for everyone to hear. He was devoted to Shauna and the twins.

Annalise might not be getting the happy ending she wanted, but she could still rejoice in Shauna's happiness. As for her own, it was a work in progress. She hated how things had ended with Jack and wished he could understand why she'd stepped away when she did. He thought she was wimping out, and maybe that was true. At least she could tell herself it was for the greater good.

Lanterns and strings of party lights still glowed around the pasture's perimeter, making the wide-open space feel like a cozy sanctuary from the shadows heralding the gathering night.

The sun had set while Walker finished his last song, painting brilliant orange-and-red coils across the sky. Those rich hues faded then shifted to dusky evening. Within the next hour, it would be charcoal black with only the stars shining overhead as natural light.

The plan was to finish the majority of the cleanup and return in the morning for the rest. Annalise hoped she'd be able to avoid Jack, at least for tonight. She was tired, and her heart ached in a way she didn't know how to soothe.

Once they were home and she'd tucked her kids into bed,

she'd regroup and spend the hours she should be sleeping shoring up her defenses.

Fake it until you make it had worked up until this point. There was no reason to believe it wouldn't carry her through this hurdle as well.

The sound of angry voices from the barn made her pause in the act of tying up a trash bag. It sounded like Everly Mae and Jack were arguing, which didn't make sense.

She met Shauna's gaze across the field as Everly Mae's shouting grew louder.

"Of course she stole the money. Who else would have a reason? She must have planned it all along."

It was difficult for Annalise to hear Jack's response over the roar in her head. Whatever was happening caused a sick pit of dread to open in her stomach.

As if they understood things were about to go down, Margo and Trey appeared at her side.

"Why is Mrs. Tinsdale yelling, Mommy?" Margo asked, her voice unsteady.

Annalise's children had heard too much yelling when Jonathan was arrested. Their father shouting at the FBI agents who barged into their home and later the clients who descended on the house looking for him. For answers. For their stolen money.

Although concert tickets had been sold online before the show, PTO volunteers had passed around donation jars during the concert.

From his place on the stage, Walker encouraged the audience to be generous in giving to a good cause.

Annalise didn't have any idea how much additional money they'd raised, but she guessed the sum was significant.

She also knew they'd locked it away inside the barn's small office, and she and Jack were the only two people with keys to that space.

"Is Chief Davis still here?" Everly Mae shrieked into the night, loud enough to wake the dead.

Annalise automatically put a hand on Trey's shoulder when the boy winced.

"It's okay, sweetheart. This has nothing to do with us."

"Mrs. Tinsdale is heading this way," her son answered. "We need to go, Mom. Now."

"No, Trey." She understood the urge to flee but forced her feet to remain still. "We've done nothing wrong."

"You took it." Everly Mae wagged a violent finger at Annalise as she rushed forward, her husband, Tobias, and Jack hot on her heels. "Somebody call the police. I want Annalise Haverford arrested."

Both Margo and Trey moved closer, but they didn't cower behind her legs. Her children stood tall, each taking a step in front of her like they were forming a pint-sized shield of protection.

Even with confusion and panic making her heart pummel her rib cage, the display of solidarity caused her chest to fill with love.

Shauna and Flynn approached as well, along with the twins and Gus.

She felt like she'd been transported to a fantasy land or a movie set, one where her allies were gathering to have her back as she squared off against her sworn enemy.

Annalise was done fighting battles. The pressure of it felt too exhausting for words. She didn't want to go toe to toe with Everly Mae or anyone.

All she wanted was to live her life in a way that would make her kids proud. She wanted to be happy, maybe for the first time.

"Is there a problem?" she asked calmly and registered the snap in Everly Mae's furious gaze. A subtle flash of uncertainty, as if she didn't recognize Annalise as a person who could respond with anything but hypothetical fists flying.

"Two thousand dollars is missing from the donations we collected tonight." Everly Mae had reached them, and the fury rolling off her in waves was a palpable force. "You took it. You planned this whole thing as a way to siphon off some of the donations for your own benefit."

Annalise huffed out a laugh at the absurdity of the accusation. "I wish two grand would solve my problems."

"You took it." Droplets of saliva pooled at the corner of Everly Mae's glossy lips like she was foaming at the mouth to make sure Annalise paid for this transgression. "You're a criminal, just like your husband. The amount doesn't matter. What did Jonathan need with all the money he stole? He ruined people because he was a monster. You're both monsters."

Annalise felt a shudder pass through Trey as Margo released a gasp of denial. Her poor children, still having to atone for the sins of their father. Jonathan was in a minimum-security federal prison in northern Virginia. The facility catered to white-collar criminals; for all she knew, her ex-husband spent his days reading and working out.

He was behind bars, but was his cell any more confining than the bars that caged the rest of them, unable to move on with their lives because they were continually condemned for wrongs that didn't belong to them?

"I'm not a monster," she said, still calm, taking each of her children's hands and giving them a reassuring squeeze. "Neither is my ex-husband. He's a man who did awful things. I'm willing to apologize to every one of his victims. If I had the means, I'd make restitution. But he's still a father to my kids, Everly Mae. Don't make this worse than it needs to be."

"You're the one making it worse by stealing," Tobias

said then caught Asher Davis's eye. "She took the money, Chief. We're trying to do a good thing here, and the Haverfords clearly think they are above the law. She's a scumbag criminal just like her husband."

"That's enough," Shauna said, moving directly next to Margo. "Annalise doesn't deserve this."

"You've fallen for her charm," Everly Mae told Shauna. "But she'll screw you over, just like she has the rest of us."

Annalise shook her head. As grateful as she was for Shauna's support, she didn't want anyone having to come to her defense. She didn't ask for any of this. Why hadn't she left Magnolia to start over where her reputation and Jonathan's misdeeds wouldn't follow her?

"You have no proof," Shauna pointed out.

"Search her," Everly Mae demanded. "Check her car."

"She didn't take the money," Shauna insisted.

Annalise dropped Trey's hand to touch her friend's arm. "It's okay. They can—"

"We don't need your permission." Tobias's tone was hot with righteous outrage. "I'm a member of town council. I demand—"

Shauna snorted. "You're not the king of this town."

"Shut up," Tobias spit out. "You—"

Annalise heard a low growl from Flynn Murphy. That wasn't good. *Don't poke the bear*, she silently willed Tobias.

But the man had obviously been stewing in his misdirected anger for months. It didn't matter that Annalise hadn't known about her ex-husband's scheme. She was still guilty by association.

Tobias sneered at Annalise. "You and your husband are low-life, trashy, despicable—"

"Enough." Asher Davis stepped forward but not quickly enough.

Annalise had been so preoccupied worrying about what Flynn might do and how Shauna was enduring the brunt of Tobias's temper that she'd taken her attention off of Trey.

Suddenly her son launched himself at Tobias. "Don't talk about my mom that way," the boy yelled in a voice thick with tears. He punched Everly Mae's short, balding husband right in his flabby belly.

For a moment there was a stunned silence. Annalise thought Tobias was going to topple over like an uprooted tree. But he swung and connected with Trey's cheek. Annalise screamed as her son fell into a crumpled heap on the ground.

Zach and Timmy let out matching war cries and rushed at Tobias, little fists flying.

Jack reached for the man, who fought back like he was being attacked by a gang of street thugs instead of a couple of kindergartners, but Everly Mae grabbed Jack around the waist and shoved him.

Asher moved in, but not as fast as Flynn Murphy. He swung and landed a brutal blow to the center of Tobias's face. Blood spurted from his nose as Tobias crumpled to the grass.

"He's dead," Timmy yelled in a high-pitched squeal.

"Daddy killed him," Zach whispered then ran into Shauna's arms along with his brother.

"He killed my husband," Everly Mae shrieked over and over. Shauna shook her head, eyes brimming with unshed tears.

Annalise felt paralyzed for a few seconds, Margo clutching her legs. But as Trey sat up, looking dazed and holding a hand to his face, she moved to her son and dropped down next to him.

"Oh, sweetheart, I'm so sorry."

The boy's face was soaked with tears, and he latched on

to her, burying his head in her shirt while Margo clutched her around the neck.

Asher knelt next to Tobias. "He's not dead," he announced. "Everly Mae, stop screaming."

His tone was pure authority, and a leaden silence descended on the group.

Asher straightened. "Two thousand is missing?" he demanded of Jack.

Tobias let out a distressed moan. "She did it."

"Not another word from you," Asher ordered then looked over his shoulder toward Trinity. "Can you get ice from the house? His nose is broken."

Trinity nodded and jogged out of the circle of light toward the main house in the distance.

"Daddy broke his nose," Timmy told Zach. Shauna pulled them closer but didn't look up as Flynn tried to meet her gaze. When he realized the effort was futile, his features turned to granite.

No.

This wasn't how tonight should go. Although Annalise hadn't taken the money, the accusation and her connection with Jonathan's crimes had still tainted the whole event.

She had no idea where Walker had gone. Dani Griggs had led him away to talk to a reporter from the local paper as the crowd began to disperse. But he wouldn't be happy with the scandal that had erupted in the past few minutes. Annalise might be innocent, but she understood how a person could be tainted just by an accusation and the resulting doubts.

Would anyone in this town trust her ever again?

"You are welcome to search me," she told the police chief. "And my car. I have nothing to hide."

“Filthy liar.” Everly Mae had removed her denim jacket so her husband could hold it to his bleeding nose.

“Let’s get you on your feet,” Jack told Tobias, hauling him up.

Flynn muttered something under his breath, then turned and stalked away.

Shauna watched him go. She glanced at Annalise, who could read the heartbreak in her friend’s gentle gaze.

No.

“Please search me.” She managed to peel Margo’s arms off her enough to stand and help Trey to his feet. “I want everyone to know I had nothing to do with this.”

Asher gave her a terse nod. He returned his attention to Jack. Annalise couldn’t help but be hurt by the fact that her former lover—a man she’d believed to be her friend—still refused to look at her.

If only she could do a disappearing act the way Flynn had and find a place to lick her wounds in private.

But she didn’t have that choice with her children holding on like she was a life raft in a raging sea.

She needed to be strong for them, even if she didn’t feel it.

“Is there another explanation other than theft?” Ash asked Jack.

Jack closed his eyes for a moment, then shook his head. “Everly Mae and I counted the donations right after the concert and locked the cash in the office.”

“Who has access to the office?”

Jack’s throat bobbed as he swallowed. “Annalise and I have the only two keys.”

“Search me,” she repeated, speaking the words more to Jack than to Asher.

His gaze crashed into hers but gave away none of his emotions.

"Mommy, I want to go home," Margo cried. Annalise's jeans were wet with the girl's tears.

"I don't think searching you is necessary yet," Asher announced.

Tobias and Everly Mae started to argue, but Trinity interrupted with the ice. "I also called a doctor friend. She's coming now to take a look at you." She nodded toward Everly Mae. "Can you walk with Tobias to the house?"

Everly Mae nodded, almost reluctantly.

Ash flashed his fiancée a grateful smile.

"I want to press charges against that brute," Tobias mumbled.

Ash stilled him with a hand on his shoulder. "You assaulted multiple children tonight, Mr. Tinsdale. Let the doctor see to your nose, then go home. I'll handle the money situation."

"Chief," Everly Mae began, her tone nauseatingly plaintive all of a sudden. "You must—"

"I'll handle it," Ash repeated, quiet but commanding.

Even Everly Mae didn't argue, but she glared at Annalise as she followed Trinity and Tobias. "Thief," she said on a nasty hiss of breath.

"Shauna, will you take Trey and Margo home?" Annalise asked her friend.

"I want to stay with you, Mommy," Trey told her. How that word *Mommy* plucked at her heartstrings.

"My love." She crouched down until she was at eye level with the boy. "I need you to take care of your sister tonight. I'll be home as soon as I can. This is all a misunderstanding."

"Who's gonna take care of you?" Trey whispered, and her gut clenched when he glanced over her shoulder.

Without turning, she knew Trey was looking at Jack. She wanted to take her son's chin in her hand and force him to focus on her. No one was going to look out for Annalise. She only had herself to rely on.

Before she could respond, he gave a slight nod, hugged her and took Margo's hand. "Come on, Margs. It'll be okay."

Shauna had lifted her sons into her arms. The twins had their faces hidden in Shauna's chambray blouse. Annalise would have thought the weight of two boys too much, but Shauna looked like she could carry Zach and Timmy all the way home without breaking stride if she needed to.

She flashed a grim smile toward Annalise but turned up the wattage as she looked at Trey and Margo. "Your mom will be home soon, and I'm sure all this nonsense is going to make her hungry. A fresh pan of brownies might be just the thing we need."

"Okay," Trey agreed dutifully. Margo only sniffed and swayed closer to Trey.

Annalise wanted to reach for her kids again, hating to see them in this state. But first, she had to clear her name and deal with the Tinsdales and their wrath.

Ash cleared his throat when it was just the three of them remaining. "I apologize in advance, Annalise. Are you sure you don't mind me looking in your car?"

"I'm the one who suggested it," she said with as much dignity as she could muster under the circumstances.

Just when she'd thought she'd left rock bottom in her rearview mirror, it felt as though she were driving in circles, destined to revisit the same dreadful scenery over and over.

"Jack, we don't need you for this part," Ash told the other man.

"I'm not leaving her," Jack said simply.

Annalise registered the police chief's surprise but didn't

react. She felt too numb. The adrenaline that had flooded her as Everly Mae came tearing out of the barn drained like a bathtub with the plug pulled, leaving her emotionally empty.

"My car's parked in front of the house."

None of them spoke as Jack led the way, their footfalls soundless on the trampled grass of the pasture.

The event had been a success, she reminded herself. Meghan's job was safe. Everything else she could manage, especially when she knew Ash would find nothing in her car.

She hadn't locked it, even with the masses coming to the property for the concert. A temporary fence was erected to keep concertgoers away from the residence.

The curtains fluttered in the living room window as Asher Davis opened the passenger side door, the interior bulbs flooding the darkness.

She saw Everly Mae peek out, the barest hint of a smug smile playing around the corners of her mouth.

And Annalise knew before she heard the chief's hushed curse that he'd found the missing money in the glove compartment.

Heat burned through her, starting at her scalp and scorching its way to her toes until it felt as though her whole body had been set aflame.

Was this a reckoning for the mistakes she'd made and the people she'd used and mistreated or a matter of revenge by association?

Maybe Everly Mae would have been content to leave her alone if Annalise had gone softly into the night. She could have crawled under a rock, hurled herself prostrate onto some reparation stone and generally remained shunned and miserable. That might have kept her safe from this obvious—and ingenious if she had to admit it—scheme for revenge.

But Annalise had the gall to overhaul her life, to change and grow and keep going. She had the nerve to be happy, and the people Jonathan had wronged couldn't have that.

Too big for her britches.

"She didn't do it."

Her gaze darted to Jack, who was scowling at Ash and the cash envelope he held.

"You don't know that," Annalise countered because she wanted to rage. Not at the dying of the light but for the hope she'd had that she deserved a second chance. She couldn't take out her temper on the police chief. Railing and kicking up a fuss would only give Everly Mae the satisfaction she craved.

The woman wanted to see Annalise undone.

Jack had seen her undone in the most intimate ways. But he'd turned his back on her when she hadn't been willing to fight.

Why was he defending her now? It didn't make sense, but his support felt unwarranted and infuriating.

"I know you," Jack said quietly, the full weight of his attention on her as if Asher Davis didn't exist.

"Annalise, I think we should talk more at the station."

"Yes, Chief."

"No."

Jack placed a hand on the police chief's arm.

"You'll want to remove that, Jack," Asher said calmly.

Jack lifted his hand then dragged it over his stubbled jaw. "You don't believe she'd do this, Ash. Hell, she practically begged you to search the car. Someone framed her and I think we both can take a good guess as to who."

"I'll get to the bottom of it," Asher assured him.

"You can't take her to the station. Her kids need her."

"It's okay, Jack." She wasn't sure why she felt the need to reassure him when panic poured through her like a summer rainstorm.

"Damn it, Annalise, none of this is okay." He grabbed her by both her arms, practically lifting her off her feet.

"Jack," Ash warned in that same even voice.

"Why won't you fight for yourself?"

She blew out a shaky breath, hating that his touch, which was hardly gentle, still soothed her. "I'm tired of fighting," she said honestly.

"Then I'll fight for you."

"Why?" The question whispered out of her mouth before she could pull it back. It shouldn't matter.

"Because I love you, you confounded woman."

Her mouth dropped open, and she thought she heard Ash curse again, but the police chief took a step back to give them some space.

"I didn't even think you liked me anymore," she told Jack, shocked to find her voice thick with emotion.

His grasp softened. "I like you. I love you. I respect the hell out of you, too, which is why it kills me to watch you let people like the Tinsdales run roughshod over you. You're a fighter, Annalise. For everyone else. You stood up for Shauna. You saved Meghan's job."

"Those things benefited me, too," she said quickly because she couldn't accept Jack's opinion of her when she'd believed for so long that she was the selfish, superficial shrew her mother had raised her to be.

"That's not why you did them. Close your eyes for just a moment, honey."

She was so bewildered by the warmth of his tone that she followed the command without question.

Jack pulled her closer and dropped the sweetest kiss on each of her eyelids. "See yourself like I do. You are brave and beautiful. Even though you try to hide it, your heart shines through in everything you do. You are honorable, Annalise Haverford. You shouldn't have to pay for your ex-husband's crimes. Be honest. Did you steal that money?"

Her eyes popped open and she glanced from Jack's dark gaze, filled with equal parts tenderness and exasperation, to where Ash Davis was watching her expectantly.

"I didn't steal anything."

Ash inclined his head. "Can you explain how the envelope of cash ended up in your glove compartment?"

She shook her head. "No, but can we take a tiny pause in discussing the stolen money?"

The chief's eyes widened, but she was already returning her attention to Jack.

"Tell me again you love me."

He gave her a slow grin. "I love you." He trailed his palms up her arms until he was cupping her face. Lord, how she'd missed being touched by this man. "Are you going to say it back to me or leave me hanging?"

She swallowed down the fear that fizzed up from her chest. After Jonathan, she'd promised herself she wouldn't rely on anyone else to make her happy. She would have her own back.

But something had changed in the past couple of months. She'd transformed and grown into not only her own best champion. She'd learned to be a friend and accept help and love in return.

Loving Jack didn't make her feel weak the way her marriage had. This man gave her strength and support just the way she was. He liked her when she was brave and independent, and she also liked herself that way.

"I love you, you ornery, stubborn, beautiful man."

"Beautiful might be pushing it," Jack said and kissed her.

"Your heart is beautiful," she said against his lips.

"And it's yours forever."

"Okay, enough with the pause." Ash gestured to the house after checking his phone. "Trinity can't hold back the Tinsdale terrors much longer." He looked pained as he held up the money. "I'm afraid I'm still going to need to take Annalise to the station to discuss—"

"The camera." Jack's expression was as triumphant as Trey's after a grand slam home run. He put an arm around her shoulder, and she felt safer than she had in a long time.

Whatever happened, this man would stay at her side. He would take care of her heart, which was exactly what she deserved. Despite the anger at Everly Mae and the worry over how she'd clear her name, Annalise trusted Jack.

Ash raised a thick brow. "A camera, you say?"

Jack nodded, his jaw set in a determined line. "I installed it because we had so many animals ready to give birth. Most recently, I have it focused on Gertie the goat. Her stall is right next to the office. As long as the battery is still good, we'll have footage of anyone who went in or came out of the office tonight."

The police chief looked almost as relieved as Annalise felt. "Then let's go back to the barn." He glanced over his shoulder at the house. "I'm guessing that tape is going to prove quite enlightening."

Jack took Annalise's hand as they headed across the pasture once more. "I've got you," he said softly.

"I know." She squeezed his fingers. "And you better never let go."

CHAPTER TWENTY-SEVEN

SUNDAY AFTERNOON, Shauna sat on the rocking chair on her front porch, sipping a glass of lemonade Annalise had made from scratch.

"You fall in love, and now you're going to turn into Suzy Homemaker?"

"It's good, right?" Annalise asked with a satisfied grin. She'd had a smile on her face ever since returning home from Whimsy Farm to report the camera footage had shown Everly Mae picking the lock on the office door.

Shauna hadn't realized people outside of movies and crime television shows employed lock picking as a skill. A few minutes later, Annalise's blond nemesis had exited the office, carrying the envelope Asher Davis had later found in the glove compartment.

She'd been wearing gloves to hide her fingerprints, which even Annalise had conceded was impressive attention to detail.

When they confronted Everly Mae, Annalise reported she'd thrown a fit and denied involvement. Then she'd burst into hysterical sobbing, lamenting the unfairness of Annalise finding a way to reinvent herself when she deserved to be punished right along with her ex-husband.

In the end, Tobias was innocent and unaware of the scheme. He'd apologized to Annalise for the awful things he'd said and had shown up at the house early this morning to apologize to the kids for his behavior.

Shauna appreciated the gesture, which had been more than Flynn offered. The infuriating man had gone radio silent since he'd stalked away last night.

"Did you get a seed?" Annalise asked, eyeing the lemonade pitcher dubiously. "I took care when squeezing these suckers. When life gives you lemons, you should order an electric juicer."

Before Shauna could answer, Meghan, who'd been absently scrolling on her phone, gasped in shock.

"What's wrong?" Annalise and Shauna demanded in unison.

"Nothing." Her voice shook with emotion.

"That's a lie," Annalise said. "We don't lie in the Front Porch Club."

When Meghan finally raised her gaze, tears shone in her eyes. "I'm so stupid. The biggest idiot on the planet." She transferred her phone to the wicker coffee table in front of the lounge chair and wrapped her arms tightly around herself.

"Also fat and boring, like my mother always told me, although I thought I'd grown out of caring and liked myself anyway."

Shauna set aside her foul mood to cross to where her friend sat. She squeezed Meghan's hand and lowered herself onto the tufted cushion.

"You are none of those things."

"Don't tell us you're scrolling through pictures of celebrities at the beach." Annalise drained her glass. "That is not the way to start summer break. Comparison is the thief of joy, as they say."

Meghan sniffed. "It's weird how social media sites can read your mind—at least that's how it feels. I had a random thought about Walker and Dani together. Suddenly, one of my country music fan friends posts a photo of the two hugging on the street in Nashville."

"Maybe it was an old photo." Shauna grabbed the phone and pulled up the site. She studied the photo. "Why doesn't it look old?"

"It's from today," Meghan confirmed. "Walker and Dani are in Nashville together today. They must have taken a private plane. I'm sure Gus was fine staying with Jack." She glanced at Annalise. "Did you know about this?"

"Not one bit."

Shauna read the headline that accompanied the grainy photo. "'After a private concert on the North Carolina coast, reunited lovebirds hit the city to record new music.'"

Annalise sat forward. "I can't believe it. He doesn't even like her."

"He kissed her on stage last night," Meghan reminded her friends.

"That was for show," Annalise insisted.

"I don't know what I expected."

"She kissed him," Shauna clarified.

"He kissed her back." Meghan wished she could pluck her miserable heart out of her chest. "I thought him kissing me back was something special, but I guess not. Isn't that the definition of stupid?"

Annalise shook her head. "If anyone is stupid, it's Walker for being drawn in again by Danielle Griggs and her web of hair extensions and lip fillers. He likes you, Meghan. I know it."

"Sure he does," Meghan agreed with an eye roll. "Everybody likes me. I'm the girl next door and everybody's friend. Dani Griggs is the type of woman a man like Walker canoodles with while the paparazzi is watching."

"She probably called the press," Shauna said. She hated seeing her friend like this.

"It doesn't matter." Meghan brushed a quick hand across her cheeks. "I've got what I need, and I have Walker and the two of you to thank for it. My job is safe, and I've already had several people contact me from foundations around the country that help fund music and art programs in elementary schools. I'm also going to work with Carrie for the summer, so everything will be fine. I'm going to be fine."

"You deserve better than fine," Annalise said. "We all do."

"Speaking of better than fine—" Meghan's smile turned genuine "—can we talk more about Jack Grainger's shocking romantic side?"

Annalise looked positively twitterpated. "He was amazing."

"You deserve that," Shauna told her. "Just as much as the rest of us. Maybe even more."

"Not more," Annalise said gently. "No word from Flynn?"

Shauna grimaced. "I told the boys he'd called to check on them, and we'd see him later. I just wonder if we'll ever see him again."

"You can't mean that. He wouldn't—"

"I saw the look in his eyes last night," Shauna interrupted. "He was..."

"Mad as hell?" Annalise supplied. "I'm not condoning violence, but I understood his sentiment. When Tobias knocked Trey off his feet and then went after the twins—"

"To be fair," Shauna said quietly, "Zach and Timmy attacked him."

Annalise hissed out an angry breath while Meghan squeezed her hand. "They're little boys," the art teacher reminded Shauna, "and they were defending their friend."

"Trey appreciates them," Annalise said. "I do, too. Just like I appreciate Flynn. I owe him a thank-you when we see him."

"If," Shauna insisted quietly. She was afraid speaking in anything but a whisper would allow her emotions to overtake her. "I say if because the look I saw in Flynn's eyes last night wasn't anger, although I think there was plenty of that watching Tobias Tinsdale lash out at the kids. He was also terrified of his reaction. Answering violence with violence doesn't work and changed the course of Flynn's life when we were younger. He thought he had a handle on his temper."

"He hit a man who was assaulting our kids," Annalise argued. "He didn't beat him to a pulp or have to be pulled away in a fit of uncontrollable rage. If Flynn hadn't stepped in, Jack or Ash would have done the same."

"Tobias was out of line," Meghan reminded her. "That's why he came to apologize."

Shauna sighed. "I don't disagree, but I'm not sure Flynn sees it that way."

"How do you see it?" Meghan asked.

Shauna realized that was the crux of the silent battle inside her. If she were going to let Flynn back into their lives and her heart, it would be all of him. Not just the softened edges but the sharp corners that could still poke and tear.

Was she ready to give him that chance? Did he even want it?

As if in answer to that question, a familiar truck rolled down the street and parked at the curb.

"Is it wrong that I want to run into the house and hide?"

Annalise shook her head. "The urge is understandable, but you're going to stay here while Meghan and I go into the house and squeeze more lemons. I'm hoping Flynn will stay for a glass."

Shivers tingled along Shauna's spine as he stepped out of the vehicle and closed the door. He glanced in her direction and then away as if gathering courage. She didn't know what to make of that, but her heartbeat sped up like she was on a roller coaster approaching the first giant hill.

"I don't want to go into the house," Meghan said with a pout that would have been adorable in another situation. "I want to watch."

"Oh, darlin'." Annalise grabbed the woman's hand and pulled her to her feet. "We'll watch from the front window. I'm an expert lip reader."

"Good to know," Shauna said as she stood and wiped an invisible speck of dirt from the front of her pleated peasant skirt. "I'll be sure to keep my back to the house."

"Spoilsport," Annalise murmured. She disappeared into the house with Meghan following.

"I didn't mean to scare your friends away," Flynn said as he approached. He wore tan cargo pants and a dark blue T-shirt, looking far too appealing even though shadows formed bruises under his stormy eyes.

He rubbed an absent finger against the knuckle of his opposite hand. There was a slight scrape, the only sign he carried from his run-in with Tobias.

"You didn't scare them." Looking down from the porch to where Flynn stood in the bright afternoon sunlight and the miles it felt separated them, she could see the muscle ticking in his jaw.

"You didn't scare any of us," she added, knowing they both needed to hear it.

He ran a hand through his hair. His throat worked as though he were fighting back the words he wanted to say.

"I scared myself," he admitted, his voice husky and raw. "I wanted to kill that guy, Shauna. Just like all those years ago. There's been so much discipline drilled into me. Years of therapy and the damn coping mechanisms I've adopted were useless in the face of my rage. One second was all it took to undo everything. He put his hands on my son, and I wanted to destroy him. Just like I wanted to annihilate the man who hurt you."

Her throat ached from the tears she tried not to shed. She'd cried so much after Flynn left for the army and then when he'd walked away from her on the heels of the night they'd shared. Her tears wouldn't do either of them a bit of good.

She wasn't sure what he read in her silence, but his shoulders seemed to deflate. She'd never seen Flynn anything but solid and intimidating. Now he appeared irrevocably broken, like a child's toy smashed to bits. It was a foolish thought because she'd been with him all during the concert, laughing and stealing kisses when the boys weren't looking.

Nothing had truly changed. Only everything had changed.

"I'm sorry," he said, devoid of emotion. "I only came by to tell you—"

"You're leaving," she supplied before he could, willing her trembling legs not to give out on her. "I guess I should have expected that." She tried for a laugh but didn't quite manage it. "I might have expected this ending from the beginning, but reality still feels like a blow."

His eyes churned with emotions so wild she couldn't read them. "I told you I wouldn't hurt you again. I wasn't coming to tell you I'm leaving, Shauna. I wanted you to know I reached out to my counselor, and she's going to refer me to somebody in the area. I never want to feel like I'm that close to losing it. I don't want to believe I've lost you because of my anger, but that's your choice."

He drew in a slow breath as if collecting his composure. "You have the power. I'm not giving up a relationship with my sons, but if you want me out of your life other than bumbling along as a co-parent, I'll respect that. It's going to be the hardest thing I've ever done. Harder than walking away, but I want you to be happy."

Shauna's mind and heart reeled as she tried to process his words. Why did he look so defeated if he wasn't leaving or giving up? She realized she still hadn't managed a response when Flynn cleared his throat.

"I can hear the boys in the back. I'm going to say hello. I want to talk to Trey as well. I owe an apology to your friends, although I suppose I could wave since they're staring at us from behind the curtains."

She breathed out a laugh. "Reading your lips."

He frowned in confusion, then sighed. "I'm sorry, Shauna. I can't say it enough. I wish I could have been the man you needed me to be. I wish for a lot of things. But we'll figure out how to do right by our boys."

Her brain still addled, she glanced over her shoulder to see Annalise and Meghan shoot her matching incredulous looks. She turned back, and Flynn was walking across the yard, snapping her out of her bewilderment.

"Wait," she shouted. He immediately paused, so she ran down the stairs, stopping short directly behind him.

"What if you make me happy?" she asked on a rush of breath. "What if you're the man I need you to be, mistakes and all?"

He turned slowly. "Am I?"

"How can you doubt it? I'm the one who said I love you."

"That was before," he reminded her in a gentle voice. "Before I showed you I still can't be trusted."

She shook her head and took his hands. They were warm in hers and precisely the right fit. "I trust you with my life and my heart. I trust you to love and protect our sons. And I trust you to throw one good knockout punch to finish a fight before it starts."

He blinked like he was as discombobulated as she felt and then laughed. "Throwing punches is one of the few things I'm good at."

"You're good at a lot of things—way too good at making me fall in love with you over and over again."

He lifted his hands and smoothed back her hair, bringing her close until their foreheads pressed together and their breath mingled in the sultry heat of the afternoon.

Another tremor traveled through him. "I never stopped loving you. The moment I saw you and Declan together sitting in the driveway outside that foster home, my heart belonged to you, Shauna. I tried to leave you in peace because I thought I was doing the right thing. I thought we were all wrong, but my heart is yours alone. That's how it will be until I take my last breath and probably beyond that. You are everything good in my life."

She couldn't help the whimper of pleasure that escaped her. "If your career in security doesn't work out, you should take up professional poker because you don't give away a thing."

"I won't make that mistake again." He leaned down and kissed her and it wasn't just their mouths joining; it was their souls. "I'm going to spend the rest of our lives making sure you have no reason to doubt me. I'm going to tell you I love you so much you'll beg me to shut up."

She wrapped her arms tight around his neck as he lifted her off the ground. "I hope so."

"Daddy's here," Zach called.

Shauna heard the pounding of little feet approaching. Flynn lowered her but kept her tucked close to his side as Zach and Timmy ran toward them.

The boys stopped, their eyes widening at Shauna's wet cheeks.

"These are happy tears," she said quickly. "What would you think about all of us becoming a family for real?"

The boys looked stunned for a moment and then erupted into joyous cheers of delight.

"Wait." Flynn held up a hand, and the twins went immediately motionless.

Fancy trick. Did boys always listen to their fathers more than their mothers? She would have to work on that.

He bent down and opened his arms. The twins came forward almost shyly then clutched at him when he wrapped an arm around each of them.

"I'm sorry about last night. I shouldn't have punched that man. I went a little wild when he—"

"It's okay, Daddy," Zach said. "We know fighting isn't good. Trey told us that sometimes you just gotta let loose with a whopper."

Shauna rolled her lips together to keep from grinning. Fighting was no laughing matter, but it was hard to hide her happiness at the moment.

Flynn looked at each of the boys. "Trey has the right of it. Mostly I'm sorry for walking away from you and your mother. I'm not perfect, but I want you to know I will be here for all of you. I'm going to love you as best I can. If I make mistakes, I'm going to apologize and do better the next time."

"That's what Zach and I do when we fight," Timmy told him. "Mommy taught us."

"Did she teach you?" Zach asked.

"Your mother taught me a lot of things. She taught me how to love and that I deserve to be loved."

"I love you, Daddy," Timmy said with a shy smile.

"I love you, too," Zach echoed.

Shauna couldn't hold back crying as she saw matching tears shining in Flynn's eyes. His gaze didn't look stormy. It was clear and calm and so precious to her.

She wrapped her arms around all three of her boys. Her forever family.

She glanced toward the front porch, where Annalise and Meghan weren't bothering to hide anymore. They stood in the window, hugging each other as they both gave her an enthusiastic thumbs-up. It may have taken a long time to get there, but Shauna had finally found her way home.

* * * * *

A CAROLINA DANCE

CHAPTER ONE

TRINITY CARLYLE STARED at herself in the full-length mirror hanging on the door in her childhood bedroom in her mother's two-story home in Magnolia, North Carolina.

"I look like a tired potato sack," she murmured.

"You look beautiful," her sister Freya countered.

"It doesn't matter," Trinity said to her reflection, ignoring her older sister, who lay on the bed, feet propped up on the filigreed headboard. "This isn't even a real date."

"You look amazing," Freya insisted.

Trinity turned away from the mirror. She smoothed a hand over the burgundy dress with ruching that gathered at a sparkly ornament on the side. Freya had loaned her the flattering silk confection for the evening.

Having given birth only three months earlier, Trinity still didn't fit into many of her regular clothes, mostly due to her increased cup size thanks to breastfeeding baby Thomas.

Not that the wardrobe she'd brought with her when she escaped her abusive ex and eventually landed back in Magnolia had included many wedding-appropriate cocktail dresses.

Luckily for her, Freya had spent years on the reality-show circuit, so she had outfits for any and all occasions. Like Trinity, Freya had recently returned to North Carolina full-time, and as she was intent on reinventing herself, she seemed more than willing to part with as many items from her former life as she could.

"The dress is beautiful anyway." Trinity tugged at the scooped neckline. Pre-Thomas, her proportions had been almost boyishly modest. But now…

"I'm not sure I can strap these girls down enough to feel confident they won't pop out at any minute."

"A little cleavage isn't the worst thing in the world," Freya told her with a wink. "Ash might appreciate your new look."

"Don't say that." Trinity's cheeks burned with a mix of embarrassment and anticipation. "You're going to make me too anxious to go through with this. It's a favor. He needed a date for a wedding, nothing more."

"Why not more?" Freya demanded as she rolled over to face Trinity, pushing a lock of dark hair away from her face. "Asher Davis has liked you since the night he found you peeing in the woods on the side of the highway coming into town. You like him, too. What's the problem?"

Trinity flattened her palm against her forehead. "Where to start? My last relationship was a train wreck of monumental proportions. I'm not even sure I'm capable of being with someone normal. I have a baby. I live with my mother."

Freya held up a hand. "Ash lived with his mother-in-law up until the new year—"

"Because he was doing her a favor. Not because he didn't have other options. He's already got a kid. He had a wife. He doesn't want the burden that I would be."

"You aren't a burden." Freya flipped her long legs over the side of the bed and stood. She took a step forward and cupped Trinity's face in her hands. "You are a treasure. Ash or any man would be lucky to have you. You can't let Dave stay in your head, Trin. He was awful, but now you're rid of him."

Trinity swallowed back the tears that threatened to overtake her every time she thought about her ex and the way he'd shown up to Thomas's christening just before Christmas. He'd been wielding a knife and making threats.

Freya's now fiancé, Christopher Greer, had been injured in an altercation with him. Ash, who was not only a stand-up guy and an amazing father but also the town's police chief, had stepped in to arrest Dave.

Trinity hated that she'd brought any manner of violence into the lives of the people she loved. For weeks after the incident, she'd had nightmares about how much worse things could have gotten.

Then she pictured the fear on the face of Ash's eleven-year-old daughter, Michaela, when her father had been forced to intervene.

Of course, the girl knew her dad's work was dangerous. Ash had shared with Trinity how much his late wife had hated his chosen career and the tension it had caused in their marriage.

Trinity would never want to be the cause of more challenges for him or Michaela, which was why she'd put some distance between the two of them, stepping away from their burgeoning friendship—and possibly more.

It had been easy enough with the holidays and everyone being busy and then Ash and Michaela moving into their own house.

He'd called and texted several times. She hadn't exactly meant to blow him off and was friendly when she saw him in passing, but that was as much as her heart could take.

"I shouldn't have agreed to this," she said, pulling away from Freya's touch. She didn't want to be comforted at this moment. "I wouldn't have if Mom hadn't practically forced me into it."

Freya's mouth quirked. "Who would have thought that

May Carlyle, women's empowerment icon, would turn into a full-blown matchmaker?"

"Not me," Trinity grumbled. "That's why I gave in—I was just so shocked."

"I think it's good that you're doing this. You need to get out. You need a life other than taking care of Mom and Thomas. You deserve some happiness, Trin."

"I am happy." She tugged on the dress's neckline. "My son makes me happy. Seeing Mom with Thomas makes me happy. The fact that you and Beth found love with great guys makes me happy." She held out her hands, palms up. "I'm bursting with happiness."

"Ash could make you happy if you let him."

Trinity forced a smile. "I'm the plus-one tonight. Mom and his mother-in-law made him ask me. Don't read more into it, Freya."

"As long as you keep an open mind."

The doorbell rang from downstairs, saving Trinity from explaining to her sister that her mind wasn't the problem. It was her heart she couldn't open.

"Trinny, your handsome date is here," May Carlyle called. "Come down before I steal him from you."

Freya choked out a laugh.

Trinity shook her head. "I'm glad Mom has recovered from the stroke, but she is not the same as she used to be."

"That's a good thing," her sister reminded her.

"Yes, mostly," Trinity agreed. She started for the door but paused as Freya wrapped her in a tight hug from behind.

"Have fun tonight, little sister."

"I'm just a plus-one," Trinity repeated, more for her benefit than Freya's.

She grabbed her purse from the dresser and hurried down the stairs before May could shout out any other embarrassing comments. But her breath caught in her throat as she reached the first floor.

May had handed Thomas to Ash, who held the baby like he was about to pose for some sort of hot-dad pinup calendar.

He wore a dark suit with a crisp white dress shirt and a robin's-egg blue tie that matched the color of his gentle eyes. His thick, wavy hair was still damp at the ends, and his strong jaw looked newly shaven. He probably smelled delicious, and Trinity had the sudden urge to bury her nose in the crook of his neck, much like her son was doing.

She'd thought he looked handsome in his police department uniform, but Ash dressed up was another level entirely.

"Hi," he said with a dazzling smile. "You look lovely tonight, Trinity."

"Hi," she managed in response, mentally commanding herself to calm the heck down.

The front door was still open, and Trinity felt grateful for the cool breeze wafting in. She was hot from head to toe, her chest burning with the knowledge of what could have been if she'd chosen better or believed she was worthy of love.

If she didn't still bear the scars of her father's abandonment of their family or her mom's self-centered affection growing up. If she'd had a normal family—if she was normal—this was what her future might have held.

A man like Ash Davis.

She blinked to clear the illusion because that's all her wayward thought amounted to. She was a plus-one and nothing more.

CHAPTER TWO

THE NIGHT WENT so much better than Asher Davis could have imagined, and every moment of it was an excruciating form of torture.

He hadn't planned to take a date to the wedding of one of his deputies just across the bridge to the resort island south of Magnolia. He'd been almost aggressively single since his late wife's death. The only date he'd been on was with Trinity Carlyle, and she'd gone into labor at the restaurant before the appetizer had arrived.

Ash didn't care about that, although Trinity had kept her distance since Thomas's birth. He tried to be understanding. She had her hands full, and then the unfortunate business of her rotten ex-boyfriend showing up at the church had been a shock.

He could deal with scumbag exes. Ash had seen a lot worse during his decade in law enforcement. That was why his marriage had been on the rocks before Stacy's death in a fiery car crash. Being married to a police officer wasn't an easy road, even in an idyllic town like Magnolia.

Stacy had hated the danger and uncertainty of his work. Her complaints had echoed through his head when he was left to raise Michaela alone. He'd moved from the city to the close-knit coastal town to be closer to Stacy's family, and because he figured being the police chief in a small town would be less of a risk than his beat in the city.

That was true. But it didn't remove the danger altogether.

He'd seen the fear in Trinity's eyes when her ex had lunged with that knife in his trembling hand. Ash had had no problem taking down the man, but things with Trinity had never been the same.

Ash couldn't blame her. She was starting over and had a baby to consider. Why get involved with a man who took a risk every time he walked out the door? He sometimes wished he could change the reality of his career and was thankful Michaela didn't know any different.

He'd resigned himself to letting Trinity go. Ash understood personal sacrifice—and she might have captured his heart with her innate kindness and sweet nature, not to mention a beauty that made his knees go weak—but he wanted her to be happy more than anything.

Still, when Helena and May had dropped the most obvious hints on the planet that he should ask Trinity to attend the wedding with him, he didn't hesitate.

Even though she was going with him as a favor, he couldn't pass up an opportunity to spend time with her.

She'd seemed nervous and almost timid on the drive to the church. He'd filled the awkward silence with questions about Thomas and stories of Michaela's new school semester and adjusting to life away from his mother-in-law's house in the three-bedroom rancher he'd bought a few blocks away.

It was easy to talk to Trinity, and eventually she'd relaxed. His chest had filled with contentment listening to her sharing sweet tidbits about her life and adventures as a new mom.

If people thought it was strange that he'd brought a date to the wedding, no one mentioned it. He hoped his affection for her wasn't too obvious—he didn't want to scare her off when he had this chance to start over.

He figured his coworkers at the station knew about his

unreciprocated crush on the beautiful single mother. One of his deputies is had gone so far as to try to give Ash grief for his feelings, which were apparently written all over his face anytime he saw Trinity in town.

She'd returned to work part-time at a popular hair salon just off the main square, so he saw her often enough.

Tonight was different.

It was how he wanted it to be—having her on his arm felt right. Unfortunately, she might disagree, as he couldn't help but notice that she'd ensured that the two of them were always surrounded by a group once the wedding was over.

He hated thinking she didn't want to be alone with him.

The lead singer for the country-western band who'd entertained the crowd at the reception announced the night's final song. They sat at one of the round tables in the banquet hall, and as the band began to play a slow ballad, the other couples at the table moved toward the dance floor.

Trinity watched them with a look of almost pained wistfulness in her beautiful blue eyes. Then she turned to Ash with the fakest smile he'd ever seen.

"This has been a great night, but I'm out of practice being social. Should we head—"

"Dance with me," he said, holding out a hand.

She swallowed and stared at his fingers for a long moment before finally slipping hers into his grasp. "Okay."

Her fingers were soft and cool.

"Already the highlight of my night," he told her as he pulled her to her feet and led her to join the other couples.

Her smile wobbled at the edges.

"You're safe with me, Trinity."

He wasn't sure what caused her to be so nervous but had to assume her past relationship was to blame. He wanted her to know that he would never hurt her, no matter what did or didn't happen between them.

She didn't answer or confirm his pronouncement, and Ash wanted to rail against her recalcitrance. He wanted to go back to how it had been when she first arrived in Magnolia, when they'd had such an easy rapport.

They were friends. He wanted to be her friend and so much more.

Michaela loved Trinity. His mother-in-law loved her. Hell, she'd been friends with his late wife when the two of them were kids.

It should be easy. Why did this have to feel so hard?

He placed an arm around her waist and drew her closer. The sweet floral scent that had been drifting toward him in tiny hints all evening enveloped his senses. He must have it bad if even the way she smelled drove him wild.

She placed her free hand on his shoulder, delicately, like a butterfly perched on a flower.

Neither of them spoke as they swayed to the music. He didn't want to ruin the moment.

He didn't want it to end.

As if an answer to a prayer he hadn't spoken out loud, she sighed and rested her head on his shoulder.

It felt right, and he adjusted his hold so there wasn't an inch of space separating them. His body almost did a jig of happiness. He'd thought about holding her in his arms so many times and wanted the song to last forever.

He wasn't sure when the energy between them changed, but suddenly the fine hairs on the back of his neck stood on end, and his limbs grew heavy. The sensation wasn't simply awareness. It was need.

He needed Trinity. He wanted her. And he knew she felt something, too.

The anxiety she'd displayed earlier drained out of her—well, maybe not drained. Maybe it was engulfed by the electric connection of attraction between the two of them.

"I can't tell you how happy I am right now," he said against her ear.

She tensed for a moment, and then a little purr of acquiescence escaped her throat. "Me, too."

Ash felt like he'd just won the lottery with her tiny admission.

All too soon, the music ended. Ash reluctantly stepped away. Trinity's face was flushed, her gaze slightly dazed. He'd never seen anything so dazzling as her shy smile.

"When do they expect you back?" Ash linked their fingers, but instead of leading her back to their table, he headed for the exit, not bothering to say goodbye to his friends.

"Freya is spending the night at Mom's, so..." She shrugged her shoulders as he glanced back at her. "I don't think I have a curfew."

"You haven't been to my new house. Would you like to see it?"

They both knew he wasn't simply offering a tour of his new home. He wanted her there with him. He wanted her in his bed.

Her eyes widened, and Ash wondered if he'd made a mistake. Was he pushing her too fast, too far?

He'd heard her tell several people tonight that the two of them were attending the wedding as friends or some nonsense about her being his plus-one.

He squeezed her fingers, willing her to trust him...to take a chance. Maybe if they had one night together, they could figure out what seemed to be keeping them apart.

Ash sure as hell couldn't figure it out on his own. "Please, Trinity." It was the closest he'd come in his life to begging.

"Yes," she said softly, and Ash picked up the pace.

When they got to his truck, he went to open the passenger-side door for her, then stopped.

Her delicate brows furrowed. "What's wrong?"

"Do you remember talking under the stars last Thanksgiving night?" He pointed to the night sky dotted with a thousand pinpoints of light.

"I was kind of a mess back then," she said with a self-conscious laugh. "You must have thought I was—"

"I thought you were beautiful," he interrupted and reached out to trace his thumb across her pink cheek. She swayed closer, and he knew for certain that he didn't imagine their connection. She still felt it, just like he did. "I think you're even more beautiful now."

And before she could argue with him, he captured her mouth with his.

Ash had wanted to kiss Trinity Carlyle practically since the first moment he saw her, but the feel of her soft lips on his was more than worth the wait.

She tasted as sweet as honey, and his body responded like he was a hungry bear coming out of hibernation. But he took things slow. He wanted to savor her and for her to know she was precious to him.

She pressed her mouth more fully to his and wound her arms around his neck. This was the moment he'd been waiting for—possibly his whole life—but then, suddenly, she let out a little cry of distress and yanked away.

"Trinity?"

Her hands had gone up to cover her chest like she needed to protect herself.

What the hell? Ash would never hurt her.

"Are you okay?" he asked, trying to make his voice soothing. "If I—"

"It's not you." She kept her eyes fixed on a place beyond

his shoulder. "I need you to take me home. To my mother's house," she clarified, as if that wasn't obvious. "I'm sorry."

She grabbed for the door and tucked herself into the passenger seat before he could form a response.

He didn't know what had spooked her so severely but honored her request.

They made the drive in silence, with Trinity angled away from him, her arms crossed tightly around her torso.

He pulled into May's driveway, and Trinity looked over her hunched shoulder at him. "I had a lovely time tonight. Again, I'm sorry for—"

Her wide blue eyes shone with unshed tears. "You don't have to apologize to me, Trin. Never."

She nodded, climbed out of the car and hurried toward the front door. He waited until the porch light was turned off before backing out of the driveway.

Maybe he'd read the situation wrong. Maybe it was finally time to let go of his feelings for Trinity. Feelings she obviously didn't reciprocate, despite the heat of that kiss.

CHAPTER THREE

"WHY DIDN'T YOU tell him what happened?" Freya asked the following day over coffee in their mother's cozy kitchen.

Trinity rolled her eyes and placed her mug on the quilted place mat in front of her. "Sure. That's what a man wants to hear while kissing the snot out of a woman—*sorry, my milk let down, and I've soaked through my pretty dress*."

"Kissing the snot out of you, huh?" Freya winked. "That sounds weirdly appealing when it involves Ash."

"Soaking him with breast milk would have been the opposite of appealing." Thomas let out a gurgle of happiness, and Trinity leaned in to kiss his tiny toes. He sat in a bouncy chair she'd placed on the table and offered her a smile. "You're worth ruining my chances at romance, little man."

"Nothing is ruined," May said from where she was stirring oatmeal on the stove. "You should have told Ash the truth. He can handle it."

"Maybe, but I would have died of embarrassment." She shook her head. "It was a good reminder that it's not the right time."

"Phooey," May harrumphed.

"Exactly," Freya agreed, taking a sip of coffee. "I think you were scared by how much you liked kissing Ash—or having the snot kissed out of you."

"Stop talking snot," May commanded. She ladled oatmeal into three bowls and spooned the berries Freya had washed on top before bringing them to the table.

"Ash knows you're a mother," May said as she placed a bowl in front of Trinity.

Trinity had thought she would have gotten used to her mother's newfound domesticity. Yet it still sometimes felt odd to be mothered by May Carlyle, famous for the book she'd written decades earlier about taking care of herself as a woman above all others.

For May, that included her three daughters and had led to their estrangement for many years. Although Trinity had a hard time wrapping her mind around thinking of her mother's stroke as a blessing, it had brought the sisters together in a way she would consider a blessing for the rest of her life.

"Ash is a good man," May said, repeating Freya's words from the previous night.

"You don't have to keep telling me. I know he's a good man. The best." Trinity swallowed around the yearning and regret currently bubbling up inside her throat. "Which is why you should agree that he deserves someone better than me."

"No one is better than you," May said, then patted Freya's head. "No one's better than any of my girls. Ash would be lucky to have you, and he knows it."

"Everyone knows it but you," Freya added. She glanced at her phone when it vibrated on the table. A small smile played across her striking features. Now the yearning and regret were joined by jealousy.

"Is that Greer?" May asked. Before Freya met him, Christopher Greer had been May's friend and literary agent. He and her sister had formed an unlikely bond over the holidays, and Trinity knew their love was the kind to last—just like their oldest sister with Declan Murphy.

Maybe she couldn't put Ash out of her mind because,

like little sisters everywhere, she'd always wanted to do what her two older sisters were doing. Falling in love might be part of that.

She stirred brown sugar into her oatmeal and took a bite, sighing around the comforting sweetness.

"I wonder if Thomas will like oatmeal as much as I do when he starts eating solid food." She tickled her baby's toes again.

"He'll be there before you know it," May said.

Trinity nodded. "Which is why I should devote myself only to him."

"Which is why," Freya corrected, "you have a responsibility to be happy. He should see you happy."

There was that word again.

Happy.

Her sister had told her the same thing the night before, but now Trinity didn't argue. She'd spent enough time in the past few years just surviving. There had been no extra energy or room to think about being happy. Emotion balled just under her rib cage as she gazed at her beautiful baby boy.

It wasn't the fear or anxiety that had settled there for so long. It felt strangely like hope.

She'd learned a long time ago that hope was a dangerous emotion, but she welcomed it anyway. The alternative was giving up, and she would never do that again.

She would never settle for less, because she wanted to show her son that he deserved more. He deserved everything good in the world. And if she could believe that, maybe she could think that she deserved a sliver of it.

CHAPTER FOUR

"Come in," Ash called, not bothering to look up from his desk Monday afternoon. He'd spent most of the day doing paperwork, which he enjoyed about as much as he would ripping off his own fingernails.

Once a month, it had to be done, and his staff knew to leave him be until he was through it. But his assistant, Mary, insisted on bringing in coffee and sustenance regularly, although she didn't speak directly to him.

He appreciated the food and the caffeine and tried not to take out his irritation on her.

"You can leave it on the desk, please. I should be done in a couple of hours. Sorry I snapped at you earlier."

"Any chance you can take a lunch break?"

He stilled and lost track of where he was in the report he was writing. The loss of concentration was worth it as he glanced up to see Trinity smiling at him, a bag of take-out balanced in front of her.

He frowned, and she blinked. "I can just leave it on the desk," she said quickly. "It's clear you're in the middle of something. Mary thought you might like a break, but—"

"Why are you always putting up shields between us?"

More rapid blinking. "I don't know what you mean." She slowly stepped forward and placed the bag on his desk. "There's no shield between us."

"Then why were you holding the bag like it was made of

titanium? Plus, Saturday night, you had your arms wrapped so tight around yourself it was a wonder you could breathe. I know you've been through a lot, Trinity, but I'm not like your ex. I'm not going to hurt you, but I can't keep trying to convince you. You either have to believe me or go on faith at some point."

She cringed, and he almost wanted to take back the words, but no. He could give her space and honor her if she didn't want to be with him, but he wasn't going to pretend anymore.

Ash and his late wife had pretended things were okay, but they hadn't been. When she'd died, he'd wished she had told him what was in her heart and found a way to be happy before the accident took her.

He thought maybe if they'd had, he could find a way to live without guilt.

Instead of fleeing, Trinity moved closer. She opened the bag and began to take out the carryout order—a turkey sandwich with a side of pasta salad, chips and a can of root beer.

Trinity's mouth curved at the edges as she studied the soda can.

"Root beer is underrated," he said, feeling slightly embarrassed that he'd ordered that instead of something more adultish like iced tea or…who cared what drink he ordered?

"I have no problem with root beer," she told him as she placed the can on his desk. "I'm also not worried you will hurt me, Ash. Not in the way I was before."

"How do you feel about trust and faith?" he asked softly, needing to know even if the answer might not be what he wanted to hear.

"I'm working on those." She laughed. "Especially having faith in myself. Trusting you wasn't the problem Saturday night."

"It was trusting yourself?" he prompted.

She shook her head, and he noticed twin spots of color blooming on her cheeks. "When you kissed me, it was…" She seemed to be grasping for the right words.

"Nice?"

"Amazing." She pulled her lower lip between her teeth. "So amazing that my body went a little haywire. Um…my milk let down."

His turn to blink.

She held up a hand. "Please don't say anything. I don't want to talk about it, as it was insanely embarrassing."

"You're a mom with a baby. That's normal, right?"

"Not when I'm in the middle of the best kiss of my life."

Well, that was good to hear.

"The best of your life?"

She opened the bag of chips. "Want to share your lunch?"

"You didn't answer."

"The best," she confirmed. "Which freaks me out, Ash."

"Because of the breast-milk reaction."

"Oh my lord. You have to stop mentioning it. No, I'm scared because trusting isn't something I do well. Neither are relationships. My life is complicated."

"I'm a single dad who just moved out of my mother-in-law's house a few months ago," he reminded her. "I have some baggage of my own."

"But you're confident and successful, and you've got a good life. I've got debt and a baby—and an ex-boyfriend in jail. Not to mention meddling sisters and a mom I still need to look after while she continues to heal. I don't have baggage. I have dumpsters full of complications."

"Trinity."

Her chest was rising and falling in ragged breaths now, like she'd run an emotional marathon warning him off. But he wasn't scared of life complications.

He came around the side of the desk, placing his hands on her arms. She wore a striped long-sleeve sweater and a pair of faded jeans. Her hair, which she normally kept pulled back, fell past her shoulders and smelled like wildflowers.

"I don't care about any of that. I care about you. I want a chance with *you*."

She searched his face. "I can't figure out why. On our first date, my water broke, and I practically soaked your suit coat with breast milk on our second date."

"It's always an adventure." He smiled and dropped a quick kiss on her forehead. He couldn't explain what he felt for her and didn't dare try, because then he might be the one who got scared.

All he knew was that being with Trinity settled his heart in a way that Ash wanted and needed more than he could say.

CHAPTER FIVE

THE FOLLOWING TWO weeks were the happiest Trinity had ever experienced. True to his word, Ash didn't seem to care about the complexities in either of their lives. He was attentive and sweet, making her feel special even with the demands on his time in other areas.

She and Thomas became regular visitors to his new house, where they'd make dinner together while Michaela entertained the baby or did homework at the kitchen table. If Ash's daughter thought it was odd that Trinity was spending so much time with her dad, she hid it well.

There were times when Trinity wondered if Michaela wasn't in the matchmaking business along with May and Helena. It made Trinity laugh to witness how Michaela lauded Ash's good points, right down to commenting how thick Ash's hair remained, unlike many of her friends' fathers'.

Trinity had laughed at the observation, but as she and Ash, who held Thomas in his arms, entered the elementary school gym on a bright Saturday morning to see Michaela's science fair display, she couldn't help but notice the girl had been right.

"You really do have good hair," she told Ash, nudging him gently.

"I can't take credit, but if that's what does it for you…" He linked their fingers and lifted her hand to kiss her knuckles.

"Not here," she admonished as she yanked her hand from his.

He paused outside the entrance to the gymnasium. "Why not here?"

"Ash." She sighed. "People will talk."

"Is that a problem for you? Because it isn't for me."

"I don't want to rush into anything." She took Thomas from him, cradling the baby close.

His jaw tightened. "There you are with the shield again."

"Thomas is a baby, not a shield."

Ash cocked an eyebrow. "Are you sure?"

"Let's go see Michaela," she said instead of answering, because she wasn't sure and hated that doubt and fear held so much power over here.

He looked like he wanted to argue but nodded.

The gym was crowded with students, teachers and family members, but they found Michaela easily with her display of a trio of plants she'd spent the past month speaking to in three different ways.

Trinity's heart rippled in her chest as she listened to the girl explain her experiment. She'd used positive words with one plant, neutral with the second and angry words with the third.

Was Trinity like that pathetic, mangled plant, ignored or spoken to harshly for so long that she'd wilted beyond measure? Maybe there was no hope that Ash could even bring her back to life.

The last thing she wanted to be was a burden—emotional or otherwise—to him or anyone.

She plastered a smile on her face as a small crowd formed around Michaela's display. Like her father, the girl was a natural at relating to people.

At the end of her short presentation, the gathered group

applauded, and Ash hugged his daughter. “And here I thought all I had to worry about was watering the houseplants to keep them alive.”

Michaela rolled her eyes at his dad humor, then hugged Trinity and kissed Thomas’s cheek.

Trinity wanted to believe she deserved the affection Ash and Michaela offered so freely but couldn’t stop the worry she wasn’t worthy of the happiness they brought to her world.

She took a step back as Ash was drawn into a conversation with a couple of dads who wanted to discuss the recent string of burglaries in a community on the outskirts of town.

“Cute baby,” a voice said at her side. She turned to the woman who’d come to stand next to her.

“Thanks,” she answered, feeling frumpy in her oversize, basic sweatshirt and stretchy leggings. She’d meant to change into something nicer before meeting Ash at the school, but Thomas had been fussy that morning, and her mother had wanted help putting together a new office chair, so Trinity had rushed out of the house in order to make it on time, a stylish outfit long forgotten.

The woman watching Ash with what could only be described as a predatory gleam in her gaze wore a fitted blouse that tapered at her narrow waist and a denim pencil skirt with a wide belt and matching heeled boots to pull the outfit together.

Her hair was long and blond, falling in delicate waves over her shoulders, and her makeup was understated but expertly applied. Trinity was lucky to remember to brush her teeth some days.

“Are you a friend of Ash’s?” the woman asked in a deceptively sweet tone.

Trinity might have lived in the Mountain West for the past decade, but she knew how to read Southern superiority like she'd never left.

"Yes," she answered, wanting to claim him even though she had no right. "We live next to Michaela's grandmother."

"How charming." The woman sighed. "My daughter and Michaela are in the same class at school. It's been a treat getting to know Ash."

A *real* treat, Trinity guessed.

"Especially since our girls are getting older and we have more free time. You're only getting started, of course, and bless your heart for that. The next few years will be...well, precious, if a lot to handle. I can't imagine going back or being saddled with the responsibility of a baby again. I know Ash feels the same."

"You do?" Trinity couldn't help the question. Ash was such a natural with Thomas that she hadn't thought about the fact they were nearly on opposite ends of the parenting spectrum.

"Oh, yes," the woman confirmed with a satisfied smile. "We were talking about the freedom that comes when kids start to get older just the other night at dinner."

Trinity swallowed around the lump that filled her throat. Ash looked over at that moment, his thick brows furrowing slightly as his gaze tracked between her and the soon-to-be fancy-free mother at her side.

He waved, and the woman waved back and...did she seriously blow him a kiss in the middle of the science fair? Trinity adjusted her grip on Thomas.

At this moment, she *was* using her baby as a shield. Who could blame her?

"I've got to go," she muttered.

"Of course you do," the woman agreed, her tone placating. "I believe I smell a little something in that diaper. Being a mommy to a baby is never-ending work, but eventually, you'll regain your life." She patted Trinity on the arm. "I'll tell Ash and Michaela you said goodbye."

Thomas was Trinity's life—dirty diapers, unstable nap schedules and all the millions of other details that went into mothering a baby. Sure, Ash liked her, but would he want to commit to loving not just her, but her son as well?

They were a package deal, and it dawned on her how the complications she'd mentioned were only the start of what she and Ash would have to navigate in a relationship.

Why would he bother when there were other easier—probably on many levels—options out there?

It was too depressing to ruminate over, so she did what she was best at—she turned and walked away.

CHAPTER SIX

ASH PULLED UP to his mother-in-law's house for Sunday supper and did his best not to let his gaze stray to the house next door.

"Are you ready to meet your gam gam?" Michaela asked the small dog visibly trembling next to her in the back seat.

"I'm not sure your grandmother will want to claim a dog as her new grandchild," Ash said and then blew out a chuckle.

"Barney is perfect, and Grammy is going to love her." Michaela placed a delicate kiss on the animal's furry snout. "Aren't you perfect, sweetums?"

"Do not call that animal sweetums, Mic. He's a proud, regal specimen."

"Sure, Dad. Keep telling yourself that."

"That's what you told me when we were at the animal rescue."

"I was trying to convince you to let me adopt him. I could tell Barney needed me."

His daughter had been begging for a dog since she could speak the word. Stacy had been allergic, and once they'd moved in with Michaela's grandmother, there had been too much to deal with besides taking on the responsibility of pet ownership.

But as soon as Ash had signed the contract to buy the home where they now lived, Michaela had been angling to add a pet to their small family.

Ash had managed to avoid the topic, but after Trinity took off from the science fair yesterday, he'd needed a distraction. And a two-year-old mutt with scraggly hair, a pronounced overbite and floppy ears apparently filled the bill.

Meredith Ventner, who ran the Furever Friends Animal Rescue in Magnolia, had introduced them to several animals, but Barney had been the one to capture Michaela's heart.

He was medium-size, underweight and not the type of dog Ash would have picked for himself. But after Michaela went to bed last night, Barney had climbed up next to him on the sofa and rested his soft muzzle on Ash's hand when he'd been about to text Trinity.

Immediately, Ash had fallen just as hard as his daughter. Who would have thought that a rescue mutt would make a good wingman? But Ash had appreciated it just the same.

The woman who had his mind and heart tied in a million knots had eventually texted him to apologize for leaving so abruptly—a dirty diaper had been her excuse, but Ash wondered if it had more to do with Monica Wheeler, the divorced mom who had been trying to put the moves on him since he'd arrived in Magnolia.

But if Trinity was scared off so easily, what did that say about her feelings for him? He yearned for a relationship where he could be all in and didn't want to settle for less in return.

Maybe things between them weren't meant to be.

"Hey, Trinity, wanna meet our new dog?" Michaela called as she exited the car with Barney on the leash. "His name's Barney, and Meredith at the rescue said he's a Heinz 57 breed."

Ash mentally put up his defenses—only to have them disintegrate as he watched the enthusiasm with which

Trinity greeted his daughter and the new addition to their family. She sat on the grass with Michaela and oohed and aahed, then laughed as Barney climbed into her lap and covered her face with wet doggy kisses.

"He's the sweetest," she told the girl. "What a lucky, handsome boy to be adopted by you."

Michaela's grin stretched ear to ear. She extolled Barney's already long list of virtues and the tricks he could do.

"Dad likes him, too," Michaela said as Ash walked up to join them. "I caught him feeding Barney a slice of bacon this morning, even though Meredith said no people food."

"A dog-owning rebel." Trinity chuckled, and the sound was like a punch to the heart for Ash. "Who would have thought the town's upstanding police chief had a secret rule-breaking side?"

"No more bacon," Michaela scolded him as she stood.

"He needs to gain weight," Ash argued.

"Meredith gave us a meal plan." His daughter tugged on Barney's leash. "We're going to stick by it." She gave Trinity a quick hug. "I'm going to introduce Barney to my grandma. Tell May I'll come over later."

"I'm sure Mr. Jingles and Barney will be fast friends," Trinity said with another laugh, referring to her mother's beloved, if cantankerous, cat.

"Me, too," Michaela agreed and trotted off with Barney in tow.

"Mr. Jingles is going to hate that dog." Ash reached out a hand to help Trinity up off the grass. He wondered for a moment if she would refuse to take it. Then she slid her cool fingers into his and he tugged her to her feet.

"You never know," she told him. "Sometimes opposites attract."

"Are we opposites?" he exclaimed before he could think better of asking the question.

"In some ways." She shoved her hands into the front pockets of the linen overalls she wore with a pale yellow tank top underneath. Her hair was pulled back into a messy topknot, displaying the graceful column of her throat.

Ash knew better than to mention it now, but her beauty never failed to overwhelm him. She was like a cool breeze on a hot day and everything good in the world.

Despite their difficulties and stumbles, he couldn't ever imagine giving up on Trinity. Unless she wanted him to—it would be hard to deny her anything.

"You probably have more in common with that woman from the science fair."

He scrunched his face as he tried to figure out who she was referencing. "Monica? The blonde?"

"She said you had dinner together."

Ash ran a hand through his hair. "It was a team dinner for Michaela's soccer club. Monica was there along with a couple dozen other parents."

"Oh." He could almost hear the gears in Trinity's mind processing this information. "So not a date?"

"Not in the slightest," he confirmed. "Did she tell you we went on a date?"

"She implied it," Trinity admitted. "Along with the fact that the two of you are both glad to be done parenting babies." She glanced over her shoulder at her mother's house. "Even though she thought Thomas was precious. Or maybe she thought I was precious. It was a very Southern conversation, and I'm out of practice with those."

"Is that why you left the school?"

"Thomas had a dirty diaper."

"That you could have changed in the restroom." Hot

and sudden, frustration boiled up inside him like a geyser about to blow. "Trinity, I can't keep doing this. I like you." He shook his head. "It's more than like, but if you won't trust me even a little—"

"I know," she agreed before he could finish his thought. "Trust is hard for me. I don't want to hold you back."

"You aren't." He blew out a breath. "Hell, I've got a dog now. You want to talk about complicated."

"Man's best friend is more complicated than a baby?"

"They are both commitments," he said with grave sincerity. She laughed, which was what he wanted.

"Ash, I—"

His phone buzzed in his back pocket, the specific ring of his deputy at the station. "Hold that thought," he told her then quickly answered the call. "Okay, I'll be there in ten." He ended the call and rolled his shoulders. "I've got to go now. One of my deputies got called to a robbery in progress just now, and shots were exchanged."

"Was anyone hurt?"

"An officer took a bullet to the leg." He was already stepping away. "Will you tell Michaela I'll be back as soon as I can? Damn it. I hate working on the weekends."

"She's fine. I'll make sure of it," Trinity promised, then surprised him when she hurried forward to kiss his cheek. "Be careful, Ash."

The breath drained from his lungs at the worry in her eyes. He'd seen that same concern in his late wife's gaze, and it had slowly morphed from anxiety to resentment as the years passed.

Talk about complicated. His job had everything else beat by a mile. As he got to his car and sped off toward the address he'd been given, he realized Trinity wasn't the only one with doubts about a relationship.

As much as he cared for—loved her, if he wanted to admit the truth—he wasn't sure he could subject her to the worry of being the partner of a law enforcement officer, knowing what it had done to Stacy.

Maybe there was more to her putting up shields than he knew. Maybe it was time he accepted the truth that he couldn't give Trinity Carlyle the happy life she deserved, no matter how much his heart wanted him to.

CHAPTER SEVEN

It was nearly midnight when Trinity blinked awake at the feel of someone gently shaking her.

She took a moment to remember where she was—asleep on Ash's soft leather couch, which answered the immediate question of whether she was dreaming the sight of his handsome face staring down at her.

"Are you okay?" she asked automatically, sitting up and wrapping her arms around his neck.

"I am now," he answered against her neck, taking a deep breath, as if her scent was some soothing elixir for whatever work crisis he'd been dealing with most of the night.

She held on tight, taking an equal measure of strength in his warm, solid body holding her. "What happened?"

"We got a lead on the people behind the recent burglaries. One of my men got shot in the takedown and the standoff…" He drew back and gazed at her, upset swirling in the depths of his blue eyes. "One of the ringleaders was killed in the raid. Two members of his crew fled into the woods, and we gave chase."

She squeezed his arms as panic gripped her heart. "You could have been the one shot or killed, Ash."

"I'm fine, sweetheart." He traced his finger over her cheek. "Tonight isn't typical, Trinity. I want you to know that. I moved to Magnolia because the work would be less dangerous than in the city."

"But it's still dangerous," she countered.

"Yes." He pulled away from her, and she wanted to scream in protest but remained silent as he sat back against the cushions on the far side of the couch. "Dirty diapers and all the other things you call complications pale in comparison, right?"

She laughed softly. "Well, wiping a poopy butt won't get me killed."

"I'm sorry if you were worried tonight." He sounded painfully weary. "Thank you for bringing Michaela back here. She could have stayed with her grandmother."

"I don't mind. I brought Thomas's portable crib, so he's sound asleep in your office." She gestured to the monitor sitting on the coffee table. "That boy is a sound sleeper. I doubt he'll even wake up for the drive home."

"I hate that he has to be disturbed." Ash frowned. "In some ways, it was easier when we lived with Helena. She was always around, and I know my daughter isn't your responsibility."

"She thought Barney would want to sleep in his crate."

"I'll have to get a crate to keep at her grandmother's."

"Ash, this isn't about a dog crate."

"No," he agreed. "It's about how wanting something so badly doesn't give me a right to have it." He scrubbed a hand over his face, and even in the dim light of the end table lamp, she could see fine lines of worry and exhaustion bracketing his mouth and eyes.

He had a face that was not only movie-star handsome but was also dear to her. If this night and her worry over his safety had proved anything, it was that Trinity didn't want to waste one more minute denying her feelings for Ash.

"I need to tell you something," she said softly.

He sighed. "I think I know what it is, and you need to know I don't blame you, Trin."

"Blame me?" she repeated slowly. She had to admire his self-confidence, although she agreed. What woman wouldn't fall in love with Asher Davis?

"All of the talk about complications and your issues. I get it now. They were excuses. You were trying to let me down easy because I'm the real problem."

Okay, maybe she'd read this conversation wrong. "How are you a problem? Ash, you're darn near perfect."

"Hardly." He shook his head. "Everyone has issues, Trin. But not many people have a job like mine. It drove Stacy and me apart, and I blame myself for her unhappiness. I wish I could have taken the burden of loving me from her. I wish Michaela didn't have to deal with it. But I don't know how to be anything else but a cop. It's in me, you know? Part of who I am and—"

"Part of what I love about you," she interrupted. As he turned to stare at her in astonishment, she scooted closer to him and tucked her legs under her.

"You love me?" His voice sounded as dazed as she felt.

She took his hands in hers. "I do. I think I have since I came out of those woods and you tried to give me a ticket."

"I didn't give you a ticket," he muttered, one side of his mouth quirking. "I wouldn't—"

"I know." She leaned in and brushed her lips across his. "Being a cop, a father and an all-around stand-up guy is part of who you are, Ash. Just like being a mother and a survivor is woven into the fabric of my being. My doubts are all mine, and I can't promise they won't keep cropping up."

"We can deal with them together," he said. "If you're willing to take a chance on us."

She wrinkled her nose. "Pretty sure I just said I love you, so I'm kind of all in at this point."

He lifted her onto his lap and kissed her deeply. The

way he held her felt like a promise that she'd always have a safe harbor in his arms.

She wanted that so badly.

"I love you, Trinity Carlyle. I want to tell you every day for the rest of our lives. I want to slay your dragons or cheer you on as you slay them yourself. I want to be a father to Thomas, if you'll let me. My heart belongs to you, and there is nothing I want more than to love and cherish you for as long as you'll let me."

"So you're all in, too?" She grinned against his mouth.

"Forever," he promised, and her heart sang with happiness.

Happy.

That was the only word for how she felt right now. So simple but so right.

"Will you stay with me tonight?" he asked, cupping her face in his hands. His eyes were warm with love and a banked desire that had heat moving through her body. "I want to start our life together right now."

Suddenly, she felt shy. Her body wasn't the same as it had been before pregnancy. She wasn't the same as the last time she'd been intimate with a man. But she trusted Ash and had faith in herself and their new love.

Happiness wasn't a stagnant emotion. It took risk, work and commitment, and she was ready to face all those challenges with this man.

"I'd love to stay," she told him. "Forever," she added, kissing him again.

Their mouths were still fused when Ash leaned forward to scoop up the baby monitor, then stood with her in his arms.

"I don't think I've ever been so happy," he said as he pulled away to gaze at her. "It's rather terrifying."

She laughed because she understood the sentiment.

"We'll navigate both the terror and the happy together, Asher Davis. Our love will get us through all of it."

Trinity might have let doubt and fear rule her life for too long, but she knew the love she felt for Ash would prevail over anything. She'd finally found her home with him.

* * * * *